# ALYSON NOËL

# Blacklist

## A BEAUTIFUL IDOLS NOVEL

YOUNG
ADULT
HQ

HQ
An imprint of HarperCollins*Publishers* Ltd.
1 London Bridge Street
London SE1 9GF

This paperback edition 2017

1
First published in Great Britain by
HQ, an imprint of HarperCollins*Publishers* Ltd. 2017

Copyright © Alyson Nöel 2017
Alyson Nöel asserts the moral right to be
identified as the authors of this work
A catalogue record for this book is
available from the British Library

ISBN: 978-0-00-821684-9

Printed and bound by
CPI Group (UK) Ltd, Croydon, CR0 4YY

*For Charlie and Rachel, my A-list friends*

No man is rich enough to buy back his past.
—OSCAR WILDE

# Blacklist

**Breaking News: Discovery of Blood-Soaked Dress Leads to Arrest of Night for Night Party Promoter!**

By Trena Moretti

Just in—Mere hours after teen heartthrob Ryan Hawthorne was called in for questioning regarding the disappearance of his former girlfriend, Hollywood A-lister Madison Brooks, Los Angeles police received an anonymous tip leading to a blood-soaked dress thought to belong to Night for Night party promoter Aster Amirpour.

While the official statement released by the LAPD states that tests are under way to determine the source of the blood, an LAPD insider assures us they've received confirmation that the blood on the dress is a match for the missing celebrity.

According to our sources, the dress was turned over to police when a W Hotel employee became suspicious.

"I was only doing my job, which requires me to double-check the number and type of clothes found in the guest's laundry bag with the number and type of clothes the guest logged onto the form," said the employee, who wishes to remain anonymous. "This is the same standard procedure we always follow before we send the laundry out to our vendor. You would not believe how many people don't know the difference between a chemise and a dress. Anyway, in the middle of checking I noticed that a black dress had been improperly marked as a blouse. When I looked closer, I saw that the dress was covered in large dark stains that struck me as suspicious. It was then that I alerted my boss and they took it from there. If it really is the blood of Madison Brooks, then all we can do is pray for that poor young girl, because it really was an awful lot of blood. The dress was completely covered in it."

At the time of writing, Aster Amirpour was being booked into LA County Jail. We'll have more as this story develops.

# ONE

## GIRL AFRAID

Madison Brooks grudgingly surrendered the fading remnants of her dream and blinked into the blackness before her. The room was soundless, still. The air hung weighty and stale. Despite the promise of sleep, her waking life remained a living hell.

While she had plenty of fears—fear of forgetting her lines during a live performance, fear of her secret past being revealed—a fear of the dark had never been among them. Even as a child she understood that the mythical monster dwelling under the bed could only pale in comparison to the all-too-real parental monsters getting high in the den.

And it was no different now.

She pushed away from the soiled mattress she'd slept on and crept toward the solid steel door, alerted to any hint of scent, sound—anything that might provide a clue as to who had taken her, where they had taken her, and why. Over thirty days spent in captivity, and Madison was no closer to answers than the night she'd been snatched. She'd gone over the incident countless times—the memory playing on a continuous loop as she searched frame by frame, hunting for revelations, some small but crucial detail she might've missed. Yet every viewing remained stubbornly the same.

She'd broken up with Ryan only to be rescued by Tommy, and after sharing a few beers (along with a few memorable kisses), she'd received a text from Paul instructing her to meet him at Night for Night, and she'd fled without question. Though she should've known the moment she arrived at the closed and empty club that something had gone terribly wrong. Paul was professional. Punctual. If he'd truly intended to meet her, he would've been there already. She'd walked straight into a trap, but that was all hindsight now. Yet another item to add to the long list of things she'd chosen to ignore until she found herself with nothing but time to second-guess and berate herself.

How could she have been so trusting? So naive?

Why had she continued to wait on the terrace, reminiscing about a past she was desperate to keep buried while ignoring her gut instinct that urged her to flee?

Last thing she remembered was a curl of wind at her back, the wisp of a scent she still couldn't place; then a hand was clasped firmly over her mouth and time folded in on itself.

And now, several weeks later, she remained locked in a windowless cell that offered little more than a sink, a toilet, a bare mattress tossed on the floor, and a succession of bland, lumpy meals served three times a day.

Not a single sign of her captor.

Not a clue as to why she'd been taken.

Her diamond-encrusted Piaget watch, the hoop earrings Ryan had given her, the Gucci stilettos she'd worn, and the cashmere wrap she now used as a blanket served as the only reminders of her former Hollywood It Girl status.

If it was money they were after, they would've stripped her of the luxuries long ago. Allowing her to keep them seemed almost cruel. Like they wanted her to remember who she'd once been, if only to show her how quickly they could strip it away.

She sprawled on the cold cement floor with her legs splayed before her, wondering, as she always did, what was happening outside the cinder-block walls. Surely the whole world knew of her disappearance. There was probably even a task force specifically assigned to her case. So why was it taking them so long to find her? And more importantly, why hadn't Paul directed them to her when he was the one who'd insisted on embedding the microchip tracker into her arm, just under the burn scar, in anticipation of this very thing?

Right on schedule, the lights switched on—sending the fluorescent bulbs flickering, humming, and washing the room in a garish green glow. A moment later, when the slot snapped open, Madison crouched right beside it, stretched her mouth wide, and screamed from the very depths of her belly.

But just like every other day, the tray of lumpy food shot past, the slot slammed shut, and Madison's cries for help languished hollow and unheard.

She kicked the food aside and glanced around the small room, searching for something she might've missed, something she could use to defend herself with. Paul had taught her how to see past the mundane. *Nearly everything has a dual purpose,* he'd told her. *Even the most ordinary item can be used as a defense.* But even if she could fashion her stiletto heel into a weapon, there was no opponent—no one to fight. She was trapped all alone in her cinder-block cell.

With a frustrated sigh, she turned her attention to the pictures of her eight-year-old self spread across the ceiling and walls. The repeating image was occasionally spliced by a random strip of mirror meant to reflect the sorry state she currently found herself in. In the photo, her hair was tangled, her feet dirty and bare, an old doll dangled from the tips of her fingers as she regarded the camera with a deep violet stare.

It was the same picture someone had sent Paul as an unspoken threat.

The one he'd assured her had burned long ago with everything else from her past.

In the ten years since the photo was taken she'd traveled such a great distance, rose to great heights, only to come full circle and find herself as powerless, desperate, and filthy as she'd been as a child.

Everything Paul had told her was a lie. Her past had never been erased. It had been there all along, patiently waiting for just the right moment to remind her of the sins she'd committed on her rise to the top.

Someone had connected the dots between the hopeless child she'd been to the triumphant star she'd become.

Someone had uncovered the darker truth of her journey— the lies she'd told, the people she'd betrayed—and now they were making her pay.

While she refused to believe Paul was behind it—he'd been protecting her for too long to turn on her now—she couldn't rule out the idea that maybe someone had gotten to him. Either way, it was clear she could no longer count on him to find her.

Absently, she ran a finger over the web of fresh scars that covered her knuckles and hands—a reminder of an earlier bid to escape that had resulted in a broken pinkie, a badly strained wrist, and the loss of three nails. She'd acted impulsively, allowed herself to be driven by fear. It was a mistake she would not make again. Her next attempt had to succeed. Failure was no longer an option.

She remained like that, staring at the wall and formulating a plan, the images of her past and present selves merging into one, until the last meal was delivered and the cell went dark once again.

# TWO

# HEART-SHAPED BOX

## BEAUTIFUL IDOLS

### Innocent Until Proven Guilty, Yo!

By Layla Harrison

Warning: If you landed on this blog looking to revel in the usual sarcastic celebrity snark fest, then you might want to get out while you can and save your clicks and comments for Perez Hilton, Popsugar, or wherever you go to fuel up on your daily dose of Hollywood gossip when you're done reading me.

Don't even try to pretend we're monogamous.
I know you've been clicking around.

While I'm usually all too happy to provide the sort of low-level, derisive, Hollywood dirt you've come to crave, today

I'm afraid I'm ~~unable~~ unwilling to come out and play.

Unless you've been hiding under the proverbial rock, you're probably aware that Aster Amirpour has been arrested for the murder of Madison Brooks. A good source confirms the Bravado Channel even cut a very special *Real Housewives of Hades* episode in order to report the breaking story, and I think we can all agree that the willingness to preempt the daily digressions of everyone's favorite cloven-heeled, cleavage-enhanced, pitchfork-wielding blondes shows just how very serious this story is.

As it turns out, it is serious, and I was there when it happened. Which means I watched in horror as an innocent person was unfairly handcuffed and hauled away in a squad car in front of dozens of paparazzi.

Until you've watched someone being accused of a heinous crime you *know they did not commit*, then you probably won't have any empathy for what I'm going through now. Thing is, I know beyond a shadow of doubt—well beyond any and all reasonable doubt—that *Aster Amirpour is innocent*. Which means I will not write about her arrest in my usual way.

While I'm more than happy to continue to report on all manner of Hollywood debauchery, I cannot and will not use this blog to bring down an innocent or perpetuate a story that simply isn't true.

Also, as we so often seem to forget during times like these, allow me to remind you that our legal system works on a little thing called the *presumption of innocence*, which translates to mean: *the burden of proof is on the one who declares, not on the one who denies.*

Look it up:

http://legal-dictionary.thefreedictionary.com/presumption+of+innocence

546 Comments:

**Anonymous**

Your a fucking idiot.

**MadisonFan101**

Your friend is a murderer and you're both going to hell.

**RyMadLives**

Aster Amirpour is a slut and a murderer and everyone knows it but you.

**StarLovR**

You're blog is as ugly and boring and basic as you are.

**CrzYLuVZomby38**

If the dress don't fit, you must acquit! But we all know it fits, so . . .

**AsterMustDie**

I hope you end up as dead as Madison.

Layla Harrison sat at her desk, mindlessly sipping her coffee and glaring at the comments section emblazoned across her computer screen. She was supposed to be working. Supposed to be making her mark by ensuring that the party to herald the launch of Ira Redman's new Unrivaled tequila label was the most hyped, most talked-about party of the season. Instead, she was using company time (along with the company computer) to read the comments a bunch of media-manipulated morons had left on her blog.

"Innocent or guilty?"

Layla looked up to find Emerson, the guy from a few cubicles over, standing too close for comfort and peering over her shoulder.

With a click, Layla minimized the tab along with the other pic on her screen—the one of a frightened and pale Aster being ushered into a police car, the headline above it screaming, *Party Promoter Aster Amirpour Arrested for the Murder of Madison Brooks!*

It wasn't like she needed to study it. She'd stood right beside Tommy Phillips and watched the whole sordid scene play out just one week before.

"Definitely, one hundred percent *not* guilty," Layla snapped. To Emerson the case was little more than a hot piece of gossip about a fellow Unrivaled employee. It wasn't personal for him like it was for her. She resented him using it as an icebreaker, and had no problem letting him know it.

"Not like it matters." Emerson regarded her through wide topaz-colored eyes that his thick lashes and perfectly groomed brows only seemed to enhance. It was Layla's first day on the job, and it was already the second time she'd been on the receiving end of his go-to condescending expression. Thankfully she'd started midweek, so there were only two more days left until the weekend.

The first was when she got lost in the maze of identical cubicles on her way back from the break room, and Emerson escorted her to her desk with an eye roll and an audible sigh. Layla had spent the next half hour silently fuming. How was she supposed to recognize hers when they all looked the same? When it came to designing his clubs, Ira Redman spared no expense. So why wouldn't she expect a cool millennial campus, brimming with espresso bars, basketball courts, spa rooms, and maybe even a yoga studio or meditation den? But the Unrivaled Nightlife corporate offices, which basically amounted to a study in greige with their matching wall-to-wall carpet and workstations, were so opposite of what she'd envisioned—so disappointingly bland—that when she'd first walked in, she was sure she'd arrived at an accounting firm.

The rest of the day was spent online, researching Madison Brooks's disappearance a little over one month before and the evidence the LAPD had managed to stack against Aster in the ensuing weeks, only to get caught slacking off by Emerson of all people.

"Cases like that are all about perception." Emerson was still standing too close, still peering over her shoulder even though there was nothing to see—her screen had gone blank. "And perception *always* drives results."

Layla allowed her gaze to roam the fine planes of his face—the high cheekbones, square jaw, finely sculpted chin, smooth dark skin—and found herself frozen, unable to breathe. Extreme beauty often had that effect—as did the paralyzing fear of getting fired on her first day of work. She could only hope Emerson wouldn't inform Ira of her less than stellar performance.

"Figured you would've known that," he said. "After all, isn't that what our department's all about? Manipulating public perception into believing Ira's clubs are the only worthy place to see and be seen, and that his tequila is the only brand worth drinking?"

Layla fidgeted, fingers picking at the strands of her platinum bob while swiveling back and forth in her seat. While she was beginning to resent Emerson's presence, even she had to admit there was truth in his words.

"Anyway," he continued, in a light, breezy tone she didn't quite trust. He had it out for her, of that she was sure. "I'm guessing this was meant for you, seeing as it has your name on it." He dropped a rectangular package onto her desk.

Layla squinted at the parcel. On the surface, it seemed innocuous enough, but something about it set her on edge. For one thing, there was no return address. For another, it was her first day on the job—she wasn't expecting any mail.

"Found it on my chair when I came back from lunch. A simple mail room mix-up, I'm sure."

Layla's fingers fumbled awkwardly at its edges, but she had no intention of opening it till Emerson was safely returned to his cubicle. "Okay, thanks," she said, her voice as dismissive as she could possibly make it. She waited until he rounded the corner and disappeared from view.

The package was substantial, but not terribly weighty. And when she shook it ever so slightly, she could sense something bulky shifting inside. All of which brought her no closer to guessing its contents.

Hoping the mail room had some sort of defined protocol for screening potential mail bombs, she retrieved a pair of scissors from her drawer, sliced through the tape, and stared perplexed at the red satin heart-shaped box she found tucked inside with a small envelope attached to its front.

It was the kind of box usually seen on Valentine's Day. The kind of box that looked very out of place sitting on her desk in the middle of a scorching-hot August afternoon. And with no love life to speak of since Mateo had dumped her, she couldn't even venture a guess as to who might've sent it.

Her dad simply wasn't the grand gesture type. And Ira—well, Ira was her boss, which made it grossly inappropriate and completely out of the question. As for Tommy . . . well, she wouldn't allow herself to consider it.

On the front of the envelope, her name was written in an elaborate curlicue script. Still no closer to determining who'd sent it, she flipped it over, ran her finger under the flap, and removed the small rectangular card placed inside, which bore a picture of a grinning cartoon cat with a noose tied snugly around its neck.

Layla stared at the card—it was hideous, creepy, and the sight of it gave her the chills. While she had no idea what it was supposed to mean, one thing was sure—it definitely hadn't been plucked from the Hallmark shelf.

With trembling fingers, she popped the card open to find a message written in the same fancy curlicue script.

Hey, Valentine!
In your effort to help your friend get out of jail
Your blog has become a total fail
And while I consider that a real shame
I think we both know, you alone are to blame
If it's clues that you want
Then trust me, this is no taunt

*Inside the box awaits a surprise*
*I truly believe it will open your eyes*
*All I ask from you*
*Is to post it for public view*
*I hope you take the bait*
*And don't make me wait*
*If this all gives you pause*
*Then remember this clause:*
*Curiosity killed the cat—but satisfaction brought*
*her right back!*
*Xoxo*
*Your Secret Admirer*

Layla set the card aside and pried open the box, only to groan in dismay as a pile of pink confetti and glitter spilled out all around her. Her heart racing, she slipped a nail under the flap of the slim manila envelope hidden beneath and retrieved a single piece of paper folded neatly in thirds.

The paper was yellowing and worn, its edges curled, the writing dramatic and loopy, with small chubby hearts dotting the *i*'s and carefully drawn stars and twisting vines of flowers trailing the length of the margins.

Layla began to read, and by the time she reached the end she went right back to the beginning and started again. By the third reading, she was left with more questions than answers, mainly: *Who on earth did it belong to and why had someone seen fit to send it to her?*

She was just refolding the pages, about to slip them back into the envelope, when a picture she hadn't noticed tumbled out and landed faceup on her desk.

The girl in the photo was young, probably somewhere around seven or eight, but definitely no older than ten. Her hair was long, tangled, and dark. She had skinny legs and dirty bare feet. The dress she wore was wrinkled, stained, and at least one size too small, while the doll she dangled by her side was missing an eye and a limb and wore a strange, somewhat malevolent, lopsided grin.

But it was the girl's eyes that held Layla transfixed. They were so intense, so arresting, so startlingly familiar it was nearly impossible to look away.

Hurriedly, she shoved the package into her bag, pushed away from her desk, and darted toward the exit. Aware of Emerson's gaze burning into the back of her head, she anchored her cell between her shoulder and ear and in a lowered voice said, "We need to meet. I think I've just found our first clue."

# THREE

# THIS SUMMER'S GONNA HURT LIKE A MOTHERF****R

Aster Amirpour shuffled into the room and took the only chair available to her—the one bolted into the floor. Despite hating every moment of being locked in her cell, she'd come to dread leaving it as well, and for that she had her parents to thank. They meant well, she knew. But every visit from them and her attorneys left her feeling progressively worse, depleted of hope and resenting the freak show her life had become.

It was strange to think how just a few months earlier she'd graduated high school fully convinced she was standing on the precipice of a bright and shiny future, only to end up arrested for an A-list celebrity's murder.

All her life she'd dreamed of being famous—the face on every magazine cover, the name on everyone's lips. Never once had she imagined she'd achieve all those things in the absolute worst, most inconceivable way.

She'd been in lockup less than a week and she already missed absolutely everything having to do with her former life. She missed her little brother Javen so much it was like a physical ache. She missed the feel of the hot California sun on her skin and spontaneous trips to the beach with her friends. She missed shopping sprees at Barneys, her large collection of designer handbags and shoes, as well as her weekly salon appointments for manis, pedis, and blowouts. And after the revolting, carb-heavy, jail-issued meals she was forced to gag down, she could honestly say she even missed green juice. Basically every aspect of her daily existence she'd once taken for granted she found herself missing with the kind of intensity most people reserved for loved ones or pets. If she was lucky enough to get out, she swore to express a lot more gratitude for the luxurious life she'd been given.

But for the moment, locked behind bars and clothed in an orange jail-issued jumpsuit, there was little to be grateful for. Her parents refused to let Javen visit, claiming they didn't want Aster to traumatize him any more than she already had. Just when she was sure she'd reached rock bottom, their comment made her realize there were still several more layers of hell left to explore.

Then there were the shackles her jailers insisted she wear

on her ankles and wrists, which were not only humiliating but completely unnecessary. Aster wasn't violent, and she certainly didn't pose a threat to anyone, but she'd failed to convince them of that.

It was hardly her fault that within minutes of being locked into the overcrowded holding cell she'd been dragged into a brawl. One moment she was eyeballing the filthy exposed toilet set smack in the center of the cell, wondering how long she could hold out before she'd have no choice but to use it, and the next, some crazy chick was whaling on her with both fists, leaving Aster no choice but to use the moves she'd learned in kickboxing class. Even though she'd acted in self-defense, there was no explaining that to the powers that be.

In the end, the incident had gained her a black eye, a split lip, the distrust of her jailers, and her very own cell, which was meant as a punishment but felt more like a win.

She slumped toward the edge of her seat and waited for her attorneys to enter, hoping they'd finally agreed to post bail. Her parents could've handled it days ago, but they wanted to teach Aster a lesson. As though the first-degree murder charge she was facing wasn't lesson enough.

And yet, as desperate as she was to get out—as much as she hated the food, the filthy mattress, the lack of privacy, the disgusting smells, the hideous orange jumpsuit she was forced to wear, and pretty much everything else—the idea of returning home to live with her parents was its own kind of prison. Sure, the environment was incomparably luxurious, but the house rules were just as stringent. Though at the moment, it was the only option she had.

The door swooshed open behind her and Aster closed her eyes, wanting to savor a few moments to herself before she took in her mother's impeccably coiffed hair and expertly made-up face, which only seemed to emphasize the judgmental look in her eyes. Though as tough as it was facing her mother, seeing her father was worse. He could barely bring himself to look at her, and when he did, it left Aster wishing he hadn't bothered. His grief was so profound Aster swore she could see it emanating from him like exhaust from a car. She'd been a daddy's girl for as long as she could remember, but now that she'd done the unthinkable, now that she'd disappointed him and brought shame on the family, she was sure there was nothing she could ever do to regain his favor.

It was a childish game, refusing to look. She'd done the same thing as a kid whenever she was faced with something she didn't want to deal with. Of course it never worked, but that didn't stop her from trying. Still, maybe this time would be different. Maybe this time she'd wake from the nightmare and rewind her life to the day her agent called with news of Ira Redman's contest. Only this time, armed with the foresight she lacked then, she'd refuse the offer and spend the rest of the summer like any other normal eighteen-year-old—shopping, sunning, flirting with cute boys, and waiting for her first semester of college classes to begin.

"Aster. Aster—you okay?"

The voice was familiar, but it wasn't the one she'd expected. She blinked her eyes open to find Ira Redman sitting before her, wearing a crisp cotton shirt folded at the cuffs, the better to showcase his sporty Breguet watch. Beside him sat the attorney she'd met with before, back when she was first called in for questioning and had no idea just how much trouble she'd soon be facing.

"I'm not sure if you're aware, but I still represent you." The lawyer centered his gaze on hers.

Aster nodded and picked at her jail-issued jumpsuit, which drained her complexion and made her look as close to death as she currently felt. It was strange to see the two powerful men sitting before her. It was so opposite of what she'd expected it took a few moments to process.

"I would've come sooner, but you forgot to put us on the list." Ira shot her a pointed look that told her they both knew it wasn't exactly an oversight.

She squinted between the attorney and Ira. The two men were probably around the same age, but Ira was clearly the one wielding the power. In a place like LA, a bespoke suit and designer silk tie was the uniform of those who answered to a higher authority. Whereas Ira's dark designer jeans and untucked shirt indicated he answered to no one.

"We want to help you. If you'll let us, that is."

Aster stared at the dull green wall just past his shoulder, the shade forever imprinted on her mind as the color of misery, despair, and lost hope. She clenched her hands in her lap, unsure which of the two evils was worse, being in her parents' debt or Ira Redman's. God knew she needed help. Her parents' idea of support was to swap one jail for another by putting her under house arrest. Not that she actually had anywhere to go outside of the family manse. She was the most reviled person in LA. The safest place for her would be tucked away in her family's massive gated Beverly Hills estate, where no one could reach her.

Yet Aster refused to play it safe. Refused to admit she'd messed up her life so badly she needed her parents' strictest guidance to get back on track. She was just stubborn enough that she could not, absolutely would not, surrender to their will. But mostly, she'd do whatever was necessary to shield them from the mess and keep their involvement to a minimum. Accepting Ira's help was a sure way to do that.

She'd made so many stupid mistakes—falling for Ryan Hawthorne was at the top of the list. She'd let her ego take over and fooled herself into believing Ryan when he said he cared about her, that he'd always be there for her. It was all lies, of course.

What had Ira said? *Never trust an actor, Aster. They're always acting; they have no off switch.* It was only now that she could see the truth of those words.

All she knew for sure was that she didn't harm Madison Brooks. She was 100 percent innocent of any wrongdoing—despite the abundance of evidence the state of California was holding against her.

"We're prepared to post your bail."

Aster glanced at them between wet, clumpy lashes, unaware she'd been crying. She did that a lot lately.

"And what do you want in return?"

Ira and the attorney exchanged a loaded glance, before Ira switched his focus to her. "Nothing."

"You know I can never repay you." She frowned at her chipped nails and ragged cuticles. Her hair was matted and dirty, her skin broken out, and she was probably rocking a major case of unibrow, but she was too depressed to care about any of that. It wasn't like she was posting selfies from her jail cell.

"You going to flee the country?"

She frowned. "Where would I go?"

Ira shrugged. "Then it looks like neither of us has anything to worry about."

"And so you bail me out . . . and then what?"

"You return to your normally scheduled life. Your suite at the W is waiting."

She inched lower still on the hard plastic chair. It was embarrassing to keep taking from him. It needed to stop. She needed to stand on her own two feet. Though at the moment, she was so far gone, so in need of a savior, she had no idea where to start.

"And how am I supposed to live?" Aster mumbled the words. "How am I supposed to support myself? Who would be crazy enough to hire me?"

Ira laughed. Actually threw his head back and laughed as though she'd said something funny. When he finally quieted down, he looked at her and said, "Call me crazy, but I distinctly remember offering you a job, and I seem to remember you accepting."

"Yeah, and then five seconds later I was cuffed as someone read me my Miranda rights." She shook her head and refused to look at him. "I'm no good to you now."

"On the contrary." He was quick to counter. "This is Hollywood, Aster, not the Republican primary. In the nightclub biz, scandal is currency. Even so, if you decide you're not interested in my offer, there's still the matter of the prize money you won."

Aster wondered if she looked as surprised as she felt. Her last memory of the prize money was the moment Ira plucked the check from her fingers and slid it into his pocket. *For safekeeping*, he'd said, though the expression he wore had convinced her she'd never see it again. Seconds later, she was shoved into the back of a squad car and hauled away, and she'd pretty much forgotten about it until now. Had she really been so wrong about him?

"You earned it fair and square. It's yours for the taking. I deposited it in a trust account under your name."

"Keep it." She dismissed the offer with a quick wave of her hand. She might be desperate and broke, but it was the right thing to do. "Put it toward the attorney's fees and bail." She glanced briefly at the lawyer sitting opposite her and ran a series of quick calculations in her head. Though the prizewinning check bore an impressive number of zeros, it was merely a start. A good defense team would plow through it in no time. It would be spent well before they even made it to trial.

She dropped her chin to her chest and scrubbed her hands through her hair. She'd moved one step forward, only to find herself right back where she'd started. She had nowhere to live and no good way of supporting herself. As a high school grad with no real skills and a mug shot that had gone viral, she was untouchable, unemployable. The independence she'd longed for came at a price she could not afford.

"I'm serious about the job offer as well," Ira said, as though reading her mind.

"The job was as a promoter. How am I supposed to bring people in? I'm a social pariah!"

Ira remained undeterred. "If you want to change public opinion, you need to put yourself out there and prove you have nothing to hide. I wouldn't make the offer if I didn't think you were capable. Remember the promise I made at the start of the contest?"

She looked at him, her head spinning with all that he'd said, all that remained unsaid.

"I promised that working for me would amount to the sort of real-life experience you can't get at school, and I'm pretty sure I delivered, no?"

This time, when a rush of tears coursed down her cheeks, Aster did nothing to stop them. It marked the second time Ira had stepped in to help her in a way her parents refused to do. But more importantly, unlike her parents, Ira didn't judge her. Didn't try to keep her feeling diminished and small. His belief in her potential was relentless, and he encouraged her to believe in herself relentlessly too.

She wondered why he did it—why he even bothered. He'd never asked for anything in return other than for her to succeed at her job. For someone who always seemed to be working an angle, she'd yet to figure out what angle he was working with her.

While she loved her family, the thought of returning home to the watchful glare of Nanny Mitra and her parents was too much to bear. She hated the fact that she needed rescuing, but was grateful to have someone other than her parents to save her from drowning.

"Thank you," she said, her throat so constricted she nearly choked on the words.

Ira smiled and stood. A second later the lawyer stood too, saying, "It may take a few hours to process your bail, but you'll be out of here soon."

Aster watched as the guard opened the door and the two men filed out of the room.

"And Aster," Ira called over his shoulder. "Don't worry so much. It's all going to fall into place. I promise you that."

As the guard led her back to her cell, Aster clung to Ira's words like the life preserver they were.

FOUR

# WHY'D YOU COME IN HERE LOOKIN' LIKE THAT

Tommy Phillips arrived five minutes later than planned, but still early enough to claim the darkest, most secluded booth in the nearly empty bar. In a city fueled by ambitious overachievers who equated success with an inflated level of busyness, the only other patrons were tourists looking to boost their Instagram accounts with a grim piece of Hollywood lore, and the daytime regulars who bore the soft, defeated look of those who'd not only forfeited the race, but had chosen never to run.

In another three hours they'd all be gone, edged out by after-work warriors willing to look past the faint smell of burnt popcorn and the antiquated jukebox playing a steady stream of deep tracks in their search for cheap drinks, willing women, and any other vice with the promise to numb them.

While Tommy wasn't exactly living the dream, at least he'd managed to avoid that particular brand of nine-to-five hell.

He settled onto the red vinyl cushion and ordered a beer from the waitress who'd flashed him a flirty look he didn't return. A month ago, he wouldn't have hesitated to flaunt the heartbreaker grin that had made him a legend back at his Oklahoma high school. But ever since Madison Brooks disappeared and the tabloids turned their focus to him for the small walk-on part that he'd played, Tommy's go-to response to a pretty girl flirting was to avert his gaze and wait for her to move away.

It wreaked hell on his love life. Never mind his nonexistent sex life.

Like the rest of LA, he was eager for the dry spell to end.

He centered his gaze on the entrance, not wanting to miss the moment Layla arrived. Though they texted often, it'd been a week since he'd seen her. A week since LA was in flames and they watched their friend get hauled away for first-degree murder.

A few moments later, when the door swung open and Layla appeared as a small, black-clad figure in a circle of light, Tommy took one look at her platinum-blond hair, gray-blue eyes, and pale lovely face, and realized he wasn't even close to being over her.

Though she was definitely over him.

Not that there was anything to be *over* exactly. The kiss

they'd shared had been a one-time thing; not to mention, last he'd checked, Layla had a boyfriend. Still, the memory had managed to stick no matter how hard he tried to forget.

She paused in the entry, scanning the room. She'd find him eventually, though no thanks to him. It wasn't often Tommy got a chance to observe her unaware—looking just the slightest bit lost and unsure as opposed to her usual sarcasm and swagger—and he planned to enjoy it for as long as he could.

"Way to pick a venue, Tommy." Layla flung her bag into the booth and slid in beside it, as Tommy tried not to notice the way her dress hitched up her thighs. If she caught him staring, she'd eat him alive. "Isn't this where they found that actress's body parts chopped into bits and stored in plastic containers in the fridge?"

"That was back in the sixties. They've remodeled the kitchen since then," Tommy said, not the least bit disturbed by the bar's grisly past.

Layla took a dubious look all around. "Looks like that's the only thing that's been remodeled."

The waitress arrived with his beer and Layla ordered a coffee, black. As the server walked away, Layla turned to Tommy and said, "Did she just roll her eyes at me?"

"They depend on their tips." Tommy shrugged. "Besides, haven't you reached your caffeine quota by now?"

Layla checked her phone and placed it on the table before

her. "I didn't call you to discuss my need for coffee rehab."

Tommy bit back a grin and took a slow sip of beer. Layla had no patience for small talk. He'd learned that the first day they'd met, when he'd made the mistake of trying to engage the cute blonde who'd rolled up to the Unrivaled Nightlife interview on an electric-blue Kawasaki. That first meeting hadn't gone well, but back then Layla had hated Aster too. And yet, here she was, determined to find some way to save her.

Tommy pressed his forearms to the table and leaned toward her. It was time he stopped fantasizing about a relationship that would never be and focused on the real point of the meeting.

"Still can't get in to see Aster." Layla sighed. "Who knew county jail was tougher to breach than the VIP list at Ira's clubs?" She frowned. "Not to mention how I'm pretty sure Trena knows more than she's letting on. But every time I bring it up, she insists on talking around it. It's like she's determined to block me and I can't figure out why. After all, I'm the one who fed her the clue about Ryan Hawthorne. Maybe she needs a reminder."

"She's protecting her intel. Doesn't want you to scoop her, or whatever you journalists call it." Tommy watched as Layla absentmindedly drew invisible circles on the table-top using the tip of a blue-painted nail. Trena wasn't the only one talking around it; Layla was holding back too. On the phone, she'd been urgent, insisting he drop everything and meet right away. But now that they were face-to-face, she was acting like she regretted her choice, or worse—debating whether or not she could trust him.

Layla started to speak, then paused as the waitress dropped off her coffee. The moment the server moved out of earshot, she looked at Tommy and said, "I told her I'm no longer writing about it. I'm taking a break from the subject, and believe me when I say my numbers have plummeted because of it. My advertisers are bailing, and I'm taking a major money hit. Still, I can't in good conscience continue to write about it. Not when I'm sure Aster's innocent." She regarded her coffee with a regretful stare. "I never should've posted those pics of her and Ryan kissing. I put the cops right on her trail, and once there, they were too lazy to look anywhere else."

Tommy could hardly believe what he'd just heard. "And what about the pics you posted of me?"

If he was expecting an apology, clearly it wasn't forthcoming. He watched as Layla shot back against the vinyl upholstery, folded her arms at her chest, and centered a steely gaze right on his. "Way I remember it, you didn't hesitate to claim your fifteen minutes of fame."

Tommy felt flush with anger. No one ever triggered him quite like she could. After a few moments of edgy silence, he'd calmed enough to concede that what she'd said was in many ways true. Though he'd be damned if he'd admit it to her.

"So why not write in her defense?" he said, hoping to move on before Layla stormed out, or worse. The solution seemed obvious enough to him. If he had a blog, that was what he'd do. It's certainly the stance he'd taken whenever he granted an interview, which was less often these days.

Having moved to LA with dreams of breaking into the music industry, Tommy had soon discovered it wasn't going to be nearly as easy as he'd hoped. The good looks and talent that had made him a standout in his small Oklahoma town barely registered in a place where virtually everyone was ridiculously beautiful and well on their way to fortune and fame. So when news of Madison's disappearance first broke, Tommy didn't hesitate to claim a piece of the spotlight. At the time, he was sure Madison was merely lying low and would surface soon enough. What he hadn't counted on was the discovery of her blood on the Night for Night terrace, much less Aster's stained dress linking her to the crime.

Layla unfolded her arms and sipped from her coffee. After crinkling her nose in distaste, she went back for more. "Clearly you don't read my blog." She returned the cup to its saucer. "Otherwise you'd know that the one time I dared write a piece in Aster's defense, it resulted in death threats." She shook her head at the memory.

"Everyone loves an easy target." Tommy studied her, watching an array of emotions play across her delicate features as she reluctantly nodded in agreement.

"Unfortunately for Aster, she's easy to hate. She's young, rich, gorgeous, a little on the prissy side. . . ."

"A little?" Tommy felt ashamed the moment he said it. With everything Aster was facing, it didn't seem right to poke fun, no matter how true the accusation. "Though actually, the same goes for you. Anytime you dare to put yourself out there, or worse, put yourself out there in a way that honors your convictions, you can expect to be dog piled."

"Speaking from experience?" Layla quirked a brow as her gaze moved over him.

Tommy shrugged and sipped his beer, remembering the backlash he'd faced—the slew of hate tweets, his car tires getting slashed—all because he'd been the last known person to be seen with Madison. The internet was the most terrifying court of all. It was mob mentality at its worst—rife with torch-wielding armchair judges ready to convict on mere hearsay alone. Luckily for Tommy, the furor had eventually died down, but only because the haters had found a new target in Aster.

"Look," Layla said. "As the former president of the I Hate Aster Amirpour Club, I get it. But now I just want to help her. For one thing, Aster's innocent. For another, it's the right thing to do."

Tommy studied her closely. She was acting odd, cagey, purposely avoiding whatever she'd come to discuss. And while part of him wished the whole thing had been an excuse just to see him, he knew better. Layla was simply not the flirty, coy type. She was the most straightforward girl he'd ever met, or at least, usually. At the moment, she clearly needed a nudge, even though she was the one who'd called for the meeting.

"So what's this evidence you found?" He pressed back against the cushion and waited for her to fess up.

With a resigned sigh, she sank a hand into her bag, retrieved a package, and pushed it across the table toward him.

Tommy glanced between Layla and the heart-shaped box, then settled in to read.

March 14, 2012

Today at school I almost gave myself away. Or, actually, I did give myself away, but since it was only in front of Dalton, it's not exactly the emergency it could've been, since everyone knows that Dalton doesn't really count as a person who matters enough for other people to actually listen to.

Still, I can hardly believe that after all the hard work I've done to successfully erase any and all traces of my former hillbilly accent, watching countless old movies so I'd sound sorta British, or, at the very least, like I could be from just about anywhere but WV, I was ~~stupid~~

careless enough to totally out myself for the hick that I am.

Anyway, it all started when I spilled a can of paint all over my smock during art class and let out a stream of curses that normally wouldn't be any big thing unless a teacher overheard (which luckily didn't happen, since Mr. Castillo was too busy updating his Tinder profile to pay attention to me), but quickly became a VERY BIG DEAL when Dalton overheard and I realized I'd ACCIDENTALLY USED MY OLD ACCENT!!!!!

Ugh.

I can't even. ☹

The second I realized what I'd done, well, I just stood there like an idiot. I swear, I could hardly even breathe!! And when Dalton's eyes met mine, I sincerely thought I would die right then and there. It felt like my whole life was rewinding—flashing right before my eyes. It was like I was literally watching all my dreams—everything I've been working toward—vanish in one horrible moment.

Or at least that's how it seemed at first.

But after a few seconds ticked past, I pulled it together enough to realize that if I wanted to undo the damage, then I needed to own what I did.

So, while Dalton was busy standing there gawking as though he was trying to process how best to handle this juicy bit of intel, I looked right at him and forced myself to smile as I said, "Tell me the truth—did that sound authentic?"

Dalton just stood there, mouth gaping like a fish at feedin' time.

So I smiled wider and said, "I'm auditioning for a TV commercial this weekend, and I'm working on my accent."

He stared at me for so long I actually started to sweat. It was like I could see his mind processing the quickest way to use my mistake to leapfrog his way to instant popularity.

"There's a kissing part too," I added, before I could fully think it through. Still, desperate times call for desperate measures, and all that. . . .

I inched closer, so close we were nearly touching, and said, "And I should probably work on that too. Maybe you can help me rehearse after school?"

Whatever he'd been thinking of doing to me before, well, he was now thinking of doing something entirely different. And even though I was reluctant to go through with it, now that I'd put it out there, I had no choice but to commit.

He waited for me after school, and I let him walk me home. Luckily, the parents were at work, so we had the whole house to ourselves. And even though I only planned to let him kiss me for no more than ten minutes max, surprisingly, kissing Dalton wasn't so bad, so I decided to bring him up to my room and go a little longer (and a little further!) than planned.

By this time tomorrow, Dalton will be popular (I'll make sure of it) and my secret will be safe. I just hope he doesn't expect me to be his girlfriend or anything, because while he may be a decent kisser, I can't risk getting close to him.

<u>Can't risk getting close to anyone, ever.</u>

I was just lucky it was Dalton and not Emma or Jessa or someone who wouldn't be quite so easy to ~~manipulate~~ distract.

In the end, I guess it wasn't too bad. If nothing else, it served as an important reminder of how I can't afford to let my guard down.

How I can never stop acting like the shiny new version of myself.

<u>How I can never stop acting, period.</u>

The diary entry was so full of contradictions it was hard to process. The proliferation of hearts, flowers, and stars was definitely the mark of a romantic, dreamy-eyed teen. But the actual content displayed the kind of ambition, maturity, and determination rarely found in someone that age. Tommy studied the xeroxed copy, having no doubt Madison had written it. And judging by the date at the top, she'd been around fourteen at the time.

He studied the picture again. Only one person had eyes like that, and the eyes never lied.

While Tommy had no idea what it might mean, one thing was sure: Madison Brooks was not at all the person she pretended to be.

The posh East Coast accent was a fake. And while the childhood she recounted in interviews might have been true for the latter part of her life, if the pic and diary entry were anything to go by, Madison's earlier years were markedly different from the story she told. Her life as she'd described it was no more than an ingenious work of fiction.

Clearly Madison had worked hard to bury her secrets, leaving Tommy to wonder if those same secrets were somehow responsible for what happened to her.

Had the truth of her past come back to haunt her?

"So . . . what do you think?" Layla leaned toward him. "It's Madison, right?"

Tommy swallowed. Not trusting his voice, he cleared his throat before he attempted to speak. "It's definitely her." He shook his head. It seemed so improbable, so unlikely, and yet, it made perfect sense. Their time together had been brief, but it left a lasting impression. And one thing was sure, the way she drank a beer, the way she kissed, and the way she'd let her accent slip left no doubt in his mind that there was more to Madison Brooks than there seemed.

"Kind of creepy, though." He glanced at Layla, who nodded in a way that encouraged him to go on. "I mean, she's so cold and calculating the way she manipulated that Dalton kid into keeping her secret." He shook his head and swiped a hand through his hair. "I mean, she was only fourteen and she was already trading sex for favors—or implied sex anyway."

"Never mind that part about how she's always acting—can never stop acting." Layla frowned. "I mean, if her whole life is make-believe, does that mean her disappearance is fake too?"

Tommy took a moment to consider the question, though he had no good way to respond. "Who sent this?" He forced his gaze away from the pic and back on Layla.

She shrugged. "My guardian angel, I guess."

Tommy held Layla's gaze. "What about Ira?" He'd warned her about Ira before, or more accurately, his suspicions regarding Ira. Ira had played Layla all through the contest, always pretending to be *this close* to firing her and yet never quite managing to go through with it. Tommy was convinced it was all an act. Layla was never really in danger of being fired, not until the very end anyway, and for that, she had her blog to thank. The sensationalistic, gossip-fueled stories she posted on Beautiful Idols were good for Ira's clubs, made them a bigger draw than they already were. At the time, Layla wouldn't even consider Tommy's theory. But after watching the way Ira reacted toward Aster's arrest, how he failed to display the slightest hint of emotion when he plucked the prizewinning check from her hands, he wondered if she'd finally woken up to see what was so glaringly obvious to him.

Ira Redman was not to be trusted.

Just because Ira happened to be Tommy's biological dad, and just because Tommy was eager to clinch the sort of success that would allow him to confidently reveal their connection, didn't mean Tommy liked him.

"Ira's more of a fallen angel than a guardian angel." Layla reached for a raw sugar packet, inspected both sides, then returned it to where it came from. "Besides, why would he bother?"

*So you'll blog about it,* he thought, but refrained from actually saying it. Mostly because he wasn't exactly sure what Ira could possibly gain from that, other than more exposure for his clubs, which seemed motivating enough, but still he just said, "I guess I thought maybe, since you and your dad are both working for him—"

Layla cut him off before he could finish. "My dad and I haven't seen much of each other. He's mostly holed up at the Vesper all day working on the mural Ira hired him to paint. You probably see him more than me."

Tommy shrugged. "The new VIP room is strictly off-limits. Apparently the artist doesn't wish to be disturbed."

"Believe me, it's the same policy when he's working at home." Layla fell into silence as they both nursed their drinks.

The sight of a pensive Layla sitting before him left Tommy with a primal longing to swoop her into his arms and protect her—that and so many other things he might do once he had her securely pressed up against him. . . .

"We need to do something."

The sound of her voice shook him out of his reverie. And when his eyes met hers, it was clear Layla wasn't looking to be rescued, or anything else.

"I'm tired of sitting around doing nothing while Aster's in jail. I think we should make a list of evidence, things we need to follow up on. Between the picture, the diary entry, and Aster's video, we have enough to start our own investigation."

Tommy wiped a hand across his mouth and placed the empty bottle before him. "I have a gig." He fielded Layla's quizzical look with a shrug.

"I thought you wanted to help." Her brow knotted as her gaze narrowed on his. "I mean, why else are you here?"

Tommy sighed, ran a hand through his hair, and glanced toward the bar, suddenly regretting his decision to meet. Aster was the only daughter of wealthy parents with unlimited resources. There was nothing he and Layla could possibly offer that Aster's family and some white-shoe law firm couldn't. Despite what Layla thought, they lacked resources and know-how, not to mention any worthwhile evidence. So what if Madison wasn't always named

Madison? She'd hardly be the first in Hollywood to create a fictional past for herself.

The only reason Tommy was sitting in that booth was because he'd wanted to see Layla again. It didn't make sense; she wasn't his usual type, but that didn't stop him from thinking about her pretty much all the time. But clearly Layla saw him only as a potential Scooby Gang member. And the way she was glaring at him left no doubt that his feelings for her would forever go unrequited.

It was time he distanced himself from Layla and the whole Madison mess she was dragging him into. He was tired of always looking over his shoulder. Tired of always being hounded by paparazzi. Tired of complete strangers tweeting so much shit about him.

He'd arrived in LA with a dream, and it was time he started taking meaningful steps toward making it real.

"Have you ever considered that maybe Aster is guilty?" he said.

Layla balked. He'd rendered her speechless. A victory of sorts, though it hardly felt worth celebrating.

"You did not just say that," she snapped.

Tommy had meant exactly that and more. In the days since Aster's arrest, he'd had plenty of time to contemplate the evidence leveled against her, and he was no longer so convinced of her innocence. "She was dating Madison's boyfriend," he said. "They found Madison's blood on her dress. Not to mention how Aster's alibi for that night just doesn't add up. She doesn't remember? Really? Don't you think that's a stretch?"

"You can't be serious."

Layla was in shock—angry, and in shock. But someone needed to say it. Might as well be him. The evidence piling up against Aster made it increasingly difficult to believe in her.

Besides, how well did he actually know her? Not well at all. His experience with Aster was mostly limited to the contest, and even that revealed Aster as cutthroat, focused, and willing to play dirty and do whatever was necessary to secure the win.

Didn't matter that the same could be said of him. He wasn't guilty of harming Madison, whereas he couldn't definitively say the same of Aster.

"I'm out." He slid an envelope across the table toward Layla, watching as she blinked but wouldn't so much as touch it. "Madison's keys," he explained. He should've turned them over to the police right from the start. But with Detective Larsen always breathing down his neck, Tommy had hung on to them, convinced Larsen would only use them against him. "Wiped clean of my prints, I might add." He exhaled long and deep, relieved to finally be rid of them. "Seriously, I want nothing to do with this." In an instant he was up, pulling a sizable handful of bills from his wallet and tossing them onto the table. He'd managed to find a place where he could drink a beer without being carded, and he hoped to keep it that way.

"But you haven't even read the card yet! There was a card that came with it—it had a cartoon picture of a seriously messed-up cat, and—"

"Don't need to," he interrupted. "I meant what I said."

"I can't even believe this!" Layla's voice was harsh, attracting the attention of the drunks at the bar, and she wore an expression so furious Tommy cringed when he met it.

He nodded toward the guy aiming a camera in their direction. "Pretty sure the waitress alerted the paparazzi. I'm guessing we have less than five minutes before we're swarmed. Guess you should've ordered more than a coffee."

Instinctively, he slung a protective arm around Layla's shoulder, scowled at the photog, and rushed her toward the door, all the while cursing himself for so quickly abandoning his vow to be done with her. First sign of trouble and there he was, jumping to Layla's rescue, willing to do whatever it took to protect her. It was the decent thing to do, sure, but it also left him wondering if he'd ever truly be over her.

He'd see her safely to her car and no more. After that, they'd go their separate ways. He wished her and Aster well, but this was the end as far as he was concerned. Tommy Phillips was officially moving on.

# FIVE

# I WOULD DIE 4 U

**Spotlight magazine exclusive!**

**Spotlight:** *We here at* Spotlight *recently caught up with teen heartthrob Ryan Hawthorne, who has been through a whirlwind of a rough time lately. Between the cheating scandal that led to the very public breakup with his girlfriend, A-lister Madison Brooks, followed by Madison's disappearance, Ryan himself being called in for questioning, and the cancellation of his show (which we just received confirmation of after weeks of rumors) . . . Well, Ryan, first things first—our condolences on all the bad news. How are you holding up?*

**Ryan:** *Thanks, but no condolences needed. Life has its cycles, and peaks are always bordered by valleys. The key is to accept each stage as it comes, find the* *lesson so you can learn and grow and try not to repeat your mistakes, and never, ever take the good times for granted, or the dark moments personally.*

**Spotlight:** *Well, that's certainly very enlightening of you. Not sure we could maintain such serenity in the face of all you've been dealing with. Maybe we need a new life coach or yoga studio!*

**Ryan:** *Is there a question here?*

**Spotlight:** *Certainly, and we'll get right to it! We know* Spotlight *readers are dying to hear your take on these recent events, including the arrest of your former paramour, Aster Amirpour, just hours after you spoke to detectives. Do you have any thoughts you'd like to share pertaining to Aster's arrest and the part she allegedly played in the murder of Madison Brooks? Was there some insight or clue you shared with police that led them to the discovery of the blood-soaked dress?*

**Ryan:** *Are you serious?*

**Spotlight:** *Well, even you have to admit the timing is extremely suspicious. . . .*

**Ryan:** *What I know is that I willingly spoke to the police. I wasn't "dragged in for questioning" or however you chose to relay it at the time. Also, I had nothing to do with the discovery of the dress or Aster's arrest. I was as surprised as you are. You have to understand that I haven't spoken to Aster since the scene at Night for Night. And though I deeply regret my actions,* *which I've stated on countless occasions, I sincerely doubt Aster had anything to do with Madison's disappearance. I also don't believe Madison is dead.*

**Spotlight:** *And the dress?*

**Ryan:** *What about it?*

**Spotlight:** *Bloodstains don't lie. And from what we've learned so far, the dress was covered in them.*

**Ryan:** *I can hardly be expected to comment on things I know nothing about. I've made my feelings clear, and I stand by my word. All I can do is continue praying for Madison's safe return, and see how it all plays out once the case goes to trial. If you're asking me to speculate, well, I'm sorry to disappoint you, but I won't do that.*

**Spotlight:** *Right. Well, we thank you for taking the time to speak with us, and like you, we're also praying for Madison's return. Before you go, any hints for what's next?*

**Ryan:** *I've got a few projects in the works, but nothing I can announce just yet.*

**Spotlight:** *Well, I hope you'll consider giving us an exclusive!*

**Ryan:** *Yeah. Um, okay. We'll see.*

**Spotlight:** *You read it here first, life moves on for Ryan Hawthorne, and we at* Spotlight *wish him all the best!*

"Why are you scowling like that?"

Mateo tossed the magazine aside and rushed to the side of his little sister's hospital bed. He brushed a concerned hand over her forehead, relieved to find her skin mercifully cool, showing no sign of the fever that had started it all just one week before.

A fever, followed by bruising, unexplained weight loss, and eventually a fainting episode at school. Acute lympho-blastic leukemia was the official diagnosis, or ALL as they called it—a scary name for when the body went rogue and decided to manufacture too many immature white blood cells. And now, because of it, Valentina's immune system was so weakened she'd succumbed to an opportunistic infection.

"How are you feeling?" He struggled to shake off any lingering traces of anger the article had sparked. But seeing his little sister looking so helpless and small among all the needles and tubes and the port in her chest awaiting chemo-therapy only managed to trigger him more.

This was what truly mattered! His fingers circled the bed rails so hard his knuckles pushed taut against his skin. Yes, a celebrity had gone missing, had maybe even been murdered, which was an undeniably terrible thing, but did it really deserve to claim every headline when there were so many innocents suffering in the world?

What made Madison's story more worthy than the

tragic tale of his sweet little sister?

Why did people care more about celebrities than the fate of everyday people?

Valentina regarded him closely. "Well, now I really need to read it." She nodded toward the magazine. "The way it got you all wound up, there's clearly something good in there, so hand it over, please!"

Mateo frowned and made no move to retrieve the magazine. "You shouldn't be reading that stuff." Even to his ears he sounded stodgy, old, and judgmental, but he assured himself he was only trying to protect her.

"Why, because I'm too young?"

In his eyes, Valentina would always be the cherished baby sister he'd give his life for. But knowing how much she'd hate hearing that, he leaned against the bed rail, brushed her long dark curls away from her forehead, and said, "No, because it's too trashy for a classy princess like you."

She tried to scowl in return, but it was only a second later when her face burst into a grin that made his heart lurch. The fact that she could even manage such a thing in light of all she was facing was almost too much to bear.

How was it possible that just a few weeks earlier she'd celebrated her birthday looking as vibrant and healthy as any other ten-year-old girl, only to end up in this horrible, sterile room with its mint-green walls and tired floors, hooked up to various tubes and machines responsible for keeping her alive?

Seeing his little sister suffer was the absolute worst thing he'd ever experienced, and Mateo had seen more than his share of sorrow. But Valentina was a child, an innocent. She didn't deserve any of this. The whole thing reeked of unfairness, and it left him wondering if the black cloud hanging over his family would ever move on.

The Luna Curse—it was the name he'd given to the unfathomable situations they continued to find themselves in. With the death of his father shortly after Valentina's birth, followed by the loss of his older brother Carlos a few years later, Mateo was sure he'd seen the worst of what life had to offer. The night they'd received the call informing them that Carlos had overdosed outside a Hollywood nightclub hadn't been entirely unexpected. Carlos had suffered from addiction for a while, had even gone a few rounds with a local rehab center. Still, the devastating news had thrown the Lunas into a spiral of grief they were only just beginning to recover from when Valentina fell ill.

Clearly the Luna Curse hadn't gone anywhere. It had merely taken a hiatus, a much-needed rest in which to gather enough strength to come roaring back—rearing its ugly head and descending on them with a vengeance they could never imagine.

He watched her lids flutter closed once again. She tired so easily, and yet she was imbued with an inner strength that surpassed everyone else's, somehow managing to remain happy and cheerful and never once complaining, no matter how bad things got. Mateo wished he could do the same.

While their mom fought hard to keep a brave face, inside she was broken. And most of the time Mateo felt broken too. In the last week alone his mom had lost her job, and Mateo had lost Layla. Both of which, while bad, weren't entirely out of the ordinary. But this—this thing with Valentina—was all the proof he needed that it was time for him to step up and do whatever it took to look after his family.

He reached for his sister's hand. It looked so small and pale folded in his. Up until now, he'd had the luxury of not wanting for much. He'd easily gotten by on the pay (plus tips) he made working as a surf butler at some of the fancier resorts. The usual trappings of success—a big house and showy car—held no interest for him. And though he recognized his lack of ambition as a growing source of irritation for Layla, he'd never thought it a problem until now.

After listening to the pediatric oncologist explain the course of treatment and all the exorbitant costs that accompanied it—the sort of costs that could easily break them, possibly even leave them all homeless—there was no denying it was time for him to grow up and shoulder the burden his mom could no longer carry alone.

Maybe Layla was right.

Maybe his lack of ambition was a much bigger issue than he'd initially realized.

Maybe it was immature, childish, a refusal to start acting more responsibly and taking the first steps toward adulthood.

Or maybe it wasn't that at all.

Maybe it was just who he was—mellow, content, interested in pursuing the kind of things money couldn't buy.

All he knew for sure was that the one time he had compromised hadn't gotten him anywhere. Hoping to bridge the growing rift between them, he'd planned to surprise Layla with the news that he'd accepted a sponsorship with a surf brand that had been after him for a while. Only before he could tell her, he'd received an anonymous text with a picture of Layla kissing Tommy, and they hadn't spoken since.

Not like it mattered. As it turned out, a sponsorship mostly consisted of a pile of logo T-shirts and swim trunks and a handful of stickers to put on his boards. It wasn't the payday it used to be. The exotic surf trips (which he didn't really care about) and the monthly paychecks (which he did) were reserved for the top few on the professional circuit—an elite tribe to which Mateo didn't belong.

Still, he wasn't without options. And though he'd once sworn against the idea of relying on his good looks to make a living, confronted by the sight of his baby sister, her life dependent on the tubes that slow-dripped various liquids into her veins, he no longer had the luxury of thinking that way. Turned out, there were some things that *only* money could buy—like the best hospitals, doctors, and lifesaving treatments for Valentina. And it was up to Mateo to find a way to provide those things for her.

"How are we doing?" The door swung open behind him, and he turned to find the nurse briskly entering the room. "Anything I can get you?"

Mateo started to shush her, warn that his sister was sleeping, when Valentina's eyes popped open and she nodded toward the chair by her bed.

"Can you hand me that magazine, please?" She shot a glance at Mateo and grinned triumphantly when the nurse promptly retrieved the tabloid and placed it onto her lap. "My brother thinks it's too trashy for me—what do you think?" Valentina held it before her, the cover displaying a picture of Madison looking angelic beside Aster's haggard mug shot—her hair tangled, face pale, as her fearful gaze stared into the camera.

The nurse took a moment to consider. "I think he's probably right." She nodded gravely as she set about checking Valentina's blood pressure. Then, brightening, she said, "But that's last week's news. Have you heard the latest?"

Valentina's eyes widened as she sat up a little straighter, and Mateo groaned in frustration. His little sister was ten going on sixteen, and like most girls her age, she idolized Madison—wanted to be just like her. Also, like most ten-year-olds, she hated being treated like a child. And while Mateo wanted to stop it—stop her illness, stop her preteen obsession with celebrities—he was powerless against both of those things.

Though there was something he could do—something he could no longer afford to avoid.

As Valentina and the nurse discussed the merits of their favorite Madison movies, Mateo pressed a kiss to his sister's cheek and stepped outside the room. Hurrying down the hall, he pulled his phone from his pocket, scrolled through his long list of contacts, and sighed in relief when he saw he'd at least had the foresight not to delete the one number that just might change his run of bad luck.

"Hello," he said, the moment the phone connected. "You told me to call if I ever changed my mind about your offer. Pretty sure I just did."

# SIX

# HOTLINE BLING

*LA Times* reporter Trena Moretti stifled a yawn and amped up the stereo on the Lexus she'd driven off the lot just a few weeks before. Having grown up in New York City only to spend the last several years in DC, she had no need for a car and considered it an unnecessary, climate-destroying convenience she would not indulge in. But LA was a car-conscious place that held fast to its motto: *You are what you drive.* If she wanted to fit in, she needed to at least make an attempt to do as the natives did.

Initially she had her heart set on a used Porsche, but when the salesperson guided her across the lot to the dark red Lexus coupe, it was love at first sight. And it wasn't long before she'd become addicted to the thrill of driving the racy convertible.

She glanced in the rearview mirror, assessing her clear blue-green eyes, dark caramel complexion, and headful of wild bronze-tinged curls she'd long ago given up trying to tame. Maybe she still looked the same, but falling in love with a car proved she was dangerously close to becoming a full-blown Angeleno.

She pulled alongside the curb and drummed her thumbs on the steering wheel as she watched the girl juggle dueling Starbucks cups as she struggled to open the passenger door.

Trena leaned across the seat and propped the door open, flinching against the rush of heat she'd let in. "Priya?" She was surprised to find that the girl with her long black hair, smooth brown skin, and flashing dark eyes was even prettier in person than she was in her picture—a rarity in a Facetune-addicted town like LA.

"My research tells me you're a chai latte fan." Priya handed over the cup, and Trena grinned in return. Sure the move was ingratiating, but Trena was appreciative all the same. After buckling in, Priya turned to Trena to say, "Before we get started, I have to tell you what an honor this is. I'm a really big fan of your work."

Trena gave a curt nod. Flattery was always nice, but she had no interest in being fawned over and needed to make that clear from the start.

"Tell me—what is it you hope to get out of this?" Trena checked her side and rearview mirrors and merged into oncoming traffic. At the charity auction, Priya had been the most aggressive bidder by far, pledging a surprising amount of money to ensure she won the "Day of Mentoring with Trena Moretti" prize. So surely she had some kind of agenda in mind.

Without hesitation, Priya replied, "An offer for a full-time position as your assistant would be a good start."

Trena took a moment to process the words. While it didn't exactly come as a surprise, she wasn't convinced it would work. Her last assistant had quit after less than a month, citing extreme boredom in the exit interview, and Trena couldn't say that she blamed her. Other than sending the girl on frequent chai runs, there really wasn't much for her to do. Or rather, there was plenty for her to do, but Trena was too much of a control freak to actually delegate anything important.

She stopped at a red light and nodded toward the billboard ahead touting Madison Brooks's upcoming movie. Madison might be missing, but her face was just about everywhere one looked—peering out from newspapers, magazines, TV screens, movie ads, and tasteless internet memes—like a specter haunting the city. In this particular case she wore her usual impenetrable expression, her face a mask of poised professionalism that gave nothing away.

"What do you think happened to her?" Trena nodded

toward the sign and watched as Priya regarded it with a long, shrewd look.

"Wherever she is, I don't believe for a second that Aster Amirpour was involved." Priya glanced between the picture of Madison and Trena. "I think someone's setting her up."

Trena held the look. The girl had a spark of fire and determination Trena could relate to, only Priya seemed a bit more composed and polished than Trena had been at her age.

"She's too pampered, too soft, a born-and-bred Beverly Hills princess if I ever saw one." Priya bit her lip, as though surprised she'd just said that out loud. "I just don't believe she has it in her to go all homicidal like that."

"Maybe not," Trena said. "But under the right circumstances, anyone's capable of just about anything, murder included—never forget that." As a journalist, it was the motto Trena lived by. After a moment she added, "And yet, I also have a hard time believing Aster's involved with whatever happened to Madison Brooks." Her words faded into silence as they passed through the intersection.

It was just too easy, too convenient. After weeks with little to nothing to go on, the clues had just popped out of nowhere, lining up like obedient soldiers awaiting inspection. Maybe that was standard practice on TV shows where crimes were regularly committed and solved in the forty-two minutes of airtime allotted between commercial breaks, but in the real world, it was never that easy. Life was messy. Murder was messier.

When it came right down to it, the whole Aster/Madison conspiracy reeked of bullshit. One hundred percent, pure grade bullshit.

Or, this being LA, free-range, grass-fed, organic bullshit—but bullshit all the same.

Trena had a nose for bullshit, able to sniff it out like a hog on a truffle hunt. Ever since she was a kid, she'd had a sixth sense for trouble and lies. Her grandmother, Noni, claimed she'd inherited "the gift" of a long line of Moretti women, but Trena had always been practical and no-nonsense, never buying into Noni's woo-woo beliefs. All she knew for sure was that her gut knew things well before her head had caught on, and that instinct, when she followed it, never steered her wrong.

It was what helped her survive the tough, crime-ridden neighborhood she'd grown up in.

It was what led her to the best stories back when she was first starting out as a journalist.

And more recently, it was what saved her from making the biggest mistake of her life by almost marrying her lying, cheating ex-fiancé.

While moving to LA wasn't exactly the career path she'd planned, and while more than one colleague (mainly print snobs) had questioned whether transitioning from her reporting gig at the *Washington Post* to spearhead the *LA Times* digital division wasn't perhaps a step down, Trena didn't care. Step down or not, one thing was sure—it was a step in a new direction. A step away from a past she was eager to put well behind her. Not only did the job get her out of DC, but it offered a whole new life she'd never considered. And what better place to reinvent herself than in the very city that specialized in extreme makeovers?

During the five hours it had taken to fly from DC to LA, Trena had decided to make her mark at the *Times* by exposing the thick layer of grime hidden beneath the town's glossy exterior. It probably wouldn't make her the most popular journalist, but it would make her the most feared, and where there was fear there was power.

While she hated to think of Madison's disappearance as a lucky break, there was no denying the articles she'd written about it had elevated Trena's byline to must-read status. She was the first to question whether Madison had been murdered—the first to point out how the LAPD wasn't doing much in the way of investigating. Though her reporting hadn't won her any fans where local law enforcement was concerned, it had worked at spurring them into action. And it was only a short time later when evidence of foul play began to appear.

"Tell me what you know about Madison." Trena

cruised past a long line of palm trees, their fronds look-ing dull and burnt, slumping beneath the relentless glare of the sun. "What do you see when you look in those eyes?" She motioned toward another of Madison's billboards, her deep violet gaze hinting at something Trena could never quite grasp.

It was the gaze of one who'd stared into the abyss and lived to tell the tale—or, in Madison's case, bury the tale so deep even a cadaver-sniffing hound couldn't track it.

Then again, maybe Trena was in too deep to see it objec-tively. Maybe a younger, fresher, less jaded perspective was just what she needed.

Priya looked thoughtful as she picked at the lid on her cup. "I see a girl with a solid grasp on her image. A girl who only reveals what she wants you to see. As for what I know . . ." She frowned. "Probably the same stuff as you. She's an only child. Her parents were killed in a house fire when she was nine. After which she was sent to live with a nice foster family in Connecticut, only to leave home at fourteen and head for LA, where she pretty much became an overnight success."

"Eight," Trena interrupted. "The fire happened when Madison was eight."

Priya cocked her head. "Really? Could've sworn it was nine."

Trena ran a quick mental review of everything she'd

read, everything she knew. It wasn't the age that mattered. Trena knew she was right, and yet it also begged a question she hadn't thought to pose until now. Her pulse quickening, she said, "Where was Madison between the fire and her foster parents? Who looked after her—where did she stay?"

"I don't know." Priya squinted. "I always assumed she was caught up in the system."

It was the same thing Trena had assumed, and it left her steeped in shame. Assuming was for amateurs. It was sloppy, lazy, and Trena knew better. Perhaps she could use an assistant, after all. More than ever she was convinced that the key to discovering where Madison had gone depended on uncovering where she'd been long before she became Hollywood's It Girl. So far, her research had gotten her nowhere, and yet one simple conversation with Priya had pointed down an alley that just might yield something good.

"It's just that . . ." Priya paused as though organizing her thoughts. "Her bio reads more like fiction than real life. It has just the right amount of tragedy, followed by just the kind of emotional punch the audience loves. Like they called in the industry's top screenwriters to craft the story of Madison's rise to the top. It doesn't ring true."

Trena couldn't agree more.

"I mean, what kind of parents cheer when their underage

teen boards a bus bound for Hollywood?" Priya rolled her eyes and shook her head, her brow furrowed in judgment.

Again, it was exactly what Trena had thought. While Hollywood was aspirational for many, it was also well known for eating its young. Which meant no responsible and loving parent would support their kid making that move on their own—and especially not at fourteen.

"Question is—who helped her get settled, and where are they now?" Trena looked at the dark-eyed girl sitting beside her. "Because one thing is sure, Madison didn't conquer this city on her own. She may be more mature than most— an old soul, if you will—but she certainly didn't navigate the Los Angeles real estate market without help of some kind."

Priya's eyes flashed. Her enthusiasm was so infectious Trena found herself uttering the very thing she'd earlier convinced herself not to. And yet she'd be foolish to miss the opportunity. Sure the girl was young and a bit too eager to please, but she was also smart, driven, and maybe exactly what Trena needed to kick the Madison story to the next level.

"What if you start out part-time and we'll see how that goes?"

Priya didn't even try to conceal her excitement. "Can I start now? Seriously, you can drop me off right here and I'll call for an Uber. Oh, unless you still want me to finish the day like we planned?"

Trena turned onto Hollywood Boulevard. The plan had been for Priya to sit in and observe while Trena interviewed Ira Redman at his new club, after which Trena would take the girl out for a meal, give her some advice, shake hands, and be done with it. But now, all of that seemed like a huge waste of Priya's talents and time.

Trena pulled to the curb. "Where will you start?" She watched as Priya slung her purse on her shoulder and jumped from the car.

"I have my sources." The girl raised her phone to her ear, shot Trena an enigmatic grin, and raced down the boulevard as Trena drove a bit farther before parking in the only available space that wasn't occupied by a work truck.

She smiled at the bouncer who met her at the back door, wondering if he remembered her from the last time she'd stopped by Night for Night—the night Madison had gone missing.

"Ms. Moretti." He gave her a quick once-over, before admitting her inside.

Trena started to enter, then thought better and paused in the entry. She was on her way to interview Ira Redman, an interview she'd been trying to secure since before Madison Brooks disappeared. Though she intended to ask the tough questions and really go after him, she was sure Ira would try to turn it into a puff piece—the sort of vanity profile she had no interest in writing.

But maybe she had it all wrong.

Maybe she'd been too focused on the front door when she should've been eyeing the back.

While she had no doubt that Ira held the key to the city's numerous secrets, she was just as sure he had every intention of keeping them sealed. When it came to her job, Trena was a pro, but men like Ira were so well versed in charm and PR it was nearly impossible to dig past the surface and make a dent in the glossy veneer.

But a guy like James . . .

Trena paused long enough to give the bouncer an appreciative look. Thanks to a solid mix of Jamaican and Italian genes combined with daily six-mile runs, at thirty-six years old Trena could still hold her own. Sure, certain parts weren't exactly as pert as they once were, but what she lacked in youthful springiness, she more than made up for in experience.

Or at least that was what she used to think until her break with her fiancé left her feeling vulnerable, distrusting, and doubting her prowess. She'd responded to his betrayal by throwing herself into work, and purposely ignoring any man who so much as looked at her. But now, with the sexy bouncer standing before her, she wondered if she might carve out some time for a little flirtation. He was younger than her, but from the considering grin he'd shot her, it wasn't like it mattered. Still, it'd been so long since she'd last been with a man, her attempt at flirting left her feeling foolish, and more than a little self-conscious.

"Isn't it a bit early for you to be watching the door?" She checked the time on her watch, then returned her focus to him. His lips were full, his dark skin gleamed, and the way his brown eyes narrowed on hers told her he sensed exactly what she'd been thinking.

"Just doing my job." His lips twitched at the corners, and she found herself wondering what they'd be like to kiss.

"Do you ever get a day off?"

His grin widened, but he refused to answer either way.

"Because I'd love a chance to interview you . . . if you could ever spare the time."

James cocked his head to the side as though weighing the offer. "I thought you were here for Ira," he said.

Trena settled her gaze on his massive arms—imagining those biceps wrapped firmly around her. Aware of the heat rising to her cheeks, she quickly dismissed the image and said, "Something tells me you'd make a far more interesting subject."

He tossed his head back and laughed as though she was joking, but Trena was entirely serious. She'd get the interview. Maybe not today, but eventually. James had secrets. Possibly Ira's secrets, and maybe even Madison's too. Luckily for her, she was persistent and patient and had every intention of meeting him again.

"In case you decide you're interested." She dipped a

hand into her bag and presented her card.

James held her gaze as he slipped the card from between her index and middle fingers—the feel of his flesh grazing hers enough to send her belly into a flutter. More than ever, she wanted that interview. What surprised her was how much she wanted him too.

She watched as he tucked the card into his pocket, then held the door wide as he ushered her inside to where Ira was waiting.

# SEVEN

# THE BITCH IS BACK

Aster stood in the middle of what could only be described as a construction zone and looked all around. Though Ira had assured her that the former souvenir shop was well on its way to its latest incarnation as his newest, chicest, most exclusive nightclub to date, at the moment it more closely resembled a serial killer's lair with its plastic-draped walls and floors and the constant background hum of power drills and saws.

It was eerie, creepy, and the look Ira's assistant had flashed her as Aster entered the space left her feeling unsettled.

Was this how it was going to be from now on? People giving her the side-eye as they quickly backed away?

She swiped a bead of sweat from her brow and sipped

from the bottle of water Ira's driver had given her on the ride over. Outside, the temperature soared into the triple digits—inside, it seemed even hotter.

Though she'd choose the heat, the incessant construction clatter, and the pervasive smell of freshly poured cement over the harsh environs of jail any day, she'd been more than a little taken aback when Ira insisted on stopping by the new club before dropping her at her place at the W.

"So, what do you think?" he asked, his face free of expression, though somehow she knew it was praise that he wanted.

"Well . . ." She bumped the water bottle against her chin, struggling to find something positive to say, when one of Ira's pencil-skirt-wearing assistants carefully picked her way through the debris in her red-soled designer heels and began apprising him on the number of urgent calls he needed to make and scheduled meetings he'd missed. Aster watched in guilt-ridden silence, knowing she was to blame for his falling so far behind on his day.

"Also, Trena Moretti just arrived. She's waiting by the back door," the redhead told him.

Ira stared blankly, not making a move.

"You're scheduled for an interview. It's been booked for weeks." Her grin was deferential, but her gaze flashed in a way that had Aster wondering if they were sleeping together.

With his good looks, power, and wealth—an LA trifecta of sorts—Ira was considered one of the city's most eligible bachelors. And though the tabloids were always trying to decode his love life, other than an endless string of rumored conquests that included an impressive number of Victoria's Secret models, A-list actresses, and a couple of infamous socialites, Ira remained maddeningly elusive—eternally linked to everyone and no one.

Ira's curt nod gave nothing away. He simply turned to Aster and said, "Why don't you wait in my office? I'm afraid it's not much at the moment, but if this runs too long, I can always recruit James to drive you home."

Aster buried her frown and forced herself to nod good-naturedly instead. She longed to return to her luxury condo, but she owed Ira. Big-time. And at least he hadn't brought her to Night for Night. Just because she'd agreed to return to her old job as the club's promoter didn't mean she was ready to see it quite yet.

For some, the VIP cabanas in the Riad—the area reserved for Night for Night's A-list clientele—were considered the height of sought-after nightlife luxury, but for her they served as a painful reminder of the night her life took a turn for the worse, leaving her to wonder if she'd ever be able to view the sexy Moroccan-style surroundings as anything other than the infamous crime scene they were.

Not only had Madison's blood been discovered on the

terrace, but according to the cops, a group of eyewitnesses reported seeing Aster leaving the club with a strange male they'd yet to ID. Unfortunately, Aster still couldn't remember any of that. Though the fact that she'd been seen leaving should count for something, or at least that was what she thought until her lawyer reminded her that Madison was also seen leaving and yet her blood had ended up both on the terrace and the dress Aster had been wearing. People left places, people returned to places. What they really needed was for Aster to identify where she'd spent the night, but she wasn't willing to share that just yet.

All Aster knew for sure was that she'd woken the next morning to a wicked hangover in a strange apartment and an empty bed, filled with regret for having wasted her virginity on someone who couldn't bother to stick around long enough to brew her a cup of coffee.

Later, when a DVD was delivered to her apartment, Aster had gaped in horror at the grainy footage of her stripping and dancing before she quickly turned it off, unable to watch any more. At the time, she thought it the single worst thing that had ever happened to her. But that was before she'd been arrested for first-degree murder.

From the moment she'd joined Ira's contest, her life had taken a turn for the worse, and yet here she was with both hands out, accepting his help and getting sucked further and further into his debt.

"Hey, you okay?" Ira regarded her with such concern that Aster fiercely shook the thought away and returned to the present. She knew how busy he was, and yet he'd still seen fit to sacrifice the better part of his day in order to help her. All of which made her feel bad for what she was about to say, but she said it anyway. "Trena Moretti?" She narrowed her gaze. "The reporter for the *LA Times*? The one responsible for the headline 'Was It Murder?'"

Ira cocked his head, but otherwise gave nothing away.

"This interview isn't about me, is it?"

He broke into a grin. His sexy grin. His charming grin. His shark grin. Like a Rorschach test, it depended entirely on the perception of whoever was on the receiving end. Aster viewed it as a mix of all three.

"Relax," he said in a tone that was meant to be reassuring. "It's a profile piece on me. She's been trying to nail this down long before that headline."

Aster's shoulders sank in relief, leaving her feeling more than a little embarrassed for assuming the worst. Still, it was just a matter of time before word spread that she'd been sprung from jail and every journalist in the world came begging for an exclusive. Should she sit down with Oprah, Diane Sawyer, or Katie Couric? She had no idea, though eventually she'd have to decide.

Ira studied her with a speculative expression as he absently rubbed a thumb against the squared edge of his chin. And just like *that*, Aster grew tense all over again.

"Though now that you mention it . . ."

She did not like where this was heading. Not. At. All.

"No." She was already shaking her head long before he could finish the thought. "I'm not ready. I mean, seriously, look at me! My hair is greasy, my face is a crime scene, and even though you're too polite to mention it, I happen to know how bad I smell, since I haven't had a proper shower in nearly a week."

Ira dismissed her excuses with a quick wave of his hand. "All of which makes you even more perfect. Aster, think about it—sure, you're not looking your best, but who would expect you to? You're fresh from the can, which makes you vulnerable, authentic, and real."

"None of which is good when you're about to be interviewed for the role you played in a celebrity's murder."

"On the contrary." Ira held firm. "You'll come off as raw, fresh, and completely unrehearsed, which will only work in your favor, since your usual high-end look can be intimidating. Look, last thing I want is to push you into a situation you're not prepared for, and if it makes you feel any better, I'll be there the whole time. I won't let her take advantage, I promise you that."

Aster's first instinct was to say *no*. Or rather, *hell no—a thousand times no—absolutely, 100 percent no!* But she couldn't bring herself to form the words.

Ira seemed so convinced it would work, and despite his many flaws, Aster greatly admired his numerous achievements in life. Ira came from humble origins, and like most people who'd made the trip west, he'd arrived in LA with a dream. Unlike most people, in just a few years' time he'd managed to turn that dream into an empire. It was pretty much the opposite of Aster's story. Having been born and bred in Beverly Hills, a Persian Princess in an extremely wealthy family, she'd had every advantage handed to her, only to make a complete mess of her life and end up in jail at the age of eighteen.

Clearly her instincts couldn't be trusted. So maybe it was time to let someone else call the shots for a while.

Next thing she knew, he was ushering her into his makeshift office and settling her in front of a fan that provided little relief against the unbearable heat. A few moments later, she heard his voice rising over the din of hammers and saws.

"And when it's ready, this will be our VIP area," he said.

Aster took a steadying breath and faced the woman with the gorgeous mane of wild bronze curls. Though they'd never met, Aster recognized Trena immediately. It was Trena who'd convinced the cops to question Ryan Hawthorne, though admittedly, that hadn't exactly turned out as Aster had hoped. While Aster had no idea what Ryan had told the police, she had no doubt he was solely to blame for turning their attention to her and planting the blood-covered dress that was the most damning piece of evidence being used against her.

If nothing else, his actions proved Ryan was guilty. Why else would he bother setting her up and framing her for the crime unless he had something serious to hide?

Maybe Ira was right. Maybe talking to Trena was exactly what she needed. While she wasn't sure where Trena stood, it couldn't hurt to befriend her, or at the very least talk to her. If public opinion was truly ruled by headlines and sound bites, then it would serve Aster well to author a few that might turn the tide in her favor.

Trena had an agenda; everyone did. And while Aster had no idea what it might be, now that Trena was standing before her, giving Aster an appraising look while Ira acted like he hadn't actually planned the whole thing, she had no choice but to play along and hope it wouldn't come back to bite her.

"Aster Amirpour, meet Trena Moretti." Ira presented the two women to each other.

"Well, this is certainly a surprise. Or at least it is for me." Trena shook Aster's hand and shot Ira a look like she recognized a setup when she saw one.

Aster looked to Ira for guidance. Seeing his nod of encouragement, she faced Trena and said, "Ira was generous enough to post my bail." She hoped it was okay to share. But Ira looked pleased, as she figured he would be. Most people loved taking credit for their good deeds.

"Ira? Not your parents?" Trena tilted her chin in a way that caused her shock of wild curls to spring across her forehead and dangle over her amazing blue-green eyes.

Aster shrugged. She was willing to talk, but she would not bash her family, no matter how conflicted she currently felt about them.

"And how are you doing?" Trena narrowed her gaze on Aster's split lip and the enormous purple shiner surrounding her eye.

Aster forced a half grin; it was the best she could do. She knew her pathetic appearance could work in her favor, but that didn't mean she felt comfortable looking so defeated, beaten, and unkempt that it served to provoke pity.

"Any chance I could get an in-depth with you? I'm sure that after a week of being locked up for a crime you didn't commit, you'll want to get your own story out into the world."

"So you don't think I'm guilty?" Aster had assumed Trena was out for her blood. But the warm smile she received instead nearly pushed Aster to tears. Someone in the press believed her. Someone powerful enough that people might actually listen to.

"Aster came directly from jail," Ira said. "I made her swing by so I could take care of a few things, and she's been waiting patiently for me to take her home. While I'm sure she wouldn't mind answering a few questions, anything more will have to be scheduled for a later date. This isn't exactly a comfortable venue—or at least not yet."

Trena shot Ira a knowing look. Clearly she recognized the game he was playing. "I'll want an exclusive," she said.

Ira nodded. "But of course."

Aster regarded them closely. The way they discussed her as though she was feeble and voiceless and not actually standing right there left her feeling simultaneously annoyed and relieved to let other people handle the weightier details of her life for a change.

*Just for a little while,* she promised herself. *Just until I get a proper sleep, a shower, a professional blowout, an eyebrow wax, and get back on my game.*

"You can film in any of the clubs—Night for Night, Jewel, the Vesper—up to you. I can give you exclusive access wherever you choose." Ira inspected his nails like he wasn't all that invested.

Aster noted the way Trena's face lit up upon hearing the word *film.* It was so predictable—so Hollywood. Aster had yet to meet an ambitious person who didn't secretly dream of being in front of the camera, and print journalists were no different. Still, it bugged her to see how willing Trena was to use Aster's personal tragedy to elevate her own profile. staying true to the media's motto: *If it bleeds, it leads.*

After only a moment's hesitation, Trena reached forward to shake on it. Switching her focus to Aster, she said, "Do your friends know you're out?"

Aster's expression was blank. Her best friend, Safi, was no longer speaking to her; most people weren't.

"Layla and Tommy," Trena clarified.

Aster closed her eyes and sighed. More proof of just how much her life had gone off the rails. The two people she'd once written off as being completely beneath her were now the only true friends she had left in the world.

She opened her eyes and met Trena's gaze. "No," she finally said. Her voice sounding more timid than she liked, she cleared her throat and tried again. "Not yet. Just got my phone back and the battery's dead. And so far, Ira's managed to keep the news quiet."

Trena considered the info. "We'll want to move fast then. The one who leaks the story controls the story."

Aster nodded gamely, though the truth was, she was growing annoyed. She knew Ira meant well, and maybe Trena did too. But she also knew better than to believe anyone ever acted purely out of goodwill. They were both working an angle, and while Aster had no idea what those angles might be, she knew it was time she stepped up her game and started working one too.

Ira had sprung her from jail, offered her a job, and given her a place to live, and for that she was grateful. But that didn't mean he owned her. And it certainly didn't mean he could use her as a means toward whatever endgame he was playing.

Or maybe it did mean exactly that.

Maybe Aster was in so deep, so indebted to him, he owned her completely.

All she knew for sure was that she needed a shower and a decent bed that didn't reek of the bodily functions of the hundred or so people who had slept there before. She needed to take control of her life, and she needed to start now. Leave them with no doubt of who was ultimately calling the shots.

While it was nice having Ira steer for a while, truth was, Aster had always made a much better driver than passenger. Spotting James on the far side of the room, Aster stood before Ira and Trena and said, "Call me tomorrow. We'll set something up. I'm sure Ira will be happy to pass on my number. But for now, I've got a date with a bubble bath, a carton of Ben & Jerry's, and some much-needed *z*'s."

# EIGHT

# SHE SELLS SANCTUARY

Mateo Luna approached the entrance of Ivy at the Shore and contemplated his choices. Technically, it wasn't too late to bolt. In fact, it would probably be better for everyone involved. Or at least it would be better for him. Though it certainly wouldn't be better for his family. They were depending on him. He literally held his little sister's life in his hands.

The thought was sobering enough to convince him to move forward and go through with the plan.

While most people wouldn't hesitate to seize the chance to become rich and famous, Mateo had no interest in fame, and he certainly didn't aspire to live the life of a Kardashian. Still, he was desperately in need of a quick and sizable money grab, and while it remained to be seen if this particular path would provide the easiest route, if things worked out as he hoped, it would certainly be the quickest. And at the moment, speed was of the essence.

"Mateo Luna?" The hostess looked him over and waited for him to confirm. He nodded, wondering how she recognized him, when she said, "Follow me."

She flashed a flirtatious grin over her shoulder and led him through the garden-like setting, past a patio known to be popular with celebrities, and toward a small table tucked away in the back, close to the fireplace. While the hostess was lovely, Mateo couldn't bring himself to do much more than notice.

His life had revolved around Layla for so long that suddenly finding himself without her left him feeling adrift. He missed her smile, her kiss. He missed the way she'd slept curled up all around him, and he knew he wouldn't be over her anytime soon.

She'd kissed another, which he'd already forgiven. Relegating it to a drunken slip, he was willing to put it behind them no matter how much it hurt. It was the lying he couldn't accept. He'd truly believed they were different from most couples he knew. That they were honest and open—that they'd left nothing unacknowledged or unsaid. But Layla had hidden the truth, and while he still had no idea who had sent the text—what kind of person would act in such a deliberately mean-spirited way—there was no denying it was time to move on.

Problem was, Layla was a hard act to follow, and the heartbreak she'd caused left him too wounded to go looking for a replacement.

"Your server will be right over." The hostess motioned to a vacant wicker-backed chair, and Mateo squinted in confusion at the pretty blonde seated among an array of colorful cushions. Her pink glossy lips curved into a grin as she slid her glass toward him.

"This is the most amazing chardonnay," she said as though she'd been expecting him. "You've simply got to try it!"

He pressed his lips into a frown and looked all around. Clearly this was some kind of mistake.

"Well, sit down, silly." She nudged his chair with her foot until he reluctantly lowered himself onto the seat. "Now seriously, try it." She slid the glass before him. "I'm dying to hear what you think!"

He grabbed the glass by the stem and took a small sip. While he wouldn't call it amazing, it wasn't the worst thing he'd ever tasted.

She leaned forward, looked at him expectantly.

He ran a self-conscious hand through his hair. "Amazing," he mumbled, forcing a half grin and returning the glass. His mind was in a whirl, trying to determine how the heck he'd found himself sitting across from Heather Rollins.

He'd met her once before, the night he'd stopped by

Jewel looking to surprise Layla at work. Only Heather had found him first, and she'd made a big show of hanging all over him. While she was undeniably pretty, she just wasn't his type. Heather was all sugar and shine—the girl equivalent of cotton candy. Whereas Layla was equal parts snark and smarts—her sweet side revealed to only a few.

He remembered how surprised he'd been when he'd complained about Heather, only to listen in shock as Layla had defended her. At the time, Mateo had taken it as further proof of just how far Layla had fallen and how fast.

"You should order one."

Mateo had been so lost in his thoughts it took a moment to realize she was referring to the wine and had motioned for the server.

"No, I'm good. Just . . . water, please."

"You in AA?" Heather whispered the moment the waitress left, eyes widening as though she'd unwittingly uncovered a secret. Then, reading the perplexed look on his face, she said, "You ordered water."

"No . . . just . . . trying to stay hydrated." He rubbed a hand across his chin, wishing he could start over, or at the very least delete his response. This was not going at all the way he'd envisioned.

"So that's how you stay so fit. Who do you train with?" At the word *fit*, she reached across the table, past the ceramic pitcher of multicolored roses, and squeezed his forearm. Though he was tempted to shrug away from her touch, he was surprised to find her hand cool, soft, and strangely comforting.

"No trainer. Mostly just . . . surfing."

Heather cocked her head, causing her long blond curls to cascade across her cheek as she mercifully settled her hand back on the stem of her wineglass where it belonged.

"You seem really nervous." She looked pleased when she said it.

He ran a hand through his hair again—he really needed to stop that. "I'm—I think there's been a mistake. I'm supposed to be meeting with—"

"With Heidi Berenkuil. I know." Heather shot him a long, considering look. "She's outside on a call. You didn't see her?"

Mateo shifted uncomfortably and looked to the untouched place setting beside her. He definitely hadn't seen her, and he was beginning to wonder if he was being punked.

"She wants to get some test shots. Of us. Together." She flashed him an amused look. "What did you think this was?"

"I'm not sure." His voice betrayed his confusion. He felt way out of his league. "I met Heidi a while back. She shoots for some of the surf magazines and does the ads for the surf brand that sponsors me. She told me to let her know if I ever wanted to get into modeling."

"So why now?"

Mateo squinted.

Heather smiled gamely and tipped her glass so the wine swirled up and down the sides. "Surely it wasn't the first time someone's approached you about modeling?"

He shrugged. He wasn't in the mood to share his long list of family tragedies and missed opportunities.

The way she regarded him left him convinced she'd gleaned more by what he didn't say than by what he did. And just when he was sure he couldn't feel any more uncomfortable, she smiled warmly and said, "Sorry if I come off as nosy. I don't mean to pry. Or maybe I do. But anyway, good for you for having boundaries. My therapist is helping me work on mine." She stopped and made a face. "And the fact that I just told you that shows just how far I have to go." She laughed and shook her head. "So here's the deal. Heidi has been hired to shoot an editorial for *InStyle* magazine. I managed to clinch the cover, which means I'll get an interview as well. But for the shoot they want to capture a casual, romantic, beachy California vibe, which is where you come in. If you're nervous, don't be. They want you as is. Just be your usual hot surfer self and it's all good. I hope you're okay with all this? Heidi thinks you'll lend an air of authenticity, and I happen to agree. But if you don't like the sound of this, or you don't like me, then you can always bail now and I'll tell Heidi it just isn't your thing."

Mateo rubbed his lips together, needing a moment to absorb what she'd said. Was it his thing? Not even close. But if all he had to do to collect a paycheck was hang on a beach with his board and a pretty girl—well, how bad could it be?

"So, what do you think?"

Mateo lifted his gaze to meet hers. "Tell Heidi I'm in," he said.

Heather grinned in a blur of bouncing curls, flashing brown eyes, and teeth that were whiter and straighter than the Hollywood sign. "You can tell her yourself," she said, waving to someone just past his shoulder, and Mateo turned to find a pretty woman with long brown hair heading right toward them.

"The light is perfect," Heidi said. "And I've already settled the tab, so what do you say we head out now and get a few quick test shots before it gets dark?"

Immediately, Heather reached into her purse and retrieved her lip gloss, but Heidi waved it away. "Not necessary. I want you as unadorned as possible. I'm thinking Kate Moss on the beach in those early Calvin Klein Obsession commercials."

"Um, except she was naked." Heather frowned. "I'm pretty sure *InStyle* wants me fully clothed."

"So, we'll put you in a slip dress or a bikini. I'm thinking

retro, but fresh. Beautiful but in a natural way. But first—"
Heidi turned to study Mateo in a way that left him feeling
so self-conscious he struggled to hold her gaze. "I need to
see how you two photograph together so I can check out
your on-camera chemistry. Sound good?"

"Perfect," Heather said. "And I have some ideas. . . ."

The next thing Mateo knew, Heidi and Heather were
leaving the restaurant deep in conversation and fully
expecting him to follow.

He did.

# NINE

# ROCK AND ROLL, HOOCHIE KOO

Tommy Phillips sat on the stool with his cherished electric twelve-string guitar strapped across his chest and adjusted the mic stand before him. He gazed out at the audience (a term he used loosely, considering how he was basically being paid to serenade a bunch of largely disinterested female shoppers) and mumbled the name of the next song from the approved list of soft hits he'd been hired to play.

The venue was a small, high-end boutique on Robertson Boulevard, and while it certainly wasn't the sort of life-changing gig he'd envisioned when he first arrived in LA, he was in no position to complain.

Initially he assumed the fifteen minutes of fame he'd gained over Madison's disappearance might really go the distance and help launch his career, only to find that while it did result in the sort of unprecedented attention he'd lacked before, it in no way resulted in good things for his music.

The videos he'd posted on YouTube might've gone viral, but the comments section was so full of vitriol, he'd quickly taken them down and seriously contemplated changing his name. Not that it would've done any good. For better or worse, he'd played a part in the biggest celebrity scandal in years. Which gave him the rare distinction of having a face that was eminently recognizable, but not at all bankable.

In the upside-down, tabloid-driven world he now lived in, Tommy was a bona-fide celebrity of sorts. Only difference between him and a true celebrity was a lack of fat, steady paychecks and revenue-producing endorsement deals.

Though there had been an offer by a start-up sneakers brand, Tommy had refused to be the face behind the brand of kicks that claimed to help you outrun whatever kind of trouble you found yourself in (which was how it'd been pitched to him). Some things you could never live down. And while the job working for Ira held promise, he didn't want to work for him for any longer than necessary.

Truth was, Tommy was coasting—had been ever since he'd arrived in LA and taken a dead-end job hawking guitars at Farrington's. Sure, it was the job that had put him in Ira's path and resulted in everything that had happened since, and while Tommy was glad for the rush of opportunities where he'd once had none, he was also just impatient enough and just ambitious enough to begin to feel restless.

He wanted more. He just needed someone to take him seriously for a change.

The irony of it all was that Tommy's dad had the ability to change his luck in an instant. In a way, he already had. But the opportunities Ira offered were more focused on building Ira's business. And though he'd given Tommy his dream guitar, he'd never expressed any interest in promoting his music.

If Ira was waiting for Tommy to ask, well, that day would never come. Tommy was no good at begging. His dad might own a string of nightclubs—one of them, the Vesper, was known as the city's hottest music venue—but there was no way he would ask for a handout. Tommy's goal had always been to earn Ira's respect by making it big on his own. Working for him as a promoter was merely a means to that end. He had big plans to make a name for himself well before he made the reveal. It was imperative that when Tommy disclosed his true connection to Ira, he did so as his father's equal.

His fingers expertly picked at the strings, strumming all the right chords, and he dutifully sang the lyrics he'd memorized just a few hours before. His gaze roamed the space, idly watching the small crowd of beautiful women juggle purses, half-full glasses of champagne, and body-skimming dresses they pressed against themselves as they swiveled before full-length mirrors and assessed their reflections.

There was one in particular who'd caught Tommy's eye. With her deep-red lips, dark waist-length hair, and thatch of heavy bangs that fell just short of her brown almond-shaped eyes, she had the sort of exotic good looks Tommy might fantasize about but would never try to approach in real life. For one thing, she was older. For another, with her body-hugging dress, designer bag, and skyscraper stilettos, she bore the sort of high-maintenance vibe he usually worked to avoid.

Still, there was no harm in looking, and Tommy watched as she posed before a mirror with a black dress clutched at her hip. A few moments later, when a pretty blonde sidled up and slipped a hand around the brunette's waist, whispering something into her ear that made them both grin, Tommy was completely transfixed.

When the brunette caught Tommy staring, she met his gaze with a look so smoldering, Tommy flubbed the lyrics and momentarily lost his place in the song.

She nudged her blond friend and the two of them came to stand directly before him as Tommy fought to regain control of his performance. But his mind was a blur of their bare shoulders pressing together, their lips just inches apart, as they whispered to each other without ever once shifting their focus from him.

It was the stuff of rock-and-roll fantasy, only it was really happening, and it took every ounce of Tommy's will to finish the song and segue into the next with even a smidge of competence.

They were flirting with him. There was no getting around it, the signals were clear. They wanted him—wanted to share him—and while he was immensely flattered, he also felt woefully out of his league.

Were they slumming?

Or worse, did they recognize him from the interviews he'd given? While they seemed more sophisticated than the usual tabloid-reading type, they probably weren't the only classy babes in LA with a secret stash of *In Touch, OK!, Life & Style*, and *Star* hidden under the mattress.

When the song ended, Tommy paused to sip from the bottle of water he'd set beside his playlist. He desperately needed a moment to get a grip on himself.

"You're Tommy Phillips."

He looked up to find the brunette had separated from the blonde and was now just inches away. He forced himself to swallow, wipe his mouth with the back of his hand, and nod politely, all the while trying not to focus on her long, toned legs, slim hips, and generous round breasts, but it was no use. She was 100 percent onto him.

Even better, he knew she was 100 percent into him too.

"I thought I recognized you." Her gaze was as direct as her voice. Strong, sure, she was undoubtedly a woman who got what she wanted.

Tommy shot a nervous glance toward the boutique owner, who was eyeballing him from her place near the register. Wouldn't do any good to piss her off by flirting with the clientele. Then again, the customer had approached him, and how rude would it be for him to ignore her?

Unsure how to proceed, he closed his eyes and started strumming the next tune. Getting lost in the music was the best default he knew. Besides, he was getting paid to play music, not set up a threesome.

He was halfway to the chorus when he realized he'd abandoned the Coldplay song he'd originally started and drifted into the one he'd written about the night he'd kissed Madison. "Violet Eyes," he called it—a dead giveaway if there ever was one. And while he'd fully intended to change the name along with the more identifiable lyrics, he hadn't quite gotten around to it, and now he was so far in, there was nothing to do but continue.

Maybe no one would notice.

Maybe they were too busy shopping and drinking to make the connection.

But when he opened his eyes again, he found the blonde and brunette standing right where he'd left them, having forfeited a fun night of shopping and champagne swilling to focus on him.

"Everything okay?" The boutique owner fussed over the women.

The blonde ignored her and maintained her focus on Tommy, while the brunette surrendered her glass of champagne and handed over the black dress she'd been carrying. "I'd like it in red as well," she said. "You can send them both to my house. You know the address."

The boutique owner was all fawning gratitude, but the woman had already moved on. As he neared the end of the song, he watched in amazement as she reached into her bag, slid a card from an engraved gold case, and flashed a sexy grin as she slipped the card into his pocket, then promptly left the boutique with her friend.

He watched them go, knowing he should be thrilled. And admittedly, part of him, most of him, was. It wasn't the first time he'd been hit on by an older woman. Solo gigs were pretty much a magnet for that sort of thing. Though it was the first time he'd been hit on by two at one time.

Still, now that they'd gone, he wasn't sure he was willing to follow through. Undoubtedly, it would result in the kind of wild night he'd brag about for the rest of his life, but Tommy was looking for something more than just a good time. As ridiculous as it was, he'd been holding out for Layla, waiting for her to come around and admit there'd been magic in the kiss that they'd shared—a waste of time that had gotten him nowhere. Layla had been drunk when it happened, and once sober, she'd given no indication of ever wanting to repeat it.

He slipped his guitar into its case and forced himself to deal with his own harsh reality. Fact was, he hadn't had a single date since he'd arrived in LA. He'd basically turned down every woman who expressed the slightest bit of interest in him, and for what? So he could win the world record for unintended celibacy?

LA had no shortage of hot females. Hell, gorgeous women were so abundant he often wondered where they hid all the plain or merely normal-looking ones. And yet, despite the nonstop beauty parade, he hadn't gotten laid since he'd left high school.

The whole thing was ridiculous. Fact was, Tommy had a life to live, and waiting for Layla to show him some interest without the aid of tequila was no way to live it. Maybe an older woman, make that two older women, were just what he needed to finally get over her.

He was young in a city where youth was the most valued currency. And yet, so far he'd chosen to live like a monk.

So what if those two women had a good twelve years on his eighteen? A brunette and a blonde was every guy's dream—and that dream was just a simple phone call away.

The boutique owner handed over his check, and Tommy

slipped it into his wallet and headed into the balmy LA night, feeling so fired up there was no way he could face his empty apartment alone.

He wondered where the women had gone. Probably back to some swanky house high in the Hollywood Hills with great city views, expensive sheets, maybe even an infinity pool.

The more Tommy thought about it, the more he grew convinced he could really use a night with those two.

Hell, you could even say he deserved it.

He retrieved the card the brunette had given him, all the while telling himself he had nothing to lose, that you only live once, and a bunch of other pep-rally platitudes he hoped would spike some much-needed courage to see this thing through.

He squinted at the card and pressed the digits onto his keypad.

"Hi . . . Malina . . ." Tommy's gaze landed on her name just as she answered. "This is Tommy. Tommy Phillips. We met at the boutique. . . ."

"Tommy." She laughed, in a way he hadn't expected. Was she flirting, making fun of him? Was he paranoid and reading too much into what was probably nothing? "That was fast." Her voice was light and teasing.

Tommy cleared his throat, then immediately wished that he hadn't. It made him sound shaky and nervous, which he was, but it wouldn't do any good to reveal that. "Yeah, well, I just, uh, I just finished my set, and I was wondering if you two might want to meet. You know, for a drink, or . . . something . . ." He leaned against his car door and waited for her reply. The silence mounted, seeming to drag on for an intolerable amount of time.

"I'm very interested in meeting with you, Tommy."

He closed his eyes. He was minutes away from the best night of his life.

"Only not tonight." Her words flowed easily, though that didn't mean they were easy for Tommy to hear.

Had he misread the signals?

He pictured them standing before him, arms slung around each other's waists, whispering back and forth and never once taking their eyes off him. . . .

No, it was impossible, out of the question. He might be only eighteen, but he'd been hit on by enough females to recognize the signs.

Tommy frowned at the phone. She was waiting for him to respond, but he had no idea what to say. Had he fallen for some kind of joke?

He tossed his guitar onto the backseat, feeling like an idiot for making the call and allowing himself to get so riled up only to be rejected by some ridiculously hot, yet clearly sadistic women.

"Tommy?" The sound of her voice dragged him away

from his thoughts and back to the very confused present he resided in. "Did you even look at my card?" Her voice was amused in a way that left him both annoyed and ashamed.

His jaw clenched, he retrieved her card again, and when he read the small print just under her name, he couldn't help but grin.

Apparently Malina Li was head of A and R for a major record label he'd actually heard of.

So it was his music she was interested in, not him.

A bigger win than he could ever imagine.

"I'm an asshole." He slid behind the wheel of his car and started the engine.

"And I'm flattered." She laughed. "Listen, why don't you stop by my office tomorrow around one? I'll have lunch brought in."

"I'll be there," he said, but she was already gone.

He merged into traffic and drove with no particular destination in mind. His luck was about to turn—he could feel it—which left him in no mood to go home. He needed to celebrate, blow off some steam, and if Malina Li and her hot blond girlfriend weren't into him, he'd find someone who was.

The air might be dry and warm with zero chance of precipitation, but Tommy Phillips was determined to make it rain once and for all.

# TEN

# BEEN CAUGHT STEALING

Aster Amirpour stirred in her bed, musing that she just might never leave. Her sheets were clean and of the absolute highest thread count; her pillow was lush and filled with pure, hypoallergenic goose down; her pajamas were woven from the finest Chinese silk; the temperature in her room was set exactly where she liked it, neither too hot nor too cold, but just right; and thanks to Ira and the maid service he'd hired, there were few visible signs of the police having ransacked the place in search of incriminating evidence while she'd been gone.

She flopped onto her belly, buried her face in her pillow, and nearly wept from the sheer joy of having an entire day rolled out before her to spend however she wanted. Maybe she'd go to the beach and take a long walk. Only this time, she'd pause long enough to appreciate all the small details she once used to ignore—the way the seagulls soared overhead, the way the sand rose and fell beneath her feet. After a week in the rage-filled environment of lockup, stripped of her freedom, her privacy, and everything else, she couldn't imagine ever taking the small things for granted again.

The thought of jail was enough to send her mood plummeting. It was crazy how easily her emotions could shift. While she mostly fought hard to stay optimistic and upbeat, there was no avoiding the reality that the frivolous life she'd once enjoyed was now forever off-limits. Even if she were cleared of all charges, the small part she'd played in the Madison drama would forever live on as a piece of grisly Hollywood lore. She'd reached for fame and wound up with infamy. She'd wanted to be an actress, and now it was just a matter of time before some casting director went looking for someone to play her in the cheesy, movie-of-the-week crime drama that was probably already in development.

Her carefree days were over. Her entire future hung in the balance. And Aster, who had once been popular, loved, and surrounded by friends, had never felt so alone in the world.

Sure, Ira had assembled a great team of lawyers to defend her—but what if it wasn't enough? What if despite their best efforts, a jury of twelve random people still decided they didn't like what they saw and convicted her of first-degree murder? The thought of going to prison was horrible enough, but knowing she'd never get out—never breathe the ocean air, never ruffle her little brother's hair—was devastating at best.

A trial date would soon be set, which meant she needed to make the most of every moment between now and then. While she still had no recollection of how she'd spent the missing hours between leaving Ryan in the Riad and waking up in the strange apartment, she was committed to using every spare second to conduct her own investigation.

Someone was setting her up—most likely Ryan Hawthorne. And while she had no idea why, she was sure that the key to proving her innocence and getting herself out of the mess depended on either finding a way to restore her memory, locating Madison, or finding a way to connect Ryan to the crime.

If it was a crime. Despite the blood evidence, Aster refused to believe Madison was dead. And yet, where could she possibly have gone?

Just the thought of all she was facing was enough to make Aster's eyes sting with tears, but she refused to indulge in them. While bed was tempting, and undeniably safe, she needed to get up and out. She needed to reclaim her life.

She shoved her feet into her slippers and padded across the room. Her fingers were just circling the door handle, when she heard voices drifting from the living room.

Was it Ira? Or possibly even the maids?

She pressed her ear hard against the door and tried to make out the words, but they were too muffled to decipher.

With her heart frantically slamming against her chest, she scanned the room for some kind of weapon, something she could use to defend herself in case it turned out to be one of her most ardent haters bent on revenge.

Unfortunately, she'd left her phone along with her purse in the living room. And, of course, being the girliest of girly girls, the best her room had to offer was a spiked Christian Louboutin heel.

Wielding the shoe like a weapon, Aster turned the knob and crept quietly into the hall, where she paused, pressed flush against the wall, and listened incredulously as a male voice said, "Relax. We have the whole place to ourselves. I told you, my sister's still in jail."

Javen?

Aster shot around the corner just in time to catch her little brother, Javen, kissing a boy on her couch.

"What the hell?" she shouted, her words stifled by Javen's surprised shrieks.

He leaped away from the boy and stared frantic and bug-eyed at Aster. "What are you doing here?" His hands fluttered wildly, raking through his dark hair and swiping at his lips as though erasing the evidence. "You scared the crap out of me!"

"What am *I* doing here? You seriously think you're the one who gets to ask questions?" Aster loomed before him, shoe at the ready.

Javen balked. "Well, kind of, yeah. And could you please lower that shoe? You could seriously hurt someone with that thing."

"Yeah, well, that's pretty much the point." Aster lowered the shoe to her side but refused to let go. Her heart was pounding, her pajamas were soaked with fear-induced sweat, and other than an initial bout of shock, her brother looked as cool, calm, and handsome as ever. "Why aren't you at school? And who the heck are you?" She stared daggers at her brother's friend, who was cowering on the couch, unsure what to do.

"I'm Dylan," he mumbled. Then, shifting his focus to Javen, he added, "Whoa, dude. I thought you said she was cool?"

"I didn't say she was cool, I said she was in jail." Javen rolled his eyes at his sister and sank back onto the couch beside his friend.

But Aster could barely focus on that. She was too busy gaping at the open bottle of Veuve Clicquot and the two half-full glasses sitting on the table before them.

"Are you seriously drinking my champagne?" She glanced between them, wondering what upset her more— that her little brother was ditching school and drinking—or that he was taking full advantage of her incarceration. Or maybe it was far worse than that. Maybe she feared her parents were right, that she really was a bad influence, and it was her fault he was here.

"We were thirsty." Javen shrugged, though he was clearly losing some of his bravado and finally starting to look as worried as Aster felt he should be.

Still, she forced herself into silence, forced herself to take a moment to calm down and catch her breath. Truth was, she hadn't seen Javen in over a week, and she'd missed him far more than she was willing to admit. Besides, it wasn't like she wouldn't have done the same thing at his age. Difference was, she would've been more careful. She never would've gotten caught. But what was worse was the realization that she was reacting just like her parents, and nothing good ever came of that.

She dropped the shoe to the floor and claimed the chair just opposite them.

"I'm sorry," she said.

Javen glared. "Well, you should be."

Aster held his gaze until he looked away. Her brother was scared. It was right there in his eyes. His tough-guy act was clearly an attempt to impress his friend. And while Aster wouldn't embarrass him any more than she already had, there was nothing wrong with drawing a boundary around that kind of behavior.

"Don't push it," she said. "Sneaking in here to drink and make out, what were you thinking?" She shook her head, torn between loving him and wanting to protect him, and all-out throttling him. It was a toss-up, but in the end, loving him won.

"Would you rather me do this at home?"

She closed her eyes and rubbed her hands over her face. That was the last thing she wanted. Her parents loved Javen, but they weren't the most modern of thinkers, and she shuddered at what they might do if they ever learned he was gay. Of course there always existed the slim possibility that they'd do little more than love him and support him and wish him the best. Though the odds of that happening were so slim, she wasn't willing to take the chance.

"How long have you been coming here?" she asked. "And don't lie and say today was the first time, because we both know it wasn't."

"Would you believe it was only the second time?"

Her eyes met his. "No, I wouldn't. And what about school?"

"We sneak off campus for lunch." He shrugged.

"You haven't been caught?"

He made a face, while Dylan remained frozen beside him. "Attendance is all computerized now, so . . ."

The shrug that followed conveyed the words he'd failed to say. Her brother was a computer whiz, which meant he'd probably hacked into the system. Looked like there were now two criminals in the family. She figured the less she knew about his illicit activities the better.

"Do Mom and Dad know you're out?" he asked, his entire tone changing as he looked at her with concern.

"Nobody knows," she finally admitted, figuring she might as well lead with the truth. "And I'm hoping you'll keep it that way." She shot her brother and Dylan each a stern look.

"I'm willing to keep the secret if you are."

She grinned. She wanted so badly to hug him, but not wanting to embarrass him, she said, "I'm guessing you two haven't eaten?"

Dylan shook his head, seeming to finally relax.

"Because the thing you should know about drinking is that it's never a good idea on an empty stomach." Aster reached for the room service menu and quickly looked it over. "And while I didn't give you a key card so you could sneak in here for a school-break sexcapade, that doesn't mean I can't buy you both lunch." She shoved the menu at them. "What'll it be?"

Javen glanced between the menu and Aster, his face flushing when he said, "Um, Aster?"

She quirked a brow and waited.

"Could you bury the phrase 'school-break sexcapade'?"

Aster grinned and headed back to her room. She had a

big day ahead, an important interview with Trena Moretti to prepare for. While she wasn't sure she was ready, it was important to move quickly. It was just a matter of time before the press learned she was out on bail, and once that happened she'd be hounded worse than any A-list celebrity.

"Order me a kale salad," she called over her shoulder, desperate to eat something healthy after all the starchy food she'd choked down in jail. Then, thinking if there ever was a time to indulge in a treat it was now, she added, "Oh, and make sure to get some truffle fries on the side. I'm going to take a quick shower, a *very quick* shower. So don't get too comfortable while I'm away."

# ELEVEN

# RUDE BOY

"Oh, Layla, you're back. Tell me, did you enjoy your day off?"

Layla stared at the coffeepot, waiting for it to finish brewing so she could get away from Emerson and back to her cubicle. She should've stopped by Intelligentsia to secure her caffeine fix on the way over like she usually did, but she'd woken up late and this was the price for hitting the snooze button multiple times. As if bitter break-room coffee wasn't punishment enough, she was now forced to deal with Emerson and whatever patronizing point he insisted on making.

"You do realize we work full days around here?"

She pressed her lips together, grasped the mug by its handle, and turned to leave.

"Since you didn't return yesterday, I thought maybe you were in need of some guidance, someone to explain all the rules."

He stood just before her, blocking the doorway. Short of plowing through him and knocking him flat to the ground, there was no way out. And his formidable six-foot-four-inch frame with its considerable muscle mass pretty much rendered that impossible. With looks like his, she was surprised he'd settled for a job in marketing when he could've just as easily been starring in some cheesy prime-time soap that required him to film most of his scenes shirtless with his pants unbuttoned just so . . .

The thought was enough to make a flush rise to her cheeks, and she fought to recover by narrowing her gaze on his and speaking through gritted teeth. "Unless you plan on reciting the Unrivaled Employee Handbook, I really need to get back to my desk. We have a party to plan, in case you've forgotten."

He leaned against the door frame, regarding her with his deep-topaz stare. "Do you have the final list of confirmed vendors?"

The urge to roll her eyes was strong, but she somehow resisted. Of course she had the list. She'd stayed up half the night working on the event to make up for blowing off the better part of the workday to hang with Tommy. She nodded curtly, sipped from her coffee, and waited for him to move out of her way.

"Good. Then that means you can sort through the boxes of gift suite contenders I placed on your desk."

Layla fought to keep her face neutral. She hadn't bothered to stop by her desk, since her first priority was to secure a large mug of coffee. She could only imagine the mess she'd find once she got there.

"It should take you the better part of the day, so no cutting out early, I'm afraid." Emerson grinned in a way that highlighted just how good-looking he was, which only served to annoy Layla more. Before Mateo, Layla had made it a point to avoid the overly pretty types, determining that they were too vain, too narcissistic, and took themselves far too seriously to be any fun. But Mateo was different. Even though he was stop-and-stare gorgeous, most of the time he seemed entirely unaware of the fuss that surrounded him.

Just thinking about Mateo left Layla glum. Mateo was practically perfect, and yet he still hadn't been enough for her. Maybe Layla didn't know how to be happy. Maybe she was one of those people, like her mom, living a bottomless life—always seeking, always consuming, but never filling up or seeing the value in what they'd left behind. Not that she was currently speaking to her mom, but the description certainly fit, and from what she'd heard, there was trouble in paradise. Husband number two was still wealthy as ever (which was what attracted her mom in the first place), but apparently he had a wandering eye. Which came as no surprise, seeing as how he was married when the two of them met. *If they'll do it with you, they'll do it to you* was the thought that first sprang to mind. But when Layla applied it to her own life, she was no longer feeling so smug.

"Anything else?" She forced her face into an expression she hoped could be read as both amenable and dismissive.

"Just so we're clear, you're accountable here. There's a hundred other people—people who are far more qualified than you—who would kill to have your job, and who also, I'm not gonna lie, are far more deserving of the position."

Layla blinked and sipped, sipped and blinked. She wouldn't give him the benefit of a reply.

"What I'm wondering is how exactly you ended up here when you're so clearly out of your league."

"I slept with Ira," she said without irony.

When Emerson rolled his eyes, Layla didn't know whether to be relieved or offended by how easily he'd dismissed the idea. "Just know that I'm watching you," he snapped.

"Then I'll try to be at my most entertaining." Layla smirked.

Though he let her have the last word, his gaze held hers for so long Layla struggled not to fidget or be the first to look away. It was a play for dominance if she'd ever seen one. Emerson was determined to prove himself as the office alpha. As far as she was concerned, he could have it. Layla wasn't looking to climb the Unrivaled corporate ladder. It was her first week on the job, and she could honestly say she pretty much hated marketing and all it entailed.

Emerson was right: she was unqualified, inexperienced, and she probably didn't deserve to be taking up space and collecting a paycheck. But for whatever reason, Ira had hired her and she had accepted, and now that she was there, her goal was the same as it ever was—to save enough money to move to New York and enroll in journalism school. She was one year away from her dream, and with the way things were going, that day would not come soon enough.

She returned to a desk that was practically sagging under the weight of so many boxes of gift suite hopefuls she stared in dismay, wondering how she could possibly get through it all in the course of a single workday. Like any good capitalist, Ira had decided to exploit all the drama and attention surrounding Madison's disappearance and the connection to his clubs to promote his latest venture into top-shelf tequila by moving the launch date up several months. Which essentially meant that Layla had arrived in the marketing department at the very worst, most frenzied time.

It also went a long way toward explaining how Ira had come to hire her in the first place. Ira was always working an angle. There were no accidents where he was concerned. Not only did he need all the help he could get to make the party a success, but Layla also had to admit, however reluctantly, that Tommy had been right all along—the popularity of her blog played a big part in Ira's decision to keep her around long after he should've fired her.

Resigned, she sank onto her chair, grabbed a pair of scissors, and started opening boxes stuffed with generous offerings of expensive designer fragrances, scented candles, wireless headphones, gift certificates offering sessions with personal trainers and house calls from nutritionists. It was her job to determine if the celebrity guests who were allowed access to the gift suite would be more excited over the offer for free laser skin resurfacing or the exclusive, all-expenses-paid Mexican Riviera getaway. It was ridiculous how much free stuff was showered on the very people who could most afford it, while their legions of fans went into crippling credit card debt in an effort to emulate them.

She opened another box and stared in dismay at a package of gluten-free, paleo-diet-approved, organic pet food, wondering if it was cool enough, chic enough, and covetable enough to excite the spoiled VIPs the gift bags were destined for. Probably not, she decided, tossing it onto the pile of things that would end up in the break room for all the marketing department employees to fight over. As far as Layla was concerned, they could have them. She'd yet to see a single thing she actually wanted.

Already bored, she sliced into the next box, dove through several inches of packing popcorn, and gaped at the sight of the envelope with her name written in curlicue script with another card featuring a picture of a cartoon cat. Only this time in addition to the noose around its neck, it had suffered a gruesome shotgun blast to the head.

> This is round two
> I'm still waiting on you
> So much is at stake
> And this is no fake
> I'm hoping my gift might make your day
> And hopefully even convince you to play.

Layla frowned and studied the sheet of paper folded inside. One glance at the flowering vines and hearts trailing the margins, along with the large loopy scrawl, told her it was another of Madison's photocopied diary entries.

She glanced all around, ensured no one was looking, and examined the box. Like the last time, it was addressed to her, though there was no sign of where it had come from.

After another look over her shoulder, she smoothed the paper flat on her lap and began to read.

> March 19, 2012
> So, I'm seriously considering keeping Dalton around

even though the original plan was to dump him after a week. But the more I think about it, the more I'm starting to believe I should maybe hang in for a while longer and not be in such a big hurry to break up with him.

Reasons to keep him:

Now that he's popular (thanks to me) everyone thinks he's way cooler than he is, and that reflects well on me.

Dalton is cute and presentable and smart enough so that he doesn't completely bore me or embarrass me.

Good Kisser.

Easy to control = does whatever I tell him to do.

The parents approve.

Parental approval makes it easier to use Dalton as a cover for when I'm really hooking up with X, who they definitely wouldn't approve of.

Being Dalton's girlfriend is like playing a role, which is good practice for my future acting career.

Won't be long before I get the hell out of here, so I may as well hang in there.

Reasons to dump him:

The whole thing is based on a lie.

Even though he's a decent kisser, I'd rather be kissing X.

???

So, I guess it's decided. Dalton stays.
At least for now anyway . . .

Layla set the note aside and clicked on her keyboard, unconsciously gnawing the inside of her cheek as she watched her Beautiful Idols landing page fill up the screen. Though her post about Aster's arrest had been her last, a quick peek at the comments section revealed that people were still actively reading it, though their responses mostly bordered on deranged and illiterate.

She sighed, unsure what to do. Part of her was tempted to delete the site and walk away while she could. While another part, a less emotional, practical part saw an opportunity that was so far untapped.

Last time she'd checked, her number of subscribers had drastically fallen, so Layla was surprised to find the count spiking again. Then again, there was nothing like a little controversy to incite the trolls into action. She imagined an army of passive-aggressive, socially maladapted, vitamin D–deprived misfits hunched before their computer screens, just waiting for her to write something unpopular so they could all pounce—the comments section being their only source of power in an otherwise powerless life.

While writing about Aster was off-limits—she wouldn't

stoop to that level, nor would she risk harming her any more than she already had—she wondered if maybe she should take the bait and use her blog to share the diary entries she'd been sent.

Then again, if she attributed the posts to Madison and it turned out they were fake, then Madison's team could go after her for libel. The last thing she needed was for Madison's pasty-faced, Dockers-wearing attorney to track her down and nail her for defamation of character, in addition to the restraining order he'd already served her.

Her phone chimed with an incoming text, and when she glanced at the display, she was surprised to see Aster's name.

I'm out & I need your help. Meet me 2nite?

Aster was out? It was the first Layla had heard of it, and she'd been keeping close tabs on the news for any and everything Aster related. How she had managed to elude the press when there was a crowd of paparazzi permanently camped outside the jail was anyone's guess. Though she'd be willing to bet Ira had something to do with it. Aster's family was rich and powerful in their own way, but only Ira had the kind of connections that could keep such a news-worthy piece under wraps.

If anyone was sleeping with Ira, it was Aster. And yet, while there was an undeniable, indefinable *something* between them, Layla still couldn't imagine it. While Layla didn't know Aster all that well, she just didn't seem like the sugar-daddy-seeking type. For one thing, Aster was already rich. For another, the ick factor was just too high to contemplate.

Layla shook free of the thought and responded.

Welcome home. Tell me when/where & I'm there.

She stared at the screen, waiting for Aster's reply.

Et tu, Tommy?

At seeing his name, Layla frowned. She hadn't realized it was a group text until then, but she didn't expect Tommy to respond anytime soon. He'd stated his feelings on the subject loud and clear.

After a few moments of silence, Aster wrote:

Tommy I'm counting on you for keys/Layla=DVD

Layla was pretty sure Aster couldn't count on Tommy for much of anything, including a reply, so she typed:

Forget T—I'll bring everything.

Layla stared at the three dots on the screen, until Aster's reply appeared.

Fine. Whatever. Address to follow.

Layla pushed her phone aside, shoved the latest diary entry into her bag alongside the first one she'd received, and stowed it safely under her desk. Since anything she posted about Madison could end up backfiring on all of them, she figured she should probably consult Aster before she made a decision.

Aware of someone watching, Layla glanced over to find Emerson standing off to the side, chatting with a fellow coworker, while pretending to ignore her. Though she'd felt the weight of his gaze on her the whole time.

Was he somehow connected to the diary entries?

When he'd handed her the first one, he'd claimed it had been accidentally delivered to him—but was that even true? And hadn't he just mentioned how he was the one who put all the goodie-bag boxes on her desk? Did that include the box containing the note?

While she couldn't say for sure, there was definitely something off about him that set her on edge.

When her eye caught his, she flashed him the brightest grin she could manage, added a little wave for good measure, then turned back toward her desk and busied herself with opening boxes and judging the contents.

# TWELVE

# LOVE DROUGHT

Somewhere in the distance, a cell phone was chiming, the sound as annoying as it was insistent. One chime. Two. Hopefully the third would be the last. Tommy had been smack in the middle of a wonderful dream, and he didn't appreciate the intrusion.

"Tommy? Tommy, you awake? I think that's your phone buzzing."

The girl's voice lured Tommy away from his dreams as a long, cool arm slipped around his waist and dropped his phone onto the sheets before him.

He worked an eye open and squinted at the screen. Aster was out and she wanted help. Tommy wasn't surprised to see that Layla had been quick to commit, but he had meant what he'd said—he was washing his hands of all of it.

He set the phone to silent, pushed it under the pillow, and focused on the pretty girl pressed up against him, the tips of her long nails gliding over his hip and working their way under his waistband with the sole intent of pleasing him.

It had started in the bar, where they'd shared a few drinks that ultimately led to a few hungry kisses. At the time, it had felt so good just to be with a girl again—to lose himself in the softness of that sweet-scented flesh. And while this girl could never compete with Layla, no girl could, he needed to accept the fact that Layla was no longer an option and it was time to move on with his life.

But now, thanks to the text, Layla had once again hijacked his brain. It was like she'd been living there, rent free, since the moment they met, and just when he thought he'd made a significant move toward getting over her, she was back. What would it finally take for him to be done with her?

He surveyed his surroundings—the building was nice, even boasted a doorman and an elevator, from what he could remember. The kind of upscale amenities Tommy's shithole was lacking. Still, it was a hell of a mess. Every available surface was piled high with clothes, shoes, magazines, candy wrappers, hair dryers, perfume—there was even a purple bong on the dresser near the bed. Tommy hadn't gotten high since high school. Not that he was opposed to it, but it was probably better avoided. He needed to stay focused, and pot made him lazy and paranoid.

He lowered his lids. God, she had talented hands, though what was her name again? Tanya? Tabitha? Teresa? Started with a *T*. Or at least he thought it did.

"Hey, Tommy—you're not going to fall asleep again, are you?"

His eyes snapped open.

*Again?*

His mind reeled back to the night before as he struggled to remember the chain of events. They'd staggered back to her apartment, kissing furiously as his hands roamed greedily over her dress, imagining the treasures that waited beneath.

She'd pulled away with a grin, moving in a way she probably considered seductive, but from Tommy's vantage point looked wobbly and unsure. She'd teetered on her heels, threw her head back, and laughed, revealing a lovely expanse of white throat that yielded to the kind of abundant cleavage that always rendered him speechless. Then she'd flung off her heels, laughing even harder when they hit opposite walls, and pushed him back on her bed among a collection of incomprehensible stuffed animals (what was it with girls and cartoon plushies?), and threw herself right on top of him.

When his head hit the pillow, he'd closed his eyes and

inhaled deeply. For such a messy room, her sheets were surprisingly soft and clean, smelling vaguely of vanilla and sweetness and girl, and then . . .

And then . . . nothing.

Tommy had fallen asleep.

With a swipe, he deleted the message and pushed his phone off the edge of the mattress. Satisfied when it landed with a muffled thud on the carpet, Tommy rolled over to face her, determined to make amends.

Aster was on her own.

Layla too.

Tommy was committed to doing whatever it took to move on, and this was the first positive step toward making that happen.

"I don't even know what to say. . . ." He gazed at the beautiful girl before him.

"Don't say anything," she purred, pouting adorably as she pressed her body flush against his, her lips trailing the length of his neck and all along his collarbone. "It's not too late to make it up to me, you know."

Allowing his eyes to feast on the bounty before him, Tommy could hardly believe his own ears when he said, "What do you say I take you to breakfast instead?"

She pulled away, her features arranged in an expression of disbelief. "You're joking, right?" Her voice was equal parts curious and offended.

He shook his head. "Not a joke," he said, hating himself for it, but saying it anyway.

There was a time, not so long ago, when he wouldn't have even considered turning down an offer like the one she presented. But if he wanted to get over Layla, then he needed to do it the right way—by opening his life to new possibilities with new people. He needed to stop living behind the wall he'd built around himself. Sleeping with a girl whose name he couldn't remember wouldn't make him forget about Layla, and at the moment, that felt like the most urgent item on his list of things to accomplish.

"Come on." He rolled off the mattress before her hand could inch any lower and he'd be rendered powerless against her. "I'll take you to République. If you haven't been, then you're in for a treat. If you have . . ." He yanked on his jeans and pulled his T-shirt over his head. "Then you already know what I mean."

She remained right in place, her fingers picking at the sheets as she contemplated the offer. "You're a really strange guy. You know that, right?" Sighing in surrender, she picked her clothes off the floor and began to get dressed.

# THIRTEEN

# CAN'T FEEL MY FACE

Mateo stood before the intimidating crew of makeup artists, hairstylists, fashion stylists, art directors, assistants, and assistants to the assistants, people wielding large white disks that reflected and deflected the light, and others running around with meters that . . . well, he had no idea what they did. Point was, they all looked so purposeful and busy. It was crazy how many people it took to shoot an editorial when all that was required of him was to flash smoldering looks at the camera.

The day before, when they'd run test shots on the beach, he'd been nervous. So when Heather suggested they grab dinner afterward, he readily agreed, thinking it might make him more comfortable when it came time for the real thing.

"It's like acting," she'd told him, while they were waiting

for their food to arrive. "It's like we're telling a story. In this particular tale, we're playing the parts of two young lovers enjoying a sultry, romantic day on the beach. I'm sure you've had your share of those, so if you feel stuck, just channel that." She'd hooked him with a gaze so direct he found himself flushing and fidgeting and looking away. "The idea is to lose yourself in the role until you become the character and it starts to feel real," she'd concluded, as though it were really that easy.

By the time their food arrived, Mateo stared at his in despair, which made Heather laugh.

"You wanted pizza, I know. But we both have too much riding on this to show up looking bloated and puffy. You'll thank me tomorrow."

Mateo had grudgingly dug into a bowl of what Heather convinced him was mostly protein, and while he thought for sure he'd hate it, he had to admit it wasn't half-bad. Besides, it was good just to be out of his element for a change, to escape his usual routine. Lately most of his meals were eaten in the hospital cafeteria or in a hurry at home while leaning over the kitchen sink.

After spending the last two years with Layla, who mostly survived on copious amounts of coffee, it was amusing to watch Heather break down the nutritional content of a meal like some kind of calorie-counting savant. Still, despite his foray into the modeling world, he loved pizza and burritos far too much to ever adopt the weird food obsessions that were part and parcel of the Hollywood set. And he certainly wouldn't be joining the three-month waiting list to secure a table at the newest *it* restaurant, which reportedly offered a full menu of raw foods, followed by a variety of colonics in place of dessert.

The dinner really had helped put him at ease, until he'd arrived on set and he became the focus of so much unadulterated scrutiny, forced to listen in as the crew discussed his various attributes as though he wasn't actually standing right there before them.

He wanted to bolt. Wanted to get the hell out of there and never return. Problem was, he had an awful lot riding on this, and no plan B to fall back on.

"You two look great. Really, really great!" Heidi circled them with her camera.

She seemed sincere, but Mateo was still tense. The moment was his to either make or break.

"Just . . ."

Uh-oh. Mateo stole a quick peek at Heather, whose expression remained open yet serene, giving nothing away.

"I need to see a little more intimacy."

Mateo froze. It wasn't like he didn't understand the word, it was that he didn't understand it in relation to him, and Heather, and the shoot they were currently immersed in.

Heidi motioned for them to inch closer, and the next thing he knew Heather had centered herself before him. Her lips parted and pressing toward his, she cupped a soft hand to his cheek and whispered, "Shhh . . . just follow my lead and don't stop until they tell us to."

He nodded imperceptibly, and when her mouth found his he did as instructed: he followed her lead.

Her arms circled his neck as he gripped her at the waist and dragged her up against him.

At first, he felt self-conscious, all too aware of his kissing prowess being scrutinized by a group of people he desperately needed to impress. But as Heather entwined her leg with his and a soft groan sounded from deep in her throat, the crew seemed to blur until it was just the two of them, exploring, playing, inciting the kind of sensations he hadn't experienced since Layla.

He kissed Heather harder, deeper, and with an urgency that surprised him. Why did this feel so easy, so good? Why wasn't he racked with the kind of guilt he expected to feel? He'd loved Layla. Loved her with his whole body and soul. So the realization that he could move on so quickly came with a jolt. Still, he was human, and the body had a mind of its own. And at the moment, his body was reacting in the usual way when a pretty girl was pressed up against him. While he didn't pretend to love Heather Rollins, he definitely was enjoying the moment. The feel of her lips on his as she crushed her breasts hard against his chest left him wishing it would never end.

With his hands buried in her soft tangle of hair, it took him a moment to realize Heidi had called "Cut!" a while ago.

"There's no denying you two have chemistry," Heidi said, squinting at the viewfinder and scrolling through the shots she'd just taken.

Mateo stood beside Heather, feeling breathless, embarrassed, and totally surprised by how much he'd enjoyed that.

"Mateo, you were perfect. A little stiff in the beginning, but you found your groove eventually."

Heather grabbed his hand and gave his fingers a squeeze.

"I'll go over these in the studio before I send them on to the magazine, but Mateo, I'd love to work with you again. I think you have a future in this, if you're interested. You'll need a portfolio, of course, but I'm more than willing to help you with that."

"He should probably get an agent too, then," Heather said, shooting a shrewd look between Heidi and him that left him feeling more like a spectator than a player.

Heidi nodded distractedly, already turning away and instructing the crew to clean up the set, they were done for the day.

An assistant tossed Mateo his T-shirt, and he yanked it

over his head as Heather ducked behind a screen to swap the bikini she'd worn for the dress she'd arrived in.

"Well done." She grinned, and placing a hand on either of his shoulders she kissed him once on each check but purposely avoided his lips, which left him feeling simultaneously disappointed and relieved. "I can help you find an agent, if you want. Because trust me, you definitely want someone looking after your interests."

Mateo had no more than shrugged when Heather was retrieving her phone from her oversize bag. After a few taps on the keypad, she held it to her ear and walked away for a bit. A few minutes later, she returned and said, "You have a meeting first thing tomorrow at my agency. And while there's absolutely no pressure to sign, it wouldn't hurt to see what it's all about."

He swallowed hard and followed her across the sand and back to their respective cars. It was all happening so fast, and while he was happy he'd succeeded at what he'd set out to do, there was no mistaking that the triumph was also tinged with great sadness.

Then again, all beginnings were endings in disguise, and vice versa. Still, it felt weird to think that it was his kissing another girl—a girl who was the exact opposite of Layla— that had won him the gig.

Not to mention how he hadn't yet gotten around to explaining why he wanted the job in the first place. For some strange reason, he needed Heather to know he wasn't just another fame seeker. He had a higher purpose, a goal.

He opened his mouth to speak, when she shot him a friendly grin. "Today was fun," she said. "Let me know how it goes tomorrow, 'kay?" Mateo watched as she slid behind the wheel and closed the door between them.

Sliding his sunglasses onto his face, he gazed out at the beach through dark-tinted lenses, telling himself there was plenty of time to explain everything later.

# FOURTEEN

# WHISPER TO A SCREAM

If Layla had to pinpoint one thing that was different about Aster, well, she could never narrow it down to just one thing. As Aster leaned against a black BMW with her arms crossed over her chest, she appeared to be an entirely different person from the girl Layla once knew.

Where Aster had once conveyed the sort of easy confidence that came from a life where unlimited beauty and wealth seemed to flow without effort, the dark-haired girl standing before her was far more muted, less haughty, and completely lacking in the sort of arrogance that once used to define her.

Though that wasn't to say she'd become timid or weak. If anything, she carried a marked air of assuredness that was missing before. Then again, arrogance was often born of insecurity—assuredness was something one earned—which left Layla wondering what the week behind bars had been like for her.

"My car's been impounded," Aster said, patting the trunk. "Apparently, it's being ripped apart in search of evidence, so Ira loaned me this." She shook her head in a way that sent her long, dark ponytail sailing over her shoulder, seeming to need a moment to shake free of the thought. "Anyway, thanks for coming." Her voice was breezy, as though she was hosting some kind of bizarre, high-end block party.

Though she tried not to be obvious about it, Layla couldn't help but gape at the giant shiner surrounding Aster's eye, never mind the thick scab bisecting her lip.

"You should see the other girl," Aster quipped, catching Layla staring a few seconds too long.

Layla shrugged, unsure how to respond.

"Please." Aster surveyed the length of the dark and quiet street. "It's the first thing you noticed. Admit it."

"I just assumed it was some kind of smoky eyeliner trend I wasn't quite up on." Layla laughed in a way that betrayed just how awkward she felt. "You know how fashion challenged I am."

Aster looked her over with a studied gaze. "You're not nearly as tragic as you used to be. You used to dress like you were asking permission. Now you just own it." She

nodded approvingly toward Layla's angled blond bob, dis-
tressed black skinny jeans, black ankle boots with gold
studs, and silk cami. Then, clearly done with the small talk
and pleasantries, she pushed away from her car and said,
"Listen, I don't want you to feel weird around me. Aside
from this black eye, nothing has changed." Fielding Layla's
doubtful look, she tried again. "Yes, I'm a little banged up,
but I'll heal. And I really wasn't kidding when I said you
should see the other girl." There was an edge to her voice
that left Layla convinced. "So don't act so careful around
me like I'm some fragile thing that might break. I'm a lot
tougher than you think, and I can't just sit back and trust
twelve people who are too stupid to get out of jury duty to
believe that I'm innocent. I can't afford to let it get to that
point. I need to clear my name now, and I need your help.
Since apparently Tommy can't be bothered to show, much
less reply to my text."

"Tommy's . . ." *A dick, a jerk, a giant douche*—while
they all fit, rather than finish the thought, Layla just rolled
her eyes and shook her head, allowing the look to say what
words couldn't.

"But you brought the keys, right?"

Layla sighed. With Aster's question, Layla's worst fear
was confirmed. This wasn't just some arbitrary address
Aster had chosen in an attempt to outwit the paparazzi—if
that had been the case, they would've met up in her luxury

apartment at the W. No, this was Madison's hood.

She shot a look around the neighborhood. The street was wide and clean, bordered on either side by a succession of thick walls, big gates, and towering hedges that were impossible to see past. It was the first tier in what Layla suspected would turn out to be a many-layered defense meant to protect the multimillion-dollar properties beyond from prying eyes, prowlers, and people like them who had no business lurking.

"You're not proposing we break into her house . . . are you?" Layla already knew the answer but hoped that, just maybe, she'd misread the signs. Night had fallen a couple of hours ago, and the dim burn of streetlamps cast everything around them in a shadowy, sinister glow. Even the stray dog on the far side of the street looked more like a hostile hellhound than the lazy Labradoodle it most likely was.

"It's hardly breaking and entering when you have a key." Aster thrust an open palm toward Layla and wiggled her fingers.

"I'm not sure that's true. . . ." Layla sounded nervous. She had good reason to be. Her hand actually shook as she surrendered the keys, not feeling the least bit relieved when the Labradoodle/hellhound moved on. Where had it gone? And worse—would it return with more demon dog friends? "Listen," she said, already regretting forfeiting the keys. Not like keeping them would've changed anything when Aster was so bent on completing her mission. Still, she owed it to both of them to at least try to reason with her. "Don't you think the cops have already been here? For all we know, they could have someone posted inside right now, just waiting for you to show up."

The thought of walking into a trap—even worse, a trap set by Larsen—was reason enough to flee. Though judging by the resolute look on Aster's face, she wasn't even close to being swayed.

"Please." Aster's voice was dismissive and brisk. "It's not like it's a crime scene. Madison's blood was found at Night for Night, not here. Sure, they probably checked out the place, but I'm also sure they're long gone by now, so I really don't think we have anything to worry about. Still, if you want to bail, now's your chance. But with or without you, I'm going in. The California death penalty may be dormant, but death row is alive and well. Just because they haven't executed anyone since 2006 doesn't mean they won't change their minds and make me the example. For the first time in my life, I can literally say I have nothing to lose. Which leaves me no choice but to risk it, even if it turns out you're right and I live to regret it."

The words hung heavy between them, and for a change, Layla couldn't think of a single good retort. "Guess that explains why you're dressed like a cat burglar." She motioned toward Aster's all-black ensemble, which seemed really inappropriate for such a hot summer night, and watched in dismay as Aster dipped an arm into a large black tote bag, retrieved two dark beanies, and tossed one to her.

"And the video?" She looked at Layla. "I'm assuming you still have it. I gave it to you right before Larsen cuffed me."

Layla reached into her bag and handed it over.

Aster seemed to breathe easier, but Layla was still on edge. What Aster was proposing could end really badly for both of them. Maybe Tommy had been right to call it quits.

"What exactly is the plan?" Layla asked. "I mean, even if the cops aren't waiting inside, then surely Madison has a serious alarm system in place. Probably even a guard dog, security cameras, a retina-scanning device . . ." She glanced over Aster's shoulder, on the lookout for squad cars, a pack of ravenous hellhounds, a random black cat crossing their path, any sort of omen she could use as a viable excuse to bail while she could. And yet, for whatever reason, she knew that she wouldn't. She just couldn't bring herself to let Aster go it alone.

"This." Aster nodded toward a row of towering hedges, fidgeting in a way that did not inspire confidence. "This is the plan. It may seem crazy, but I have to do something, and to me this makes sense." She turned away, tugged her beanie onto her head, and started walking purposefully toward the nearest house. Stopping before the formidable gate, she squinted at the address on her phone. "Last chance to turn back."

As tempting as it was to flee to the safety of her car, for better or worse, Layla had committed to this point; she might as well see it through to the end. She watched as Aster pulled on a pair of black leather gloves, headed for the keypad, and punched in the code. The two of them unwittingly held their breath as they waited for the gate to inch open.

"Someone must've changed the code," Layla said, struggling to hide her relief when the gate didn't so much as budge.

"Here, you read it. Maybe I transposed the numbers or something." Aster thrust the phone at Layla and flexed her fingers as though warming up for a race.

Layla slowly repeated the numbers as Aster punched them into the pad. Then they stood back and waited, staring hard at the gate. Aster sighed in relief when it slowly eased open. Layla sighed in defeat.

Together, they began the walk down the long stone drive that led to the house. From the lawn plagued with brown patches and weeds, to the run of untamed rosebushes dropping dead buds along the path like forgotten offerings, it was clear the yard hadn't been tended to since Madison went missing.

Still, the garden lights were aglow, which meant the electricity was still humming. Though in light of what they were about to do, Layla took it as an ominous sign. At best the alarm system was still working and fully engaged. At worst, Larsen was inside, raiding Madison's wine cellar and watching all her premium cable channels, just waiting for the moment they walked through the door.

What would become of the property and all of Madison's belongings—the bits and pieces of the life she'd worked so hard to assemble? Just how long would her team of managers keep feeding the banks and utility companies, waiting for her to return, before they decided to call it quits and begin the long process of dismantling the estate?

There were so many unanswered questions, though Layla chose to voice the one closest to the matter at hand. "So, what exactly are we looking for?" She watched as the heel of Aster's boot came down hard on a deadhead. The squished and rotted rosebud rocked her off balance for a moment before she righted herself and angrily kicked it aside.

"Clues, signs, evidence—anything that might hint toward what really happened that night," Aster whispered, sounding irritated in a way Layla couldn't ignore. Here she was, risking her life to clear Aster's name, and Aster had the nerve to get annoyed?

"Pretty sure the cops already did that," Layla grumbled.

Aster paused before the massive front door. "Maybe, maybe not." She tapped her gold-and-diamond hamsa pendant for luck, though in Layla's mind Aster was better off ditching that thing. She'd been wearing it the day she got booked for first-degree murder; clearly it didn't work in her favor. "From the moment they zeroed in on me as their main suspect, I have no reason to think they looked anywhere else. And even if they were here, they didn't know what to look for, and we do."

"We do?" Before Layla could finish, Aster was already rolling her eyes.

"Anything that bears the name Della, for starters. We need to determine if it's merely her Starbucks alias, or if it means something more. Also, if we can find anything tracking back to that apartment I woke up in, see if it's somehow connected to Madison . . . And speaking of Ryan, what's going on with him?"

Layla shook her head. "He's been pretty low profile. Claims he's trying to sort things out, and is asking the press to respect his privacy during this difficult time."

Aster smirked. "That's code for 'Don't bother me until I've had a chance to destroy all the evidence.' Or worse, he's pointing the evidence toward me to make me look guilty. And now . . . the moment of truth . . ." She gave the door an anxious glance that did not inspire confidence.

Again, Layla wondered if it was too late to bolt. But the

next thing she knew, Aster had inserted what appeared to be the house key into the lock and was slowly turning it until they heard the dead bolt retreating and the door eased open.

"If the alarm goes off—run!" Aster whispered, taking a tentative step into the entry as Layla stood frozen behind her, waiting for something terrible to happen. When a few moments passed with no sign of chaos, they ventured farther inside.

"Doesn't she have a dog?" Layla cringed at the way her voice seemed to echo in the high-ceilinged room.

"Blue." Aster nodded. "Not sure who has him now—maybe her assistant, Emily?" Aster turned a slow circle, gazing from the enormous chandelier that dominated the entry to the collection of large black-and-white photographs that covered most of the wall space.

While the house was decorated in a sort of eclectic, modern Regency style, the oversize prints really stood out. They were haunting, and not at all what Layla expected. Though they were obviously professional quality, pictures of run-down trailer parks and decrepit interiors featuring sagging couches and broken TVs weren't usually paired with Carrara marble floors and seven-foot-tall hand-blown glass installations that had easily cost somewhere in the six-figure range.

"It's a Chihuly." Layla nodded toward the glimmering

cobalt-blue sculpture. "A real one, not a copy. The only other one I've seen is in the Bellagio Hotel in Las Vegas."

"Does that mean something?" Aster squinted between the chandelier and Layla, but Layla just shook her head.

"No. Madison could definitely afford it." She forced her gaze away from the photo of a gleaming gun placed on a beat-up coffee table and surveyed the rest of the room. She felt shivery and unsure, her limbs gone suddenly heavy, reluctant to move. "It just feels so spooky to be in her space, knowing she may never return."

"What's that supposed to mean?" Aster whirled around to face her.

"We have no idea what happened—no way of knowing if she's dead or alive. And why are you looking at me like that when you know it's the truth? I mean, it *was* her blood on the terrace," Layla ventured. "And all over your dress . . ."

"So why are you here if you assume that I'm guilty?" Aster was enraged, but Layla was too.

"First of all, I wouldn't be here if I thought you were guilty. Still, it does seem a little strange that not only is your dress the state's most valuable piece of evidence, but now you know the code to her gate?"

Layla remained rooted in place, beginning to regret her decision to come without taking the time to properly think it through. It wasn't like her to act so impulsively. And yet, somehow she knew Aster wasn't the killer. Though that didn't mean she couldn't do with a little more proof.

"Seems like a topic we could've discussed earlier." Aster tapped her foot impatiently against the shiny white floor and struggled to contain herself. "But fine, whatever. For the record, I left the dress in the trash in that strange apartment I woke up in, and it certainly wasn't bloodstained then. Clearly, I was set up and someone purposely planted it in the W laundry. As for the code—" Aster fought back the anger creeping into her voice. "I lifted it from Ryan's phone. I'm not proud of it, but there it is. I'd been obsessed with Madison for a really long time—long before I hooked up with Ryan, but not in a creepy way or anything like that. Mostly, I admired her. She had everything I wanted to achieve for myself. So one time, when Ryan wasn't looking, I looked up her contact info and forwarded it to myself, then erased the trail before he could notice. So, yeah, I did that. And if you think it makes me guilty, then fine, you're free to leave." Aster was shaking with a mixture of fury and fear, and Layla could relate. She'd feel exactly the same if she were the one being falsely accused.

"So—" Layla gazed around the luxuriously appointed space. "Where do we start?"

It took Aster a moment to process Layla's intention to stay. But once she had, she sprang into action. "I think it's better if we split up. We want to be thorough, but quick.

We've wasted enough time already, don't you think?" She shot Layla a pointed look. "I'll take the upstairs, you check down here. Text if you find anything, and I'll do the same."

Without another word, Aster made for the staircase, as Layla headed out to the garage, figuring she'd start there and work her way in.

Compared to the quaint Venice Beach bungalow Layla had grown up in, Madison's house seemed far too big for just one person and a medium-sized dog to inhabit. Though compared to current Beverly Hills, Bel Air, Holmby Hills, Platinum Triangle standards, with their penchant for thirty-thousand-square-foot giga-mansions, it seemed downright modest. Still, Layla couldn't help but wonder if Madison ever got lonely or scared living single among so many unoccupied rooms.

She moved into the four-car garage, also considered small by the new subterranean twenty-car standard, and with Madison's car still missing, the empty space seemed almost eerie.

There was a stack of clear plastic bins piled against a far wall, but a quick check proved they were filled with used, discarded items that were marked for Goodwill. There was a supply of dog food and other assorted dog accessories neatly arranged in the corner, but other than that, the space with its unmarked walls and clean tiled floors made for the most uncluttered, immaculate garage Layla had ever seen.

A moment later, she let herself back inside, planning to poke around the kitchen and den, when she heard Aster scream, and Layla raced for the stairs, taking them two at a time.

Aster screaming could only mean one thing—they weren't as alone as they'd thought.

When the screaming abruptly stopped, Layla feared the worst but quickened her pace. Landing at the top of the stairs, she rounded a corner and shot down the hall, where she stopped in the entry of an elaborate bedroom she guessed to be Madison's and grabbed the first thing she saw, a large and surprisingly heavy candlestick. With the makeshift weapon clutched in her fist, she heard the muffled sound of a struggle in progress and sprang into the closet, where she froze in place, gaping in fright at the unimaginable scene unfolding before her.

# FIFTEEN

# ALL APOLOGIES

Aster had first read about Madison's massive walk-in closet in an *InStyle* magazine profile piece, where the normally cool and reserved Madison had exhibited a rare and palpable excitement as she went into great detail describing the inspiration and intricate craftsmanship behind it. At the time, Aster had gazed in envy at the pictures of the luxury dressing room/retreat. With its soft neutral tones, hand-knotted rugs, and rows of lighted shelves displaying a seemingly endless collection of designer handbags and shoes, it was every girl's dream, and Aster, who was no stranger to luxury, had found herself practically salivating.

Her in-person reaction was no different.

Until Ryan Hawthorne attacked her.

She fought hard against him, bucking, kicking, and

biting at the hand he'd clasped firmly over her mouth, despite his pleas begging her to stop.

"Let her go."

Layla loomed in the entry, brandishing a candlestick she clearly intended to use. Still, they were no match for Ryan. If he wanted, he could easily take them both down.

"Seriously?" Ryan groaned at the sight of her. "This is escalating way out of control, and someone's gonna get hurt. Put that thing down and let me explain."

"Let her go," Layla repeated. She had no intention of folding, much less retreating.

Ryan surveyed the room and considered his options. "Fine," he relented. "But just—nobody scream, okay? Nobody do anything stupid." He removed his hand long enough for Aster to start howling again, as Layla raced menacingly toward him. But Ryan reacted by flashing his palms in surrender and sinking onto the couch. "For the last time, ditch the candlestick, and try to convince your friend to power down." He shot Aster a worried look.

Aster was frantic, fumbling for her phone as she shrieked, "We need to call the police! Ryan killed Madison, and now he's living in her house!" She kicked Ryan hard in the shin and smirked in satisfaction when he clutched his leg with both hands in a mix of surprise and pain.

"Was that really necessary?" Ryan regarded Aster through bloodshot green eyes.

He looked like hell, but that was nothing compared to what he'd look like when the cops were done with him. She was punching the final digit into the keypad when Layla snatched the phone from her hands.

"Are you kidding me?" Aster glared accusingly. "Whose side are you on?"

"Mine. I'm on my side." Layla stuffed the phone in her pocket where Aster couldn't get to it. "I really don't need a B and E on my record, and neither do you."

"But he . . ." Aster motioned toward Ryan, who, at the moment anyway, was in no position to harm anyone. Sitting with his head in his hands, he'd clearly run out of steam. And if the scent in the room was any indication, he'd been well on his way to getting high when they'd interrupted him, which explained the bloodshot eyes.

Ryan lifted his chin. With his tousled blond hair falling over his forehead, he was even more gorgeous than she remembered, but also weary beyond his years. "What are you going to tell them, Aster? That you broke into Madison's house and found me in her closet, taking bong hits and listening to music that reminds me of her?"

"I'll tell them you killed her . . . that you . . ." She was totally out of ammo, and everyone knew it.

"And what kind of proof will you offer?"

He looked at them both, and in that moment, he appeared so bereft Aster wondered how she ever could've doubted him. His was not the face of a killer. But something inside her wouldn't give in just yet. Maybe he hadn't killed Madison, but he'd done other things. Things she'd been blamed for.

"I'll tell you what I'm guilty of. I'm guilty of fucking everything up. I'm guilty of going along with Madison's crazy plan. I'm guilty of believing her when she claimed she had it all under control. I'm guilty of so many things, but I absolutely, one hundred percent did not harm her, and I don't know who did."

"So what are you doing here then? What are you looking for? How'd you get in?" Aster fired the questions in rapid succession, hoping to rattle him into revealing something he didn't intend to.

"I used a key, same as you." Ryan nodded toward the key ring Aster held clenched in her fist. "Madison gave me mine. How'd you get yours?" He quirked a questioning brow, and Aster scowled in return. "As for what I'm doing here . . ." He lifted his shoulders and casually glanced all around. "I guess you could say I'm trying to figure out what the hell happened, how my life slipped right out from under me, who the hell I've been dating for the last six months, and how you ended up implicated in all this. Because I'll tell you one thing, while I wasn't a perfect boyfriend, not by a stretch, Madison Brooks was hardly a model girlfriend. Half of what she told me is lies, and now I'm left trying to sort it all out. All I know for sure is that girl is not at all who she pretended to be. She had us all fooled."

When his eyes met hers, Aster averted her gaze and stole a quick glance at Layla instead, trying to determine what she made of all this. Ryan was an actor, which put everything he said under a cloud of suspicion, yet there was no mistaking the ring of truth in his words.

Ryan lifted his hands in the universal sign of surrender. "Can we at least call a truce—even if it's temporary? Will you at least consider trying to believe me?"

"I believe you," Layla said, the simple statement enough to shock Aster speechless. "Or at least I don't think you killed her. But I do think you know more than you're letting on. You were closer to her than anyone else. So it's time to fess up and tell us what you know."

Ryan sighed and glanced between them. "Don't believe everything you read," he grumbled. "Truth is, our agents set us up. It was a relationship of convenience, and we played it up for the press, but we both knew the score."

Aster remained fuming before him. It wasn't that she didn't believe him, but she wasn't about to let him off the hook quite so easily. He'd have to work a lot harder than that to even begin making up for everything she suspected him of doing. "While you may have succeeded in convincing my friend," she finally said, "unlike me, Layla has no idea the level of deceit you're capable of."

"Fair enough." Ryan shrugged and stared longingly at the bong as though he was actually considering sparking it up.

She was losing control of the situation. Ryan's sudden appearance had set her off balance—both literally and figuratively—and Aster needed a moment to collect herself.

She stared at the wall reserved for displaying framed photographs of Madison, the neat rows spanning from the floor all the way to the ceiling. A mix of the magazine covers she'd graced—*Vogue, Harper's Bazaar, InStyle, People's* "Most Beautiful" issue—along with pics of her posing beside a variety of high-profile public figures—fellow celebrities, studio heads, athletes, celebrity chefs, even the president.

In every photo, Madison's unknowable gaze seemed to be staring right back at the viewer. The girl had secrets. It seemed so obvious now. And Aster was convinced that the key to finding her lay in discovering just what it was Madison was so determined to hide.

She returned her focus to Ryan. Despite what he claimed about the relationship being one of convenience, he'd still been closer to Madison than anyone else. She needed to know what he knew, though she couldn't afford to let him know just how desperate she'd become.

"Five minutes." She stared pointedly at her watch. "That's all you've got to convince me. So why don't you start with where you were the night Madison went missing, since, as it turns out, you went missing too."

Ryan froze. "I didn't go missing." His words were slow, halting, as though he'd carefully selected each one. "You're the one who went missing."

Aster fumed. It was exactly what she'd expected him to say. Deny, deny, deny. Well, not anymore, and not on her time. "Not exactly," she snapped, staring him down until he visibly cringed. "Try again."

Ryan looked to Layla as though she held the script that contained all his lines. Returning to Aster, he said, "You went to the bathroom and never came back. I polished off the rest of the champagne while waiting for you to return. I even sent one of the waitresses to check on you. It wasn't until James told me he saw you leave and get into a car with some other guy that I took off with my friends."

She was as equally outraged as she was stunned. If what he said was true, then they'd never slept together. But that didn't mean she hadn't slept with someone else. Possibly the nameless, faceless stranger she'd supposedly left the club with?

A wave of nausea rushed through her as everything she'd feared about that night made the leap from bad to so much worse. She felt dizzy, unsteady. Gazing longingly at the couch, she thought how nice it would be to sit for a bit until she found her footing again, but quickly ruled it out. She could not, would not, show any weakness. She'd survived a week in jail. She'd survive this too.

"You were pretty upset." Ryan's tone was tentative. "I figured you just needed to blow off some steam."

His words were a blur as she turned to search Layla's face, in desperate need of a second opinion, an ally, someone to translate and make some kind of sense of everything Ryan was saying.

Ryan ran a hand through his hair, removed the earbuds that hung from his neck, and placed them on a table next to the bong and his phone. "Truth is, the breakup was staged. Mad thought she was doing us both a favor. She knew I was seeing you, knew how much I was beginning to care for you. . . ."

Aster rolled her eyes, shook her head, and groaned in a way he couldn't possibly miss. He might have sideswiped her a moment ago, but with that single bullshit statement, she was back in control.

"Okay, fine." He sighed and rubbed at his eyes. "I was attracted to you, which isn't exactly a crime, is it? You were always so elusive, so impossible to get, it drove me crazy and made me want you even more. When I admitted as much to Madison, she didn't hesitate to jump on it. She said she needed to get away for a bit. She had some business to handle, something personal, though she refused to divulge any details. She claimed a public breakup would provide the perfect excuse to disappear for a while."

"Why'd you agree to go along?"

Ryan looked at Layla. "Because I needed the press. Even bad press would do. My show was getting axed, I had nothing lined up, and I knew Aster wanted to get noticed and I—we—Madison agreed it might help. She ended up going off script and taking it way further than planned. I guess she got caught up in the moment, or maybe she got caught up in her anger toward me for stepping out on her. All I know is I was shocked at the level of drama that ensued, and yeah, I guess I was also a little annoyed, which is why I didn't try to check on her to see if she was okay. In my defense, I really did believe it was all part of the plan. It wasn't until they found the blood evidence that I realized something had gone terribly wrong. Then, when Aster's dress was linked . . . well, that's when I knew that someone else had been pulling the strings all along." He looked at Aster, eyes pleading.

"Thirty seconds." She glared in return.

He pressed his lips together, ran a hand over his perfectly chiseled face. "I don't think you're guilty. I also don't think Mad set you up. I think something far darker is happening, and that's why I—"

"Time."

Ryan hung his head. "For the record," he said, voice broken, "I really do care what happens to you. I feel partly responsible for getting you into this mess."

"Yeah, like in all those interviews when you called me a mistake?"

He shook his head. "Not a day goes by that I don't wish I'd handled myself better and that I refused to go along with Madison's ploy. Not that I'm blaming her, or at least not entirely. I'm sorry for everything that's transpired, for all the horrible fallout."

"Fallout! You consider a first-degree murder charge *fallout*? Because that's what I'm facing."

"I don't expect you to forgive me."

"You know what I really hate?"

He looked at her with bleary, red streaked eyes.

"I hate when people knowingly screw you over, then say they're sorry and assume that's all that's required. You want my forgiveness? Go out and earn it! Your words are worth nothing to me—your actions are your only true currency, and so far they've failed on every level. You said you'd be there for me, that you wouldn't let me face this alone. Less than twenty minutes later, you disappeared from my life."

"You're the one who disappeared! You left the club without me."

"I don't remember any of that. I don't remember anything after I left the Riad."

Ryan's face looked troubled as he continued to study her. "I had nothing to do with that."

Aster's shoulders sank. She was losing steam but was unwilling to surrender completely. "Tell me what you know about Della," she said.

Ryan balked, then just as quickly he collected himself. "MaryDella. It's Madison's real name."

"And her last name?" Aster quirked a brow and waited.

Ryan sighed. "No idea. But it's not Brooks. Her last address before LA may have been Connecticut, but that's not where she came from."

"That's a lot of info for someone who claims to know nothing."

"I dated her for six months. Not sure that's a lot of info when you take that into account. Though I can tell you she was cutting deals all over town. Madison had a very extensive payroll."

"Meaning?"

"Aside from the usual lawyers, managers, agents, stylists, publicists, assistants, and the like—she was also paying James—"

"James—the bouncer at Night for Night?"

"Whatever their arrangement, I've no doubt it required his discretion. She also had a fixer." Fielding their confused looks, he said, "Someone who handled her . . . stuff."

"What kind of stuff?"

"The kind of stuff her team of professionals didn't, couldn't, or wouldn't, I guess."

"So, basically, other than her first name you really don't know anything."

"Listen, I'm as eager to solve this mystery as you are."

"Doubtful." Aster glared. "I have a lot more at stake."

"I'm willing to help, if you'll let me. Let me prove that you really can trust me."

Aster studied him. He seemed sincere, and there was no doubt that the more insiders they had on their side, the better. But she kept her expression as smooth as freshly poured concrete. Better to let him sweat it out until she decided.

After a moment's silence, she said, "We're not friends. Not even close. We're just trying to solve a mystery and clear my name, nothing more. And, for the record, this isn't one of your stupid Hollywood sitcoms. We're not some zany group of superheroes out to avenge the world of evil. My very life is at stake. Which means, if I so much as catch you not taking this seriously, I'll make sure you regret it."

Ryan didn't hesitate to offer his hand.

After a long moment, Aster shook on the deal. Then, dropping his hand just as quickly, she settled onto the rug, looked at Layla and Ryan, and said, "So, where do we begin?"

# SIXTEEN

# MUSIC TO WATCH BOYS TO

There was no logical explanation for why she was feeling so grumpy. Sure, she'd barely gotten any sleep, having spent the bulk of the night at Madison's, talking and strategizing and forming a plan with Ryan and Aster, but Layla was used to late nights, and she wasn't much of a deep sleeper anyway. Going to bed for her was more like switching to *do not disturb* mode for a handful of hours while the rest of the world powered down.

Maybe it was because she missed blogging—connecting to an audience through the stories she wrote.

Maybe it was because she hadn't fully adapted to life without Mateo. More than once she'd found herself in the midst of texting him after seeing something funny she knew he would like, only to remember just before she hit Send that, for the moment anyway, they were no longer friends.

Or maybe she was still miffed at Tommy for bailing on Aster when she needed his help. And maybe, just maybe, she missed him a little bit too.

Whatever the reason, Layla took it out on Hollywood Boulevard, swerving in and out of traffic while cursing all its tour buses and rubbernecking tourists driving their oddly colored rental cars well below the speed limit. Didn't they realize there was nothing to see?

Okay, maybe there were a few semi-interesting sights like Grauman's Chinese Theater and the Walk of Fame stars, but the majority of the boulevard was an eyesore of sagging buildings, cheesy souvenir shops, and smelly costumed weirdos charging people ridiculous fees just to pose with them. Despite Ira's bid to turn it into the new Sunset (or rather the old Sunset, seeing as how the once-legendary strip of celebrated nightclubs was giving way to swanky hotels, luxury condos, and exclusive designer boutiques), it was the same old seedy freak parade Layla had always known.

She glared at the vanity plate before her. Was there anything dumber than a plate that announced the type of car it was attached to? *Just in case you missed the insignia on the trunk, behold the very clever, phonetically spelled license plate to remind you of the type of car you are currently tailgating!*

Layla had no shortage of petty annoyances. Her list of pet peeves was so lengthy it often left her feeling more like some old curmudgeon than the eighteen-year-old girl that she was. Maybe she should lighten up, open her heart, and embrace the fact that the person before her was a very proud Ferrari owner, and rightfully so.

But when she read the plate again, she realized the best and only recourse for someone like her was to maneuver around it until she could no longer see it.

She weaved in and out of traffic, scanning her rearview and side mirrors for radar-gun-wielding cops. Last thing she needed was a ticket; she was already running late as it was. While the BMW was comfortable and drove like a dream, if she'd taken the Kawasaki she would've been there by now. Still, the use of an Unrivaled company car was a major job perk she'd be a fool to pass up, and yet the fact that she hadn't left Layla uneasy. It was more than the fear that she was turning into yet another shallow, materialistic, mall-worshipping zombie like her mom. Now that Layla and her dad were both working for Unrivaled, the car was like another hook connecting her to Ira.

Having started the day getting reprimanded for deeming the organic, gluten-free, Paleo-approved pet food as not goodie-bag-worthy when, according to Emerson, there was no shortage of celebrities wanting their dogs to eat like cavemen, Layla desperately needed to end her first week on the job by accomplishing at least one assignment she could feel proud of.

Emerson had jumped all over her when he caught her ducking out early, convinced she was getting a jump on the weekend. The astonished look on his face when she informed him she was on her way to meet with Malina Li at Elixir Records made the humiliation almost worth it.

For whatever reason, Ira had specifically asked her to handle the music for the tequila launch, which seemed like a pretty important task—one that would definitely be better handled by someone with far more experience. She'd even gone so far as to question why the Vesper's booking agent didn't handle it instead. *Because I'm asking you*, had been Ira's terse reply, and Layla had been smart enough to leave it at that.

After turning left on a red (the only way to turn left in LA, thanks to the constant flow of heavy traffic), she found a space in the parking structure and rode the elevator to the very top floor, all the while trying not to feel completely out of her league, which she undoubtedly was.

The office walls were covered with framed photos of Elixir's numerous rock star clients, and Layla tried not to fidget as the receptionist gave her a thorough once-over before ushering her into a sleek, modern, yet decidedly feminine space decorated in brushed golds and rich creams, where a gorgeous woman with long dark hair and deep red lips sat frowning behind a large ebony desk.

Malina Li, the head of A and R, was exactly the kind of woman Layla dreamed of interviewing. Her rise to the top of a male-dominated industry was the sort of story Layla dreamed of writing. But at the moment, Malina was scowling, and because of it, Layla was cringing.

"You're not Ira," Malina snapped.

Layla stood awkwardly before her. "I'm here on Ira's behalf." She hoped it was the right thing to say. The way Malina shook her head and leaned back in her seat, silently regarding Layla through a thick fringe of lashes and a judgmental brow, told her it wasn't. "I'm going to be honest," Layla said, figuring it was better to be frank and not even try to bluff her way through the meeting. "I'm not entirely sure why I'm here. I don't usually handle these things."

Malina sighed and crossed her legs at the knee. "Leave it to Ira to send a newbie to punish me." The sour expression that followed only served to punctuate the sentiment. "Okay. Fine," she said as though resigned to her fate. "I don't know how much Ira's told you, but the short version is the artist he booked for the launch just canceled due to reasons I will not get into. Suffice it to say Ira is furious. And while I understand his predicament, I've recently signed someone new who's destined to blow up really big. If Ira agrees to book him, it will only raise the cachet of his brand, as he'll be able to lay claim to being the first to showcase him."

"Sounds exciting," Layla said, but the baleful look

Malina shot her told her she would've been better off saying nothing at all.

"So, seeing as Ira saw fit to send you, that means the future of my bright and shining star, my great new hope, rests entirely in your inexperienced hands."

Layla swallowed. That sounded ridiculously overdramatic, but she knew better than to respond.

"What do you know about music?" Malina demanded.

Layla gnawed the inside of her cheek. In her panic, her mind had gone blank and she couldn't recall a single song that she liked. Thanks to her dad's creative influence, Layla had grown up listening to some pretty cool bands. Much of her childhood had been spent touring art galleries, museums, and going to concerts. Because of that, she had no embarrassing boy band crushes that could ever come back to haunt her. And yet, with Malina warily eyeing her, the best Layla could do was mumble, "Um, I mostly like rock. I listen to a lot of classic rock, actually."

"How classic?" Malina uncrossed her legs and leaned forward. Her chair squeaked in protest as Layla gulped. This was a test she would either pass or fail. There was no gray zone with Malina.

"Classic like . . . Zeppelin, Hendrix, Bowie, Nirvana . . . oh, and the Cure," she said, remembering how Mateo had introduced her to them, and while she could no longer remember if she'd liked them, it was out there now and there was no retrieving the words.

"Nirvana is classic rock?" Malina quirked an amused brow.

"They were playing 'Smells Like Teen Spirit' when I bought guacamole at Gelson's the other day." Layla met her gaze and held it.

"Touché." Malina grinned, well, barely, but still, Layla would take what she could get. "So reassuring to know my high school soundtrack has survived the test of time only to end up in the local produce aisles." She tapped her fingers against her desk, then pulled a demo CD from a folder and pushed it halfway between them. "It's not a proper studio recording, which means it's a little rough. Also, we haven't had time to schedule a professional photo shoot, but trust me when I say this guy is hot, hot, hot and has the talent to match."

Layla nodded and waited for more, waited for Malina to remove her perfectly manicured index finger from the CD so she could stuff it into her bag and get the hell out of there.

"Originally, I was positioning him to debut at the Vesper. But now that this opportunity's opened up, I think the Unrivaled tequila launch would work just as well. He's new, but he's ready. I've no doubt he can handle the crowd. Now it's all up to you . . ." Malina's eyes narrowed, her voice faded; clearly she'd already forgotten who she was talking to. Could this meeting get any worse?

"Layla," she supplied, her voice as tight as the expression she wore on her face.

"Yes, so my hope is you'll give him a chance, *Layla*."

Malina emphasized the name as though committing it to memory, and suddenly Layla wished that she wouldn't—wished that the moment she left, Malina would forget she existed.

"I'm sure you know how hard it is to make it in this town. The industry is very competitive, and . . ." Her phone buzzed then, and she glanced at the screen and pressed her lips into a frown. "Just—give it a listen." She rushed to stand and pressed the demo into Layla's hands as she promptly stood too.

"I expect to hear from you soon. We're only days away from the event, so we need to move quickly." She was already at the door. Layla was just a few steps behind her.

"And the artist's name?" Layla asked. She knew nothing about the music biz, but it seemed weird that during the entire time Malina had been singing this unknown rock god's praises, she'd yet to mention his name.

"Don't worry about that. Just give it a chance."

Layla left the office and made her way to her car. It felt so good to be out of that corporate environment—away from Malina, free of Emerson. She thought she might even open her sunroof—something the sun-phobic LA native rarely did.

She plucked a flyer from under the windshield wiper, about to toss it when she realized it wasn't a flyer at all.

It was another card. Her name was carefully scripted on the front of the envelope in that all-too-familiar curli-cue scrawl, while the card itself bore a picture of the same cartoon cat from the first one. Only now, in addition to the noose around its neck and the bloody gunshot wound to its head, its front teeth were knocked out, making for an even more sinister grin.

Inside, someone had written:

*Your reluctance to play is making me sad*
*Better move quickly before sad turns to mad*
*It would be a real shame*
*If you mistook this for a game*
*If you continue to delay*
*There will be a hefty price to pay.*

Layla's gaze darted frantically around the parking garage as she tried to catch a glimpse of whoever might've delivered it. Were they hidden away somewhere, watching her every move? She shook away the thought, buried the paper deep in her bag, and slid inside her car.

The only one who knew about her meeting was Emerson. Even Malina had expected to meet with Ira, not her. Had he really driven all the way out here just to slip the message under her windshield? She supposed it was possible, and yet, something about it didn't make sense.

Eager to rule it either way, Layla phoned the office and asked to speak to him. If Emerson was there, then she'd know he didn't do it. She hadn't been in Malina's office long enough for him to make the round trip.

But if he wasn't there . . .

The call connected and Layla was immediately put on hold.

"I'm afraid you've just missed him," the receptionist said, her voice terse and hurried. "Can I take a message?"

Layla sat behind the wheel of her car, her gaze shifting between her side and rearview mirrors. "How long ago did he leave?"

The receptionist heaved an annoyed sigh. "I don't know. Not long. Look, do you want to try his cell? We're really busy here what with the launch and all."

Layla ended the call and started the car. Someone was playing her—using her as a pawn in hopes of exposing Madison's lies. And the worst part was, Layla had no clue as to who was behind it. Though the threatening tone had given her pause, to fold now would be to surrender what little power she had, and that she would not do. If they wanted her to post the journal entries, then they'd have to send something a lot juicier than the adolescent angst she'd received so far.

With the sun blaring overhead, Layla fed the CD into the

stereo, cranked up the volume, and merged onto the street. Maybe she didn't plan on making a career out of marketing, maybe she loathed the corporate hierarchy, which bore an eerie resemblance to her junior high cafeteria, but there was something to be said for getting paid to drive around the city listening to a demo CD.

The sound of an electric guitar burst through the speakers, and like Malina had warned, the sound quality really was rough. But the opening refrain was catchy enough to convince Layla to turn up the speakers.

A few chords in, a male voice began to sing. The lyrics were so wistful, Layla unwittingly slowed at a yellow, causing a flurry of horns to honk all around her. But she was too captured by the singing to focus on the driver behind her flipping the bird with both fingers. The voice coming through her speakers was strangely and hauntingly familiar.

She listened closer . . . something about kissing a girl in a bar . . . a girl with deep violet eyes . . .

The light turned green. The car behind her slammed the horn hard. But Layla remained right where she was. Listening to Tommy Phillips sing about the night he hooked up with Madison Brooks, knowing she now held the power to either make or break his debut.

# SEVENTEEN

# 'TIS A PITY SHE WAS A WHORE

Transcript

*Trena Moretti Exclusive Prime-Time Interview*

Episode Title: "What Happened to Madison Brooks?"

Air Date: August 19, 2016

Topic: Did Aster Amirpour Murder Madison Brooks?

**Trena Moretti:** Aster, I'd like to thank you for agreeing to talk with me today. After nearly a week in jail, you were just released on bail. What was it like for you living behind bars?

**Aster Amirpour:** A complete and total living hell.

**TM:** I can't help but notice your injuries. Can you tell us about how you sustained those?

**AA:** I was jumped.

**TM:** You were jumped by . . .

**AA:** Another inmate. I'd just been put into the holding cell and the next thing I knew, I was being attacked.

**TM:** Was there any indication as to why?

**AA:** (sighs) Listen, jail is a sad, depressing, and desperate environment that doesn't operate according to the usual social niceties. People are locked up in cages, locked up like animals, and so they begin thinking and acting that way. I have no idea what motivated the attack; maybe she was a Madison fan.

**TM:** A Madison fan. According to our records, you were once a Madison fan too.

**AA:** (looks directly at the camera) I still am. Listen, what people don't understand and what I'd like to make clear is that I'm one of Madison's biggest fans. I love her, and admire her, and I'd never, ever do anything to harm her—

**TM:** (interrupts) And yet you had no problem having an affair with Madison's boyfriend at the time, TV star Ryan Hawthorne. Or are you denying your involvement with Ryan?

**AA:** I'm not denying anything, though I'm not sure that what I had with Ryan constitutes an affair.

**TM:** Well, it's no secret you accepted the presents he gave you, and there were pictures of the two of you kissing. . . .

**AA:** Yes, and while all of that is true, it still wasn't quite as . . . intense . . . as people like to assume.

**TM:** Meaning?

**AA:** Meaning, Ryan and I never slept together. I was a virgin the entire time I was with him.

Ryan gripped the transcript so tightly Aster could hear the paper crumple in protest. "Is this true?" He stared at her bug-eyed.

Aster focused hard on the road before her. She was working from memory—a memory that was foggy at best. While she couldn't remember anything about arriving at the apartment, she remembered leaving it all too well. And yet, the sting of shame had been so strong, she'd grabbed a cab and gotten the hell out of there as quickly as possible without once looking back.

If only she had the luxury of not looking back now.

How was she to know that the one night she couldn't recall would end up being the basis for her entire defense?

Between the diary entries Layla had received, Madison's numerous lies about her past, and the odd mix of people she'd kept on her payroll, there were a lot of moving parts, none of which seemed to connect. Though Aster was determined to prove they fit nicely together, at the moment it was like having all the corners and edges of a puzzle but not a single piece to fill in the center.

Her first task was to retrace her steps that fateful night, beginning with locating the mystery apartment. Though Ryan had insisted on joining her, she drew the line at letting him drive. She needed the time behind the wheel, needed to feel in control of when and where she was going. She'd given Ryan the transcript in a bid to keep him occupied. At the time, she hadn't given much thought to its contents and how it might affect him. Now that he had, she realized she would've been better off waiting for it to air later that night.

"I guess I didn't tell you because I didn't think it mattered." Defiantly, Aster lifted her chin and focused on Ryan. His expression was grim.

"C'mon, Aster, at least give me the benefit of the truth. A girl as beautiful as you doesn't lack for opportunity—if you chose to remain a virgin this long, then clearly, it was important to you."

She exhaled deeply, wishing she could shut her eyes and block him out completely, but the bumper-to-bumper LA traffic wouldn't allow it. "Most of my friends couldn't wait to get on with it, like it was some kind of burden they were desperate to be rid of. But I didn't see it that way. I wanted it to matter—to mean something more than just some crazy night with a boy I felt nothing for." She stole a glance at him. "That night at Night for Night, I was ready to go through with it. I'd convinced myself you were the one. Turns out I was wrong." When she dared to look at him, she found his expression so bereft it made her heart squeeze in spite of herself.

Her spine straightened, her shoulders stiffened. She needed to do whatever it took to defend against the conflicting emotions his mere presence incited. *Ryan is an actor—he's not to be trusted.* The phrase had become like a mantra she continuously repeated.

Ryan studied the transcript. "You say here that the entire time you were with me you were a virgin—does that mean you're not anymore?"

"What the hell does it matter?" She punched the brake at a red light and silently fumed as the car pitched forward and her gaze caught on yet another billboard featuring Madison's face.

"If it was your choice—your conscious choice and your conscious consent—then it's absolutely none of my business, you're right. But Aster, if someone assaulted you, then that's a very different scenario."

"You already know about the video," she snapped. "So draw your own conclusions." The second the light turned green, she pressed hard on the gas and shot out of the intersection. There was nothing like driving for blowing off steam.

"You said you were alone in the video."

"Well, clearly someone was holding the camera." She rolled her eyes and turned up the radio to drown out his voice. Ryan was seriously starting to get on her nerves.

"You need to tell someone."

She shrugged, in no mood to discuss it.

"I mean like your attorneys, or the police, or even your parents."

"No!" The word came out more forceful than she intended, but she was seriously regretting her decision to tell him. More than anyone, her parents could never know. And if she told the police or her attorney, then they'd confiscate the DVD so they could introduce it at trial, and no good would come of that. When it came to sexual assault, people loved to blame the victim, and unfortunately, slut shaming was all too real. If her parents found out, it would destroy them in a way from which they'd never recover. She'd caused them enough pain already—she refused to add any more.

Ryan flashed his palms in surrender and settled back in his seat. Aster was sure that was the end of it until he piped up again. "I'm just saying if you were assaulted, then you need to get checked by a physician."

It was all she could do to keep from screaming in frustration. She needed to focus, needed to locate some kind of landmark telling her she was on the right path. But with Ryan going on the way he was, it was nearly impossible. Through gritted teeth she glared at him and said, "And what good would it do? That was weeks ago. Besides, what are they going to do—conduct a virginity test?"

"Aster." He placed a hand on her arm, but the way she flinched in response saw him quickly retract. "I know a doctor who can help. She has a large celebrity clientele and knows how to keep the press away. Look, I don't want to cross any boundaries, and I apologize if this is coming off all wrong, or offending you in any way. It's just . . . well, I'm worried about you, and I want you to know that I'm here to help in any way I can."

Aster closed her eyes, but only for a moment. She was way beyond shutting out the sort of things she wasn't ready to face. It was time to put that particular game to rest. Besides, she needed to take steps toward reclaiming her memories and clearing her name. Maybe seeing a doctor would help in some way.

"Also . . ." He shot her a tentative look. "From everything

you've said, it sounds like someone drugged you. You only drank half your champagne and you can't remember a thing. I drained the bottle while waiting for you to return, and I was fine."

Aster froze, forced herself not to react, at least not out-wardly. Though there was nothing she could do about the wild trembling inside her belly.

"Who poured the champagne?" Her voice shook as she fought to recall.

Ryan looked right at her. "Ira."

Aster slammed the brakes hard, causing the car to skid to a stop and just narrowly miss the SUV right before her. She gripped the wheel tightly and struggled to catch her breath, unsure if her pounding heart was because of what Ryan had said, the near miss, or the view just beyond the windshield.

"That's it!" she whispered.

"You seriously think Ira had something to do with it?" Ryan made a surprised face. "I mean, why would he go after Madison—and why would he frame you for it? What could he possibly gain from something like that?"

Aster could think of a few things Ira could gain—namely the kind of PR for his clubs that money could never buy. Still, she shook her head in dismissal. She couldn't even think about that. She was too busy counting the seconds until the light turned green once again.

"Aster? You okay?"

Ryan shifted in his seat and leaned toward her, as Aster pushed through the intersection. Once she'd cleared it, she jammed the wheel to the right and parked alongside the curb. "This is it." She nudged her chin toward the high-rise looming tall and wide before her. "This is the building."

Without a word, Ryan popped his door open.

"Where do you think you're going?"

"I'm investigating."

"You don't even know what to look for."

"And you do?"

"I remember everything from that morning."

The look he gave her was doubtful.

"Okay, maybe I didn't remember the address, but everything else is clear as a photograph. Besides, you're too recognizable."

"And you're not?"

She reached into the backseat and retrieved a slouchy black beanie for him and a large floppy brimmed hat for herself. Paired with the dark sunnies she was already wearing, she reasoned she could be mistaken for just about anybody.

"You really think it's this easy?" He assessed his reflection in the lighted visor mirror.

"Look, it's now or never," she said in frustration. Ryan's skepticism only served to magnify her own, and she couldn't afford to take on his doubt. She needed to move before she lost all her nerve. "For the moment, no one even knows that I'm out, which means this may be my one and only chance to move about without the paps on my trail. Ira can only hold back TMZ for so long, you know. Besides, once Trena's interview airs, it'll be a whole other story. And it's not like you can stop me."

Ryan shook his head, slipped out of the car, and walked alongside her toward the building's entrance. "Pretty sure this is it," she said.

"How sure?"

"Eighty to ninety percent sure."

"What will it take to get a hundred?"

"The artwork in the lobby. It's big, bold, colorful, and definitely memorable."

Ryan frowned. "All these buildings have modern art in their foyers. . . ."

"Trust me, I'll know it when I see it," she said, cutting him off. "Now try to be quiet and pretend you don't know me." She pushed through the revolving glass door, crossed the gleaming stone floor, and approached the guy behind the concierge desk tucked away in the corner. He definitely hadn't been there the morning she'd fled. Then again, she'd left just after sunrise, so it was probably hours before his shift began. "I was wondering if there were any available units I could see?" She stole a quick glance at Ryan, who was somewhere behind her, discreetly taking pics with his cell phone.

She held her breath as the guy looked her over. His gaze shifted from her hat, to her sunglasses, to her expensive designer bag, before he finally got around to replying. "You can check with the leasing office if you want, or I can save you the trip and tell you there're no vacancies."

He returned to his phone as though expecting her to leave, but Aster remained firmly in place. "Nothing at all—not even short term?"

The guy looked her over again. This time studying her so intensely, Aster was sure he recognized her as the girl in the picture, right next to the one of Madison, featured on the cover of the newspaper he'd recently abandoned to the far side of his desk. But all he said was, "No short terms allowed."

He was back to ignoring her, but Aster had no intention of giving up so easily. Leaning against the desk, she flashed him the best grin she could manage, considering the scab bisecting her lip. "Just because they're not allowed doesn't mean they don't happen. . . ." She slid a thick roll of bills toward him and pushed her lips wider.

"You two together?" He glanced between her and Ryan, who was wandering around the lobby.

Without hesitation, Aster shook her head.

The guy paused as though considering whether or not to believe her.

"Fine." He relented and slid a plastic key fob toward her. "Twelfth floor, unit seven."

"And the price?"

"Two K a week, plus a five-hundred-dollar deposit."

Aster nodded and made her way toward the elevator bank. She'd just hit the call button when she heard the guy address Ryan. "Hey, bro, you need something?"

"I'm wondering what you can you tell me about this piece." Ryan gestured toward the large painting Aster had recognized from her last visit.

"Local artist. Signed at the bottom." The guy shrugged, frowned, and went back to his phone.

"Yeah . . ." Ryan bent to get a closer look at the bottom right corner. "I can't quite make it out." He glanced between the guy and the painting.

The elevator chimed, the doors slid open, and Aster stepped inside. Last thing she heard before the doors squeezed shut was the guy's annoyed voice telling Ryan, "It's by H. D. Harrison." Followed by, "You know there's no loitering, right?"

Aster rode the elevator all the way to the twelfth floor, trying to think of why the artist's name was so familiar. By the time the car arrived, she'd given up and gone in search of unit seven.

She tapped the key fob against the reader and felt a small burst of triumph when the light flashed green, allowing her entry. Despite all the mental prep she'd put herself through, the moment she stepped inside, her heart clenched like a fist and she was forced to grasp frantically at the glass console in an effort to steady herself.

This was it. She was sure of it.

The oversize modern furniture with its leather couches and mirrored surfaces, and the black satin sheets in the bedroom (the sight of which made her skin crawl), all of it was familiar—terribly, hauntingly familiar.

She was glad she'd made Ryan stay behind. He meant well, she knew, but this wasn't the sort of moment she was willing to share. While she had no idea what had transpired here, chances were it wasn't good. Either way, she couldn't afford any distractions when there was so much she needed to process.

After peering inside the closet and drawers and finding them empty, she sighed in frustration. The events of that night remained as elusive as ever.

Was Ryan right? Had someone gone to the trouble to drug her? Ira had poured the champagne, and yet she had a hard time believing he was responsible. Maybe she was being naive, but really, why would Ira go to the trouble to frame her, only to go to even greater trouble to help her disentangle herself from the mess? It just didn't make sense.

She moved through the apartment. There was no telling how many people had occupied the space since she'd left. But who had rented it that night? And had they done so with the sole intent of setting her up? Surely her attorneys could subpoena the records, but that would require her to confide that she'd been here, and that she wouldn't, couldn't do.

There had to be another way.

She took pics of all the rooms, including the one where, according to the DVD, she'd acted out her shameful striptease. First standing in the spot where the person with the camera might've stood, and then from the place where she'd danced. She closed her eyes and tried to rewind to that night, when she heard the muffled sound of something moving beside her.

Her eyes sprang open, her pulse jammed into overdrive, and she whirled all around, trying to determine who had managed to sneak in without her noticing.

She heard the sound again, insistent but hollow. "Ryan?" she called in a shaky voice that betrayed the full extent of her fear. Her body tensed, she crept toward the door, nearly tripping over her bag, which had fallen to the floor.

What the—?

The sound repeated, followed by a soft knock at the door. Slinging her purse onto her shoulder, she crept toward the entry and peered through the peephole, then frowned as she let Ryan in.

"You scared the hell out of me," she whispered as her phone vibrated from inside her purse and she recognized it as the sound that she'd heard.

"I sent you a text."

Without a word she moved back into the living room, as Ryan looked all around. His hands involuntarily clenched into fists, as though ready to lash out at the specter of the person who'd wronged her.

In a way, it was sweet. But Aster refused to be swayed.

"This is where I was standing when that video was made," she said, hating the way her voice shook when she said it.

"So, how far away was the person filming you?"

She looked at him, not quite comprehending.

"I mean, was it a close-up, or a bit farther away?"

Aster swallowed hard, and said, "A bit farther away. Like, you could see most of me . . . or at least to my knees . . . maybe my shins. I can't really remember. But I don't think you could see my feet."

Ryan nodded and squinted at the painting. "So, someone was standing here." He went to stand just in front of it. But before he reached it, something caught Aster's eye.

"Wait—is that . . ."

Ryan turned to see what she was pointing at.

"Do you see that? Right there—toward the middle. Is that a hole?"

They moved closer, and as Ryan brushed his fingers over the canvas, they caught in the small hole that had been punched into the painting.

The artwork was large and vibrant, another H. D. Harrison, according to the signature at the bottom. And though the puncture was small and easily missed, upon closer inspection there was no doubt it'd been purposely placed there. She'd started to lift the painting from the wall when Ryan rushed to help. Then the two of them gaped in dismay at the crudely constructed shallow shelf that could easily hold a portable video surveillance device or even a cell phone set to record.

"Maybe it wasn't as bad as you think?" Ryan had barely finished the thought when Aster whirled on him, ready to let him have it, and he quickly flashed his palms in surrender. "I know. I just heard it, and I'm sorry that it came out all wrong. What I meant was, maybe you were alone. Maybe no one was ever here with you."

She felt the air rush out of her as the real words, the ones he wanted to say, but either couldn't or wouldn't, played in her head. *Maybe your worst fear never happened. Maybe no one raped you. Maybe you can let go of this particular burden you've been dragging around.*

The thought was worth clinging to, but at the moment, it was pure speculation. There was no proof it was true.

All she knew for sure was that someone had gone to great lengths to set her up. The thought of this nameless, faceless enemy intent on taking her down was almost impossible to imagine, and yet Aster no longer had the luxury of living in denial.

After taking a series of pics of the find, Ryan replaced the painting, and they made to leave. Checking her phone on the way out the door, she gasped audibly as she read Ira's text.

"What is it?" Ryan slung a protective arm around her, and for a change, she made no attempt to push him away.

Wanted you to hear it from me first—your trial date just set for Sept 20. Earlier than hoped, but judge won't budge. Not to worry, your defense is on it.

She stood rooted in place, on the verge of hyperventilating. "I can't even believe this!" She gazed imploringly at Ryan. "I'm a little more than a month away from sitting in a courtroom, forced to passively look on as my attorneys try to convince twelve strangers to believe in my innocence, and they probably won't even let me testify on my own behalf. The defense is always so afraid the defendant will get tripped up under cross-examination they rarely allow that. Meanwhile, the jurors all naturally assume that if you really are innocent, then you should get up there and proclaim it. So when you don't, it's like a major strike against you. There's no getting around it—I'm doomed!"

Her knees started to give as she saw the floor rearing up to meet her. And the next thing she knew, Ryan had folded her into his arms and was smoothing a hand over her hair, whispering softly into her ear. "It's all right—you're all right—it will all be okay. . . ."

She wanted to believe him, wanted so badly for it to be true. But a moment later, she broke free of his grasp, steadied herself, and said, "But what if you're wrong?"

His worried gaze met hers, but it was nothing compared to the brand of panic stirring within her.

"Way it stands now, there's just not enough to support my plea of innocent. My only hope for acquittal lies in finding a proper alibi—one that can't be contested. Which means I have to fill in the missing gaps of that night or find Madison. Either way, I need to move fast. Every moment spent is a potential moment lost. The countdown has begun."

She moved toward the elevator bank and impatiently jabbed the call button with one hand, while texting Javen with the other and asking him to meet after school. Then, looking at Ryan, she said, "Wait a few minutes before you make your way down. Then meet me outside by the car."

She rode the car to the lobby and returned the key fob to the concierge.

"And?" The guy gave her a squinty look. Or maybe that was how he always looked.

"I'm definitely interested," Aster told him, her voice a little shaky in a way she hoped he wouldn't notice. "How does this work?"

He slid a card toward her. It was completely blank other than a web address.

"Log on, fill out the form, and make your deposit online."

"That's it?"

He shrugged noncommittally. "You want more?"

For someone playing fast and loose with the rules, he sure was a prick. Still, Aster just shot him another bright grin and made for the door. She'd just passed the painting hanging in the entry when the thought hit her.

H. D. Harrison was Layla Harrison's dad.

# EIGHTEEN

# PAINT IT BLACK

"Where you headed?"

Tommy froze in his tracks and stared longingly at the door. He'd been so close—just a handful of steps from freedom—only to get caught checking out early. He waited a beat, sucked in a breath, then turned to face Ira.

"Uh, I've got a meeting, so . . ." He jabbed a thumb toward the door as though Ira hadn't realized that was his intended destination. As though his sole purpose for interrupting him hadn't been to stop him from leaving.

Ira eased around the bar and came to stand before him. Between the expensive designer clothes he wore like armor, and his usual unreadable expression, he was intimidating as hell, and pretty much the last person Tommy wanted to displease. Though he guessed it was too late for that.

"And this meeting of yours—does it happen to be work related?"

*Not really,* Tommy thought. What he said was, "Of course."

Ira looked him over. "VIP room's shaping up nicely," he finally said. "You been up there lately?"

Tommy shook his head. Though Ira's tone seemed friendly enough, it was never a good idea to relax around him. Like any fierce predator, it was impossible to tell when he might strike.

"Don't you think you should take a look? Seeing as it's your job to promote it."

Tommy shrugged, raked a hand through his hair. "Just trying to give the artist some privacy. Besides, pretty sure the room will promote itself once it's ready."

"So what am I paying you for?" Ira's features sharpened.

Tommy stood before him, doing his best not to cringe or display any visible signs of weakness. There was something so primal about dealing with Ira—it was all about survival of the most cunning and fittest, though unfortunately, Tommy had just unwittingly rolled onto his back and displayed his soft white belly.

Still, it was a good question—one that Tommy often wondered himself. While he hadn't exactly hesitated to take the job, the last few days he'd found himself with so little to do while the room was being readied he figured he might as well work on promoting his music career. Though sharing that with Ira was the quickest route to getting canned.

"Not sure how you want me to answer," Tommy said, realizing immediately after that it was the absolute worst thing he could've said. Still, Ira had a way of wearing him down with little to no effort on his part.

"Pretty sure I warned you a long time ago about ever trying to second-guess me, or tell me what you assume I want to hear, because I guarantee you will always be wrong. In the future, when I ask you a question, do yourself a favor and answer honestly, regardless of how you think I'll respond."

Tommy nodded. There, he'd been properly chastised, maybe now Ira would allow him to leave. Unfortunately, Ira's challenging gaze told him a quick escape was out of the question.

"So . . . you're telling me I should ignore the sign on the door and go take a look?"

"How can you possibly promote something you've never seen?" Ira asked, allowing no time for Tommy to respond before he turned on his heel and started walking away. It was a moment before Tommy realized Ira expected him to follow.

After climbing the narrow set of stairs, Ira unceremoniously threw open the door and impatiently motioned Tommy inside, all the while studying him for his reaction.

But the sight had rendered Tommy gobsmacked.

On the surface, the room was a mess of paint-spattered floor coverings and shrouded furniture piled high and shoved against walls, while the speakers blared an old Rolling Stones song Tommy hadn't heard in a while, but that he instantly vowed to add to his playlist. The walls featured a riot of color that was impossible to take in at one glance, and at the center of it all stood Layla's dad. Paintbrush in hand, he seemed totally unaware of their presence as he created a mural that was so vibrant, so full of life, so massively impressive, it was impossible to define.

Tommy let out a low whistle—the sound giving voice to the words he was unable to speak.

"He doesn't come cheap, but he's worth every penny." Ira nodded toward the masterpiece in the making. "Do you know how much money these walls will be worth when it's finished? And it will only increase from there."

Tommy had no idea how much they'd be worth. The whims of the art world completely eluded him. Though he was captivated by the story unfolding—every brushstroke adding yet another layer to the history of rock and roll—the origins of the world—the soul's journey—the almost supernatural ability of music to inspire, heal, and connect seemingly disparate people from all over the world. It was all there, and it was magnificent to behold.

Tommy had always been biased enough to believe music

was the highest art form, but watching Layla's dad illustrate what it was music did best, he had to admit that in the hands of the right artist, an artist who truly loved and understood his subject, maybe no one medium was better than the other. Maybe they were never meant to compete, but rather exist separately but equally.

"H.D.," Ira called, displaying no qualms about disturbing what appeared to be the artist's deeply meditative state. "I want to introduce you to Tommy Phillips."

When H.D. swung around, Tommy once again was struck by the resemblance to Layla. He also saw that H.D. clearly remembered the last time they'd met.

"Good to see you." H.D. offered a paint-crusted hand, and Tommy didn't hesitate to clasp it in his.

"You two know each other?" For whatever reason, Ira looked more interested than Tommy thought the situation warranted. But maybe that was just because Ira was a control freak who prided himself on knowing things long before they had a chance to occur.

Tommy hesitated, unwilling to share the story of how he'd taken Layla home the night she'd overindulged in Ira's top-shelf tequila.

"Tommy stopped by the house once." H.D. cracked a knowing smile that sent a riot of creases around his blue eyes.

Ira's calculating gaze moved between them. "Well, we

don't want to keep you. Just wanted Tommy here to get a sneak peek, since it's his job to make this room profitable once it's ready."

"It's amazing," Tommy said, feeling humbled and in awe and a little guilty for the way he'd recently blown off Layla.

H.D. nodded, wiped his hands on the sides of his jeans, and went back to work, as Ira led Tommy out of the room and back down the stairs.

"Since I'm going to be stuck here for a while," Ira said, "and since I'm clearly not keeping you busy enough, I've got an errand you can run."

Tommy stood in the doorway of Ira's office and tried to look amenable, but he was running seriously late for his meeting with Malina, and she was not the type to keep waiting.

Then again, neither was Ira.

Ira retrieved something from a drawer and was circling around to hand it to Tommy when his hip inadvertently brushed the edge of his desk and sent a handful of papers scattering to the floor.

Tommy watched the papers flutter and land, his gaze catching sight of one in particular with a picture of a cartoon cat bearing what looked to be some serious injuries.

Before he could get a better look, Ira took another step forward and covered the image with his black Gucci loafer.

Had he done it on purpose?

And what was it about the image that seemed oddly familiar?

Tommy searched Ira's face, but his gaze was impassive and gave nothing away. "Drop this by Night for Night on your way out and give it to James. No one else, just James."

Ira handed Tommy a thick envelope that was most likely filled with cash. Having once been on the receiving end of one of Ira's donations, he recognized the signs. Though he couldn't help but wonder what James had done to earn it, or would be doing soon.

Tommy glanced between the envelope and the gleaming gold horse bit on Ira's shoes, still unable to define exactly what was nagging at him.

"You don't want to be late for your meeting," Ira said, by way of dismissal.

Tommy nodded, slipped the envelope under his arm, and headed outside, steeling himself against yet another scorcher of a day. It wasn't until he was climbing into his car that he flashed on Layla's fearful look as she'd told him about the card she'd received along with Madison's diary entry.

*But you haven't even read the card yet! There was a card that came with it—it had a cartoon picture of a seriously messed-up cat, and—*

Only he'd cut her off before she could finish.

Was it the same cat he saw?

And if so, did that mean Ira was involved?

He adjusted his rearview mirror and looked back toward the Vesper, wondering if he should find a way to get inside Ira's office and find that paper so he could bring it to Layla. His guilt over blowing her off was becoming increasingly difficult to ignore. And what about her dad? Was H.D. getting sucked into this mess without even realizing?

Tommy knew Layla's dad was short on cash and desperate for work, which was how Ira found most of his employees. It was certainly how he'd found Layla, and Tommy grudgingly included himself as well. And while it wasn't exactly true for Aster, moments after she accepted Ira's offer to stay on as a Night for Night promoter, she'd been arrested for first-degree murder as Ira . . . Tommy thought hard on the best way to describe it. While he couldn't definitively say Ira had been expecting Larsen to show up at the Vesper with an arrest warrant, at the time, Ira had handled the detective's sudden appearance with such calm calculation it bordered on eerie. And now, from what Tommy had heard, Ira had taken on the role of Aster's only hope for salvation.

While it was no secret that Ira was a control freak who liked to surround himself with people who were wholly dependent on him, the question was why?

Was it so he could keep a team of loyal minions on call?

Or did it go much deeper and darker than that?

And now that Ira had succeeded at snaring them all in

his web, would they ever be able to find their way out again?

He sank deeper into his seat, thinking he should call Layla and relay his suspicions. But a moment later, Malina texted, demanding to know where he was. And just like that, Tommy was reminded of his earlier vow to get serious about his future and stay away from problems that weren't his to solve.

If Tommy was ever going to fulfill his dream of not only leaving Ira's employ, but confronting him with the truth of their connection once and for all, then he needed to do whatever it took to launch a successful music career.

Besides, they were all adults, and they'd made their own choices. And as Layla liked to remind him, LA was an ambitious place where friends were in short supply.

Without another thought, he jerked the mirror back into place, pulled away from the curb, and headed for the recording studio.

# NINETEEN

# BUILDING A MYSTERY

Trena Moretti sipped her red wine and reviewed the video of her interview with Aster for what she guessed to be the seventh time, or possibly even the tenth—she'd lost count after five. The first two viewings had been mostly celebratory in nature, with Trena grinning the entire time, reveling in the fact that she was headed for prime-time TV. Each subsequent viewing was watched with an eye toward critiquing her performance—the areas where she could stand to improve, openings she might have missed due to her nervousness.

When it came to her performance, Trena was merciless, tougher than most critics would ever venture to be, though her brutality served a purpose. Once she cataloged her mistakes and committed them to memory, she rarely, if ever, repeated them.

For the most part, she had to admit that the interview had gone well. Aster proved to be a much more challenging subject than Trena had expected, which would only help to increase the ratings. Trena saw herself as a storyteller, a narrator, and like any good story, the protagonist was only as good as the antagonist pitted against her. Aster's feistiness and refusal to fold ensured that Trena stayed sharp, focused, and on top of her game. It was just a matter of time before the interview went viral and earned itself the hashtag of #mustsee status.

Early word from the network chiefs proved they were pleased, which Trena hoped would lead to more TV opportunities. Now that she'd gotten a taste of life before the camera, the idea of returning solely to print journalism seemed inconceivable.

It was time she set her sights higher, forged a plan to move up in the world. And there was no doubt in her mind that the Madison disappearance was her first-class ticket to permanent prime-time.

Thanks to her good luck in meeting Layla early on, Trena had been uniquely positioned to break the story in a way all the other competing journalists lacked. It didn't hurt that Layla had looked up to her and viewed Trena as a mentor. Hell, there was no denying the girl had been totally starstruck, and Trena had willingly embraced her new role as a sort of journalism guru.

But lately, Layla had been acting slippery and elusive,

making it nearly impossible to pin the girl down. And with the trial date set, Trena's source at the LAPD claiming there was nothing new to relay, and Priya, her new assistant, so far unable to uncover anything meaty enough to be of any use, Trena found herself in the unenviable position of having to chase after Layla in the way Layla had once chased after her.

While the Madison scandal wouldn't be fading from public consciousness anytime soon, Trena was far too competitive, and way too ambitious, to lose the momentum she'd worked so hard to gain. Meeting Layla at the quietly elegant Palmers, with its faux suede booths and large sepia-toned photos of wild mustangs lining the walls, was her first major step toward remedying that.

She checked her watch and frowned. Layla was eighteen minutes late, which was something the once eager-to-please girl never would've chanced before. Clearly she was aware of the shift in power, and she was playing the moment for all it was worth.

"She's here."

Trena removed her earpiece and squinted in the direction Priya was looking. "I don't see her."

"She's talking to the hostess." Priya nodded in that direction.

"How'd you recognize her—have you met?"

"I do my research." Priya started to gather her things. "They're heading over now."

For a moment, Trena considered letting her stay, then quickly decided against it. Layla was more prone to talk if it was just the two of them.

Priya had just slid away from the table when Layla arrived. The two paused, stared briefly at each other, before Priya moved on and Layla claimed her side of the booth.

Trena studied her carefully. Layla seemed upset, more tightly wound than usual. The way she ran a hand through her hair and looked all around as though she was rethinking her decision to meet left Trena uneasy.

"It's been a while," Layla said, visibly calming as her gaze finally met Trena's.

"I assumed you've been busy." Trena took a small sip of her wine and settled her fingers at the base of the stem. It was better to proceed slowly and let Layla lead.

"Everyone's busy in LA." Layla rolled her eyes. "Our social status is entirely dependent on our ability to keep the appearance of a jam-packed schedule."

Trena grinned. Slowly, the ice was starting to crack.

"Aster says the interview went well."

Trena lifted her shoulders and, in a display of false modesty, said, "It airs tonight, so we'll see."

"You haven't watched it?"

"Haven't had time." Trena tapped her fingers on the base of her glass. No point in alerting Layla to just how much she had riding on this and whatever information she might or might not choose to divulge. "Have you seen a lot of Aster?"

"She just got out." Layla's gaze drifted toward the door, which was not a good sign.

"I meant that in relative terms."

"Compared to her family, yeah, I guess I've seen her a lot." She fidgeted in her seat, picked at the edge of her woven place mat.

"She still hasn't met with her family?"

Layla's features sharpened. "That's a complicated situation, though it's not really my place to discuss it."

Damn. Trena had played that poorly by sounding too eager, and now she was forced to pull back and switch gears if she had any hope of moving forward again. "Should we order?" She motioned toward the menus placed on top of the square glass chargers. "They're known for their perfectly aged grass-fed steaks, but trust me, the kale salad is not to be missed."

Layla shook her head. Acting like she hadn't even heard Trena, she said, "Who's that girl?"

Trena met Layla's questioning look with one of her own.

"The one you were sitting with."

"You mean my assistant?"

"Assistant or bodyguard?"

Trena followed Layla's gaze all the way to where Priya was seated at the bar with a clear view of their table.

"She didn't want to disturb us," Trena said, though in truth Trena was just as surprised to find Priya watching as

Layla was. She'd thought for sure she'd moved on.

"I know her." Layla's brows pinched together as though she was trying to place her.

"Priya?" Trena glanced over her shoulder again, watching as Priya spoke furtively into her phone. It wasn't all that unusual that she and Layla might know each other. After all, they were both young, both interested in journalism.

"I never knew her name, but I could swear she interviewed for the Unrivaled contest."

Trena watched as Priya, still on her phone, slung her bag over her shoulder and left. It wasn't until the door swung closed behind her that Trena turned back toward Layla. "Are you sure?" Trena's mind reeled in reverse. She was positive Priya had never mentioned that, and it seemed like the kind of thing that would be strange to leave out. Especially in light of the Madison story Priya was helping her research.

"Well, I can't be one hundred percent positive, no." Layla shrugged. "There were a ton of people there, and we mostly kept to ourselves."

"So she wasn't chosen to be one of the contestants?"

Layla shook her head.

"Well, I guess that's not all that surprising. She doesn't seem like the nightclub-promoting type," Trena said, less because she believed it to be true, and more to salvage her faith in her own instincts.

"And I do?" Layla laughed, took a quick glance at the menu, then pushed it away. "Who knows what Ira was thinking when he said no to her and yes to me?" She shrugged. "Anyway, I can't stay. I just wanted to stop in and say hey."

Trena fought to keep herself from groaning. Great. A hit-and-run. Not what she'd envisioned when she'd set up the meeting. Also, the brief mention of food made her realize she really was hungry.

"You seem upset." She leaned across the table and peered at Layla with a look she hoped passed for concerned. "Is everything okay?"

Layla squared her shoulders as though summoning a strength she was beginning to doubt. "My friend's on trial for a murder she didn't commit, and now . . ."

*And now WHAT?* Trena wanted to shout, but instead she forced herself to sip her wine slowly and pretend as though it didn't matter in the least whether or not Layla continued.

Layla shook her head in dismissal, and Trena was sure she'd just lost her, when she suddenly blurted, "What do you know about libel?" She pressed her lips into a thin, grim line as her cheeks flushed ever so slightly. "As a journalist, I mean. Under what circumstances can someone go after you and sue you for being libelous?"

"Is this about Madison?" Trena sensed it was, but she

needed Layla to confirm it.

Layla hesitated, but ultimately conceded a nod.

"Well, Madison's a public figure, so . . ."

"Yeah, yeah, I get that." Layla waved her hand impatiently. "What I meant was, what if someone posted something like a piece of writing or something they attributed to Madison? But then later, it turned out they'd been tricked and that it wasn't from Madison at all. Could that be considered libel?"

So this was why she was acting so jumpy when she first arrived—she was haunted, afraid someone was setting her up. After what had happened to Aster, Layla had good reason to be paranoid. Whoever was behind all this had considerable reach.

Trena leaned back in her seat and pretended to put serious thought to the dilemma. "If I knew about your situation, then I might be of more help."

Layla clamped her lips shut, as though forcing herself to keep from saying something she feared she'd only live to regret. Though the way she pulled her purse onto her lap and toyed with the strap hinted at a deeper desire to reveal whatever she was hiding in there.

Trena sat across from her, silently willing her to hand over the goods, when the next thing she knew, Layla clutched the bag to her chest and shot up from the table.

"I gotta go," she said, voice edged with panic.

Trena forced herself to remain calm. "Sure you can't stay?"

Layla shook her head and shifted her weight from foot to foot as though she couldn't get out of there quickly enough.

"Okay. Well, call me if you need anything." Trena kept her tone cool and her expression cooler. "You know I'm here for you."

Layla nodded distractedly, looked all around, and bolted past the hostess stand and out the front door.

A moment later, Trena tossed a handful of bills onto the table and slipped out behind her.

Careful to keep a few car lengths between them, she followed Layla all the way to Aster's building, where she parked outside and debated what to do.

Layla knew something, something that maybe Trena could use. But at the moment, the girl was too paranoid to confide anything, leaving Trena no choice but to follow Layla and keep her under surveillance until Trena found a way to regain Layla's trust.

She adjusted her seat and prepared to settle in. There was no telling how long it might take. Lowering her window in search of fresh air, she was instantly slammed by a blast of heat so intense it was like sitting in a dry sauna. She was tempted to put it back up and rely on the air conditioner instead, but with less than a quarter tank of gas to spare, she had no choice but to make peace with the sweat.

*But it's a dry heat!* the locals liked to say. All Trena knew was that the thought of sitting in a car for an interminable amount of time on a triple-digit day was a miserable fate either way.

Her belly grumbled, and Trena cursed herself for not grabbing a bite at the restaurant while she'd had the chance. Who knew how long she'd be forced to sit in her car, waiting for Layla to emerge?

She popped open the glove box in search of an energy bar, a bag of M&M's, something to tide her over so she wouldn't faint from starvation. Spying an almond biscotti she'd picked up at Starbucks a week earlier, she tore open the wrapper and popped a small broken piece into her mouth. It was stale, and she couldn't help cringing a little as her teeth crushed against it. She was seriously considering spitting it out when she noticed what looked to be an unmarked police car parked on the opposite side of the street.

Forcing down the biscotti with a sip from the bottle of water she always kept on hand, Trena leaned out the window, lifted her shades, and squinted into the sun. Her gaze widened in surprise when she saw it was Detective Larsen slumped behind the wheel of the unmarked car, his gaze fixed on Aster's building.

# TWENTY

# I KNOW WHAT YOU DID LAST SUMMER

"It's official, I have a stalker." Layla dropped dramatically onto the couch and glanced between Aster, Ryan, and Aster's little brother, Javen, who was hunched over a computer, typing furiously while Aster and Ryan anxiously looked on from their place on the couch. "Someone left a note on my car threatening my well-being if I don't post Madison's diary entries on my blog."

"So why don't you?" Ryan asked.

Layla shrugged. "Because they're only interesting if they really are written by Madison. And even then, they're only interesting because they reveal a side of her no one has seen."

"Sounds like reason enough to me," Aster said, never once taking her eyes off her brother.

Layla pushed away from the couch and headed for the

window, wondering why she hadn't shared her suspicions that Emerson might somehow be involved. "I guess I just feel like I need more proof," she said, musing on how the statement applied equally to both her suspicions about her coworker and the diary entries. She needed more proof. They all did. They had plenty of bits and pieces, but nothing concrete, nothing real to go on. "If I just randomly publish them without revealing who wrote them, no one will care. If I claim they're from Madison's diary and it turns out they're not, then I can be sued for libel, which I really don't need."

"Maybe you should consult Trena?" Ryan ventured. "You know, get some feedback on the best way to handle it."

Layla made a considering face, but it was mostly for their benefit. "Journalists can get kind of competitive, and I'm not sure I trust her," she said, deciding not to tell them about their meeting, and how she wasn't questioning just Trena, but also the company she kept. It was probably just a coincidence that Trena's assistant reminded her of someone she'd seen at the Unrivaled interviews, except Layla didn't believe in coincidence, and as a journalist, she'd learned to rely on her instincts.

"I'm not sure you should trust anyone." Aster shot Layla a look she couldn't quite read. Though if she had to guess, she'd say there was something deeply suspicious lurking behind it.

"What exactly are you getting at?" Layla asked, figuring

she might as well put it out there. She had enough games in her life. She didn't have the patience to take on another.

Aster and Ryan exchanged a meaningful glance before Aster stretched her long bare legs before her, flexed her ankles, and said, "I guess I'm just wondering why your dad's artwork is all over the building I woke up in that morning."

"You found the building?" Layla looked from Aster to Ryan, wondering why they hadn't bothered to mention it until now. This was big news—really big, in fact.

"Don't change the subject," Aster snapped.

"But . . . that *is* the subject." Layla frowned, not getting what Aster was suddenly so worked up about.

"Just answer the question!" Aster was agitated, and when Ryan tried to calm her by placing his hand over hers, she promptly snatched hers away and focused on where her brother was working in the corner.

"Listen, I don't know what this is about." Layla spoke carefully, afraid of setting her off and inciting a meltdown. "Actually, let me rephrase that. I do know what you're getting at. And before we both say things we cannot take back, let me assure you that my dad is a well-known artist. Which means his artwork hangs in many spaces, both private and public, throughout the city and beyond. So, if you saw his work somewhere, that doesn't mean—"

"Two pieces. I saw *two pieces* in the same building!"

Aster narrowed her eyes on Layla's. "That seems a little excessive, don't you think?"

"Not really, no." Layla struggled to not take offense, which was virtually impossible with Aster seeming to imply that Layla somehow had something to do with setting Aster up. Or was she implying her dad was at fault? Either way, it was crazy, mind-boggling proof that Aster was seriously starting to lose it.

"And there was a hole in one of the paintings."

Layla wondered if she looked as incredulous on the outside as she felt on the inside. "Well, I can assure you that I'd *never* do that. It's like book burning—it's unholy, sacrilegious."

Ryan shook his head at Aster before turning to Layla with an apologetic look. "Listen, I think we're all a little on edge here. So . . ." He frowned as Aster sprang from the couch and went to check on her brother.

"Did you find anything?" Aster's tone was impatient, her body jumpy and restless.

"Maybe." Javen stopped typing and swiveled around to face her, and once again Layla was struck by how much he resembled his sister. He might even be the slightest bit prettier, as impossible as that seemed.

"Don't mess with me, Javen." Aster thrust a hand on her hip. "This is important. My life is at stake."

"But *why* is it important?" His dark, long-lashed eyes

flashed on hers. "Why should this place possibly matter? How exactly does it fit in?"

Aster looked away. Her expression completely shut down in a way Layla found frustrating. If she didn't want to tell her little brother, so be it. But why wouldn't she at least confide in her lawyers? Why did she continue acting so stubborn, insisting on doing things her way, which as far as Layla was concerned, was veering more and more toward the wrong way?

Well, if Aster wouldn't tell anyone, then maybe Layla would. With the way she'd acted so nice and ingratiating, as opposed to her usual, hurried, superior self, Trena was clearly desperate for info. Layla fingered her phone, tempted by the idea of setting up another meeting just as soon as she left.

"Is this where you spent the night when you came home that morning wearing some guy's clothes?" Javen looked as though he already knew the answer; he was just willing his sister to show a little faith and confirm it.

Aster glared. "Are we really doing this? Are you really going to play me when I'm this desperate? What do you want this time—the keys to my car? Because you can't have it—it's been impounded."

"I don't want anything." Javen spoke quietly, though he didn't seem particularly stunned by the comment. Layla could only imagine what it must've been like to grow up in

Aster's shadow. "I'm just wondering why I'm seeing footage of you entering that apartment."

"Wait—*what*?" In a flash, Aster was practically on top of him and grasping at the computer, but Javen was quicker and slammed the lid shut.

"I have answers," he said. "But first I have questions." He guarded the laptop in his arms as Aster stood shaking and furious before him. "As a reminder, hacking is illegal. Just because the feed was particularly easy to hack into doesn't mean I can't get in serious trouble for the things you're asking me to do."

Layla watched as Aster visibly softened, but only a little.

"Fine," she finally relented. "I was there. Obviously, I was there. Question is, who was there with me?"

Javen studied her for a long moment. "I only saw them from behind."

Aster stood before him, holding her breath.

"But from the long hair and clothes, it looks like a girl. And just so you know, the apartment was secured in your name."

Aster wobbled precariously, looking as though she might faint. In an instant, Ryan shot away from the couch and appeared right beside her, though Aster was quick to recover and push him away.

"I'm all right," she snapped. And then to Javen, she said, "I need to see that. I need to see everything."

Without a word, Javen propped open the lid and walked them through the hallway's surveillance video, which showed Aster weaving down the hall, hanging on to someone shorter, with long brown hair. When they reached the room, the girl sank a hand into Aster's purse, procured the key fob, and let them both in.

"I don't get it," she said. "There are witnesses who swear they saw me get into a car with some unidentified guy. No one ever mentioned a girl. And why was the key fob in my purse? Until that moment, I'd never been there before."

"Maybe she was waiting inside the car and no one saw her, or maybe she met up with you at the building. As for the key fob, she probably slipped it in there on purpose, knowing the surveillance video would make it look like you rented the place. Not to mention, did you ever actually finish watching the video?" Layla asked, causing Aster to whirl on her in anger, as a knowing look crossed Javen's face.

"No," Aster finally admitted.

"Well, maybe you should." Layla refused to be deterred. "Maybe it's not at all what you think."

"So, you're saying I ditched Ryan at the club so I could go back to my secret luxury love nest—a place so secret I didn't even know about it—so I could hook up with some chick with long brown hair wearing Rag & Bone skinny jeans?"

"You can tell the designer from that?" Layla pointed at the screen. She knew it was unimportant, but in a strange way, it was undoubtedly impressive. Aster was like a fashion detective.

Aster stood before them, her fingers nervously working the gold-and-diamond hamsa pendant that hung from her neck.

"Keep watching." Javen fast-forwarded for a bit, before hitting the play button again. A moment later, they watched the girl leave, her head dipped in a way that made it impossible to make out her face. According to the time stamp, about fourteen minutes had passed.

"So, it was a quickie then." Aster sank to the floor and dropped her head in her hands.

"Is anyone thinking what I'm thinking?" Layla glanced at each of them. "That maybe the girl was Madison?"

Aster groaned, Ryan looked intrigued, and Javen just shrugged.

"I know it sounds like a stretch, but Ryan, you said yourself that Madison talked about hiding out for a while. You also mentioned that she went a little overboard with your staged public breakup. So what if she planned this whole thing? What if she's hiding out somewhere on some white-sand tropical beach, laughing at all of us? What if she's just trying to punish Aster for a bit, before she resurfaces and reclaims her spot as the world's most loved celebrity, thereby getting Aster off the hook for her murder?"

"That's insane," Aster said, though her face seemed to question the possibility. "I mean, it *is* insane, right? Because as much as I want to believe it, wouldn't that make Madison a total sociopath?"

Layla shrugged. "Vindictive, yes. But a psychopath? Not necessarily."

"But what about the blood?" Aster asked.

"And the dress," Ryan said.

"I can continue watching the footage, and I'll let you know if I see anyone else coming or going," Javen said. "But there's no telling how long that might take. I do have school, you know. Not to mention, Mom and Dad and Nanny Mitra are breathing down my neck, sure that I'm sneaking out to come here, despite their strictest orders to steer clear. As if." He rolled his eyes, prompting Aster to laugh, but only for a second before her face fell serious again.

"Okay," Ryan said. "So far we know that someone rented the apartment in Aster's name, someone drugged Aster, and someone led Aster to the apartment, where they spent fourteen minutes and change—"

"Which is long enough for them to have convinced you to do a striptease, put you to bed, and messed up the room to make it look like a wild party occurred," Layla finished.

"So what do we do now?" Aster's shoulders sank in exhaustion. "Or, more accurately, how do we find Madison?

How do we convince people that she really is alive?"

"Listen," Layla said. "This all makes perfect sense and I know I'm the one who brought it up, but what about the diary entries? Why would Madison send us those and threaten me to post them? They make her look kind of awful and expose all her lies."

"Who said Madison's behind that?" Ryan said. "Maybe it's just a Madison hater being opportunistic."

"Like they're sick of her being hailed as a saint, and they want the public to know who this chick really was." Javen nodded assuredly, as though he'd just solved the case.

"So they're parallel crimes, but not necessarily connected?" Aster took a moment to consider it.

"Well, I know what I'm going to do," Layla said, taking a moment to review the plan in her head before she divulged it. "I'm going to issue a challenge on my blog and see where it leads. It's the only way I can think of to communicate, since my stalker always seems to know exactly where to find me, but I have no idea where to begin looking for them. Mind if I borrow that computer?"

Javen passed the laptop to Layla, who quickly logged in and posted a brief message on her blog.

## BEAUTIFUL IDOLS
### The ~~Tail~~ Tale of the Not-So-Curious Cat

If you want the cat to play

Then give her something juicy to say

You'll need to go the extra mile
And send her something worthwhile
Otherwise, don't waste her time
With your pitiful list of petty crimes.

"What's with the rhyme?" Aster peered over her shoulder.

"It's our thing." Layla cringed as she reread it. "And don't judge. I'm a journalist, not a poet. This is the best I can do on short notice."

"You sure you want to post that?" Ryan's voice was skeptical.

"It's already done." Layla returned the computer to Javen. "Now we wait and see if they bite. And Aster, it's time you watch that DVD. I'll watch it with you, if you want. For all we know there could be a clue on there. But either way, we need to get a better idea of exactly what happened to you, once and for all."

# TWENTY-ONE

# GUILTY FILTHY SOUL

Aster Amirpour pulled the brim of her hat so low it nearly covered her face as she pumped the gas pedal impatiently with her foot, inching the car forward bit by bit as she waited for her parents to open the gate.

With the crowd of paparazzi gathered outside her car, banging on the windows and shouting her name, the intervening seconds seemed to drag on for an eternity. Finally the gate slowly eased open and Aster shot forward, leaving the swarm in her wake as she sped down the drive and came to a skidding halt in front of the garage.

She paused in her seat and gripped the wheel hard, her breath coming hectic, too fast, as she willed herself to relax and get a grip on herself.

She could do this.

She *had* to do this.

Inside, her parents were waiting, and she'd put them through enough hell already. Last thing she needed was to bail on their agreement to meet.

Sliding out of the car, she hurried across the stone drive and made her way to the door, wondering who she'd find waiting on its other side—the maid or Nanny Mitra. She was hoping for Javen, thinking a friendly face might set her at ease, when the door swung open, she took one look at her father, and instinctively barreled into his arms.

He nudged the door closed with his foot and returned the embrace. But it wasn't his usual hug. His demeanor was perfunctory, stiff, and not nearly as warm and welcoming as Aster once remembered him being.

A moment later, she pulled away, swiped a hand over her face, and said, "Hi, Dad."

He returned her greeting with the saddest gaze she'd ever seen.

She looked past his shoulder to find her mother standing just behind him, though Aster settled for nodding, knowing better than to try to hug her. Nanny Mitra stood by the grand staircase, but Aster, still feeling the sting of her betrayal, chose to focus on her brother instead.

Remembering their agreement to pretend they hadn't seen each other until now, she hugged him fiercely and ruffled his hair, until he finally whispered, "Jeez, Aster, don't overdo it." And she quickly released him and stood awkwardly before them, unsure what came next.

She'd gone over the moment so many times in her head, but now that it was happening in real time, she could no longer remember the speech she'd prepared. While an apology seemed an appropriate place to start, there was a part of her that doubted it would do any good. It seemed they'd moved way beyond that.

"We'll talk in the living room." Her mother's voice was stern and commanding, bordering on harsh. To Javen, she said, "Now that you've seen your sister, it's time for you to go back to your room."

"But Mom—" he started to protest, but Aster shook her head in warning. Last thing she needed was for him to agitate her mother any more than she already was.

She watched as Javen pounded up the stairs with Nanny Mitra close on his heels; then she followed her mother's rigid, Chanel-clad back to the sofa, where she was ordered to sit.

Aster sank onto the French silk cushions, which weren't nearly as welcoming as they appeared. But then with the abundance of stiff-backed chairs and priceless antiques Aster had been forbidden to touch as a kid, the house had been designed more with an eye to impress than to comfort.

Not surprisingly, her mother was the first to break the silence. "I'm sure you can imagine how distressing it was for us to learn that you were out on bail and you'd failed to contact us."

Aster stared down at her hands. She'd expected this, and yet she still hadn't come up with a satisfying answer that would explain her actions without hurting their feelings. "I needed some space," she finally said. "And I guess I figured you did as well."

Her mother tilted her chin in a way that made her appear even more poised and regal than usual. And with her dad standing behind her, his hand resting on the back of her chair, they looked so imperious, so impenetrable, Aster wondered why she'd ever thought it a good idea to visit them.

She gripped the edge of the cushion and started to rise. This was a mistake. She needed to leave before it could get any worse.

"We saw the interview."

Aster was crouched in a half-standing, half-sitting position when her father's voice jerked her away from her thoughts.

"You held your own with that reporter. I was proud of the way you handled her." Aster slowly lowered herself back onto the cushion and prepared to settle in, if only for a little longer.

Her father was proud of her.

She'd made her father proud.

She was close to weeping from the sheer joy of hearing his words, but forced herself to merely nod in reply.

"We know you didn't do it, Aster."

The last statement came from her mother, and Aster wondered for a moment if maybe she'd somehow imagined it. It was the very last thing she'd ever expected to hear. She'd been sure her mom had assumed she was guilty of every imaginable atrocity from the moment she'd caught Aster sneaking into the house dressed in boys' clothes.

"Though that doesn't excuse the actions you took that landed you in your current predicament. Nor does it excuse the hell you've put this family through."

*And . . . she's back!* Aster slumped low on the sofa. She'd expected exactly this and much worse. Hell, she deserved it. She'd hurt them in every conceivable way, and there was no making up for it. All she could do now was try to shield them from the freak show her life had become. Unfortunately, with the upcoming trial, the public scrutiny was about to amp up in ways they could never foresee.

She ran her fingers over the custom upholstery, aware that every touch, every look, was the last until she could put the whole mess behind her. And if things didn't go her way, then it was entirely possible she'd never return.

Her father patted her mother's shoulder in a vain attempt to calm her, but Aster's mother, as usual, refused to be silenced.

"Your brother's studies are slipping, we're plagued by paparazzi who continuously manage to sneak inside our community, not to mention our company stocks are plummeting."

"They're not *plummeting*," Aster's father corrected, but her mother shook her head and held firm.

"Our business interests are being adversely affected."

Aster swallowed hard, unsure exactly what was expected of her. There was no use defending herself when they'd already confirmed they believed she was innocent. As for all their other grievances, there was no denying she was 100 percent guilty of causing them.

All except for Javen's poor grades, which probably had a lot more to do with his new boyfriend than her. Though it wasn't like she'd ever reveal that. It was his secret to share.

Aster threw up her hands. "I'm not really sure what you want me to do here."

"Move home," her father said. "So we can look after you."

The pleading look on his face nearly saw her agreeing. But a moment later, Aster shook her head. "You think it's bad now with the paparazzi? It'll be ten times worse if I move back. And while I can never make up for all the trouble and heartache I've caused, I can do my best to protect you from at least some of the circus that surrounds me. And the only way to do that is to distance myself entirely."

"But I've hired a team of lawyers!" her father cut in. Edging around her mother's chair, he came to stand before her. "They want to talk to you about discussing a plea bargain."

Aster nearly shot out of her chair as her gaze darted wildly between her parents. "A plea bargain? Why would I even consider that when I'm innocent?"

"This has nothing to do with whether or not you're innocent," her mother said as Aster stared incredulously, hardly able to believe what she was hearing. "Aster, you have to realize there's an overwhelming amount of evidence stacked against you. The prosecution is already threatening the death penalty."

Aster gaped in astonishment. They couldn't possibly believe this was the best path to follow. She was willing to do whatever it took to protect them, shield them, and most of all stop hurting them. But not at her expense. Not like this.

"We can get you a reduced sentence with the possibility of parole for good behavior," her father said. "You'll be out in a matter of years."

"So they'll let me out when I'm eighty years old and my life is nearly over?" Aster shook her head, refused to even consider it. The week she'd spent in jail had been an absolute nightmare, and that was like a country club compared to the harsh reality of a state prison.

"No." Aster stood before them, her legs as shaky as her voice. "I'm sorry, but I can't do that. I *won't* do that. I'm going to trial, and I'm going to fight. I refuse to plead guilty for a crime I didn't commit."

"Aster, please—don't be so naive . . . ," her mother started, but Aster had already turned away, was already crossing the precious hand-woven Persian rug that had been passed down through multiple generations of Amirpours, and heading for the door. Her eyes swimming with tears, she blindly felt her way out of there.

"At least speak to our lawyers." Her father chased behind her.

Aster paused with her hand on the knob. She knew they meant well—that they were panicked and fearful and desperate for a way to end the nightmare. But people driven by fear were known to make notoriously bad choices. What they were asking her to do was inconceivable at best. She had a little more than a month to further her investigation and prove them all wrong, and she intended to take full advantage of every second of freedom she currently had. Rushing to make an agreement with the prosecution would only succeed in her being locked away for a very long while.

"I have lawyers," she said. "Good lawyers. Ira hired them."

"And how are you going to repay him?" her mother asked, her face clouded with the worst sort of suspicion.

Aster cringed under her glare. She'd asked herself the same thing many times, and still had no ready answer. "I know it's a lot to ask," she said. "But I need you to trust that I just might know what I'm doing, despite all immediate evidence to the contrary."

Her parents stood silent and united before her, and knowing that was the best she could hope for, Aster leaned in to hug them both briefly, then made her way back to her car.

To think the day had started on such a positive note, with Aster filling in some of the missing pieces she'd been unable to recall. With Layla's support, she'd finally summoned the courage to watch the DVD in its entirety, which amounted to just under six minutes of a completely mortifying striptease, before she grew increasingly wobbly on her feet and the footage abruptly cut off. As embarrassing as it was to watch that with Layla, at least they were able to confirm there was no sign of assault. Though it wasn't until Javen also confirmed that no one else had entered the apartment between the time the mystery girl left and Aster rushed out the next morning that she could truly experience the relief of that particular burden being lifted. And yet, despite the bright start, the visit with her parents had sunk her right back into the familiar depths of despair.

And now she had to go meet with Ira to discuss her appearance at his upcoming tequila launch scheduled for next weekend. The event would mark her first public debut since her interview with Trena had aired on TV the night before, and Ira, as usual, would leave nothing to chance.

Aster started her car and drove toward the gate. With her trial looming near, she resented both the intrusion on her time, and Ira expecting her to appear at his party like some kind of scandalous show pony. Though for the moment, she was in no position to argue. Accepting his help kept the burden off her family, which meant she was indebted to him, for better or worse.

# TWENTY-TWO

# EX'S & OH'S

"Don't be so nervous—it's gonna be fun!"

*Easy for her to say.* Mateo crawled out of Heather's car and gazed up at the towering manse, feeling woefully out of his league, which was how he often felt these days. Between the numerous photo shoots required to build a portfolio, the meetings with agents, editors, and advertisers, not to mention the crash course in media training taught by Heather, who insisted he'd thank her later, his days were long and full and ran at a much quicker pace than he was used to. The sort of full-throttle lifestyle most Angelenos claimed to thrive on was something Mateo had always worked to avoid. And now, only a week in, he felt like a passenger in a runaway car with no brakes. There'd been no time for surfing, and ironically, he'd barely seen much of his family. The simple pleasures he'd once taken for granted suddenly seemed like a luxury.

He ran a thumb over the woven friendship bracelet he wore on his left wrist—a gift from Valentina, who'd made it for his birthday a couple of years before, and he hadn't taken it off since. In the life he now found himself living, it was one of the few remaining tokens that anchored him to his former self, and he cherished it more than ever.

"Try not to look so impressed," Heather hissed, grabbing him by the elbow and maneuvering him toward the security tent set up just outside the gate. "Or, more accurately, try not to look so horrified." She laughed and squeezed his arm, as they waited for the bouncer to check them off the guest list and usher them inside.

"People actually live like this?" Mateo gaped at the ultramodern, multistory, over-the-top residence. It was like something out of a movie. A glass-and-steel fortress rumored to have over fifty bathrooms and thirty bedrooms, not that he planned on counting them. He'd also heard something about an on-site bowling alley, a subterranean twenty-car garage, and a working diner and hair salon. The whole thing reeked of the worst sort of excess.

"No one actually lives in this place," Heather said. "It's more of a party house."

Mateo frowned. Here he was, worried about paying his little sister's medical bills, while others were building multimillion-dollar homes so they'd have a place to host elaborate parties. Before the rush of bitterness could completely take over, he looked at Heather and said, "Sounds like you've been here before."

Heather shrugged nonchalantly, refusing to commit either way. Then, pushing through the crowded entry, she grabbed two shots of Unrivaled tequila from a passing waiter who was too overwhelmed to actually card anyone and handed one to Mateo. "We don't have to stay long, but it's good PR to appear at these things. As long as you don't get carried away and drink too many of these, that is." She hoisted her glass, tossed an arm around Mateo's neck, and grinned for a nearby photographer. The whole scene was over and done with before Mateo could even process what'd happened.

Heather had a knack for spotting photogs and making every moment seem as though it were tailor made for Instagram. She clinked her glass against his and drained it with a toss of her head. Her eyes gleaming, cheeks flushed a light pink, she encouraged him to follow her lead. "Drink up so you can tell Ira how much you like it, even if you don't."

Mateo drained his shot, surprised by how smooth the tequila went down. Returning the empties to another passing waiter, Heather grasped Mateo's hand in hers and led him through the house and outside to the backyard, toward the large, rectangular infinity pool that seemed to spill off the face of the earth.

Thanks to Heather's insisting they arrive late, the party

was in full swing. "Not only does it spare you the horror of appearing overeager," she'd claimed, "but more importantly, it gives you the sober advantage. Nothing like showing up fresh and clearheaded while everyone else has spent the entire night drinking. You'd be amazed at what those notoriously private A-listers get up to once they start hittin' the sauce. 'Loose lips sink ships,' as they say. But I say, 'Better to watch their yacht go up in flames than your own.'"

Not only was Heather full of sayings like that, but she also had an entire rundown on the inner workings of the A-, B-, and C-lists (the D-list weren't worth knowing, and so she didn't). Most of the time, her incessant chatter made Mateo's head spin. He could barely keep up with all the names, much less the gossip surrounding them. Even when he'd been with Layla, and he offered to proofread her blogs, he mostly looked for structure and typos; the actual content had never held any interest for him.

While Heather considered herself a solid member of the B-list, she was convinced her new show would propel her straight to the top of TV royalty and was constantly reminding Mateo of how she could help introduce him to all the right people whenever he got tired of modeling, which she insisted he would.

Truth was, Mateo was already tired of modeling, but he was resigned to being in it for as long as it took. The money was good, more than he'd ever seen on a single paycheck with his name on it, so there was no reason to stop, no matter how foolish he felt posing for the camera.

Still, Heather had gone out of her way to help him. And while he had no interest in adding *actor* to his résumé, he was grateful for all that she'd done. She'd even promised to set him up with her financial adviser—an absolute necessity, according to her.

"How good are you with money?"' she'd asked, just after he'd received his first check.

Mateo had shrugged. "I've never had enough to know."

The look Heather had given him was long and considering. "I know the money sounds like a lot at first, but trust me, between agents and taxes, it gets chipped away pretty quickly. Which is why so many once-promising entertainers end up broke and in rehab."

"That won't happen to me," Mateo had said, though the skeptical look on Heather's face left him unsettled.

Actually, Heather left him unsettled. Ever since the photo shoot on the beach, Mateo had been distracted by the thought of kissing her again. Probably because their kiss marked the only moment since Valentina fell ill and he broke up with Layla that he'd been able to lose himself in the moment and forget just how desperate his life had become.

For the first time ever, Mateo understood why people

like his brother Carlos gravitated toward the numbing effect of alcohol, drugs, and other addictions when life got too rough. Carlos never forgave himself for surviving the car accident that claimed their father's life. Even though they ruled out driver error early on, Carlos refused to ever get behind the wheel again and dedicated what little remained of his own life in pursuit of numbing and forgetting, instead of accepting the fact that sometimes life just didn't make sense.

Kissing Heather could easily become an addiction, a way to temporarily mask his painful reality. But he refused to use Heather in that way. And Mateo had never been one for random hookups. He was a solid relationship guy.

"Where have you gone?"

Mateo blinked at Heather's curving pink lips, just inches from his.

"You're a million miles away." She tucked a renegade curl behind her ear and grinned in such a warm, appealing way, he could feel himself relenting on the deal he'd just struck with himself. "The stars are aligned." She motioned toward a surprisingly clear and starry sky, courtesy of the late summer Santa Ana winds that had swept away the usual blanket of smog before mellowing to a much-welcomed breeze. "I don't want to jinx it, but I truly believe we're both on our way to greatness, and what better way to celebrate than in this ridiculously tacky, oversize party pad?"

Greatness translated to multiple zeros in his bank account and the best care for Valentina—a total win. And yet, so much had happened in the span of a week, his feelings were all over the place, though they didn't necessarily veer toward celebratory.

His gaze met Heather's. With her long golden hair cascading over her bare shoulders and her blue eyes flashing on his, there was no denying the attraction pulsing between them, like an invisible string pulling them together.

Next thing he knew Heather was leaning into him, pressing her body flush against his as his arms instinctively circled her waist. In his pocket, he felt his phone vibrate with an incoming text, but with Heather's lips so warm against his, it was easy to ignore, easy to forget they were in a public place. Easy to forget he shouldn't be doing this.

"Uh-oh, blogger alert."

Heather pulled away and straightened her dress, as Mateo followed the length of her gaze all the way across the yard to the place where Layla stood watching.

# TWENTY-THREE

# USED TO LOVE YOU SOBER

Layla had arrived at the party unfashionably early, but that was only because she wasn't there to have fun; she was there to do her job and make sure everything ran smoothly, or at least that was her assignment, according to the speech Emerson had given upon meeting her at the door.

She was only an hour in when she'd decided it was a lot more fun to be a nightclub promoter. Which was really saying something, considering how she'd been as completely unsuited for the job promoting Jewel as she was in her current position as junior marketer, or party fluffer, or whatever the hell Ira was paying her to do.

Still, the crowd was starting to grow, packing the expansive space with so many big-name athletes, actors, musicians, and models that the celebrity blogger inside her couldn't help but feel gleeful at all the possible stories surrounding her. Though she'd been warned, by Emerson no less, that gossip blogging was strictly off-limits, she was encouraged to write about the event, but only in the most complimentary, product-friendly way. And even then, using only the preapproved photos supplied by the hired photographers. In other words—the usual obligatory, snooze-fest puff piece she had no interest in writing.

A quick trip to the gifting suite told her it had come together nicely, and there was no shortage of sexy, barely clad girls serving endless shots of Unrivaled tequila, which seemed to keep the male guests happy and sated. There was a DJ set up in the disco, and thanks to copious amounts of tequila, people were already dancing. There was also a putting green, a bowling alley, a game room stocked with purple felt billiard tables and vintage pinball machines, so many bars she lost count, and a multitude of bedrooms that, by the looks of the crowd, would be put to good use at some point.

There was even a cigar den on offer that was rumored to be well stocked with Cubans. Last she'd looked she'd found herself gaping in horror at the sight of her dad, haloed by foul-smelling smoke clouds while a woman Layla had never seen before perched on his knee. For one thing, her dad didn't smoke. For another, her dad didn't flirt or date or hook up or whatever it was he was doing with the blonde. As if seeing her dad at a party wasn't bad enough, even worse was the nagging worry that it was all due to Ira's influence.

Ever since her dad had started working for Ira, his nights were spent painting the mural and his days spent crashing for a few hours while Layla was at work. Ira had him on such a tight leash, Layla barely saw him. Initially she was worried about his health and well-being—he was really pushing himself. But after seeing him smoking a Cuban and acting so out of character, she wondered if she should be even more concerned.

Then again, maybe he just wanted to cut loose and have a little fun. It was a party, after all. And maybe, just maybe, Layla should stop acting like she was the parent and lighten up a little.

For the moment, she resolved to not only shelve her concerns, but to do whatever it took to avoid going anywhere near that room.

She glanced across the long stretch of lawn, where a stage was set and one of Ira's minions fussed with the mic in preparation for Ira's official greeting, after which Tommy would make his debut.

Only no one knew it was Tommy. Malina had made Layla promise to keep his identity under wraps, and Layla was still struggling with the decision to go along with her request. Malina had reasoned that Tommy was too easily linked to Madison's disappearance—that the connection would only hinder his chances of people taking him seriously. While it made perfect sense on the surface, something about it didn't fully add up. Layla was sure there was more going on than there seemed.

She'd held off on booking Tommy for as long as she could, prompting Malina to leave a string of feverish messages before Layla got around to returning her calls. Though she was tempted to reject him, if for no other reason than to get back at him for acting like such a giant douche, in the end, her sense of ethics won out. Tommy deserved a fair shot at his dream. As for everything else, that was for his conscience to deal with, not hers.

Not to mention that if he nailed the performance, it would reflect well on her. If not, then she'd probably get canned, which might not turn out to be such a bad thing. Either way, someone would win.

She moved through the throng of Hollywood elite, spotting Trena over by the bar deep in conversation with James, while Ira made the rounds, looking slick and sleek and in total control. For a moment, when his steely navy-blue gaze met hers, Layla felt the tug of something familiar— there was someone he reminded her of that she could never quite place. Then, just as quickly, Ira moved on and Layla caught a glimpse of Tommy chatting up a curvy blonde in a minuscule dress she was seriously close to busting out of. Typical. Layla rolled her eyes and looked away.

So far she hadn't seen Aster or Ryan, and while she could hardly blame them for bailing, she doubted Ira would view it so generously. No matter how crowded the party, Layla had no doubt Ira ran it much like his clubs—with his finger on the pulse of everything and everyone.

All around her, people were talking and laughing, and when she heard someone calling her name, she was surprised to find Emerson approaching. His arm was linked with that of a beautiful girl Layla soon recognized as Trena's assistant, Priya.

Emerson was grinning, which was such an odd sight Layla wasn't sure what to make of it. And though Priya grinned too, her eyes remained cold and dark and fixed right on Layla's.

"Priya, this is Layla, the one I was telling you about." Emerson motioned between them as Layla felt herself tense.

Whatever it was Emerson had told her, Layla guessed it wasn't good. Around the office, Emerson made no attempt to hide how much he disliked her. And yet here he was, grinning like they were old friends. Was this for real? Or was this just Emerson's way of putting on a party face?

"What could he have possibly told you?" Layla forced her lips into a bit of a curl. There, now he'd seen her party face too.

Priya gave her a long, considering gaze. Starting at

Layla's ankle-wrap sandals, she worked her way up the snug off-the-shoulder dress before landing on her artfully smudged eyeliner, where she paused and said, "He told me you write a very popular blog. But of course I already knew that. I used to read it religiously. But other than that cryptic message you posted the other day, it seems you've stopped writing. May I ask why?"

The question was innocuous enough, but the delivery was as probing as Priya's gaze, and it left Layla wondering what was really going on. This wasn't just small talk.

"Just . . . taking a break." Layla shrugged, shooting a quick look at Emerson, who seemed a little too interested in her answer as well. Returning her attention to Priya, she said, "So how's it working out with Trena?"

Emerson glanced between them. "You two know each other?"

"Not exactly," Priya said quickly—a little too quickly.

And again with the intense gaze. What was her problem?

"Well, now I'm confused." Emerson laughed. Only it didn't seem real. But then, everything about the conversation leaned more toward surreal.

"We both work for Trena," Priya said.

Layla frowned. Clearly Priya knew that wasn't true, so why would she make a point of saying it? "No," Layla said, doing nothing to mask the edge creeping into her tone. "I don't."

Priya cocked her head to the side and furrowed her brow

as though giving deep consideration to the matter. For Trena's sake, Layla hoped Priya was better at researching than she was acting.

"Sorry, my bad," Priya finally said. "I could've sworn you were one of her sources."

Though Priya's arm was still linked with Emerson's, she kept just enough distance between her body and his that Layla couldn't tell if they were merely friends, or something more. Not that it mattered, and not that it was any of her business. But at the moment, she'd welcome any sort of clue as to what was really going on here. Layla felt fairly confident that Trena would never reveal her sources. Not to anyone. And especially not to a part-time assistant she'd recently hired. Clearly, Priya was fishing, but what was she fishing for? All Layla knew for sure was that the two of them were giving her the creeps, and the sooner she got away from them, the better.

"Listen, I'm gonna . . ." She jabbed a thumb in the opposite direction and took off before they had a chance to respond.

Why were they so interested in her blog? Were they somehow involved with the creepy notes she'd been getting? While she wouldn't put it past them, for the moment she had nothing that connected them to Madison. But after that strange encounter, she wouldn't rule them out either.

She moved through the crowd of partygoers, desperate

to shake off the bad vibe they'd given her. It seemed every-one was either happily paired off, or flirting to a degree that they were soon to be paired off. Hell, even her dad was poised to get lucky—a thought that elicited an image so horrifying Layla shook her head fiercely in a desperate attempt to dismiss it.

Still, all those happy couples left Layla feeling lonely. She missed having a partner, someone to flirt with and get excited about. Once again she found herself wondering if maybe letting Mateo go without a fight was something she'd always regret.

Instinctively, she reached for her phone. She could text him. Just to say hello, nothing more. Maybe she'd even include a pic of her current over-the-top surroundings and add a snarky quip to go with it. Mateo hated this sort of extravagance, and it would be a fun, harmless joke between them. After all, they had a history, and just because they'd decided to take a break didn't mean she'd stopped caring about him.

She took a pic of the pool, filled with oversize white-and-gold swan floaties with bikini-clad models riding their backs and typed:

#SwanGoals

The moment she heard her phone swoosh, informing her that the text had been sent and there was no going back, she swiped a shot of tequila from a passing waiter and drained it in hopes it might help dim some of the panic.

In less than a minute she'd committed two regrettable acts she might never live down. Though while her last experience with tequila hadn't ended so well, Layla was older now. Wiser. Besides, she could pretty much guarantee she wouldn't be kissing Tommy Phillips ever again.

She turned toward the stage, where Ira was preparing to take the mic, and where just off to the side, Mateo—her Mateo—was kissing Heather Rollins.

Wait—*what?*

Layla squinted. Blinked. And yet, the view remained stubbornly the same.

Ira was speaking now, but Layla couldn't make out the words. It was as though everything around her had paused, while Mateo and Heather continued mauling each other in the most gruesome display of PDA she'd ever been forced to witness.

When Heather finally came up for air, Layla couldn't help but notice the small smile that spread across her face as Heather's gaze veered directly to hers.

A moment later, Mateo looked too, but Layla couldn't bear to meet it.

She pressed a palm to her belly, sure she was about to be sick, and glanced around frantically, searching for an exit. But the wall of people made it impossible to escape.

Somewhere behind her, Ira made a joke, and the crowd

surged with the usual obligatory laugh, as Layla fought to squeeze free, desperate to make her way to one of the fifty bathrooms so she could lock herself inside and try to make sense of the horrifying sight she'd witnessed.

She'd just found an opening and was about to make a run for it, when someone grabbed hold of her and Layla turned to find Heather's fingers circling her wrist.

"I have an exclusive for you!" she sang, in her usual giddy, breathless way. "If you're still blogging, that is. I noticed you haven't been writing much lately."

Layla glanced blindly between Heather and Mateo, wondering if she looked as confused, injured, and dazed as she felt. But Heather continued yammering, seemingly oblivious to Layla's fragile emotional state.

"He has an ad debuting tomorrow," she stage-whispered. "But if you write it tonight, you'll still get the jump on everyone else. You'd like that, wouldn't you?"

Somewhere in the distance, Ira was pushing his tequila. She should be there, standing alongside the rest of the Unrivaled marketing team and supporting him from the sidelines. Wasn't it her job to check his shirt for lint and laugh the loudest at all his jokes? Maybe. Probably. Undoubtedly. And yet, somehow she couldn't convince her brain to make her legs move. The sight of Heather and Mateo together had rendered her speechless, useless. It was too much to process.

Heather was grinning, her hands waving about in a dramatic display. "Meet America's next top model!" She gestured toward Mateo as though he was a shiny new car some lucky person was destined to win. "Obviously, you've already met, but I thought you should be the first to know that Mateo is about to become the newest teen heartthrob!"

Layla swallowed past the lump in her throat and turned toward Mateo. The simple act of meeting his gaze was unbearably hard and depleted her strength, but she forced the words anyway. "Congratulations. That's uh . . . that's great." Her voice rang as hollow and wooden as she currently felt.

Last she'd checked, Mateo despised Heather, abhorred Hollywood parties, and had accused her of being changed for the worse thanks to her involvement in such a phony, shallow world. And now, here he was, wearing designer jeans, an expensive T-shirt, and some stupid fucking fedora it was too hot to wear.

Without a word, she turned on her heel.

"Layla . . . ," Mateo called after her, but Layla ignored him and raced blindly away.

# TWENTY-FOUR

# DRINK YOU AWAY

Tommy had been dumb enough to invite Tiki to the party, and he was already regretting it. He barely knew her, and he certainly didn't think of her as a girlfriend or even a potential girlfriend. Truth was, he wasn't even sure why he'd done it, other than he'd been scrambling for something to say to fill the awkward silence when five minutes into breakfast he'd discovered they had virtually nothing in common and so he'd blurted the only thing he could think of—he invited her to his debut and she'd been quick to accept. He would've been better off making the usual halfhearted promise to call, but Tommy had never been any good at that either.

Malina had ordered him a limo, and for the entire ride there, he watched Tiki take selfies as she posed provocatively across the long bench seats, while Tommy mentally rehearsed the playlist. It was only a handful of songs, but the gig was more important than most. He'd be singing for A-listers, tastemakers, influencers with unlimited reach—the kind of celebrities and Hollywood players who had the power to make him if they liked what they saw.

The fact that he had Layla to thank for the gig left him uneasy. When Malina had informed him of her meeting with Layla, Tommy had groaned and figured he was doomed. Malina had raised a brow, but Tommy refused to explain.

"You're in no position to be making enemies," she'd told him.

To which Tommy replied, "Then you've definitely got the wrong guy. Thanks to the Madison mess, I have way more haters than fans."

"It's handled," Malina had assured him, before going on to inform him of her decision to keep his identity under wraps. Which was how he came to be billed as "Special Surprise Performing Artist."

Tommy thought for sure the idea would backfire. That sort of contrived vagueness only worked for real artists like Bono or Springsteen or some other Rock & Roll Hall of Famer who people would actually get excited about. Using it for some young, dumb unknown was bound to disappoint.

"You *are* famous," she'd said. "Just not the right kind of famous—or at least not yet. But trust me, you will be." When Malina's dark eyes met his, it was just like she'd said: he was in no position to make enemies, much less disagree with people who knew more than him.

And now, after having just finished his set, he was filled with what could only be described as elation. The initial shocked silence when the crowd first recognized him as the thug tied to the Madison scandal had been more than a little disconcerting. But after a shaky start, Tommy found his voice, and it didn't take long before the crowd forgot who he was and gave him a chance. The enthusiastic applause and screams for an encore when he finished his set proved Malina was right.

Someone handed him a water, someone else a shot of tequila, and the next thing Tommy knew, he was surrounded by the kind of gorgeous models and actresses that had once only populated his dreams. And yet, here they were in real life, telling him how amazing he was, while Malina was swarmed by execs wanting to set up meetings and talk about how working together could be of mutual benefit.

Tiki squeezed inside the circle of models and clutched his arm in a proprietary way—a move that worked to deter some of the models, but not all. Still, he had only himself to blame. Tiki was pretty and nice and eager to please. Problem was, she just wasn't Layla and never would be.

Luckily, it wasn't long before Malina saved him by introducing Tiki to an actor rumored to be newly single, before deftly pulling Tommy aside.

"You okay with losing the girl?" she asked.

Tommy shrugged. By the looks of it, Tiki had already moved on.

"Good. You need to be single. Your star will rise quicker if every girl in America thinks she has a shot at you."

"Just America? Why are we limiting ourselves?"

Malina grinned. "Last I checked, every girl in America wanted to kill you, so we have a bit of a PR crisis on our hands. Nothing I can't handle, though, as long as you do what I say."

So far he was fully aligned with whatever she planned. "Have you talked to Ira?" he asked, trying to keep his voice from betraying his nerves. But in his mind, it was Ira's response that mattered most.

"Not yet. Though my spies tell me he looked pleased."

Tommy frowned. "Then they're lying. Ira never looks pleased."

"Why don't you ask him yourself, then?"

Tommy turned to find Ira standing just behind him.

"I hate surprises." Ira's gaze was flat as he shifted between Malina and Tommy.

"Most people do." Tommy fought to determine what was really going on behind the immaculate mask, but as usual Ira was impossible to read.

"It's my night. Been planning it for weeks. And somehow you two manage to pull a fast one."

Malina started to speak, but Tommy beat her to it. "I just seized an opportunity when it was offered to me. Isn't that what you would've done?" He was tempted to end the sentence with *Dad—Isn't that what you would've done, Dad?* But if Ira didn't like the surprise of Tommy replacing his headlining musician, there was no telling how he'd react to that particular bombshell. Besides, Tommy wasn't quite ready to make the reveal. His career was just starting. He had a long road ahead.

Ira clenched his jaw and stared at the glittering city skylights beyond. "How does it feel to have your dream come true?" he asked, returning his focus to Tommy.

Since he'd arrived in LA, Tommy's dream had been to hear Ira praise him. Praise him in a way that proved he'd be proud to claim Tommy as his son. But if anything, Ira only seemed annoyed to have lost a small margin of control over his launch. And while Tommy considered it a small victory, it was hardly the stuff of his fantasies.

"I'll let you know when it happens." Tommy tossed back a shot of tequila and turned to leave. "Oh, and congrats on your party," he called over his shoulder, leaving Ira to stare at his retreating form as he made his way across the lawn to where Layla stood, contemplating her own shot of tequila while looking sexy as hell in an off-the-shoulder red dress.

"I hear I have you to thank." Tommy grinned, though his smile vanished as soon as he took in her blurry, unmistakably tear-stung gaze. "Uh, Malina told me about your meeting," he added, watching Layla awkwardly dab at her face in an attempt to appear as though everything was fine. "Something tells me that's not a celebratory drink." He looked pointedly at the shot glass clutched in her hand.

"Either way, the effect is the same—it helps you forget."

Tommy squinted and rubbed an uncertain hand over his chin, unsure how to respond. He knew he owed her an apology, but clearly, this was not the best time.

"Mateo and I broke up." The words seemed to stumble forward in a rush, as though she was desperate to be rid of them, pass the burden to someone else. After a moment of silence, she said, "How come you don't look even the slightest bit surprised?"

Tommy shrugged. He'd heard some vague rumor about Mateo being seen out and about with Heather Rollins, and while he'd felt bad for Layla, part of him hoped it was true. To her he just said, "You okay?"

She nodded confidently, but Tommy wasn't buying the act. Layla hated to be pitied. Anyone could see that.

"Happily ever after is for movies and books." She tilted her chin and forced her gaze to meet his. "In the real world, everything has a beginning, middle, and end. There's no such thing as forever."

Tommy regarded her with a skeptical look. "You saying you don't believe in the big, splashy Hollywood ending?" When their eyes met, Tommy felt a stream of energy pulsating between them. But maybe that was just him. Layla seemed preoccupied and oblivious.

"Even as a kid I wanted Cinderella to pretend the shoe didn't fit so she could do something more interesting with her life than marry a prince."

A slow smile broke across Tommy's face. All around them, the party raged on, but at that moment, he was immune to it all. All he could see was Layla's lovely face hovering just inches from his.

"Anyway, cheers!" She hoisted her glass and drained the shot in a single gulp.

"Did it work?" He cocked his head and waited expectantly.

Layla shrugged. "Too soon to tell. So, where's your date?" She glanced all around as though looking for the blonde he'd arrived with, but in that particular crowd, it was a needle meet haystack situation.

"Last I saw she'd latched onto someone way more famous than me."

"In this crowd, that could be just about anybody."

Tommy laughed. "According to Malina, in order to

build my fan base, I need to stay single."

"That sounds a little . . . controlling."

"It's as good an excuse as any. Not like Tiki was a contender."

"Tiki?" Layla made an exaggerated gaping face.

"Don't mock. It's not like I named her."

Layla burst out laughing, and Tommy began to relax. It felt good to be back on friendly terms. He'd missed her feistiness, her friendship, and the easy banter they shared.

A waiter passed and Tommy was quick to claim two glasses and hand one to her. "How many of these have you had?"

Layla took a moment to think, then wiggled two fingers before him.

"Good." He handed her a glass. "From what I remember, things don't get interesting until number four." When his gaze met hers, to his delight, he found she was grinning. "To Ira," he said, clinking his glass against hers. "For better or worse, we have him to thank for all this."

"To Ira!" Layla pressed the glass to her lips at the same moment the power went out.

# TWENTY-FIVE

# THE KILLING MOON

Aster and Ryan were heading up the hill toward the infamous party house when she turned to him and said, "Be honest, how many times have you come here before?" She shot him a sideways glance.

"Who, me?" Ryan flashed a coy grin; then, remembering who he was talking to, he copped to the truth. "One or two lingerie parties a few months back, that's all."

Aster took a moment to process. "So you're a cross-dresser, or do you consider that cosplay?"

Ryan laughed, which, admittedly was the reaction she was after when she'd made the joke, and yet his casual attitude set her on edge. Here he'd been sleeping with Madison Brooks, arguably the most beautiful girl in the world, and yet he still couldn't resist attending a party filled with half-naked girls. While his honesty was admirable, the male species' seemingly insatiable appetite for eye candy left her deflated.

"Some Russian tycoon was trying to transform the place into the new Playboy Mansion, and a friend, who shall remain nameless, scored me an invite."

"So now you're friends with Voldemort?" She rolled her eyes. "Seriously, what's with all the mystery? What do you think I'm going to do with the guy's name—hand it over to Layla to post on her blog?"

"I'd just rather not drag him into the story without his consent, that's all."

Aster sighed in frustration. While Ryan was uncommonly transparent when it came to his own stuff, he took a much stingier approach when it came to doling out gossip. *You'll have to ask them—it's not my story to tell*, was his go-to reply whenever she questioned him about anything outside of Madison's disappearance. It was annoying as hell.

"So . . . what was it like? The lingerie parties, I mean." She couldn't help it; she was totally intrigued by the things men did when their girlfriends weren't looking.

After a moment's hesitation, Ryan said, "Let's just say Hef's still the king. At least for now, anyway . . ."

"Viva King Hef." Aster frowned, feeling suddenly grumpy.

"You asked." Ryan playfully bumped shoulders with her, reminding her of the pact they'd made that night at

Madison's when they agreed to be totally honest with each other, no matter what. It was the only way they could successfully work together, they reasoned. And while Aster mostly liked their new open way of communicating, she realized she'd become so used to (and so good at) playing the usual games between guys and girls that the honesty didn't come quite as easily as she'd thought it would. Or maybe that was just her. In the short time they'd been working together, Ryan had divulged all sorts of secrets that, in retrospect, Aster wasn't sure she actually wanted to know. Even for an actor—which she constantly reminded herself Ryan was—it was impossible to believe he was faking.

Where sex was concerned, Ryan was quick to put it all out there. Lingerie parties, naked FaceTime dates with Madison—nothing was off-limits. His easy, open attitude both amazed and frightened her. It also made her realize she hadn't been as ready to sleep with him as she'd thought. At least she'd managed to dodge that particular bullet, though under the circumstances, it wasn't by choice.

"On a scale of one to ten, how mad will Ira be that we're arriving so late?" She was eager to change the subject. Only before Ryan could answer, the lights blew and the entire neighborhood was plunged into blackness.

"What the hell?" Aster stumbled and fought to grab hold of Ryan in an effort to steady herself as she blinked into a blanket of darkness. She'd been born and raised in the city and she'd never seen it like that. And with the Santa Ana winds stirring, combined with the chorus of startled shrieks echoing from the house, the eerie factor was at an all-time high. "No way am I going in there." Aster stopped dead in her tracks, refusing to budge another inch.

"You got your cell phone handy?" Ryan set his to flashlight mode, and Aster did the same. A moment later, he was leading her back down the hill.

"Ira must be furious." She glanced back toward the house.

"Because we're so late, or because of the blackout?"

"Both."

In the not-so-far distance, a coyote howled, causing Aster to shiver and Ryan to loop a protective arm around her. Normally, she'd waste no time pushing him away, but between the pitch-black night and the razor-fanged predators, she was glad she didn't have to face it alone.

And yet, there was something about being plunged into darkness that left her feeling oddly safe and unseen. For the first time in a long time she felt freed from the burden of constantly needing to hide her identity. She'd been so over-exposed for so long, it was nice to know that the only ones aware of her immediate presence were Ryan Hawthorne and a pack of coyotes. Okay, maybe not the coyotes.

"What now?" she asked. "We told the driver to go."

Ryan's features lit up like a Halloween mask as he stared down at his phone. "And unfortunately, the next Uber is forty-two minutes away."

"Which may as well be an eternity," Aster groaned.

"Maybe we should stop and sit and wait it out? Surely the lights will come back on eventually. These brownouts never last very long."

It sounded reasonable on the surface, until the coyotes started yipping like they did when they were surrounding their kill, and Aster started moving tentatively down the hill.

"You're going to break your neck trying to navigate in those things." Ryan shined his phone on her four-inch Aquazzura sandals.

"I know." She sighed. "I should probably get over the ick factor and go barefoot instead."

She stopped and grabbed hold of his shoulder, about to slip off her shoes, when Ryan said, "Or I could carry you."

Aster laughed, until she realized he was serious, and next thing she knew, her arms were wrapped around Ryan's shoulders as her legs straddled his back. "I'm not sure this is the best idea," she said, feeling suddenly self-conscious, both at being a burden to him and how good it felt to embrace him.

"You got a better one?"

At the sight of people fleeing the party and barking at

the valets to bring them their cars, Ryan and Aster moved toward the edge of the street. Funny to think how rich and famous most of them were, and yet, in a power outage everyone was rendered equally helpless, left to rely on someone else to fix the problem and return their world to normal.

Ryan maneuvered around the long line of cars the valets were busy positioning, when, without warning, he darted toward one in particular with its lights on and doors open.

"Quick, get in!" Before she could stop him, he'd deposited her onto the passenger seat, shut her door, and raced around to his side.

"What are you doing?" Aster cried in horror as Ryan slipped behind the wheel, shifted into drive, and raced down the pitch-black street.

She pressed a hand hard against the dashboard as though that would somehow stop the nightmare from happening.

Had she misjudged him?

Had he been plotting against her this whole time?

Was he really stealing a car and making her an accomplice?

Whatever it was, she wanted no part of it.

She was just about to tell him as much, when the GPS spoke, instructing him to make a right at the end of the street.

Aster fumbled for the door handle, ready to bail the

second he slowed. "What the hell is going on here—where are we going?" she yelled.

Ryan looked at her, eyes wide, voice filled with disbelief when he said, "Wherever she takes us." He nodded at the screen. "This is Madison's car."

# TWENTY-SIX

# DEAR FUTURE
# HUSBAND

Rather than ending the party, the blackout only served to kick it up to a whole other level as the juiced-up, uninhibited revelers found themselves in a well-stocked, paparazzi-free paradise where anything went.

Candles and lanterns were swiftly procured, and the generator, once discovered, was promptly put to work. While everyone around them seemed to be coupling up and drifting off to the manse's numerous bedrooms, Tommy and Layla used the blackout as an excuse to slip out unnoticed.

Just outside the gates, a swarm of paparazzi had gathered, and unfortunately, Layla and Tommy were instantly recognized. Layla shielded her face with her hands and rushed past them. "Vultures," she mumbled under her breath, realizing just after she'd said it that the same could be said of her.

As a chronicler of the very culture she loathed, she resented finding herself at its center. She had never been in it for the fame. Or, maybe she had, but not the sort of fame that she'd found. She longed to be known for her work, not her dubious connection to a star's disappearance. And though she wasn't entirely sure she was in line with the idea of karma, even she had to admit her recent turn as tabloid prey built a pretty solid case for its existence.

Tommy slid a protective arm around her and told the photogs in no uncertain terms to back the hell off. For a moment, Layla allowed herself to relax into Tommy's embrace, enjoying the brush of his skin—the way his body felt so solid and sure pressed tightly to hers. But just as quickly she reminded herself how the sight of Mateo and Heather together had left her feeling lonely and sad, and she ducked out of his reach.

Loneliness—that was all it was.

It had absolutely nothing to do with the way Tommy's tousled brown hair fell across his forehead in a way that perfectly framed his intense navy-blue eyes.

And it certainly had nothing to do with the way his dark denim jeans dipped enticingly low on his hips.

Or how his soft gray tee stretched taut across his shoulders and chest before perfectly skimming his abs.

"C'mon." Tommy ushered her toward a limo waiting just outside the gate.

"This is yours?" Layla wasn't sure what to think. After

just a single performance, Tommy was already living like a rock star.

"For tonight anyway."

She slid across the long bench seat and started to direct the driver to her car until Tommy stopped her.

"Not happening," he said. "I'm not letting you drive after four shots of tequila. You can come back and claim it tomorrow."

"Three—only three shots," she corrected, watching as Tommy unearthed a bottle from the limo's well-stocked bar.

"So why stop there?" He uncapped the bottle and offered her the first sip.

Layla sighed. She knew from experience that Tommy and tequila were a dangerous mix, but maybe that was her problem. Maybe she'd been living too cautiously. Maybe she should just turn off that annoying, insistent, fun-hating voice of her conscience and see where things led.

She closed her eyes and tipped the bottle to her lips. The memory of their kiss bloomed large in her head . . . the feel of Tommy's hands at her waist . . . his lips meeting hers . . . She'd been trying to forget the kiss since the moment it'd happened. And though she'd briefly convinced herself that she had, there was no denying she'd give just about anything to kiss him again.

"You know what would be perfect right now?"

Layla blinked at Tommy, his face looming close, those navy-blue eyes flashing on hers as his lips broke into a mischievous grin.

"In-N-Out." He swiped the bottle from her grasp and took a swig, as Layla sprawled across the black leather seat and laughed.

"It's official," she said, taking the bottle from him. "You may never qualify as a native, but you've earned yourself some serious California foodie cred."

At Tommy's orders, the driver swung by the drive-through, where Layla and Tommy ordered enough food to host their own party. Before they'd even merged back onto the street, Layla was already digging into her burger and fries.

"You know what I like about you?" Tommy sank low on his seat and regarded her with a hooded gaze.

Layla froze. Aware of the sound of her heart beating frantically, she couldn't even begin to guess what might follow that statement, though she was eager to hear.

"Your appetite."

She cocked her head, sure she'd misunderstood.

"So many girls pick at their food, or fret over their food, or talk incessantly about how they shouldn't be eating the very thing that they're eating and how they'll have to pay penance later, like they committed some sort of crime against humanity by enjoying a burger." He shook his head. "Kind of sucks the fun out of going out for a meal. But you—you just dig in as though you're actually enjoying yourself. It's a thing of beauty to behold."

Layla was stunned. It was one of the strangest compliments she'd ever received, and yet part of her felt the need to defend her fellow sisters by explaining the food-phobic, body-shaming culture they'd all been boxed into living.

In the end, she chose to stay quiet and take another big, juicy bite.

"What time does your ride turn into a pumpkin?" She placed a hand over her mouth as she chewed.

Tommy shrugged. "Why—you want to go somewhere? Should I have him drop you at home?"

Layla thought about home—thought about the possibility of her dad hooking up with his new lady friend in the room just down the hall from hers.

"Why don't we go to your place?" she said, unsure if she was emboldened by the tequila, the compliment, or her revulsion at the thought of her dad shagging in a vintage Venice Beach bungalow that was anything but soundproof. Whatever it was, she was committed to seeing it through.

Tommy looked her over. The way his lip tugged at the side as his brow quirked high, it was impossible to tell if this was a look of interest or surprise.

"Just for a little while," she said, not entirely sure that she meant it, but she didn't want to seem pushy, eager, or

God forbid, desperate. "I'm too amped to go home. Not yet anyway."

Tommy gave the order, and the driver dropped them off just outside a modern high-rise building Layla didn't recognize. "Welcome to paradise," Tommy said, opening the door and motioning her toward the entrance.

"Wait—where are we?" Layla stood on the sidewalk, squinting as she tried to get her bearings. "This is Sunset Boulevard—I thought we were going to your place?"

"This is my place—my new place. Which, I should probably warn you, happens to be a major step up from my last place. Not a shag carpet or popcorn ceiling in sight." Tommy grinned proudly; then, seeing the way Layla hesitated, he said, "Though if you prefer a more down-market vibe, we can always head over there. It's still mine until the end of the month."

Layla blinked at Tommy. Had steady employment and a shiny new record deal turned him into yet another status-obsessed Angeleno? Money changed people. She'd seen it happen before. Question was, how much had it changed Tommy?

Slowly, she looked him over. The thrashed motorcycle boots he'd once worn had been replaced with a newer, more stylish pair. And though he'd stuck with his usual uniform of jeans and a T-shirt, they'd clearly been upgraded too. She shifted uncertainly from foot to foot, unsure what to make of it. But when she lifted her gaze to meet his, he met her with a look so open and inviting she knew that despite a few superficial upgrades, deep down inside he was still the same Tommy she'd known from the start.

Besides, didn't she essentially want the same thing—to live a bigger and better, more upgraded life than the one she'd been living?

Was it possible her rush to judgment was no more than a pathetic, knee-jerk, jealousy-fueled reaction at seeing how quickly he'd progressed toward his dream?

Maybe. Probably. But at the moment, she preferred not to think about it.

She followed him inside the large, well-lit lobby and smiled to herself as he greeted the doorman by name. It was cute to see him feeling so proud of himself, and after riding the elevator to the sixth floor, they entered an apartment that showed just how big a leap in the pay grade he'd made.

"Wow." It hardly conveyed the full extent of her amazement, but in her current state of awe, it was the best Layla could manage. She crossed the pale hardwood floors en route to the balcony, which offered a stunning view of the Hollywood sign.

"Did you notice the keyless entry?" Tommy was just behind her. "The whole place is controlled by tablet—the heating, air-conditioning, TV, even the lights." He tapped the screen on his iPad and grinned when the bulbs flickered on and off.

Layla stood at the edge of the terrace. With the wind in her hair and the city sprawled out below, she was equal parts admiration and envy. "You're living the dream." She turned to face him, her gaze moving from the grin that lit up his eyes to the room just beyond. It was a beautiful space, done up in the sort of high-end, West Coast, aspirational cool you saw on reality TV shows featuring families with lives far more posh than yours. A mix of soothing neutrals with its white walls, natural fiber furnishings, and custom oak cabinets and limestone countertops in the kitchen beyond, it was environmental chic at its best.

"There's an on-site restaurant, a rooftop pool, and a gym with personal trainers and yoga teachers on call. It even comes with weekly maid service, which, I'm not ashamed to admit, is the amenity I'm most excited about. Though in the spirit of full disclosure, Malina helped set me up. I'm paying rent, of course, but for the moment, it's at a really deep discount."

"I'm assuming it came furnished as well?" Layla followed him back inside, noting how the lumpy old couch and the old crate that substituted for a coffee table were missing, though she was pleased to find his collection of well-worn paperbacks was still on display.

Nice as it was, what really impressed her was Tommy's unerring pursuit of his dreams. She was used to people talking about their plans to hit it big—and yet, when it came down to it, most lacked the incentive to leave their parents' couch long enough to actually go after the very thing they claimed to dream about.

But Tommy was the exception. When he cared about something, he was all in. As different as she, Aster, and Tommy were on the surface, they all shared the same sort of unwavering drive and ambition, which was undoubtedly how they all ended up working for Ira. Clearly he'd seen in them the same trait he valued most in himself.

He moved into the kitchen and started pulling plates and napkins and glasses together as she made for his prized vinyl collection. "Any new additions?" she asked. Last time they'd listened to Led Zeppelin, and it hadn't gone well. And though she didn't blame Jimmy Page, she figured it was better to go in another direction.

"Having a bit of an eighties moment." Tommy set the plates on the coffee table and started divvying up the contents of the In-N-Out bags.

"Eighties as in Air Supply and Wham?" Layla crinkled her nose in distaste, as Tommy shot her a look of mock outrage.

"Eighties as in the Smiths and the Clash." He came to stand beside her, and when his arm inadvertently brushed against hers as he leaned toward the stack, the brief moment of contact was all it took to send a jolt of electricity spinning through her veins. "*Hatful of Hollow*." He waved the album before her. "Do you know it?"

Layla squinted, fought to gain control of herself.

"Trust me." He pressed his lips together as he placed it onto the stereo deck and dropped the needle on the first track. "You will not be disappointed."

A burst of static filled the room, soon followed by a hauntingly mournful voice as Tommy headed back to the kitchen to fetch them some water. He handed her a bottle, then settled onto the couch and motioned for her to join him. Overcome with an unexplainable bout of shyness, she sipped and ate in an odd, nervous silence.

"Layla . . . ," Tommy started, his voice thick, hoarse, the sound of it causing her belly to flutter as she lifted her chin and studied his face, waiting for the words that would follow. His questioning gaze held hers, the moment seeming to unravel slowly, and the next thing she knew Tommy was kissing her.

Or maybe she was kissing Tommy.

It was impossible to tell who really started it.

All she knew for sure was that his body was warm and strong and felt like it was meant to be pressed against hers.

It was nothing like the last time they'd kissed. Sure, they were both fueled by tequila, but there was no more denying she'd been attracted to Tommy from the first day they'd met. No more denying she wanted him now just as much as she'd wanted him then—back when she was still dating Mateo. If that made her a horrible person, so be it. If it made her disloyal like her mom, well, at least she got it honestly. Despite the alcohol, they were two consenting adults, and Layla was ready to consent to anything Tommy was willing to do.

His mouth moved hungrily over hers before abandoning her lips in favor of her neck. His lips nipping, tasting, leaving a trail of sparks in their wake as his hands moved over her snug off-the-shoulder dress and tugged it down to her waist.

He gazed at her appreciatively. "God, you're so beautiful . . . so *perfect*." He dipped his head low to kiss her there too, as Layla arched to meet him. Her fingers pulling at his belt and unzipping his jeans, she swung a leg over his hip and straddled him at the waist, when he suddenly stopped, clasped her hands in his, and repeated her name. "Layla . . ." His voice was breathless, eyes glazed, as he pressed his forehead to hers. "Is this really about being with me—or is it about being against someone else?"

She frowned, moved to kiss him again, but when he pulled away, she glared and said, "What are you talking about? Why are you doing this?"

"I saw Mateo with Heather and—"

"And you're afraid you might be a rebound?" Her face was incredulous.

"I'm afraid you're trying to exorcise the memory of him through me. And I just want you to be sure you really want this. That you won't end up regretting it, or worse, blaming me or hating me."

At first she was furious—why did he have to wreck the moment by talking about logical things that might very well be true but that she absolutely, positively did not want to think about? But once she'd had a chance to digest the words, the anger seeped right out of her.

"Truth?" She exhaled. "I don't know, but I'm not sure it matters. We're over. Mateo and I are over. Which means I'm free to move on."

"But are you over him?"

Layla studied the paint on the wall just before her, unsure what to say. "It was a bit of a shock to see him with her, I'm not gonna lie. Still, Mateo and I weren't really as compatible as you might think."

"And we are?"

"Most of the time I hate you." She laughed. "But you are a pretty good kisser, so . . ."

"Pretty good? That's it?"

She shrugged, folded her arms to cover herself.

"Can I get an excellent?"

"You can certainly try." She cocked her head and arced her brow high. "But that'll require you to stop talking." She flashed him a flirtatious grin and leaned in to kiss him.

He met the kiss eagerly, his hands at her back, and crushed her body to his. "One more thing . . ." His lips moved against hers. "I like you. Which is why I want to make sure we're on the same page. I don't want things to be awkward between us."

"Look," she huffed, quickly losing patience. Either they were going to do this, or they weren't going to do this. And if they weren't, she'd just as soon leave. She had no interest in talking. Not about this. "You're not allowed to have a girlfriend, and it just so happens, I'm not looking for a boyfriend. So why can't we enjoy ourselves and see where we land?"

Calling an end to the argument, Layla reached for him again and Tommy made no move to stop her. She kissed him hard, exploring, tasting, her tongue melding with his. She nipped at his full bottom lip, a little harder than he'd expected, but Layla just grinned and pulled him back to her. And this time, when she tugged at his jeans, he did nothing to stop her.

He just watched with a heavy-lidded gaze as she dragged them down to his knees, and melted into her touch.

## TWENTY-SEVEN

# DIRTY DEEDS DONE DIRT CHEAP

"I don't like this." Aster shut the glove compartment and gazed worriedly out the windshield. It was the understatement of the year. After searching the front and back seats, she hadn't found a single thing that could be considered out of the ordinary, and certainly nothing that could lead them to Madison, or at least hint at what'd happened to her. "What if it's a setup? It feels like a setup." She stared at Ryan, torn between wanting him to stop the car and wanting him to keep driving. In the end, her curiosity prevailed and she settled for seeing it through.

"Oh, it's definitely a setup." Ryan gripped the wheel so hard his knuckles paled. "What are the chances of us just randomly bumping into Madison's car?" He looked at her for so long that she gestured frantically for him to focus back on the road. Last thing they needed was to wreck a car the cops were undoubtedly looking for. "Clearly someone wanted it found. Still, there's no way they could've known we'd be right there at that exact time . . . unless we're being watched." He shot Aster a sideways glance.

"If you were trying to calm my nerves, consider that a fail." Aster shivered. "Question is, if they did leave it for us, was it so they can call the cops and get us arrested for grand theft auto, or—?"

Before she could finish, Ryan said, "No, this is about the Ghost."

Aster looked at him. She had no idea what that meant.

He nodded toward the GPS. "That's the name of the destination."

Aster squinted. How had she missed that? Now that she'd seen it, she couldn't help but wish she hadn't.

"So . . . the Ghost is a place?"

Ryan looked at her. "We're about to find out. According to this thing"—he nudged his chin toward the monitor—"we're not all that far."

At the GPS prompt, they pulled into a parking lot facing a small, two-story, nondescript office complex comprised of a U-shaped building set around an open courtyard.

"I don't get it." Aster frowned at the view as Ryan parked in a spot that was shielded from the street, then busily scrolled through his contacts list.

"I knew it," he mumbled under his breath as he tucked his phone in his pocket and set about wiping down the gearshift and steering wheel with the cuff of his sleeve. "Better get your prints off that glove box, the door handle, and anything else you might've touched."

She shot him a questioning look.

"It's too risky to keep driving it. We'll find another way home. Just after we check out this place."

"Mind telling me what's going on?" she whispered. "Because it seems like you know where we are, and it would be nice if you clued me in too."

Ryan grimaced. "It's a hunch, nothing more. I'll let you know if I'm right."

Aster followed him to the directory. She was barely able to make out the names before Ryan was racing up a flight of stairs and across a landing to where he stopped before a door bearing a plaque reading *Banks Janitorial*.

"Guy's got a sense of humor." He glanced at Aster when he added, "He cleans up celebrity dirt."

He tried the knob only to find the door locked, and was just making for the window when Aster said, "Maybe this'll work." She unfolded her fingers to present a single gold key.

"Where'd you find that?" Ryan stared at her suspiciously.

"Glove box," she mumbled, sliding the key into the lock.

"And you didn't say anything?"

She shrugged and pushed the door open. "Wasn't sure it mattered till now."

Her hand went directly for the light switch, but Ryan was quick to grasp it in his before she could reach it. "It'll attract too much attention," he said. "Better to work in the dark."

"Attention from who?" It was time for Ryan to talk. She was sick of being left out. "Why should we care about this janitor ghost guy? This just looks like some boring office park to me. So what exactly are you expecting to find?"

Ryan leaned against a wall and shined his phone discreetly around the small space. The light moved from a messy desk towering with papers, to a beat-up metal filing cabinet that had seen better days, to a set of well-worn chairs separated by a cheap plastic table, to the obligatory office spider plant that, from the looks of it, was desperately in need of watering.

"This is where Paul works," he said. "He's Madison's fixer. Also known as the Ghost."

Aster fell silent. She had so many questions and no idea where to start. "Why the nickname?" she asked, knowing it was probably the least important on the long list of things she could've asked, but then again, it could prove revealing.

Ryan pushed away from the wall. "I guess because his job sort of depends on him being invisible, and apparently he's good at it." He shuffled through a stack of files on the desk and glanced at Aster when he said, "It's not like Madison talked about him much. But once, I saw her talking to this guy and when I asked her who he was, she tried to brush it off, but I wouldn't let it go, so she claimed she didn't know his real name, but that he went by the Ghost and he handled security detail for certain celebrities. Said she'd considered hiring him but ultimately decided against it. I pretended to believe her, but later, I did a little poking around and discovered his name is Paul. Officially, he works as a private investigator, but from what I hear, he does a lot more than that. And, despite what she told me, Madison did, in fact, hire him."

"Why did she lie?"

"Add that to the pile of questions I have about her. Anyway, we should probably hurry. Someone knows we're here, and there's no telling how long they'll extend the hospitality."

While Ryan checked the desk, Aster went straight for the filing cabinet. Despite the lock on every drawer, they were left purposely open, as though someone wanted her to look. She started flicking through the files, but they were arranged by a series of numbers and letters that made no immediate sense, or at least not to her.

"Anything?" Ryan whispered, but Aster frowned in reply.

"Maybe," she said. "I'm not sure how this works."

Ryan abandoned the desk and came to stand beside her.

"I know there's a system, but it's a mystery to me." She motioned toward the files and moved aside to let Ryan try.

She watched his fingers deftly move among them as though he actually knew what to look for. A moment later, he plucked a file from the pile and quickly flipped it open.

"I recognize the indexing system. My mom's an attorney," he said, his voice distracted. "I used to work for her during summer break, doing filing and stuff."

Aster hovered beside him. Other than her job promoting Night for Night, she'd never worked a day in her life. To be so easily stumped by a filing system left her feeling like a pampered, useless princess.

"This should be it, but . . ." Aster peered over his shoulder to better see. "The file is empty."

"You sure?"

He showed her the inside.

"No, I mean, you sure that's her file?"

"According to the tab." He shrugged and placed it back where he found it. "But this is weird." He rose onto his toes and reached all the way to the back of the drawer to retrieve a box full of . . . something, Aster couldn't quite make it out in the dark until he held it before her. "Blood-collection needles," he said.

Aster stared blankly.

"And it looks like there's another box just beneath full of blood collection tubes."

"What the—" Before Aster could finish, Ryan snuffed the light on his phone, dropped to the ground, and pulled her down with him. In his rush, he lost his grip on the box and the needles flew free and clattered around them.

Aster unwillingly slumped down beside him, ready to unleash her full fury for his unnecessarily scaring her, when she heard a set of heavy footsteps approaching the door and a moment later, someone aimed a flashlight right through the window.

She cringed, tried to make herself smaller in hopes of avoiding the bouncing beam of light that landed just shy of them.

Ryan reached for her hand and squeezed it tightly in his, as Aster huddled against him, praying the person would leave. The two of them remained frozen, afraid to so much as breathe, until the torch cut, the office fell dark once again, and the person moved on.

"Probably just security making the rounds," Ryan whispered, more to make her feel better than out of any real belief in his words. He reached toward her and brushed the back of his hand softly across her cheek. "You okay?"

In the dark, she could just barely make out the elegant lines of his face, the slant of his brow, his mouth just inches from hers. Instinctively, she reached up, clasped his hand to her cheek, and entwined his fingers with hers. It would be so easy to kiss him, to close the gap between them and press her lips against his. From the way he returned the look, the way he pushed into her space, it was clear he was thinking it too.

She raised a finger to his lips, softly tracing the peaks and valley of his perfect Cupid's bow, all the while remembering how good his mouth had felt crushed against hers, and how she longed to feel that again.

He shivered under her touch, ran a hand along the line of her jaw, then lingered at the base of her throat. With his body lying flush against hers, the moment was so charged with promise and heat, Aster had no choice but to force herself to retreat, force herself to remember all the reasons why they couldn't be together. Soon, she'd be on trial—her fate at the mercy of twelve people who knew nothing about her. She couldn't waste a single moment on anything other than building her defense. Kissing Ryan Hawthorne was a luxury she could not indulge in.

"We should go," she whispered into the dark, watching as Ryan exhaled deeply and reluctantly stood. "If they call in that car . . ." Aster didn't bother to finish the thought. Ryan could fill in the blanks on his own.

He peered out the window. "Coast seems to be clear." He glanced over his shoulder at her. "I don't see anyone."

Aster squinted into the darkness, but after the scare, she

was reluctant to rely on her phone. "Maybe we should get in front of this and call it in anonymously."

"And say what?"

"That Madison's car is parked out front, and that this Paul guy not only works for her, but he has a whole blood-collecting kit he keeps next to her file."

"I'm not sure that proves anything."

Aster frowned.

"Hey, just playing the devil's advocate here. Don't shoot the messenger."

"Okay," she said, struggling to make sense of it. "I'm just thinking, either Paul went rogue and harmed Madison, or more likely, he's still working for her and he helped her disappear. What if they've been planning this whole thing for a while? And what if, let's say, over the course of the last few months, Madison's been steadily giving blood in order to fake her abduction and make it look real?"

Ryan remained silent, but in the dark, Aster couldn't tell if it was because he was actually considering her idea, or trying to determine the most polite, most inoffensive way to tell her the whole thing was crazy. A moment later, his phone lit up as his fingers moved over the screen.

"Who you calling?" she asked.

"Arranging for an Uber," he started, but Aster quickly swiped his phone away and ended the call before he could finish.

"No. No Uber. No electronic record that can prove we were here."

"So how do we get out of here?" he asked, but Aster was already on it, already moving for the door.

A second later, when an alarm went off, they ran like their lives depended on it.

# TWENTY-EIGHT

# YOU SHOOK ME ALL NIGHT LONG

Layla was still awake, and she used the moment to roll onto her side and watch Tommy sleep. There was something so intimate about watching a guy sleep. Especially a guy like Tommy, who blazed through life as though he had something urgent to prove. Who he was trying to impress was anyone's guess. Maybe it was just something he needed to do for himself. Though somehow she felt it went deeper than that.

Looking at his arm casually tossed over his head, lips slightly parted, hair tousled and falling into his eyes, Layla realized just how little she knew about him. For one thing, his concern regarding her reasons for sleeping with him had taken her by surprise.

Was she trying to exorcise the memory of Mateo as he'd

suggested? It was entirely possible, and in the end completely futile. Mateo had been her first love. She'd never be fully free of him, and she wasn't entirely sure that she wanted to be.

While sleeping with Tommy probably wasn't one of her wisest moves, for the moment anyway she chose not to care. Besides, she didn't want anything from him, and she was pretty sure he felt the same way. In bed he'd been surprisingly tender and sweet, and just wild enough to thoroughly satisfy her. It was enough. More than enough, really.

She stretched her legs before her and lifted her arms high, unable to remember the last time she'd felt so fulfilled, so relaxed. The movement caused Tommy to stir in his sleep, hovering somewhere on the precipice of waking. Layla rolled toward him and lowered the sheet, taking a moment to appreciate the sight of his body, his lean muscular build probably honed from long days of working as a ranch hand, or maybe running track in high school. She tried to imagine what his life might've been like back in Oklahoma. Had he been the star of his school, always surrounded by pretty girls hoping he'd notice them long enough to write a song about them?

She ran her fingertip over his hip, about to wake him again, when her phone buzzed with an incoming text and she reached toward the nightstand instead.

"Ignore it." Tommy's voice was warm and sleepy as his

eyes fluttered open. He reached first for her breasts, then her waist, before tugging her arms and pulling her down so his mouth could meet hers.

She returned the kiss, eager to repeat all the things they'd done earlier, along with a few more things they hadn't yet tried. Only she'd glimpsed just enough of the text to know it was from Aster and that it was urgent.

"It's Aster." She fumbled for the phone, struggling to read the words on the screen as Tommy licked his way down her body.

"Aster can wait," Tommy mumbled, pausing to appreciate the gold-and-ruby ring in her navel before heading due south.

"Actually, she can't." Layla sat up so quickly, Tommy's face hit the mattress. Still, there was no time to apologize. She was too busy plucking her clothes off the floor.

Tommy gazed at her sleepily. "Where are you going?"

Layla stepped into her dress and shoved her feet into her heels. "I know you want no part of this, but Aster needs help, so I really gotta go."

In an instant, Tommy was up and getting dressed too.

"You're coming?" Layla combed her fingers through her hair, going for a look of purposely tousled, as opposed to just a bad case of bed head. No need for Aster to see her looking so disheveled and guess what they'd been up to.

"You actually think I would send you out there on your

own in the middle of the night?"

"Tommy—" Layla watched as he pulled on a T-shirt and jeans before slipping into an old pair of leather flip-flops. "Just because we . . ." She motioned toward the bed with its skewed pillows and rumpled sheets, feeling suddenly self-conscious about putting a voice to all the delicious things they'd done to each other. "Doesn't mean you have to come with me, or do anything for me, really. I have no expecta-tions. You don't owe me anything. We're both adults here, and—"

Tommy stood so close she could see the individual flecks in his irises. "I thought you said it was urgent." He rubbed the tip of his thumb across her cheekbone and tucked a loose strand back behind her ear. The move was so innocu-ous and yet so intimate, it gave Layla chills.

"I did, but—"

"So don't you think we should get going then?" He jan-gled his keys.

Without a word, Layla thrust her bag over her shoulder and followed him out the door.

"Driver's gone." Tommy led her toward the parking garage. "So we'll have to take my car."

He clicked the key fob and unlocked the doors. The chirping sound seemed to boomerang against the concrete walls as Tommy moved to open her door before getting his.

A small grin crept onto Layla's face. Who would've guessed Tommy Phillips was so well-schooled in old-fashioned manners? It made her wonder what his mom must be like. Though Tommy rarely talked about his parents or his life before he arrived in LA.

His fingers found the handle and he yanked the door open, motioning Layla inside. But Layla remained frozen in place, staring unblinkingly at the elaborately wrapped gift box sitting on the passenger seat with a card bearing her name.

Instinctively her hand flew to cover her mouth, as Tommy looked on from beside her. "How did they get into your car?" she whispered.

Tommy stared uncomprehendingly. "I know I locked it. I always lock it. And while I'd love to take credit for the gift, I'm afraid—"

"No." She was quick to cut him off. "Trust me. You don't want to take credit for this. It's not a gift." She looked all around the parking garage, but of course, they were alone. Whoever had left this was long gone.

She slid onto the seat and held the box on her lap, as Tommy went around to the driver's side and settled beside her. Since the car had been parked in the garage for the last few hours, the interior was hot, and yet the package felt cool to the touch, as though it had only recently been delivered.

Someone had been watching them. Following them. Though another quick glance around the parking garage assured her they were the only ones there, the thought of being stalked without knowing gave her the chills.

Sliding her finger under the flap of the envelope, she removed the note tucked inside and frowned at the disturbing image of an abused cartoon cat.

It marked the fourth card she'd been sent, and this time in addition to the noose, the gunshot wound to the head, and the missing front teeth, he bore a gruesome-looking black eye. Inside was the familiar curlicue script.

Received your message loud and clear
Seems you're convinced you have nothing to fear
While I can assure you that you're wrong about that
If you're in need of more proof, look no further than
the poor battered cat
If it's convincing you need
I've procured a few things to fill up your blog feed
Now that we've struck a deal
Things are about to get very real
It's time for you to do as I say
Or else you better prepare to pay.

Layla handed the card to Tommy, noting the way his eyes went wide as his chin practically dropped to his chest.

He cast a troubled glance her way, and said, "I've seen this." He shook the card in his fist. "Not this exactly, but the picture of the cat. I saw the same image on a piece of paper in Ira's office."

Layla was stricken by his words, wondering what the connection might be. Tommy had warned her about Ira before, but she'd never taken the warnings seriously. Though maybe he'd been right all along. Maybe Ira was far worse than any of them ever realized.

Wordlessly, she removed the ribbon, tore through the wrapping paper, and opened the box, finding a stack of diary entries, along with other random documents pertaining to Madison.

"We need to go." She looked at Tommy. "I'll get you up to date, I promise. But right now, we really need to hurry. Aster and Ryan are in far more trouble than they think."

# TWENTY-NINE

# OUR LIPS ARE SEALED

Tommy was shaken. So shaken he wondered why they didn't just call the police, hand over the box, and let them take it from there so they could all walk away and get on with their regularly scheduled lives. But when he mentioned it to Layla, she instantly dismissed the idea.

"Not happening." Her tone was nonnegotiable. "Pretty sure this transcends the LAPD. They found their suspect, case closed. Anything you or I do to intervene is only going to be met with suspicion. Besides, Aster can't really go back to her life. Which is why we need to help her."

While Tommy couldn't exactly dispute what she'd said, that didn't mean he wasn't tempted to try.

"Still . . . ," he muttered, leaving the thought to dangle unfinished, since he had no idea what could possibly follow that would bear enough impact to change Layla's mind. They drove the rest of the way in silence before he pulled into a church parking lot, where Aster and Ryan were supposedly waiting. "Do we know what this is about? Seems like a pretty strange meet spot." He peered through the side and rearview mirrors and watched as Aster and Ryan cautiously crawled from the shadows and looked all around, before darting for the car.

"It's about Madison." Layla sighed. "Everything's about Madison." She shifted toward the backseat, watching as Aster and Ryan climbed in. "Where to?" she asked.

Aster glanced between them as though trying to determine what they were doing together. "My place," she said. Then, narrowing her gaze on Tommy, she added, "Though I didn't expect to see you. What's with the change of heart?"

Tommy glanced over his shoulder and put the car in reverse. It was a good question, and one he certainly deserved after blowing her off after she was released from lockup. Thing was, his heart hadn't changed at all, no matter how hard he'd tried. His attempts to keep his distance and try to convince himself he could be interested in a girl like Tiki were futile at best. It was Layla he'd wanted since the first day they'd met, and after the intimacy they'd just shared, there was no more denying it. For better or worse, he was all in. Which meant he would do whatever it took to try and protect her. Though that didn't mean he was ready to pour his heart out to a car full of people.

"I became part of this the night I took Madison to the Vesper," he said. "So, like it or not, I'm in." He pulled onto the street and focused on driving as Aster and Ryan breathlessly filled them in. The two of them continued to talk over each other until Tommy noticed a car with flashing lights zooming up from behind them, and he moved to the side of the road.

He lowered his window and watched through the side-view mirror as a guy wearing sneakers, dad jeans, and a blue button-down shirt rolled at the cuffs made a slow but purposeful approach.

"Tommy Phillips." Detective Larsen leaned through the driver's-side window and flashed a squinty-eyed grin as though reuniting with a long-lost classmate he had fond memories of bullying. "Been a while." He curled his meat-slab fingers around the door-trim panel.

Tommy shrugged, tempted to say something about how it hadn't been nearly long enough, but wisely chose to keep his mouth shut.

Larsen angled his head farther inside and craned his stump of a neck toward the backseat. "Looks like the gang's all here." His beady green gaze moved among them, lingering on Aster for a moment before returning to Tommy. "So, where you all headed at"—he checked his watch—"one fifteen a.m.? Seems a little late, no?"

Tommy could ask Larsen the same thing. Was he even on duty—or had he been trailing them the whole time, looking for a reason to stop them? Not that Tommy had given him one. Larsen was out to harass, and there was nothing Tommy could do but stay cool and answer his questions in the least incriminating way possible.

Knowing that whatever he said could and most certainly would be twisted in a way Larsen wouldn't hesitate to use against him, Tommy cleared his throat and said, "Just taking everyone home."

"Looks like you've got quite a few stops to make." His red scrub-brush head bobbed at each of them. "Or you all planning a slumber party?"

Tommy clamped his lips shut. If Larsen wanted him to bite, he'd be sorely disappointed.

"How about you all hop out of the car for a minute?"

Tommy hesitated. Larsen was clearly up to no good.

"Sorry if that sounded like a question, because it wasn't. Everyone out," Larsen barked.

Reluctantly, Tommy propped the door open and slipped out of the car. A second later, Layla, Aster, and Ryan followed.

Larsen instructed them to line up alongside the car; then he stood before them, legs planted wide, arms crossed menacingly over his bulky chest. He wore the kind of shifty expression that left no doubt their full compliance was in their best interest.

"Now, let's start over." He studied each of them. "Where are you coming from?"

"Ira Redman's launch party," Aster said, as Tommy stifled a groan. It was the worst thing she could've said.

Larsen's interest was obvious as he moved to stand before her, brow lowered in scrutiny. But to Aster's credit, she didn't so much as flinch. "Guess you figure you have reason to party now that you're out on bail?"

Tommy snuck a sideways glance at Aster, relieved to see that while she clearly wasn't about to fold, she was keeping her cool enough not to get confrontational either. It was the best he could hope for, seeing as how she'd decided to take the lead on this one. Though he secretly wished she would've just kept her mouth shut and taken the Fifth.

"I'm employed by Ira," she said. "We all are—except for Ryan, of course."

*Good. Bravo. Well done. Now kindly keep quiet and stop feeding the beast!*

"Y'all been drinking?"

Tommy decided it was time to step in. "'Course not. We're underage." His gaze met Larsen's, watching as he threw his head back and roared with laughter as though Tommy had said something hilarious.

"You got anyone to verify your whereabouts?" Larsen said, once he finally quieted down. He paced before them, slowly, leisurely, letting them know who was calling the shots in case that wasn't already clear.

"I performed there," Tommy said. "Plenty of people saw me."

"That right?" Larsen stopped before him and faked like he was impressed. "You're really moving up in the world, aren't you? What with your star billing at Ira Redman's launch party, and your fancy new ride." He nodded admiringly at the black BMW, though the way his lip curled when he spoke Ira's name left no doubt he wasn't a fan.

On the surface at least, Tommy resisted the urge to fidget and forced himself to meet Larsen's penetrating stare with an impassive gaze as though he had nothing to fear, though inside was a whole other story. His heart was slamming, his gut was wrenching, and rivulets of sweat raced down his chest.

"Reason I pulled you over is because there's been a disturbance reported at an office park about a mile from here. Any of you know about that?"

Tommy shook his head and fought like hell to leave it at that.

"Seems there's been a break-in at one of the offices."

Tommy lifted his shoulders, shifted his weight from foot to foot. The Santa Ana winds were kicking up again, the hot gusts mostly stirring up dirt while providing little relief from the heat. Tommy focused on the stream of cars going past, ducking his head each time one slowed to get a better look at the lineup of unfortunate slobs unlucky enough to get pulled over on a Saturday night. A moment later, he heard what sounded like a bomb going off, and he swung around just in time to see a plume of smoke shooting high into the sky.

Larsen opened his mouth, about to say something more, when his radio crackled with an urgent call and he lifted a finger and moved back toward his car.

"You didn't have anything to do with that, did you?" Tommy whispered under his breath, as he nodded toward the smoldering sky just behind them.

"Of course not!" Aster snapped, rolling her eyes for good measure.

A few moments later when Larsen returned, he looked at each of them and said, "Go home. All of you." They nodded and started to climb inside the car, when he added, "And Aster—"

Tommy watched as Aster turned toward him, their eyes meeting for what seemed like an eternity, but was really only a handful of seconds.

"See you in court," Larsen spat. Dipping his head, he turned on his heel and made for his car, as Tommy crawled back behind the wheel, started the engine, and eased onto the street.

# THIRTY

# BURNING DOWN THE HOUSE

"You sure this place is safe?" Ryan paused in the threshold of Aster's apartment and looked all around, as though he expected the very walls to be bugged.

Though after the run-in with Detective Larsen, Aster figured he couldn't be blamed. The ride home had been fraught with tense silence, and Larsen's parting words had left her deeply shaken. She could only assume they all felt the same way.

"Ryan thinks Ira might have something to do with this mess." Aster peered into the fridge. "But honestly, I don't see why he'd bother."

"I'm just not convinced he can be trusted." Ryan rubbed a hand over his chin, refusing to give in. "Not only have his clubs benefited from the scandal, but he is the one who served you that champagne," he reminded her.

Aster distributed bottles of water and sank onto the couch beside him. "He's also the one who hired my attorney and gave me a place to live," she snapped. "The idea of him setting me up doesn't make sense."

Tommy turned away from the floor-to-ceiling windows. "Don't rule him out just yet." He cast a glance toward Layla. "I think he deserves a place on the list of possible suspects."

"Care to elaborate?" Aster was tired of people always questioning Ira's motives. It wasn't as if she didn't have her own suspicions, but for the moment, with her future entirely dependent on Ira's continued goodwill, unless someone gave her something concrete to go on, she'd just as soon call a halt to the speculating.

Tommy seemed to hesitate, then just as easily dismissed it.

"Look, can we just call a truce on Ira for now and focus on these papers instead? I think I might've scored something big." Layla seemed annoyed. Tired and annoyed. Well, join the party.

Aster settled onto the couch, watching as Layla placed the box she'd found in Tommy's car on top of the coffee table and lifted the lid. "You recognize this?" she asked, when Ryan mumbled under his breath, and Aster gasped.

Aster shook her head. "No, Not exactly," she said. "But

remember how I told you we found Madison's empty file in Paul's office? I'm pretty sure whoever sent this got to it first."

"And they're probably the same person who delivered Madison's car." Ryan nodded as though it was confirmed. Still, Aster was willing to bet he was right.

"This almost seems impossible." Tommy spoke in a mix of wonder and awe. "For one person to have so much reach."

"Who said it's one person?" Layla looked at him.

"And, if it is Paul, who, by the way, is number one on my list of suspects"—Aster tapped the lip of her water bottle against her chin—"then it wouldn't be so hard for him to arrange all of this."

"They don't call him the Ghost for nothing." Ryan shrugged.

"Well, assuming this did come from the Ghost, don't you think it's kind of weird that he still relies on paper when it seems the whole world has converted to electronic?" Layla plucked a piece of paper from the top of the pile and frowned.

"I guess it's less vulnerable this way," Aster said. "I mean, look how easy it was for Javen to hack into that apartment website."

"If it's less vulnerable, then why are we sitting here looking at it?" Tommy asked.

"Because someone obviously wants us to see it." Layla abandoned one piece of paper for another. "Though I have a feeling they might be doling it out as they see fit. This looks like it's mostly diary entries."

"Have you decided what you're going to do about those? Are you going to post them?" Aster looked at her.

"Haven't decided. Though someone out there really wants me to. The rhyming threat level is only increasing. But I don't like being told what to do." She sifted through the pile and stopped on one in particular.

Aster leaned in to get a better look. Layla's hand was shaking, and it was pretty easy to guess why. The photo was dark and grainy, but there was no mistaking the subject was Layla and Tommy. They were kissing. On a dance floor. In a club that looked a lot like Jewel. Seemed her suspicions had been valid after all.

"What the hell?" Layla whispered, as Tommy snatched it out of her hands, his cheeks flaming in a way Aster read as embarrassment.

"Who took this?" he asked, unable to keep from staring at it.

"Apparently, Madison did," Layla said, though her tone seemed uncertain, or maybe she was just stunned. "Someone sent this to Mateo. It's why we broke up."

Tommy reeled on her. "Why didn't you tell me?" His voice was edged with emotion, his face a mask of outrage.

Aster sank deeper into the cushions, as Ryan fidgeted uncomfortably beside her.

"Can we not talk about this now?" Layla shook her head, snatched the photo from his grasp, and angrily shoved it into her bag.

"I think the real question is, why would Madison do that?" Aster asked, figuring it needed to be questioned.

Tommy fell silent, as Layla nervously twisted the cap on her bottle of water and said, "Maybe she did, maybe she didn't. All I know for sure is that someone has it out for her, and apparently they want me to have it out for her too. By giving me all this stuff and making it look like she's responsible for sending the pic, it's like they're trying to alternately threaten me and/or anger me into posting her diary entries. Either way, don't you think it seems weird that Paul would keep this picture in a file?"

"Maybe that picture didn't come from the file," Ryan said. "Maybe whoever planted the box in Tommy's car tossed it in there to make it look like it did. Then again, it's not like Mad wasn't capable of that kind of thing, because the truth is, I could totally see her doing something like that. The girl has a dark side, that's for sure. Along with a very low tolerance for people who try to mess with her, which you did the moment you chose to write those old blog posts about her. She kept a blacklist of people who dissed her. You were on it."

Layla's cheeks reddened in a way that had Aster wishing Ryan hadn't revealed that. They were on the verge of veering wildly off track, and she couldn't afford for the whole thing to blow up into a bickering match.

"Okay, so suppose for a moment that the picture didn't come from the file," Aster said, determined to keep them focused and on point, "but that it did come from Madison. You had access to her house well before we arrived—did you notice anything missing? Anything incriminating like that?"

Ryan narrowed his gaze on hers. "Am I a suspect again?"

Aster closed her eyes and counted to ten. It was impossible to talk rationally with everyone so on edge. "Honestly, at the moment, everyone's a suspect." She forced her gaze on his. "Some more than others. Though, if it makes you feel any better, you've fallen to one of the bottommost positions. I guess I'm just wondering if you noticed Madison's stuff had been disturbed in any way."

"Of course her stuff was disturbed." From the tone of his voice, Ryan seemed annoyed, though he was quickly losing some steam. "The cops ran a thorough search."

"Do you think it's possible that maybe one of the detectives lifted the picture and is responsible for this?" Layla asked, not giving anyone a chance to reply before she shook her head and dismissed the thought with a wave of her hand. "No, never mind. That doesn't even make sense. If they did lift the pic, they wouldn't give it to me and try to bribe me to post it. They'd sell it to the tabloids and retire early on the proceeds."

"What about Emily, her assistant? Or even Christina, her stylist?" Ryan shifted closer to Aster, and for once, Aster didn't shrink away. "Then again, I'm not sure why either one of them would do that to her. They seemed pretty loyal."

"What was she like to work for?" Aster asked, half of her hoping he'd say she was awful, a total diva, a raging bitch, if only to validate some of her growing suspicions about the spoiled celebrity she'd once admired.

"Exacting, demanding." Ryan shrugged. "But that's only because she's a world-class control freak. It was never personal, though. And when she liked something, she was generous with the rewards. Overall, I'd say she was a lot nicer than a lot of celebrities with half the stature."

"Okay, so, now that we've confirmed we have no idea who's behind this"—Aster shook her head and sighed— "let's go over what we do know. Madison is missing, and someone went to the trouble of drugging me and setting me up to look responsible. It's also possible the same person who framed me is trying to smear Madison by trying to scare Layla into posting Madison's old diary entries. Diary entries that pretty much prove Madison lived a very different life than the one in her bio."

"What if—" Layla paused as though weighing whether or not to continue. "I mean, I know I may be reading too much into this and it might be far-fetched, but what's up with those photographs hanging in Madison's entryway?"

Aster squinted as Ryan shifted beside her.

"I mean, they seemed so odd—so incongruous." Looking at Tommy, she explained, "She has these oversize black-and-white prints of run-down interiors, guns resting on broken-down coffee tables with sagging couches in the background. Like, seriously low-rent images, when the rest of her house is super high-end. And for some reason, it's been bugging me for days. It's like—you know how liars always have a tell? Well, what if that's Madison's tell? What if her lie is right out there in the open—hanging on her walls—for anyone to see? Or at least anyone she invites over. What if those pictures are almost like a taunt, or a dare to uncover the truth about her?"

Aster took a moment to consider, then looked at Ryan and said, "Did you ever ask her about them?"

Ryan scrubbed his fingers over the spread of stubble shading his jawline. "I didn't. But then again, our relationship was superficial at best. Our agents set us up, and we both went along. Though we did our best to play the part of perfect boyfriend and girlfriend for each other, in the end, when we finally came clean, it was the first time I realized just how tough she really is. Aside from her delicate, patrician looks, there's absolutely nothing fragile about Madison Brooks. Every now and then I'd get a glimpse of the real, less-refined Madison. But it wasn't often. Mostly she stuck to the role she'd created for herself. But yeah, with that in mind, the pics don't seem all that out of place."

"You say she was tough—but do you think she was tough enough to drain her own blood and fake her own abduction?" Aster said. "Because those needles and collection tubes in Paul's office have me leaning in that direction."

"But again, why would she frame you?" Layla asked. "According to what Ryan just said, she wasn't all that upset about you guys hooking up. If anything, she found a way to use it to her advantage."

"Honestly, I don't know what to think anymore," Ryan said. "Madison is definitely capable of all of it, sure. She may very well be hanging out on some tropical island, laughing at all of us, like we said before. But while I really hate to think she'd be so calculating and vindictive, well, the opposite scenario isn't much better, because it means she really is in deep trouble."

He closed his eyes and sighed, and Aster couldn't help but marvel at how far he'd come from the shallow celebrity she'd first fallen for. Then again, intense public scrutiny and a show cancellation would do that to a person, leaving them with no choice but to grow or fold. After all she'd been through, the old Ryan was someone she couldn't even imagine falling for now. But this new version was well on his way to earning a place in her heart.

"One more thing about Ira, if I may . . ." Tommy went on to tell them all about the paper with the cartoon cat Tommy had seen in Ira's office, followed by the fat cash-filled envelope Ira had instructed him to deliver to James. "I don't know if it means anything, or if it's even connected, but I'm also not sure we should be so quick to call it a coincidence either."

A hush fell over them as they took a moment to contemplate and Aster dumped the rest of the papers onto the table, leaving them for everyone to sort through. Aside from occasional shuffling, the room was otherwise silent.

Until Layla said, "Guys—I think I've got something." She waved an old yellowed newspaper clipping before them. "It's brief—just a piece from the police blotter—but I think it proves Madison wasn't lying about the fire that killed both her parents and left her an orphan."

**West Virginia**—*Two people are dead and two injured, one critically, in a house fire that took place early Thursday morning. The fire was called in shortly after four a.m., and by the time firefighters arrived on the scene, the house was completely engulfed.*

*While the exact cause of the fire remains under investigation, fire officials said they are looking into the possibility of a double homicide and arson.*

*The identities of the victims are being withheld pending notification of family.*

*We'll have more as this story develops.*

"It says two are injured." Ryan frowned. "Madison was for sure one of them, but who was the other?"

"Did she have a sister or brother?" Aster sipped from her water.

"Not that she ever mentioned, though of course that doesn't mean anything. She wasn't big on sharing. And what's this about a double homicide? Does that mean the fire was intentionally set in order to cover the crime?"

"This is giving me the creeps." Aster pulled a baby alpaca throw from the arm of the couch and wrapped it around herself.

"Is there anything else? Any follow-up articles?" Tommy asked.

Layla flipped quickly through the stack. "Not that I can see, though I'm not sure it matters. I mean, maybe it has nothing to do with Madison."

"Oh, it's about Madison," Ryan said. "It's from a West Virginia paper, and we've already discovered that's where she's really from, thanks to those journal entries."

"So, what do we do—run a Google search on West Virginia trailer park fires dating back to what—2006?" Aster asked.

"Doesn't say anything about a trailer park," Layla

snapped. "In fact, you may not know this, but there's a whole world that exists outside of swanky gated communities and luxury condos, and it's not just relegated to trailer parks. In fact, it's how most people live."

Aster stared at her, speechless, watching as Layla sprang angrily from the couch and went to stand before the window.

"You okay?" Tommy called after her. Though despite his concern, Layla ignored him and focused on her phone.

Were they a couple? Aster's gaze darted between them. However they chose to define it, something was going on between them. As long as it didn't interfere with the work they were all trying to accomplish, she figured it was none of her business.

It'd been a long, crazy night and the sun would be coming up soon. Aster was feeling tired and cranky, and the last thing she needed was to get worked up over one of Layla's signature snarky comments. Sure, she'd made an assumption, but it was based on Layla's own theory regarding the photographs in Madison's house. Though Layla was so incensed, Aster decided to let it go. No point in antagonizing her more.

"What was the name of that office building you guys were at earlier?" Layla looked up from her cell to focus on Aster and Ryan.

Aster squinted, unable to recall, as Ryan said, "Uh, I

don't know—something like Acacia Business Park, maybe?"

Layla held up her phone to show a picture of what appeared to be a burning building.

"Apparently, there was an explosion," she said. "The whole thing is in flames."

Instinctively, Aster reached for the gold-and-diamond hamsa pendant, only it was no longer there.

"Omigod! Oh no!" She jumped from the couch and checked where she'd been sitting. Then, upending the cushion, she checked under there too. Her hand clutching uselessly at her neck, her mind fiercely rewound to where she might've left it. "My necklace! I think I lost it—it's gone!"

"Is it sentimental?" Ryan asked, a confused look on his face.

Layla said, "I know you're fond of it, but as far as good luck charms go, it didn't seem to be working."

Aster shook her head. Overcome with panic, she struggled to push the words past her lips. "I think it might be in that office! I think it fell off when Ryan pulled me to the ground when that security guard came to the window! We have to go back—we have to go get it!"

"Aster, we can't." Ryan reached for her hand and clasped it firmly in his. He spoke slowly, calmly, like one does to a child. "The building's on fire—it's swarming with cops and firefighters. Besides, there's no way to know if it fell off there. You could've lost it anywhere. When was the last time you noticed you had it?"

Aster sank to the floor and buried her face in her hands. A second later, Ryan was kneeling beside her, pulling her into his arms. She wanted so badly to be comforted, but the gnawing pit in her stomach told her she was doomed. With all the crimes she'd been falsely accused of—all the manipulated evidence pitted against her—she could hardly believe she'd just dealt herself a very real, possibly fatal blow. "I don't know," she whispered into his shoulder. "I can't remember."

He ran a soothing hand over her hair. "It's okay," he promised. "Everything will be fine. There's no need to panic. I'm sure it'll show up eventually."

"I'll check the backseat of my car when I leave," Tommy offered.

Aster untangled herself from Ryan's arms and swiped a hand over her cheeks. "Okay," she said, forcing herself to breathe, forcing herself to believe that Ryan was right, she was overreacting, and it would all be okay.

Outside the window, a new day was dawning. Maybe, just maybe, this one would work in her favor.

# THIRTY-ONE

# WALKASHAME

Trena Moretti propped a pile of pillows behind her head and watched as James walked from the bed to the bathroom. As far as men went, James was as fine a specimen as they came, his body so finely honed it was a thing of beauty to see. And Trena enjoyed looking as much as James enjoyed being looked at.

She ran her hands over her skin and kicked her legs out before her, confident she looked as good as she felt. Between her interview with Ira, which had been picked up by news outlets across the globe, and the recent airing of her exclusive televised interview with Aster Amirpour, which had aired well before most of the world even realized Aster was out on bail, Trena found herself suddenly sought after by just about every news station that mattered, including those that'd once rejected her.

Her phone buzzed from the nightstand where she'd

placed it, but Trena opted to ignore it. A journalist was rarely off duty, but for the moment anyway, her only plan was to revel in the glow of her recent bout of success. Last night, for the first time since she'd arrived in LA, she'd stood among the glittering masses and felt at home.

Normally, a glitzy product launch was exactly the kind of invitation she'd snub. Her party-going days were well behind her, not to mention how she found that sort of commercial hype especially annoying. But Ira Redman's party was not to be missed. While it wasn't exactly the Met Ball, there was no doubt it would be widely photographed and endlessly talked about. She also had Ira to thank for the sudden uptick in her star meter. And then there was the matter of the guest list—comprising the hottest celebrities, many of them members of Madison's circle. And the very fact that James would be there as well had given Trena something to look forward to.

While seducing him hadn't been nearly as easy as she'd assumed, it didn't take long to determine that the key to getting with James was to let him think it was entirely his idea, and not hers. Clearly he was a guy who enjoyed the chase, and after an initial reluctance, Trena gladly gave up the reins and let him believe he was in charge.

By the time the lights had gone out, the deal was well on its way to being sealed. The heat between them was incendiary—the only thing left to determine was how soon and where. While there were plenty of bedrooms to choose from, Trena was too discreet for a semipublic hookup. So when the lights came back on about fifteen minutes later, she simply looked him in the eye and said she should probably head home. Next thing she knew, he'd invited her back to his place, and the rest was . . . Trena grinned to herself . . . the rest was worthy of remembering next time she found herself feeling lonely and unloved.

"I'm gonna shower." James peeked his gorgeous shaved head around the corner. "Care to join me?"

Trena grinned and rubbed one long leg against the other. "Sure, let me know when you've got the water good and hot."

James laughed and disappeared back inside, and the next thing Trena heard was the sound of water hitting the marble tiles and the whoosh of a shower door opening and closing. Then she sprang into action, wasting no time fishing his cell out of the back pocket of the jeans he'd dropped on the floor the night before.

Of course the screen was locked, which meant she wouldn't get very far. Still, there was a string of partial text messages that were visible, one of them mentioning something about a building that had exploded in the middle of the night.

Trena frowned. Why would James be getting a text about a burning building? What connection could there possibly be? Was he somehow involved?

She glanced around the well-appointed room, taking in the king-size bed with its black leather tufted panels and gray sateen sheets, the ornate silver table lamps resting on top of matching charcoal-stained sand-blasted night tables, the cream-colored flokati rug at her feet. The room was sexy, sophisticated, decorated with an eye to high-end design, and the building he lived in was far nicer than hers. Also, if she remembered correctly, he drove a customized Cadillac CTS-V coupe. All of which left her to wonder, how did he afford it?

What sort of odd jobs did he do on the side?

"You coming, babe?" he called, his voice competing with what sounded like a powerful set of showerheads.

She swallowed hard, her hand shaking ever so slightly, and said, "Actually, I . . . think I'll take a rain check. . . ."

Quickly, before he could get suspicious and catch her in the act, she snapped a pic of James's cell phone screen with her own, and was just replacing his phone when she found him standing dripping in the doorway. His muscled physique was slick, wet, and coiled for action.

"What's going on?" He kept his voice light, but his gaze was dark and unkind.

She pretended she was merely folding his pants, and carefully placed them at the foot of the bed. "You should be careful where you leave these." She laughed, a high, false note she was sure he would see right through. "I just tripped over them. Nearly knocked myself out."

He remained dripping onto the rug, his gaze so studied, so intense, she cringed under its glare.

"I don't like snoops." His voice was quiet, calm, and loaded with menace.

Trena fought to keep from shaking as she wiggled her dress over her hips and said, "Who does?" She moved in an exaggerated way, hoping to distract him, all too aware of the reality of the situation she found herself in—half-naked, vulnerable, and at his absolute mercy. "So how about I promise not to stalk you on Facebook or Twitter and you do the same?" She forced herself to approach him, turning her back as she looked over her shoulder and murmured, "Zip me?"

It was probably the most dangerous, foolish move she could make. Never turn your back on the ocean, bears, and shifty men who are onto you. And yet she needed him to think she had nothing to fear, that she hadn't crossed the very line he suspected her of crossing.

She sucked in a breath as she felt the zipper slowly climb its way to her neck. He paused at the top, his breath hot on her flesh, his hands kneading the skin at her nape, until his fingers gently circled to the front and he pressed the tips tightly together.

"Be careful out there." His lips nipped at her ear, as his

body pressed hard against hers. His fingers tightened for an agonizing moment, before he finally released and nudged her away.

"You too," she croaked. Hurriedly fishing around for her shoes, her purse, she waved a shaky good-bye and found her way out of the apartment.

Barefoot, she raced down the hall and had just rung for the elevator when her phone buzzed in her purse. Glancing at the screen, she saw it was from her source at the LAPD.

Madison B's car found outside office building that burned.

Was it the same office building she'd read about on James's phone? Impatiently, she punched the call button again, desperate to flee, all the while reminding herself that it was hot, they were in the middle of a drought, the Santa Ana winds were at gale force, and fire season had been officially declared one month before. Which meant it wasn't at all out of the question to think there had been more than one office park that had burned over the course of the night, and yet . . . She checked the pic she'd taken of James's text. There was no name attached—just an odd series of numbers that provided no clue to his source, probably sent from a burner phone.

Had the rest of the text, the part she couldn't view, made mention of Madison's car being found?

And if so, why was James receiving a message like that?

He wasn't press, wasn't an investigator. He had nothing

to do with any of it—or did he?

From somewhere down the hall Trena heard the click of a knob being turned, a lock disengaging, followed by the prolonged creak of a door slowly opening.

Deciding not to stick around long enough to see whether or not it was James, Trena raced for the stairs and fled from the building as though it was on fire.

# THIRTY-TWO

# VICTIM OF LOVE

Mateo slumped over his breakfast and stared blearily at his phone as he contemplated what to do about Layla.

Technically, he wasn't required to do anything. Though they'd pretended they were "taking a break," they'd both known at the time there was no going back.

And yet, the memory of the hurt and angry look on her face after seeing him with Heather left him feeling awful, like he needed to explain.

Back when they'd first met, he'd thought Layla was the most authentic girl he'd ever known, and her brutal honesty was one of the things he'd loved most about her. Turned out she'd lied about more than just kissing Tommy. She'd also lied about interviewing for the job at Unrivaled, and her plan to go to journalism school in New York without him.

In the end, she wasn't really all that different from anyone else. She lied when it suited her, in order to spare another's feelings, or when the lie made her seem like a better person than she actually was.

And yet, the sting in Layla's eyes was not an image he could easily shake. It wasn't until much later that he saw the text that she'd sent, and by then, the damage was done and it was too late to reply.

He ran a hand through his hair, took another half-hearted bite of his eggs, then got up from the table and dumped the rest down the drain. His appetite was gone, he had a list of things to do, and yet he wouldn't be able to concentrate on any of it until he somehow made amends with the girl who'd once meant the entire world to him.

Can we talk?

He pushed Send before he could overthink it, then busied himself with washing the dishes to distract himself from the gnawing fear that she wouldn't respond.

When the reply did finally come, it read:

Not necessary.

"Shit," he mumbled, at the same time his mother walked in.

"Watch your language." She patted his shoulder and ruffled his hair before retrieving a clean dish towel from the drawer and drying the stack of plates he'd left to drain on the rack.

"Leave it. I'll get it," he told her, debating whether he

should text Layla back and try to convince her.

"I thought you had to work today." His mother glanced at him from over her shoulder. She looked tired, worn. Her gray roots were beginning to show, and there was a fresh set of lines etched across her brow, along with a sad tilt to her brown eyes. She'd faced more grief than any mother rightfully should, and it made Mateo's heart ache, wishing he could somehow erase all her pain and set the world right once again.

"Mom, please." He swiped the dish towel out of her hands and gently pushed her aside. "Go on, say hello to Father Gregorio. I'm going to swing by the hospital to visit Valentina."

"He always asks about you. Wonders when you'll come back to church."

"I know, I know," Mateo mumbled, watching as his mother grabbed her purse and keys and wiped the sheen of sweat from her brow. Life without an air conditioner was taking a toll, and the unrelenting summer heat showed absolutely no signs of abating.

She'd reached the door when she turned back to say, "It was just on the news that they found that poor girl's car."

Mateo squinted. He had no idea what she was getting at.

"The actress," she said, reading his face.

"Where?" Mateo dutifully asked. His mother never showed any interest in Hollywood, but then again, the

Madison story had transcended the tabloids and taken on a life of its own. He waited, not entirely interested in the answer. His mind was still caught on Layla, trying to decipher whether she'd responded in anger or if she really had meant what she'd said.

"Some office park burned down and they found her car parked outside. They're investigating for arson. Apparently, a male and female were seen running from the scene."

Suddenly she had Mateo's full attention. "Were they able to identify them?"

His mother shook her head, made the sign of the cross, and kissed her son on the forehead. "You're eighteen now, so I can't tell you what to do, not that I ever could." The smile she flashed him was fleeting. "That's a crazy world you're getting involved in. Please be careful," she said. "I've already lost one son. I won't lose another."

Her words took Mateo by surprise, though in retrospect he realized they shouldn't have. Despite his continued assurances that everything he was doing, he was doing to help the family, she couldn't keep from worrying about him.

"*Mamá,* please." He cupped a hand to each cheek, startled by just how small and fragile she seemed. "I'm here and I'll continue to be here. I have no interest in playing a bigger part in that world than I already am. I can be in it, but not of it, you know."

His words seemed to appease her, and once she was

gone, he finished putting away the dishes, then grabbed his own set of keys. It was Sunday morning, which meant there were a myriad of places Layla might be, but he decided to start at the top of the list, and he headed for her favorite coffee haunt on Abbot Kinney Boulevard.

He caught her leaving just as he arrived, an extra-large coffee cup clutched in one hand, car keys fisted in the other.

"Am I really that predictable?" Layla stopped in the middle of the sidewalk, forcing people to move around her, as she tilted her chin toward him.

Her hair was tousled, her face makeup free, she wore a tight white tank top, a pair of faded old cutoffs with a red plaid flannel shirt tied at her waist, and black rubber flip-flops, and at that moment she looked so insanely beautiful it took all his will not to pull her into his arms, hit rewind, and pick up where they'd left off before Ira Redman's contest upended their lives.

Instead, he settled for saying, "Sorry for the ambush. I just really had to see you."

It was the wrong thing to say, because the next thing he knew, she'd shaken her head and was walking away.

"I really don't want to hear about it," she called over her shoulder as he raced to keep up. "You're free to hook up with whoever you want."

"It's not what you think," he said, staring in disbelief

when she stopped beside a black BMW as though it was hers.

From the looks of her grim lips and narrowed eyes, she wasn't buying it despite it being true. After all the awkwardness between Heather and Layla, Mateo had ordered himself an Uber and found his way home. And while Heather hadn't exactly applauded his decision to leave, in the end, she let him go without a fuss.

Layla sipped her coffee and lowered her sunglasses onto her nose, adding yet another barrier for him to work through.

"Do you seriously want to do this?" she said. "Because I don't. I don't want to keep score of each other's conquests. There's no point. Your life is yours to live however you best see fit. You don't owe me anything. And you certainly don't owe me an explanation for kissing Heather Rollins."

"I know," he said quietly. And maybe that was part of the problem. At first kissing Heather had felt like some kind of vindication for Layla's kissing Tommy, and he'd enjoyed it, there was no point denying it. But later, when it was over, it left him feeling strangely off-kilter and confused about what it was he really wanted out of life. "Listen . . ." Knowing he was seconds from losing her, he reached toward her, then watched as his hand fell away when Layla turned and slid behind the wheel of the car. "I just—" He shook his head, ran a hand through his hair, and started again. "Valentina's sick, and I just thought . . . I thought you should know that."

"Where is she?" Layla propped her glasses onto her head, her gray-blue eyes searching his.

"Well, I'm hoping to get her transferred to another hospital today, but . . ."

"She's in the hospital?" Her jaw dropped, as she shifted the car into drive. "So what are you waiting for?" she shouted. "Get in!"

A moment later, he was buckling his seat belt and settling in beside her as Layla sped down the street.

# THIRTY-THREE

# ENTER SANDMAN

This time, when dawn arrived, Madison was ready.

She'd spent weeks going over her plan, and though it was far from foolproof, she no longer had the luxury of delaying. Though she couldn't put her finger on it, something told her that change was in the air. Whoever had been holding her captive would eventually grow bored with the routine they'd established, and it was anyone's guess what they'd do once that happened.

Would they kill her?

Madison didn't plan to stick around long enough to find out.

A quick peek in one of the mirrors reflected back the image of a grimy, scruffy, bedraggled girl with nothing to lose, and it was entirely true. She'd gone along and played the victim too long, and where had that gotten her?

Well, soon all that would end. She had every intention of fighting her way out, or she would die trying.

For the past week, she'd forced down all her meals and endured vigorous workouts that would rival even the most brutal cross-fit class. Though she was far from the top of her game, she felt capable and strong and it would have to suffice.

A few minutes before sunrise, she wrapped her cashmere shawl tightly around her hand, arced her Gucci sandal back behind her ear, and rammed her arm forward. Punching the spiked heel straight toward a long splice of mirror, she caught a glimpse of her wild eyes and determined face as the glass shattered all around her and splintered to the floor.

With no time to waste, she picked up a wide jagged piece, wrapped one edge in her shawl to avoid cutting herself, and swept the rest out of the way. Then, with her body pressed flush against the door, she stood back and waited.

A trickle of sweat rolled down her neck as her breath flared in her cheeks. Wasn't much longer before the lights would switch on and her captor would come, but when they tried to thrust her meal through the slot, the door would be stuck.

The move was a risky one, but it was all she had.

Her regular three-square-a-day schedule indicated they were intent on keeping her alive—at least for now, anyway. But what if she'd fooled them into thinking she'd given up?

That she'd forfeited the fight and was calling for her own personal hunger strike?

At that point, they'd be forced to come inside and check on her, and that was when she planned to strike.

That was when she'd surprise them at the door and stab them with the shard of broken mirror if necessary. Whatever it took to get the hell out of there.

Glancing between the watch on her wrist and the fluorescent light box overhead, she waited for the usual daily routine to begin.

Only it was already one minute past seven and the room was still dark, no one had come. And just like that, Madison's thoughts darkened too.

What if something had happened to her captor?

And what if they were the only one who knew where she was?

She would die in here—slowly starving to death.

It was entirely possible she'd never be found.

She shook the thought away, refusing to entertain it. She needed to stay focused. Needed to stay strong, think positive thoughts, and stick with the plan, no matter how flimsy it appeared on the surface.

Twelve minutes past the hour she was losing the battle against total despair. Her body sagged with defeat, her head hung low, as the sting of hopelessness burned deep in her throat. How had she come so far, risen so high, only to end up filthy, alone, and forgotten?

She sank to the ground. It was over. She'd waited too long, and now she would die with no one ever knowing the truth of what had really happened to her or who was responsible for abducting her.

Her list of unknown suspects was infinite.

Her list of known suspects was comparatively shorter.

Aster, Ryan, Layla, Ira, James, Paul, even Tommy—she couldn't afford the luxury of ruling anyone out. Though she had a hard time believing Tommy was behind it. He was too starstruck, too in awe of her, to pull something like that. Still, maybe kissing him had been a mistake. She'd let down her guard and allowed herself to relax and allow her West Virginia accent to slip through. Had Tommy mistaken the moment of vulnerability for weakness? And because of it, had he decided to follow her, kidnap her, and keep her locked up in this stinky, filthy, eight-by-ten cell? And if so, to what end?

Or maybe it wasn't Tommy at all. Maybe while she'd been making her plans, Ryan and Aster had been busy making their own. Had she fooled herself into thinking she was in charge, when all the while they'd been plotting against her?

And what about Layla? Was this some messed-up revenge plot she'd hatched because of that stupid restraining order Paul served her? It seemed like such a disproportionate act, but from what she'd seen, the girl had enough of a dark side, Madison would be a fool to rule her out.

Even Ira—greedy, ruthless, vainglorious Ira. Was it possible he was involved—maybe even conspiring with James? Either way, Madison had no doubt Ira was playing it up in the press. A star of her caliber disappearing from one of his clubs would ensure his place in the tabloid news cycle for many years to come.

But Paul . . . Madison shook her head in denial. She refused to believe it. Paul was the keeper of her secrets—the only one who knew the truth of her past. Together they'd conspired to turn small-time trailer-park MaryDella into big-time Hollywood star Madison. Together they'd covered up evidence that, if discovered, would've led her down an entirely different path. It couldn't be Paul. He would never do that to her. But, in the event that it was, then she truly was doomed. There wasn't a single person on the planet who would ever root for her as hard as he did. If he'd decided to turn on her now, then she literally didn't have a single real friend left in the world.

Truth was, it could be any of them or none of them. Hell, it could even be that annoying journalist Trena Moretti. Maybe she'd gotten so tired of hunting down stories that she decided to create one of her own.

At the moment, all that mattered was getting out of this place. Once that was behind her, then Madison could start the process of hunting down those responsible and making them pay in ways they'd never see coming.

The screech of scraping metal dragged her away from her thoughts and back to the present, as Madison rose and sprang into position.

The lights still hadn't come on, and no one even tried to open the slot, but the next thing she knew, the door flew open and Madison rushed toward the faceless dark figure that stood in the entry, haloed by light.

The shard of mirror clutched in her fist, she brought it down hard on the first bit of flesh she could find.

"*Fuck!*" The scream seemed to reverberate throughout the small space, but the competing sound of Madison's heart slamming hard in her chest and the rush of blood pounding in her ears made it impossible to discern if her captor was male or female.

The important thing was, her plan had worked.

Madison was just inches away from escape.

Spotting an opening, she raced toward the light.

She took one step. Then another. The next one would free her.

Her foot hit the ground just as the other one lifted. Her muscles coiled, about to propel her toward safety, when she felt a sharp, stinging jab at her thigh and the next thing she knew she was stumbling, falling, spiraling headfirst into a world of permanent midnight.

# THIRTY-FOUR

# CALLING ALL ANGELS

Layla had acted impulsively. Hadn't even considered the fact that she wasn't a Luna, which also meant she wasn't allowed to see Valentina. She'd just finished rubbing antibacterial gel onto her hands and adjusted her mask, when the nurse promptly stopped her from entering.

"I'm sorry," she said. "Immediate family only."

Layla looked at Mateo, tempted to lie and say they were siblings, cousins, husband and wife, but the skeptical nurse had heard it all before and was already turning her away.

"The waiting room is down the hall," she called. "You can wait for Mateo there."

"This is exactly why I want to move her." Mateo scowled at the nurse's retreating form. "Valentina needs to be around people who care, whether or not they're related."

"I doubt it will be any different wherever you go, and

I'm sure they have their reasons." Layla pulled off her mask, rolled it into a ball, and tossed it into the trash. "Listen, don't mind me. Go see your little sis, and tell her I said hello. Take as long as you need."

Mateo shot her an incredulous look. "That's it? Since when do you give up so easily and cave to the rules?"

A moment later, Layla was donning a new mask, pulling on a fresh set of gloves, and following Mateo inside to where his little sister had fallen asleep watching TV.

They settled into the two available chairs and stared blankly at the screen. While the Nickelodeon channel wouldn't have been Layla's first choice, it was better than some depressing news station where the reporters gleefully chronicled all the various ways humanity was going to hell. The pediatric oncology wing was depressing enough on its own; she didn't need further proof of just how bleak the world really was.

Surprisingly, the canned laugh track proved to be oddly soothing, and Layla spent a few blissfully empty minutes staring mindlessly at the show unfolding before her.

Layla had the worst poker face of anyone she knew, and so she'd been secretly relieved to find Valentina asleep. She needed a moment to adjust to the sight of Mateo's little sister—a perennially upbeat and happy girl who was always bursting with energy—looking so sickly and pale.

God, she couldn't even remember the last time she'd seen Valentina. She'd blown off her last birthday party with the excuse of needing to focus on winning the Unrivaled contest, which, looking back, she'd never really stood a chance at. Then again, she could see all sorts of things now that she'd refused to acknowledge back then. Hindsight truly was a bitch.

The show faded to commercial, and Layla scrolled through her Twitter and Facebook feeds, though she didn't bother with checking her Instagram or Snapchat accounts, having abandoned them as soon as she became ensnared in the Madison fiasco. She was tired of people hijacking her personal pics and using them for derogatory memes that had quickly gone viral.

She skimmed through her emails, half expecting to see one from Emerson chewing her out for leaving the launch party early, but finding that wasn't the case, she figured he was holding out for Monday. She was just about to click over to her blog when she noticed an unsent message sitting in her drafts folder—the sight of which gave her pause.

It had been a hectic few weeks, but Layla couldn't remember drafting a single email she hadn't yet sent.

Clicking on the folder, she blinked in confusion when she found an email message addressed to her that she definitely hadn't written.

> I know you think you're running the show
> But here's a tip you really should know
> It's all too easy for me to hack your life

And the things I'll do will cut like a knife

If you're thinking of alerting the cops

Then let me remind you, I'm prepared to pull out all the stops

If you think you should forward this message to someone
    who cares

Let me assure you, I'll unleash some big scares

While you don't see me, I can see you

And I'm telling you now, here's what you're going to do

Very soon a surprise will appear

It's your job to claim it without causing too many tears

Somewhere deep inside awaits yet another surprise I know
    you'll enjoy

Either way, it's time you do what I say, cuz I'm done playing
    coy.

Just after reading the message, Layla watched as it vanished from her screen and disappeared from both her drafts and trash folders as well.

Someone was watching her, electronically, remotely, up close and personal, or most likely, all of the above.

The thought caused Layla to spring from her chair so quickly it slammed back against the wall and caused Valentina to wake with a start.

"Layla?" Valentina's brown eyes went wide as she struggled to sit up in bed.

"Sorry. I'm so sorry," Layla whispered, feeling like an

idiot as she watched Mateo rush to his sister's bedside.

"Are you guys back together?"

The sight of Valentina's pale and drawn face lighting up at the thought of them reuniting almost convinced Layla to lie and say that they were. She loved the kid so much Layla would do anything for her, but even though it broke her heart to tell Valentina the truth, Layla couldn't bear to lie to her.

Layla shook her head. Then, realizing she was still clutching her phone to her chest, she placed it gently onto her chair and joined Mateo at Valentina's bedside. "But we're still good friends." She swallowed hard. *Good* friends. Why'd she feel the need to qualify it? Maybe the fact that they were standing there together proved it wasn't a total lie, but things between them were still strained enough that it felt like a stretch.

Valentina granted them each a hard stare. "Please. You sound like a celebrity press release." Adopting her version of an adult voice, she went on to say, "We've decided to end our relationship. This is a very painful decision, but we remain fully committed as friends. We ask that you respect our privacy during this difficult time." She rolled her eyes and went on to add, "RIP Mayla."

"You've been reading way too many tabloids in here." Mateo frowned.

At the same time, Layla asked, "Who's Mayla?"

"You." Valentina wagged a finger between them. "You're Mayla. Only not anymore." Her sad puppy-eyes look tugged at Layla's heart. "Just because you got tired of my brother doesn't mean you can't still come see me, you know? I thought we were friends."

"We *are* friends," Layla said. "Actually, no. We go deeper than that. I consider you family." She was barely able to eke out the words. As an only child, Layla considered Valentina the little sister she never had. But the girl was right. Layla really had abandoned her. And sadly, it began long before she and Mateo broke up. "Also, just so you know, I'm not tired of your brother. He's a . . ." She needed a moment to ward off the sob that threatened from the base of her throat. "He's a really great guy."

"And yet, you still broke up."

"It's complicated," Mateo interjected, clearly uncomfortable with the direction the conversation had taken. "Life is complicated."

Valentina shook her head and stared stubbornly at the TV. "I don't believe that. Life is easy. It's all about breathing, and doing, and making a series of choices that lead you to the next step. It's people who muck it all up by losing focus, creating drama, and making it more difficult than it needs to be."

"When'd you get so wise?" Layla asked.

"I read a lot of tabloids." Valentina laughed.

Though Layla laughed with her, she couldn't help but wonder if Valentina was right. Like her brother, she had a firm grasp on the things that mattered most—friends, family, and home. While Layla was out chasing dragons and myths and the sort of things that led one farther and farther from home, without any real proof they even existed.

And yet, she couldn't imagine living any other way. Maybe contentment was for other people, not her. Maybe it just wasn't part of her genetic makeup. All she knew for sure was that while she'd always love Mateo and his little sister, and would always be there for them in whatever way they might need, at her core she was guided by a restless soul, willing to chase her dreams all the way to the edge of the world if that was what it took.

And then, of course, there was the issue of Tommy. But the thought left her feeling so disloyal she marched it quickly out of her mind.

"Are you keeping up with your homework?" Mateo asked. "Do you need any help?"

"Homework?" Layla feigned like she was aghast. "They're making you do homework in here?"

Valentina shrugged good-naturedly. "It was my choice. I didn't want to get too far behind. Besides, it didn't take long for the thrill of watching TV all day to wear off."

Layla was about to respond, when the same nurse who'd forbidden her from entering barged into the room, took one look at Layla, and said, "I'm going to pretend you're not here."

"What, her?" Valentina nodded at Layla. "She's my first cousin once removed."

"Yeah, yeah." The nurse deposited a beautifully wrapped package on the bed and said, "Seems you have a secret admirer. There's no card attached."

That was all it took to send Layla's pulse rocketing. But shy of snatching the box from Valentina's fingers, which she hadn't completely ruled out, she didn't know what else to do but stand back and wait to see what happened next.

Would the box contain another diary entry?

Would she be forced to leap on top of the poor sick child and wrench it free before Valentina could see the horrible thing it most likely contained?

With a frantically beating heart, Layla watched Valentina work through the layer of wrapping paper and tape to reveal a plain brown box underneath that bore no identifiable markings of any kind. Though Layla had no idea what it was, she knew without a doubt it wasn't good. They'd reached the part of the poem where she was supposed to *claim it without causing too many tears*. And she needed to act fast.

She rubbed her lips together, wondering how best to handle it. With the nurse and Mateo both watching, her position was an awkward one.

Valentina had just started opening the box when Mateo

moved in to help, but Layla, in a rush, beat him to it.

"Here, let me!" Fingers trembling, she ran a nail under the tape, unfolded the flaps, and held her breath in her cheeks as she looked inside. It was a bear. An adorable stuffed bear—the kind with hinged arms and legs and soft, plushy fur.

"Uh, are you going to let me see it?" Valentina asked, as Layla became aware that everyone was now staring at her.

"Yes. Um, of course!" Trying to sound cheery and upbeat, which was always a stretch even on a good day, she freed it from the box and gave it a quick but thorough inspection before Valentina pretty much demanded she hand it over.

Layla's stomach churned. She watched Valentina grin as she lifted its arms, patted its fur, and made its legs kick back and forth. Would she be forced to wait for the nurse to leave and Valentina to fall back asleep so she could slice it open and get to the surprise that was waiting for her?

She was contemplating doing exactly that, when her gaze dropped to the bottom of the box and she saw an envelope bearing her name in the familiar curlicue script.

*Somewhere deep inside awaits yet another surprise . . .* Did that refer to the message hidden deep inside the box, as opposed to something far more sinister lurking deep inside the bear? Layla could only hope.

Valentina continued to play with the bear. It was amazing how one moment she was like some ageless sage—a dispenser of wisdom—and the next, an average ten-year-old girl who'd received a lovely new toy from a secret admirer.

"Who do you think sent it?" Valentina asked, barely able to take her eyes off it.

"Probably some cute boy in your class who misses you and wants you to get well soon," Layla said, laughing when Valentina responded by crinkling her nose in distaste.

At that moment, Layla wanted nothing more than to place Valentina in a bubble and keep her safe from the world.

But the world was patient, and in the end, there was no good way to avoid it.

"I think that's enough excitement for one day," the nurse said, giving Mateo and Layla each a stern look.

"Don't be a stranger," Valentina said as they were preparing to leave.

Layla looked from the bear to Valentina, hoping she'd done the right thing by letting her have it. But what choice did she have?

"I won't," Layla promised, shooting a questioning look toward the nurse, who refused to respond either way.

With the door closed behind them, Layla tossed the box in the bin, shoved the envelope in her bag, and told Mateo to hurry.

# THIRTY-FIVE

# WATCHING THE DETECTIVES

## BEAUTIFUL IDOLS

### Through the Looking Glass

By Layla Harrison

Ever look at the dark side of a mirror?

When you were a kid, did you ever flip it over to see how it worked?

Were you surprised to learn your reflection was the result of nothing more than a thin sheet of glass with a metallic backing?

And if so, did its magic dim just the tiniest bit?

Maybe that was just me, but I do believe celebrity works in much the same way.

When a Hollywood starlet first appears on the scene, they're like the shiny surface of the mirror, all gleaming and bright. While we, as potential haters or fans, are like the dingy metallic backing, reflecting all sorts of attributes the celebrity may or may not deserve.

Which brings me to Madison Brooks.

Since she disappeared, there's been an outpouring of emotion and wild proclamations of love—all of which begs the question:

Just how much do we really know about Madison?

Are the Princess Di and Mother Teresa comparisons (a notion yours truly finds completely absurd) actually valid?

As it turns out, we don't know nearly as much about Madison as we think.

And while you may hate me for what I'm about to do next—in fact, I'm counting on the fact that you will—over the course of the next several weeks, I double-dare you not to follow this feed.

So, without further ado, I present to you the first installment of Madison Brooks's journal.

Make of it what you will, but please note that I did not make this up, this is not a work of fiction, and it came to me via a reliable source.

As always, feel free to exit through the comments section on your way out.

*October 5, 2012*

*I'm so over it!!!!*

*So over absolutely EVERYTHING!*

*Including my so-called friends, my family, my stupid fake boyfriend, but mostly, this stuffy, boring, stick-up-its-ass town.*

☹

*UGH! I feel like I'm dying here, suffocating, drowning—and it's time to make a move and get the hell out before these uptight, small-town morons take me down with them.*

*People like to tell me how grateful I should be. Constantly reminding me of how lots of kids who find themselves orphaned at my age end up staying that way until they age out of the system and are forced to move on to dead-end jobs, multiple divorces, jail sentences, drug addictions, unplanned pregnancies, and whatever bleak clichéd scenarios those self-righteous judgmental assholes who don't even know what real hardship is can drum up on short notice.*

*Whatever.*

*I mean, yah, so my parents agreed to raise me—big fuckin' deal. Fact is, they benefited from the arrangement in ways they'd be smart to never reveal. But of course they won't hesitate to* take all the credit once I'm famous. Just watch!

Totally pathetic but completely true.

And unfortunately, I'll have no choice but to go along with whatever bullshit story they unearth for the press about all the heartwarming times we all shared.

But let's make one thing clear: when my face is on every magazine cover and every billboard—when I'm the most sought-after actress/singer/performer in the world—the only one truly responsible for helping me get there is P.

If it wasn't for him fabricating my past and arranging my present, I'm not sure where I would be.

The Ghost saved me—spared me from a future too horrible to contemplate. One much worse than the scenario above.

I guess you could say I owe him my life.

Then again, he owes me his too.

Turns out, justice isn't quite so black and white like most people think. There are lots of varying shades, and it's better not left to chance.

And now, because of the choices we made—because of the way P went out on a limb for me and put his whole life on the line—our destinies are forever entwined. If I ever go down, he's going down with me. Though I'm pretty sure that only works one way. Because if P goes down first, he'll go down alone. And he'll take all my secrets with him as well. He already proved it six years ago when he made a choice to save me. Which is why I guess, in a lot of ways, I consider him my real father.

Anyway, tomorrow is the day I board the bus to LA and never look back.

P says he'll handle my parents, all I have to do is write the note he already dictated.

At first I'll stay with him until I'm old enough to get my driver's license. Once that's done, he'll help me score a sweet apartment I'll have all to myself!

Luckily, P knows a lot of people—the influential kind that can help kick-start my dreams so I can get on with my life.

I guess I should be feeling more reflective, or melancholy, or something, to be ending the life I've lived all these years. But the truth is, tomorrow can't come quickly enough. I've been waiting for this moment since the day I was born.

Though I guess I might end up missing X just the tiniest bit. I mean, he was my first after all!

*(Just not my first-first like he thinks ☺). Though he is the first person I sort of found myself kind of caring about.*

*Which is another reason why it's time to move on. I can't waste my time on small-time boys with minuscule dreams and no future to speak of.*

*Besides, I'm sure it won't be all that hard to move on.*

*It's crazy to think how next time I write in here, I'll be living an entirely different life!*

Tommy stared at the screen long after he'd finished scrolling down it. Yeah, Madison's diary entry was juicy—in an ambitious, starry-eyed, teenage-girl way. And it also helped to prove their theory that Madison was hiding some deep, dark secrets and that Paul, aka the Ghost, aka her fixer, had, for whatever reason, buried them for her. Still, he hoped Layla wasn't seriously planning to post it. Though the threats she received seemed serious enough, he feared that caving in to the sender's demands would only cause them to escalate. After all, blackmailers rarely went away quietly.

But Layla refused to involve the police, and it wasn't like he blamed her. After Larsen had pulled them over for no other reason than to flex his muscle and show them who was boss, he agreed they couldn't be trusted. Still, there had to be some other way to handle it—someone who could help make it all go away. Question was who?

He rubbed at his eyes, having spent the bulk of the morning trying to overcome some major sleep deprivation, thanks to the crazy events of the previous night, while fielding constant texts and phone calls from Malina, who'd booked him for a long list of meetings that would take up the better part of the upcoming week.

"And what about my job working for Ira?" he'd said, voice groggy and partially muffled by his pillow.

"Quit," she'd replied, as though he was in any position to do that.

While it was undeniably tempting, Tommy was smart enough to know that one semi-successful gig did not a rock star make. Quitting his real job before things truly took off for him wasn't something he could even consider. For now, his rock god dreams were primarily fueled by speculation and wishful thinking. The future was hopeful, but at the moment, it ended with a question mark, not a period.

Though when it did come time to quit, Tommy knew exactly how it would go down. The plan was to look Ira right in the eye and tell him (in the most casual voice possible) that he was about to embark on a sold-out world tour, and then, oh yeah, just so you know, I'm the long-lost son you never knew about. Got the birth certificate right here to prove it. Then, after Ira had time to review the document and adjust to the shock, he'd gaze at Tommy with eyes filled with pride and maybe even give him a dad hug.

But he wasn't ready yet, not even close, and he'd told Malina in no uncertain terms that quitting wasn't even negotiable.

The rest of his day was spent fighting the urge to call Layla. He missed her. Wanted to see her—like, *really* wanted to see her. But Layla was skittish, and any display of interest might push her away. So instead he'd worked on a new song about a snarky waif of a girl who'd cast a spell over him.

When Aster had texted and told him everyone was meeting up at her place, Tommy had readily agreed, only to discover Layla was already there, with Mateo sitting comfortably, a little too comfortably, beside her. And for the first time in his life Tommy felt the sharp sting of jealousy. Like a blunt object to the side of the head, it rocked him so off balance, he had no idea how to deal.

"So, now that you're up to speed . . ." Aster spoke pointedly, as Tommy stared blankly. "I mean, you have finished reading it by now?"

He set the laptop on the table before him, and ran a hand over his face.

Were Layla and Mateo back together again?

Was Layla so horrified by their hookup she'd gone straight from Tommy's bed to Mateo's in an attempt to erase what she'd done?

Was last night really the quickest rebound in the history of rebounds?

"Just wondering what your thoughts are?" Aster shot him an annoyed look, and Tommy sat up straighter, forced himself to focus on the subject at hand.

"Uh, yeah, well, I'm not sure Layla should post that," he said, worried for Layla's welfare both if she did, and if she didn't.

"Me neither." Layla frowned and studied his face. Her look was so scrutinizing, Tommy quickly averted his gaze. "I don't like being threatened. But I have to admit, part of me is afraid not to post it. Whoever it is has access and reach—they seem to always know where I am. This latest message was sent to me in Valentina's hospital room! That alone changes everything. It's one thing to threaten me, but when it extends to innocent people . . ." She paused for a moment. "Anyway, for now at least, I'm still holding out. But in the future, who knows?"

Tommy nodded, relieved to know she was taking the time to think it through, as opposed to being driven by fear, which would only lead to a reckless act that might make the situation worse. He pushed away from the couch and went to stand before the window. His emotions were all over the place, and though he was aware of Aster sighing in frustration behind him, he needed a moment to get a grip on himself.

"But what if they post it for you?" Ryan said. "You already said they hacked into your email account, so what's to stop them from hacking into your blog and publishing whatever they want?"

Layla shrugged. "If they do, then maybe they'll leave some sort of electronic trail that Javen might be able to trace?" She cast a hopeful glance in his direction, but Javen was too busy working to respond.

"So, what if this X guy is real?" Mateo ventured. The mere sound of his voice instantly filled Tommy with an irrational hatred he could barely contain, so he didn't.

"So what if he is?" Tommy turned away from the window and glared at Mateo. His tone was so combative, everyone met it with a confused stare—all except for Layla, who seemed to see right through him. He looked away and sank his hands in his pockets, feeling ridiculous for being so transparent.

"What I meant was," Mateo continued, completely undeterred, "what if X isn't just a fill-in—what if it stands for a real person? Like the X is short for Xander or Xavier or something? Wouldn't it be worth looking into? Maybe even tracking him down?"

Tommy frowned. It made sense. Not that he'd ever admit that.

"But how would we even begin?" Layla asked, and Tommy breathed easier knowing Layla didn't just automatically applaud everything Mateo said. She was no lapdog. She was too smart for that.

"Good point," Aster chimed in. "She kept him a secret, which means he probably didn't go to her high school. So where would we even begin? Maybe we should look up Dalton instead? Or even those friends she mentioned in that first entry—Jessa and Emma, I think they were?"

"Didn't Trena do a story on Madison's past?" Ryan asked. "I seem to remember her interviewing the people who raised Madison, along with her group of friends back in Connecticut."

"She did, and I read it." Layla nodded. "But I don't remember any mention of a mysterious X in Trena's article. Which was pretty much Madison's whole point, right? I mean, from the way she writes about him—" Layla reached for the laptop and took a moment to skim the entry she'd written. "The part about him having no future sounds like he might be from the wrong side of the tracks, which is probably one of the reasons she kept him a secret. Like he didn't correspond with the image she was trying to project. And so I doubt she would've told anyone about him. That's not how it works."

At that, Tommy cast a sharp glance her way. Clearly Layla should know, being an authority on secret lovers. Question was: *Who was the secret lover in her world—him or Mateo?*

"Hey, Javen—" Aster looked toward her little brother, who was off in a corner, hunched over his computer. "What are the chances of you locating a guy between the ages of fifteen and thirty-five who may or may not live in the town Madison grew up in and who goes by the name of X, which may or may not be his real name?"

Without missing a beat, Javen said, "About as good as you agreeing to read the first fifty pages of *The Great Gatsby*, which I need to be proficient in by first period tomorrow."

"Just a thought . . ." Mateo shrugged, prompting Tommy to smirk, and Layla to shake her head and roll her eyes at Tommy for smirking.

"Though I will run a search on Dalton, and let you know what I find."

"What about all that stuff about Paul, or P as she calls him, and their destinies being entwined because of the choices they made six years before. You think that's just histrionic teenager talk, or do you think it's real?" Tommy snuck a peek at Layla, feeling proud to have asked a valid question as opposed to the nonsense Mateo had come up with.

"I think there could be something to it," Layla said, checking her laptop again. "Six years before the time the entry was written puts Madison at age eight. Same age she was when her house burned down and she lost her parents.

Do you think she had something to do with it?"

"You mean like, she murdered her own parents as a child and an adult helped her cover the crime—is that what you're saying?" Ryan looked appalled, and while Tommy agreed it was indeed appalling, they should at least take a moment to consider it.

"She writes that he put his life on the line, that he knows all her secrets." Layla frowned. "What else could it mean?"

"Maybe it was an accident," Aster said. "Maybe she was playing with matches or something and the next thing she knew her house was in flames."

"Maybe," Tommy conceded. "But is that really worth working so hard to bury and invent an entirely new past for yourself?"

"Maybe it was the only way she could adjust. Maybe—"

"I'm hearing a whole lot of maybes," Mateo interjected.

"Just trying to build a theory, bro." Tommy scowled.

"Well, *maybe*," Layla emphasized the word, "Mateo is right. And *maybe* it's better if we stick with the facts that we know, which are that Paul helped Madison out of a jam when she was eight, and their lives have been entwined ever since."

Mateo nodded, seemingly pleased. Tommy nodded too, but only because he knew Layla was annoyed with him.

They all fell quiet for a moment until Javen piped up. "If anyone's up for a little road trip, I think I just found our first real lead." He wagged his eyebrows and grinned, as Aster bounced from the couch and went to stand beside him. "Turns out, Paul kept a cabin. A rather remote cabin, way out in Joshua Tree."

Aster pumped her foot against the rug, making a dull thumping sound. "Are you sure? Because that just seems so unlikely. It's just such a hipster, whiskey-swilling, spiritual-seeking, boho-chic getaway . . . and from what we know about Paul, he doesn't seem like the type to hang in a place like that." Her skeptical tone matched her expression.

"But what do we really know about Paul?" Tommy came to rest on the arm of the couch. "The guy's a fixer, which probably makes him a little scary to deal with, but does that also mean he lacks appreciation for deeper meditation on the meaning of life or even the occasional whiskey shot?"

Layla rolled her eyes, which wasn't exactly the reaction Tommy was after. Then she turned to everyone else and said, "Does anyone have a picture of Paul, so we can at least know who we're looking for?" A second later, Ryan whipped out his phone and passed it around. By the time it reached Layla, she gasped. "Oh my God, I *know* him."

The room fell silent, as five heads swiveled toward her, waiting for her to explain.

"He's the one who served me the restraining order that Madison filed against me."

"Are you sure?" Mateo's voice was just caring enough,

and just gentle enough, to make Tommy seethe.

"Definitely." Layla continued to study the picture. "I mean, he's so beige he's easy to forget, and yet I have a really similar picture." After scrolling through the pics on her phone, she held it up beside Ryan's. "Tell me this isn't the same guy."

"Where'd you get that?" Ryan leaned closer, taking a moment to study the pic.

Layla paused a beat before saying, "Heather." Her gaze settled on Mateo when she said, "She used to feed me pics for my blog. It's a little arrangement we had. She told me to send myself whatever I wanted. She had tons of pics of Madison too, which I found kind of weird. She seemed a little obsessed with her."

Ryan nodded. "Mad couldn't stand her. Said they used to be friends, but then Heather freaked out and started acting really jealous when Madison hit it big. She copied everything Madison did. It drove her crazy."

"Do you think Heather has something to do with this?" Aster's eyes went wide, but Mateo was quick to dissuade her.

"Heather's a little intense," he said. "And she's definitely ambitious, but I hardly think she'd take Madison down in hopes of taking her place, which is what you all seem to be implying."

"It does sound a little too much like a *Dateline* special," Aster conceded.

"Which are all based on *true crime* stories," Tommy pointed out, more than willing to throw Heather under the bus, at least temporarily, if for no other reason than her connection to Mateo. Guilt by association, as they say.

"Point is"—Layla looked directly at him—"Heather is competitive as hell, and more than a little conniving, but I'm pretty sure it ends there. Seriously, forget I even mentioned it. We can't afford to get sidetracked."

"So, if Paul served you those papers, does that mean the restraining order was faked, since he's not really a lawyer—at least not that we know of?" Mateo asked.

Layla shook her head. "Unfortunately, Detective Larsen was all too aware of it, which means Paul could've been acting as a process server. Lots of law firms use PIs for stuff like that."

"So, where does this leave us?" Aster asked.

"Taking a field trip to Joshua Tree?" Tommy ventured, hoping Mateo would have the good sense to stay behind. No one liked a fifth wheel.

Aster checked her watch, then stood and stretched her arms high overhead. "What is that, like a two-hour drive?"

"Two and a half," Javen said. "I'm printing the address along with a map. Pretty sure this place is way off the grid, so your GPS may not recognize it."

Aster moved around the apartment, collecting her keys and bag, preparing to leave.

"One more thing," Javen said, his voice adopting a high, worried pitch. "I found a weird code on one of those papers you gave me last time I helped you."

Aster impatiently jangled her keys in her hand. "Go on."

"It was a series of numbers, like a bar code or something. It was the only thing on it, and I didn't know what it was, so I decided to run a search on it."

"And . . ."

Javen swallowed, his big brown eyes moving among them, and said, "It's a tracker."

Aster waited for him to continue.

"Madison had a tracking device, a microchip implant."

"Like . . . the kind you put in your dog in case it gets lost?"

Javen nodded. "It's not as uncommon as you think, or at least not among the super rich, the super famous, the super powerful, and other super people who receive lots of death threats."

"Did Madison get a lot of death threats?" Layla asked.

"Fame attracts haters, and Madison had more than her share," Ryan told her.

"Did you know about the tracker?" Aster turned to Ryan, but he just shrugged.

"I had no idea. And I never saw any sort of weird markings or scars . . . other than that burn scar on her arm, but she got that from the fire. Or at least that's what she claims.

I don't know what to believe anymore."

"Well, we know the house burned down, so there's a good chance the scar really is a result of that event," Tommy said. "But maybe it's also where they decided to hide the tracking device, you know, in order to conceal it better."

"Why would Madison even have a tracking device unless she was worried about this exact sort of thing happening?" Aster asked. "Could it just be because she's famous—or is it connected to whatever the Ghost covered up in her past?"

"More importantly," Layla said, "if Madison has a tracking device, and Paul knows about it, then why hasn't he found her by now? Why is she still missing? Is it no longer working? Are they both in on her fake disappearance? Or is she really in danger and her kidnapper, who may or may not be Paul, ripped it out of her?"

The room fell silent as the question hung heavy between them.

"I'm really starting to think the Ghost is behind all this," Tommy said.

"But why would he go after her?" Mateo asked. "Why now?"

"Who knows why people do what they do?" Aster frowned.

"While I can't answer any of that, I can tell you that the tracker is, in fact, still working," Javen said. "There are different kinds, but this particular one charges whenever it's in a Wi-Fi zone. And if I'm not mistaken, it's transmitting a signal at this very moment somewhere near the Joshua Tree address I just printed for you. I think we should hurry."

"Oh, no." Aster plucked the address from the printer and shoved it into her oversize bag. "While I appreciate all you've done so far, there's no *we* in this scenario. Your next destination is back to Beverly Hills before Mom and Dad implant a tracker in you." Javen started to protest, but Aster quickly shot him down. "Seriously, Javen. Go home and read *The Great Gatsby* so you don't get kicked out of school and end up a delinquent like me."

He crossed his arms and glared, but after a moment he relented. "Fine." He sighed. "But you'll need to call me when you get there, so I can lead you right to it."

"And how will you do that?"

"I'll track your whereabouts through the location device on your phone."

Aster shook her head and swooped in to hug him. "What would I do without my computer whiz of a baby brother?" She squeezed him until he laughingly pleaded for mercy and worked himself free.

Mateo was the only one who remained on the couch, wearing a skeptical face. "Uh, don't you guys think we should maybe call the cops and tell 'em what we know?"

He'd barely finished the thought when everyone turned and shouted, "No!"

"I don't think that's a good idea," Layla said, trying to soften the blow, which annoyed Tommy to no end. Why did she insist on putting baby bumpers around him? If Mateo couldn't handle the sharp edges, then clearly he should leave.

Aster stood before Mateo and said, "My trial is less than a month away. My attorneys aren't all that forthcoming with their strategy, and I can only assume it's because they don't actually have one. It's on me to figure this out, but so far, there's not much to go on—nothing that will hold up in court, anyway. I'm pretty sure I lost my necklace—my easily identifiable necklace—at what has now become a crime scene. And if that wasn't bad enough, the blood-collecting kit I found at that same crime scene is probably reduced to a pile of melted plastic by now, thanks to the explosion and resulting fire that took place just after we left. I know you mean well, and you're eager to do the right thing, but as you can see, with my future looking so bleak, I can't possibly call the very people who are actively prosecuting me, and expect them to help me."

Tommy was awestruck. He couldn't have delivered it better.

Mateo responded by flashing his palms in surrender and following them all out the door. "Listen," he said, "I think I'm going to sit this one out."

Tommy grinned. The news had never been sweeter.

"I have a dinner meeting I can't miss, and there's no way I can go all the way out there and do . . . whatever you plan to do, and make it back in time."

"And Heather?" Tommy fixed his gaze on Mateo's. "Will she be at your dinner meeting?"

Mateo raised a brow.

Tommy shrugged and looked to Layla just in time to catch her narrowing her eyes and frowning at him.

While he didn't exactly enjoy being on the receiving end of her judgmental look, in the end, his point was made. Mateo was missing the field trip so he could hang out with Heather. He figured Layla could use the reminder.

"Oh, and I think we should take two cars," Aster said, ushering everyone to the elevator bank. "Just in case, you know?"

"In case what?" Layla squinted.

"In case you two change your mind." Aster shot them each a pointed look, and Tommy made no move to argue. A couple of hours alone in the car with Layla was something he looked forward to.

# THIRTY-SIX

# EVIL WAYS

**Breaking News: Office Park Explosion Possibly Linked to the Disappearance of Madison Brooks?**

By Trena Moretti

Two firefighters were injured when a five-alarm fire tore through the Acacia Office Park in West Hollywood early Sunday morning, according to fire officials.

Though details of the firefighters' injuries were not readily available, sources tell us both were taken to Cedars-Sinai hospital, where they're expected to make a full recovery.

The fire broke out shortly after 1:25 a.m., caused by a series of explosions that tore through the building's first and second floors.

According to authorities, an anonymous call was made to 911 at one a.m. to report an alarm sounding. When first responders arrived on the scene, they found no signs of smoke or flames. It was only upon checking the premises that the explosions occurred and quickly ripped through the building.

An abandoned car was discovered in the adjacent parking lot, and though there's no official word from LAPD, an insider tells us the car is thought to belong to missing celebrity Madison Brooks.

Madison Brooks went missing in July, and authorities have been searching for her car ever since. Night for Night club promoter Aster Amirpour has been charged with Madison's murder and was recently released on bail while she awaits trial for first-degree murder.

We've also learned that a witness has come forward who claims to have seen two people running from the building shortly before the explosion. Though the witness was unable to identify the suspects' age or sex, authorities are asking anyone with information regarding their identities to please come forward.

We'll have more as this story develops.

Trena Moretti posted her story and sipped her chai tea in disturbed silence. There was nothing new there—nothing that hadn't already been previously reported or at the very least hinted at. And the last bit about Aster left Trena feeling unsettled. It seemed to imply the girl was somehow involved, when Trena's only intent had been to relay the facts as she knew them.

And yet, there was no denying that Aster's recent release overlapping with suspected arson and the discovery of Madison's car wouldn't be viewed as coincidence by most. Though what Trena had failed to include, as she was still awaiting confirmation, was that the fire had originated in an office occupied by a private detective who was directly linked to Madison.

Clearly someone was out to frame Aster Amirpour, but Trena was no closer to guessing who that might be. And while Priya assured her she was close to pinning down exactly where Madison had been during the time between losing her parents and moving to Connecticut, she'd yet to provide anything useful. Was it possible the girl was leading her on? One thing was sure, if Priya didn't produce something soon, Trena would have no qualms about firing her.

She reached for her phone and purposefully scrolled through her contacts. Maybe she should call Layla and see what she knew. Trena had spotted her briefly at Ira's tequila launch, though Layla had disappeared long before Trena had a chance to approach her. And at the time, Trena had been too busy flirting with James to care.

*James.* What was his part in all this? Trena was sure that he had one. Hell, that was why she went after him in the first place—or at least it was one of the reasons. Though after the events of the morning, she couldn't help but wonder if she'd gotten in too deep. The look he'd given her—the way his fingers had circled her throat, demonstrating just how easily he could crush the life out of her with one single squeeze—had left her deeply regretting her rush to get involved with him.

She polished off her tea and made for the shower, eager to wash away the dark thoughts and the film of sweat covering her body courtesy of her daily six-mile run.

After stepping out of her tank top and shorts, she turned on the taps and ducked under the luxurious rain showerhead, which had the seemingly magical ability to instantly quiet her mind and send her troubles shooting straight down the drain.

Her eyes shut tightly against the spray, she was blindly reaching for her shower gel and sponge when she heard a noise that seemed to be emanating from the kitchen.

Only that was impossible. She always locked the front door without fail. Having grown up in a crime-ridden neighborhood, she'd learned that lesson early on. Also, for the entire month of August she'd kept all the windows closed, favoring the cool relief of the air conditioner over the blistering LA heat.

When she heard the scuffling sound again, she shut the taps and stood naked and shivering with her ear cocked toward the door. Finally convincing herself she'd imagined it, she went about sudsing her body, when the sound was repeated.

She yanked a towel from its hook, wrapped it tightly around her, and crept toward the kitchen. She told herself it was nothing—that the morning had left her paranoid and imagining things—that her only immediate problem was the soap she was dripping all over the rug.

Until she stood in the doorway of her kitchen and gaped in horror at the sight of a large black cat sitting on the counter beside her computer, its front legs heavily bandaged.

Trena glanced around the small space, ensuring no one was there, before she approached the unhappy cat, which hissed and swiped at her as she struggled to remove the small note that hung from its neck:

*He may have nine lives, but you don't.*

"James," she whispered. Somehow, he'd gotten past her locked door and found his way inside her apartment. She'd made a huge mistake thinking she could use him to further her story, and this was his way of letting her know.

Tentatively, she reached for the cat again, taking a moment to pet it and convince it she wasn't a threat. Then she slowly went about unwrapping the gauze from its legs, relieved to find it was only for show, the cat was unharmed. If nothing else, at least James drew a line at harming animals.

She thought about calling her source at LAPD and reporting the incident, but just as quickly decided against it. Other than a deep sense of knowing, Trena had no physical proof it was James. Though she vowed to avoid him at all costs, she knew better than to not take his message seriously.

"So," she said, addressing the cat. She ran a palm over its soft, silky fur and reached for the heart-shaped tag hanging from its pink satin collar. "Someone out there clearly misses you. What do you say we give them a call and tell them you're okay?"

With the cat cradled in her arms, she punched the number on his tag into her phone and waited for the call to connect, all the while wondering who would miss her if she should ever disappear.

# THIRTY-SEVEN

# INTERSTATE LOVE SONG

"Thanks for letting me drive." Ryan snuck a quick peek at Aster before directing his focus back on the road. "I just think it's better. You seem kind of anxious."

"Of course I'm anxious. I have good reason to be!" Aster rolled her eyes and sank low in her seat as she stared out the side window at a depressing landscape dominated by superstores, strip malls, and chain restaurants.

Beside her, Ryan fell silent, which only served to annoy Aster more. Aside from feeling anxious, she also felt jumpy, easily annoyed, and vulnerable as hell. It was the vulnerability that grated most. There was something about being alone in the car with Ryan that left her feeling like they were encapsulated together, suspended from time. The destination was confirmed, but the road between seemed malleable, theirs to define.

"Listen," she started, not really knowing what would follow. But overcome with the need to speak from her heart and get it all out there, she forged on. "I need you to stop being so nice to me."

There. She'd said it. And there was no missing the uncomprehending look on Ryan's face.

"Okay, maybe that was the wrong way to phrase it." She shook her head and tried again. "What I mean is, please stop treating me so delicately. Stop being so overly ingratiating. And stop acting like you're afraid you might break me."

He took a moment to digest the words, then nodded in a way so agreeable she couldn't bring herself to rail against it, though she desperately wanted to. "Just . . . can I ask why?"

Aster frowned, crossed her arms against her chest, and silently fumed. She was mad about the kiss that didn't happen—the kiss that almost happened—the kiss that part of her desperately wished she'd let happen—but there was no good way to share that with him. A few miles later she'd calmed down enough to reply. "Because your acting so nice makes me think it's okay to like you."

Her hands clenched in her lap, as she waited for him to mock her or say something sarcastic in return.

"I get it," he said, without a trace of cynicism. "Really, I do. And unfortunately, based on my past behavior, particularly the awful things I've said in the press, I can't blame you for not trusting me. But just so you know, I'm not asking you to."

"Oh, really? Then what's all this about?" Her hand gestured wildly around the interior of his car. "Why are you even here? Insisting on helping me when there's so many other things you could be doing with your life!"

"This is me attempting to prove my true intentions the only way I can—through my actions. Look—" He raked a hand through his hair and worked his jaw as he collected his thoughts. "It's like you said that night you found me at Madison's. A verbal apology is nothing more than someone humbling themselves enough to admit they were wrong. And while it's an important first step, it's what follows the apology where the real work begins. I heard you, loud and clear, and I've been thinking about it ever since. And so, I've come to the conclusion that whether you like it or not, I'm going to be nice to you. And I'm going to continue to be nice to you no matter how hard you try to push me away. And I'm going to do that because I truly believe you're a person who's worth being nice to. And, as it happens, I've come to care about you a great deal. Which is why I plan to stand by your side and help you get through this mess you currently find yourself in. Then, once it's over and done with and we've successfully put the whole thing behind you, we can decide how to proceed. But for now, that's my plan—my not-so-secret agenda. My only wish at the moment is that you try to make peace with it."

He kept his eyes on the road as Aster replayed his words. Despite doing her best to harden her heart against him, there was no doubting he'd meant what he said.

Just as there was no denying she still cared for him too.

Overcome with shyness, she closed her eyes and whispered, "Thank you."

Then she slipped her hand over his and kept it there for the rest of the drive.

# THIRTY-EIGHT

# ALL THE YOUNG DUDES

"Mind telling me what the hell happened in there?" Layla took her eyes off the road long enough to glare hard at Tommy.

He fiddled with the stereo. Finally settling on an old David Bowie song, he sat back and gazed out the window contentedly. A little too contentedly, which was why Layla demanded an answer.

"I'm referring to your pissing match with Mateo. And don't pretend you don't know what I'm talking about. You were like a dog with a fire hydrant, and I was the one getting sprayed."

Tommy shook his head and cringed. "Jeez, you really have a talent for visuals, you know that?" He tried to make light of it, but Layla wasn't having it.

They'd had the whole talk. Hell, he was the one who'd insisted on it. All she'd wanted was to get between the sheets and have a little fun. And yet, despite coming to the joint conclusion that they were two more or less responsible adults acting on an undeniable attraction to each other with absolutely no expectations to follow, the second Mateo entered the scene, Tommy had started acting like a big, possessive weenie.

Considering how much effort he usually put toward maintaining his cool guy veneer, it was kind of cute to see him feeling so challenged. And yet, the last thing Layla wanted was to have to answer to someone. Especially when that particular someone had claimed less than twenty-four hours before that they weren't looking to start a relationship.

At least when she'd said it, she'd meant it.

"So . . . what do you have to say for yourself?" She refused to let it go. "Because if you think you can avoid the subject and pretend it didn't happen, then allow me to point out that according to the GPS, we have another hour and twenty minutes left on this journey, which may or may not provide an accurate read of unforeseen traffic patterns. Which means this may take even longer. Which also means I've got you captive. There's no wriggling your way out of this one."

"God, you're impossible!" Tommy's face reddened and

he tossed a frustrated look her way. "You can't let things go. You have to examine every little detail of every little thing."

She rolled her eyes and gripped the wheel hard. "Don't act like you didn't know all that when you decided to sleep with me."

Tommy groaned, knuckled his eyes, turned up the stereo, but Layla held firm.

"Okay, fine," he finally said. "You're right. I was a jerk. You think I don't know that? And while I'm not exactly proud of my actions, I just—" He clenched his jaw, picked at the hole in the knee of his jeans. "I guess I was stupid enough to believe you when you said you guys were over. Seeing you together like that, sitting all snugged up and cozy, left me feeling like I'd been played."

Before she could stop herself, Layla burst out laughing.

"Oh, so now this is funny? This is all a big joke to you? Because let me tell you, Layla, you are one sadistic—"

Before he could finish, she said, "No." She shook her head. "Not a joke—not at all. It's just—you gotta admit, the phrase *snugged up and cozy* is kinda hilarious. Not to mention that if anyone in this car is a player, I'm pretty sure it's you. Let's not forget how you arrived at the party with one girl, only to go home with another."

Tommy shrugged and stared out the passenger-side window. After a few moments he said, "Whatever. Listen, can we just rewind?"

Without hesitation, Layla shook her head. There was no erasing the past. It was out there and done with and there was no going back.

"No," she said. "There's no rewind."

Beside her, Tommy sighed.

"But what we can do is move forward from here."

He turned to her with his best Tommy grin. Between the dimples, the irresistible lips, and the deep denim-blue eyes, Layla could only imagine how many broken hearts that smile was single-handedly responsible for. She hoped she wouldn't someday count herself among them.

They drove in companionable silence for the next several miles, until Layla said, "Does it ever bother you to know that someone, somewhere, knows exactly what happened to Madison—maybe even someone we know—and they have no problem letting Aster take the fall?"

After a long, considering look, Tommy said, "Every moment of every day." His words hung heavy between them until Layla turned up the stereo in hopes that Ziggy Stardust might chase them away.

# THIRTY-NINE

# JANIE'S GOT A GUN

Trena strode into the dimly lit tavern, an homage to wood with its paneled walls, beamed ceilings, and plank floor. It looked exactly like what it was—a popular cop bar known for cheap drinks and cheaper eats. She inhaled the scent of a decade's worth of spilled beer and passed by a row of empty stools. Within the next hour it would be standing room only.

Grabbing a seat across from her source, she pretended not to notice the way he studied her from under a lowered brow. "You're late," he grumbled.

Trena shrugged and reached into her bag. Retrieving the note she'd found earlier attached to the cat, she pushed it across the table toward him.

He looked it over and let out a low whistle. "Looks

like you found yourself a hater."

"I'm told it comes with the territory." She grabbed the menu and looked it over—carbs, more carbs, and fried carbs. She quickly discarded it.

"Want me to check it out?"

She shook her head, already regretting her decision to show him after having decided not to. Still, if something should happen to her, it would be good to have someone in law enforcement know she'd been threatened.

She plucked it from his meaty fingers and dropped it back in her bag.

"Anything?" He leaned toward her.

Trena took a look at Larsen's half-eaten cheeseburger and said, "No thanks, I'm not hungry."

His lip twitched at the side. "I'm asking if you have any intel for me."

"Isn't that usually your department?" She arched a brow and looked him over, well aware that his testosterone-fueled meathead routine was mostly an act. Underneath all the overblown muscles and machismo, Larsen was a cool and calculating detective with a serious dark side she did not want to test.

"Tit for tat is always nice." He took a slow sip of his Coke.

Trena rubbed her lips together, caught in an internal debate. Knowing it was better to give him something, even if it was really just a hint of something, she said, "What do you know about James?"

Larsen squinted until his eyes nearly disappeared behind a set of heavily freckled lids.

"James, the bouncer at Night for Night."

She watched as he leaned back in his seat and took a moment to consider. "Ambitious, untrustworthy, a thug." He lifted his shoulders. "Why?"

Trena drummed her fingers on the table, enjoying the ritual of making him wait. "Tit for tat?" Her gaze met his impatient one. "A source claims he was close to Madison. Possibly even on her payroll."

"We already have our suspect." Larsen was too quick to dismiss the idea, leaving Trena to wonder what he might know that he was keeping from her.

She nodded agreeably. Keeping her voice light and even, she said, "But what if there's more to it? What if it goes way deeper than that?"

His lip curled up at the side as his tongue worked to dislodge something from between his back teeth. "Always does."

Trena waited expectantly, sure there was more, and trying not to cringe in aversion when he replaced his tongue with his finger and started actively picking at one of his molars.

"You ready for this?" At first Trena wasn't sure if they

were still on topic, or if he was about to reveal the culprit that had gotten wedged in his gums. Then he went on to say, "That office park that burned down? The fire started in an office leased by Paul Banks, aka the Ghost—"

"Aka Madison's fixer," Trena said, as though speaking to herself. Then, knowing how much he hated being interrupted, she shook her head and said, "Sorry. Go on."

He heaved a dramatic sigh and shot her an annoyed look, but a moment later, he was talking again. "Anyway . . ." He dragged out the word. "We're trying to track this Banks guy. Haven't been able to locate him yet, but considering his line of work, that's not all that unusual. But get this, you know how Madison's car was found in the lot?"

Trena mumbled that she did and urged him to continue.

"Madison's purse—some Céline bag that costs over three thousand dollars, if you can believe that—was found stashed in the trunk. Phone's still missing, though."

Trena forced herself to be patient. So far, other than the purse, none of this was news. Though she hoped he would get to it soon.

"Oh, and something else," he said, as though it were an afterthought, when clearly it was anything but. "You know anything about this?" He slid his phone across the table and displayed a picture of what looked to be a slightly singed gold charm encrusted with diamonds.

"It's a hamsa hand," Trena said. "It's worn as an amulet

for protection against the evil eye." She continued to study the picture as a familiar gnawing stirred in her belly.

"That's right." Larson tapped the photo with the tip of a surprisingly neatly buffed and filed nail. "And you happen to know who wears one of these?"

Trena swallowed. She knew exactly who wore one of those. Aster had worn it during the interview and had occasionally fiddled with it when the questions got a little too heated. She chose to remain silent, however. She knew better than to flub his reveal.

"Aster Amirpour." Larsen's eyes gleamed when he said it, and Trena could've sworn she saw a small glob of spittle soar from the corner of his mouth. "Found it inside that office building. Must've fallen right off her."

"Lots of people wear those, so how can you be so sure it's hers?" she said, choosing to remain unimpressed for two reasons—one, because it was true, lots of people did wear them—and two, because Larsen's obsession with the girl was veering toward disturbing.

"Let's say I'm operating on a hunch. Though there is a witness who recalls seeing a girl who fits her description running from the building."

"I thought the witness couldn't identify age or gender."

"Turns out there was more than one witness." Larsen pocketed the phone and leaned back in his seat, seemingly satisfied with the way things had gone.

Trena kept her face neutral, but inside, her mind was reeling with all the myriad possibilities. This was potentially big, really big, promising huge rewards for whoever broke the story first, and of course Trena had already decided it would be her. Though it would prove devastating for Aster, Trena had never pledged allegiance to anyone but herself. And if it did turn out to be Aster's necklace, then the girl was beyond hope.

"It's in the lab as we speak." Larsen spoke with palpable excitement. "Got a rush order in place. As soon as I get the call, which I'm expecting any minute, well, let's just say I hope Aster enjoyed her vacation at Camp W, because it's about to come to an end."

"I don't understand why she'd risk it," Trena wondered aloud. In her head, she was already piecing the article together, and yet, something about it just didn't make sense.

"Desperate people do desperate things." Larsen shrugged, as though he'd just provided a brilliant explanation, as opposed to an oft-repeated cliché. "And sometimes, most times, spoiled-brat rich girls forget the rules are meant for them too."

When his gaze locked on hers, Trena found herself transfixed, unable to breathe. The realization finally dawned on her that the reason she despised Larsen so much was because they were so much alike. They'd both fought their way out of tough neighborhoods, only to emerge mostly unscathed aside from the giant chip they both wore on their shoulders. They resented the rich, the pampered, those to whom much was given and little was expected in return. In Larsen's eyes, Trena recognized the dark, shadowy part of herself she preferred to keep hidden. But at the moment, there was no avoiding it, it was like gazing into a mirror and seeing her most driven, most ambitious, most unscrupulous self staring back.

The spell finally broke when Larsen's phone buzzed with an incoming call and he stepped out of the booth to take it, leaving Trena to grip the edge of the table and fight like hell to center herself.

"Bingo!" he said, returning a moment later. "You mind getting that?" He nodded at the check the waitress had left. "Seems I have an arrest to make."

"So, it was hers?" Trena figured it was, but as a responsible journalist, she needed Larsen to confirm it.

"Oh, it's hers. Her prints are all over it. You're welcome to come, if you want to witness firsthand. If not, give me an hour, then feel free to post whatever you want."

Trena watched as he made his way out the door; then, reaching for her wallet, she tossed a twenty onto the table and followed.

# FORTY

# HIGHWAY TO HELL

Ryan pulled to the side of the road as Aster studied the map Javen had printed for her. He was right about the cabin being remote. The car's GPS had just quit and there was nothing in the vicinity that even resembled a place where someone might live.

A moment later, Layla pulled up beside them, and Tommy rolled down his window. "I think it's right up the road there."

Aster stared grimly in the direction Tommy was pointing. The sun had fallen, and aside from the moon, a constellation of stars overhead, and the headlights on their cars, the area was enveloped in darkness.

"Seems kind of spooky," she said, mostly to herself, though she felt comforted when Ryan was quick to agree.

"You want to turn back?" Tommy asked, only partially joking.

Everyone looked at her then, like it really was hers to decide. And in a way, she guessed it was. She had the most riding on the outcome. Which was exactly why she needed to keep moving forward.

"No. Let's do this," she said, thinking if she spoke with conviction she might start to feel it. "You guys follow us."

She motioned for Ryan to go, then held fast to the door handle as the car bumped along the deeply rutted drive, occasionally scraping the bottom.

"There goes the transmission," Ryan quipped. "Not to worry, though, we'll fetch it on the way back, along with the tailpipe."

Aster squinted into the darkness, unable to discern much of anything other than the ghostly form of a few random Joshua trees, their skeletal limbs reaching up toward the sky as though praising some invisible deity known only to them. "Shit," she groaned, shaking her phone. "I can't get a cell signal! You?"

Ryan checked his cell and shook his head.

"Great. That's just great." She groaned in frustration. "How's Javen supposed to lead us to the tracker if we can't reach him?"

"The tracker's with Madison," Ryan reminded her. "If she's here, then I'm assuming we'll find her soon enough. According to Javen, it's a small cabin, which leads me to believe there's not a whole lot of places for someone to hide." Aster was about to concede he was probably right, when he said, "Look—just up there—straight ahead. I think that's it."

She leaned forward in her seat and peered through the dust-covered windshield, able to make out a small, one-story structure that, from what she could see, resembled more a shack than a cabin.

"Jeez," she mumbled in disdain. "I know the whole point of a second home is to escape the daily grind, but this is ridiculous."

"But maybe that's not the whole point of this place," Ryan said. "Maybe this isn't about getting away so much, as it is keeping other people away."

Aster took a moment to consider his words. "Sounds kind of Unabomber-ish, don't you think?"

Ryan shrugged. "Good place to hide a hostage, that's all I'm saying."

The cabin glowed under the beam of their headlights, and a moment later, Aster directed Ryan to pull over and park. "I don't want to get too close," she explained, as Ryan stopped the car and started cranking the wheel hard to the left. "What are you doing?"

"Positioning for a quick escape, just in case."

"Good thinking." She nodded, impressed with his fore-sight.

"Learned that on set for a mystery pilot I shot that was

never picked up. Never thought I'd ever use it to aid my own real-life investigation."

With both cars situated for a speedy getaway, they relied on the lights from their phones to find their way to the property.

"How do you feel about snakes?" Layla asked.

"Do you seriously have to ask?" Aster cried, furious with Layla for mentioning that. Despite the unrelenting desert heat that made LA feel like a mild day at the beach, Aster found herself shivering at the mere thought of snakes slithering around her feet.

"Not to worry, they only come out during the day," Ryan said.

"More movie-set wisdom?" Aster spat, feeling jumpy, on edge, as Ryan laughed and reached for her hand, entwining his fingers with hers.

"Either way, I'm choosing to believe it," Layla said.

They stopped beside an old metal mailbox set on a rusted steel post, and Tommy tugged on the latch and checked out the contents.

"Mostly all mailers and junk." He quickly sifted through it.

"Mostly or all?" Aster asked.

"You interested in paying his electricity bill?"

"Maybe." Aster plucked the envelope from his fingers and plunged it into her purse. "Who knows? It might contain some info we can use later."

"Like what—his gross wattage usage?"

"Like the name he used, his account number, which Javen might be able to use to hack into and find something useful. Or not. Either way, I'm in no position not to take whatever I can successfully walk away with."

Tommy flashed his palms in mock surrender and followed them up the dirt path to the single-story cottage with the covered concrete porch. "Now what?" Tommy stopped before the weather-beaten front door.

Aster nudged him out of the way and tapped her knuckles hard against the wood a few times. "Hello?" she called softly. "Anyone home?"

"Seriously?" Ryan whispered. "You think that's a good idea? Announcing us like that?"

"What—you thought we'd kick the door down instead?"

Tommy and Ryan seemed disappointed, Layla looked worried.

When the knock went unanswered, Aster tried her luck turning the knob, but of course it was locked. "Guess we'll have to work a little harder at this clue, since we weren't exactly led here." She glanced between the door and the window. "Looks like we'll have to break it," she said.

"But won't that set off an alarm?" Layla asked.

"Providing there is one." Tommy looked doubtful.

"I'm not sure he'd bother with an alarm." Ryan frowned. "It's pretty much a desert shack, so what would be the point? If he uses this place as a getaway, then I doubt he stores any sensitive information in there."

"No sensitive information, just an A-list celebrity." Layla smirked.

Tired of the bickering, Aster grabbed a rusted metal table from the porch and said, "Everybody—stand back!" Then, before anyone could stop her, she thrust it right through the window, grinning in triumph when the glass shattered into a million satisfying bits.

She moved to climb inside, when Ryan stepped in to stop her.

"Let me," he said. "Like you said, we have no idea what we might find in there."

Aster hesitated a moment, but eventually backed off and watched as Ryan cleared the sill of broken glass before hoisting himself over and inside in one swift, graceful move.

"Anything?" she asked. Hearing the thud of his feet hitting the floor, Aster rose onto her toes and tried to peer inside, but it was as dark in there as it was on the porch where she stood.

After what seemed like an agonizingly long moment, Ryan opened the door and stood wide-eyed before them. "Hurry," he said. Shooting a suspicious look beyond the porch, he quickly ushered them in. "You are not going to believe this."

# FORTY-ONE

# HOTEL CALIFORNIA

The first thing Madison noticed when she woke was the heat.

The unbearable, stifling, relentless heat.

With her flesh dripping with sweat and her hair fiercely clinging to her cheeks and the back of her neck, she swiped a hand across her forehead and slowly blinked her eyes open.

The second thing she noticed was that someone had relocated her.

She sat up with a jolt, then instantly regretted the move when her head pounded with a deep, stabbing ache as a constellation of stars spun before her. Clutching the side of the dirty mat she'd slept on, she willed the pain to subside. When it finally dulled to a more tolerable throb, she forced herself to stand and take a look all around.

How long had she been here?

Her mind reeled toward the past as she fought to recall. She'd tried to run—tried to outwit her captor—only to be outwitted by them.

Last thing she remembered was the sharp pinch on her thigh and then . . .

And then nothing.

While she'd managed to escape, it hadn't been on her terms. Someone had moved her, but where—and why— only they knew for sure.

Had someone come looking for her?

And if so, how close had they gotten?

Or had her captor simply thought it prudent to never stay in one place for too long?

All valid questions best left for another place and time. While Madison had no concept of how long she'd been out, now that she was conscious again, she needed to move quickly. Needed to get a better sense of her new surroundings, then work out a new plan for escape. And this time, there was no room for mistakes.

The relentless heat, as unbearable as it was, provided her with new hope.

While the last room hadn't been air-conditioned, it had been very well insulated, which not only kept it several degrees cooler than the outside temperature, but also made it much more difficult to break out of. But in this room, when Madison pressed her palm flush against the wall, it proved solid enough that it wouldn't give easily, but not so solid that she couldn't feel the surge of hot air emanating from beyond.

Was it possible that if she screamed very loudly someone might actually hear and come running to help her?

At the moment, she deemed it better not to try. She needed whoever was keeping her to assume she was still knocked out cold.

Though the room was dark, it wasn't so dark that Madison couldn't discern the vague outlines of her various belongings. Locating her cashmere scarf abandoned a few feet from the mat, she wrapped it snugly at her waist and tied the loose ends in a knot. While it was clearly too hot to wear, it could come in handy once she was outside, since there was no telling where she might find herself.

After exploring every square inch of the floor and running her hands along the walls, checking for shelves, she determined her shoes hadn't made the trip with her, which was really too bad. Those four-inch stiletto heels could easily take out an eye.

Other than the mat she'd slept on, and a lone bucket placed in the corner with a roll of toilet paper just beside it, the room was not only decidedly empty but also a major downgrade from her earlier digs, which in comparison seemed downright luxurious. Either she was in a temporary holding cell, or whoever had taken her no longer needed her and they'd dumped her there to die.

She didn't plan to stick around long enough to find out.

The door was locked, but then she'd expected as much, though she was encouraged to find it was made of wood and not metal like the previous one. Metal was impossible to break through. But wood was an entirely different story. And wood in a hot, dry climate was prone to aging, weathering, and splintering, which would only work in her favor.

While whatever they'd given her left her feeling frailer than she was used to, Madison summoned what remained of her energy and sprang into action. Grasping the bucket from the corner, she repeatedly rammed it hard against the door, until she stumbled back in fatigue and despair, riddled with grief to see the door hadn't so much as budged.

She lay sprawled on the floor, sweaty and breathless as she searched for other options. There had to be a way out of there, had to be. . . .

Her gaze caught on a spot in the middle of the wall that, while impossible to fully discern in the darkened room, appeared patched, as though it were covering something.

Something like a window, maybe?

Without another thought, Madison jumped to her feet and started pulling at the wood. Tearing her flesh and bloodying her hands in her efforts, she had no choice but to work through the pain.

She continued punching and tugging until she heard that first, deeply satisfying crack as the wood began to give way and separate from the wall, ultimately revealing a small broken window she could easily fit through.

Flipping the bucket upside down, Madison balanced on it for one precarious moment, before she inhaled deeply and dove straight into darkness.

She landed with a muffled thud and quickly scrambled to her feet. Stealing a handful of seconds to catch her breath and get her bearings, Madison darted forward and raced headlong into the night.

# FORTY-TWO

# WELCOME TO THE JUNGLE

"I don't get it." Aster squinted at the long brunette wig Ryan waved before them as though it were somehow significant.

"This proves Madison really was here!" he cried. "This is her wig!"

"How can you be so sure?" Tommy asked. "Considering Paul's a PI, it could just as easily be his."

Ryan continued to examine it. "Madison kept a collection of wigs. She used to create these elaborate disguises so she could move about anonymously. I'm pretty sure this is one from her collection. I remember her wearing it."

"Did it work?" Layla asked. "Was she able to go unnoticed?"

"Usually." He nodded. "She was a master at disguise. She'd create entire characters with elaborate backstories.

She seemed to really enjoy it."

"Kind of like how she created herself." Layla wore a deeply contemplative expression.

"And why are you just now getting around to telling me this?" Aster took the wig from Ryan and plucked at the seams lining the scalp as she studied it from all sides.

"I guess it didn't seem relevant until now. Anyway, I found this sitting on that chair over there."

Tommy studied the hideous vinyl recliner and frowned. Since Paul worked with Madison and a long list of celebrities, it seemed safe to assume he made them pay dearly for the kind of shady services they required. Which made the chair even more incongruous. Why wouldn't he at least spring for one that wasn't ripped at the arms with the stuffing spilling out?

Then again, maybe this was less a hideaway for Paul, and more a place for hiding others. And if that was the case, did those people hide willingly, or were they held against their will for a much darker purpose?

"Has anyone noticed how much this resembles the hair on the person in the video?" Aster's troubled looked found each of them. "Do you think it was Madison who took me there?"

Tommy was the first to doubt it. "I guess it's possible, but that makes for a really tight timeline. We hung out at the Vesper for a while."

"Not that tight of a timeline," Layla piped up. "Aster

and Ryan hung at Night for Night as Ira served them champagne. It is possible."

"Well, one thing's sure." Ryan took the wig from Aster. "I can think of two reasons why this thing was left here. One is neither Paul nor Madison believed anyone would ever find this place. The other is one or both of them knew we would most definitely find this place." Ryan stared at the wig as though the answers were written somewhere in the strands. "And while I'm hoping for the former, I'm betting on the latter."

"Well, if Madison was here, she clearly isn't here now." Tommy looked around the small rectangular room with its beamed ceiling and wood-paneled walls. There was a small kitchenette in the corner, an ugly plaid couch that looked as though it served double duty as a bed, the crappy lounge chair, an eyesore of a coffee table that had seen better days, and a tiny bathroom just off to the side with a toilet, a sink, a cracked mirror, and a minuscule stand-up shower with a serious grime issue that kicked in his gag reflex. Paul's cabin was the definition of simple, rustic, grubby living at its best.

"Well, she might not be here now, but that doesn't mean she won't return, and I plan to be here waiting for her when she does," Aster said. "Anyone have a cell signal?" She took in a collective shaking of heads and sighed.

"So . . . that's the plan? To sit here and wait for an

indeterminate amount of time, until Madison or Paul or both either does or doesn't return?" Layla watched as Aster shrugged and idly picked through a stack of ancient *National Geographic* magazines before placing them back on the table where she'd found them. She didn't look thrilled by the news—well, neither was Tommy.

"You have a better idea?" Aster said. "At least this gives us a chance to poke around and see what else we might find. I mean, if Madison really is or was staying here, then there must be something more than just a wig left behind. I think we should check through all the drawers, the cupboards, and even dig through the trash." Then, looking at Ryan, she said, "What kind of food did Madison eat?"

He rubbed his chin and thought about it. "Healthy food." He shrugged. "If you find random chia seeds and empty Pressed Juicery bottles, then you'll know for sure she was here. Listen, you guys search inside. I'm gonna have a look around the property."

He swiped a flashlight from a wall hook by the door and disappeared outside, as the rest of them went to work.

Tommy poked around as instructed, but his heart wasn't in it. Besides the wig, which did seem a bit out of place, it didn't appear as though anyone was currently in residence. The small fridge was empty, the few dishes and glasses were all put away, the trash had been taken out, and no one had bothered to replace the plastic liner bag. The only sign of life came from the multiple spiderwebs hanging from the light fixtures and draping the corners. With his luck they were probably woven by black widows—the females were considered the most venomous spider in North America, and the desert had no shortage of them. He worked his jaw and surveyed the room, on the lookout for deadly black insects with red hourglass symbols hidden on their underbellies.

"Someone planted that wig," he muttered, though what he really wanted to say was, *I think we've made a huge mistake by coming here, and I'm more than ready to leave!*

He met Layla's eye and they exchanged a worried look. He was just about to propose that they cut their losses and go, maybe even find a way to alert the local police, when Ryan burst through the door.

"I think I might've found something," he said. "Come on!" He led them all to a small bunker-like structure that stood a dozen yards away from the property. "Gotta belong to Paul, right? I mean, since there's nothing else around?"

Tommy studied it, figured Paul probably used it as a garage, or a shed, or a place to hide the bodies his celebrity clients hired him to dispose of. . . .

He started to walk around it, check it out from all sides, when Layla leaned against him and he decided it was better to stay right where he was.

"Guys, are you sure about this?" Layla said, her voice

betraying a high level of nervousness. "I mean, what if Madison *is* in there, only she's not exactly alive?" In spite of the heat, Tommy slipped a comforting arm around her, and to his relief she did nothing to stop him. "I mean, do we really want to trample all over what could possibly be viewed as a crime scene?"

"Isn't it a little too late to question that now?" Tommy said, though he kept his tone gentle.

"Never too late," Aster replied in all seriousness. "If you guys want to make a run for the car and forget this ever happened, I wouldn't blame you. But since I don't have that luxury . . ." Without another word she pushed at the door, but it refused to so much as budge.

"This looks exactly like the kind of place where you'd keep a hostage." Ryan studied the door as though looking for a weak spot, a way in. "Maybe Paul really did go rogue and this is where he's keeping her."

Softly, Aster pressed against the door and called Madison's name as they all paused to listen. "Madison? You in there?" she called again.

"We need Javen," Layla said. "If the tracker signal really is transmitting from here, then we need to know if it's coming from inside. And since we can't reach him, I'm really starting to think we should let the cops know what we've found and let them take it from here."

"Still no signal," Aster said. "And forget about the cops.

Seriously. I don't trust Larsen. For whatever reason, he has it out for me."

"Pretty sure this is out of his jurisdiction," Layla said.

"Yeah, and as soon as he gets wind of it, he'll find a way to manipulate the evidence and use it against me—against all of us, probably. Which leaves me no choice but to knock that door down and see what the hell Paul is hiding in there."

"Guys, never mind the door, I think we just found our way in." They followed Ryan to the back of the shed, where he aimed the flashlight on a broken window. "Who wants to go first?"

# FORTY-THREE

# FIGHT SONG

A long day of relentless desert sun had left the earth so scorched it burned straight into the soft soles of Madison's feet.

But that paled in comparison to what the jagged rocks and low-lying shrubs with their razor-sharp spikes had done to her legs, fiercely biting into her flesh and leaving her limbs a bloody, pulped mess.

Madison fought to ignore the excruciating pain and focused on moving instead. Her pace was labored and slow, her breathing staggered, but as long as she could continue placing one foot in front of the other, she would put enough distance between herself and the shack that she might even start to feel safe once again.

Somewhere in the not-so-far distance, a pack of coyotes howled. Their eerie chorus combined with the incessant chirping of crickets seemed almost maniacal, as though intended to taunt her, while things slithered at the ground under her feet. Were they snakes? Lizards? She figured it was better not to know.

Overhead, a constellation of stars shimmered and dazzled, but there was no time to stop and admire them. It was mindless stargazing that had landed her in this mess in the first place. She wondered if, once she finally found her way out, she'd ever be able to view the night sky in the same way again.

The moon was in its waning phase, making the shadowy landscape appear abstract, almost alien, while providing very little light in which to navigate.

It was the perfect place to hide a cache of secrets.

The perfect place to bury a girl.

A small formation of boulders sprang into view, and Madison changed course and raced toward it. The rocks would provide temporary cover. A place to hide for a moment, long enough to catch her breath and regroup.

She pushed herself faster, harder, all too aware of how vulnerable she must look—a small, lone figure left to the mercy of the environment, the weather, and predators—both animal and human.

Her next step saw her foot coming down hard and landing all wrong, with her ankle violently twisting one way, as her body soared in the opposite direction.

The moment she was falling seemed almost surreal,

like time had purposely paused so she could fully experience the horror of what was happening to her. A shriek of pain strangled her throat, her vision blurred to a haze of searing-hot misery, as the ground rose up to meet her and she landed with a thud, curled her knees to her chest, and writhed in a moment of agony so extreme, she was sure she'd never survive it.

How was it possible for her to have made it so far, only to render herself lame in her eagerness to flee?

Why had a life that had once seemed to favor her turned so resolutely against her?

Ripping her scarf from her waist, she wrapped her leg tightly and forced herself to stand.

Forced herself to work past the screaming white throbbing and start moving again.

The injury would slow her, but it would not, could not, stop her.

Calling upon the same infinite reserve of strength she'd used to propel herself out of her impoverished childhood to the top of the Hollywood elite, Madison Brooks gritted her teeth and dragged herself through the night.

# FORTY-FOUR

# GANGSTA'S PARADISE

The chime of Aster's phone ringing was so startling it was a moment before she finally got around to answering it.

"Aster—Aster, you there?" Javen's voice was cutting in and out. ". . . been trying to . . . you."

"Hold—hold on!" Aster shouted. Exiting the empty shack, she put him on speaker so everyone could hear. "Let me find a place with more bars. . . ." She traced a wide circle, frantically searching for a spot where she'd be able to hear him. "How's this—better? Javen, can you hear me?"

"A little. Listen . . ."

"What?" Aster made a face at the phone, as everyone huddled around. "Javen, can you repeat that?"

". . . got your location."

"And?"

". . . you need to keep moving . . . so . . ."

"Details, Javen, and make it quick! The reception sucks. I could lose you any second."

"You're going to . . . hike . . ."

Aster stood outside the shack and looked all around. "For a second I thought you said hike."

"I did."

"But . . ." She looked around again. "There's nothing out there."

"There is . . . on my screen."

"Sure you're not looking at a coyote—or rather a pack of coyotes? We can hear them howling."

". . . trust . . . it's the tracker . . . weak ping . . . needs Wi-Fi from your phone . . . lead you to it . . ."

She gazed into the dark, dreading the idea of venturing into it. Other than the wig that might or might not belong to Madison, the cabin and shack hadn't offered anything of real use, though they had provided more than enough creep for one night. What Javen was asking her to do was unthinkable. And yet, they'd traveled all this way; there was no point in stopping until the search was complete.

"Fine." She sighed, resigning herself to the task. "Which way?"

"Take a few steps . . . I'll direct . . . there."

"What if I lose you again?"

"We'll deal . . ."

Aster took a step forward, and her friends instantly followed.

"A little . . . right," Javen said. ". . . straight."

"Right or straight?" Aster made a frustrated face at the phone. After several steps right and then straight, she said, "Anything?"

". . . still a ways . . ."

They trudged along in formation, walking four across as their shoes audibly crunched over the dirt, kicking up great clouds of dust.

"Closer . . ." Javen's voice was fading, and Aster stared at her phone in dismay. She was losing bars with each step.

"I might lose you," she said.

"Just keep . . . you'll find her . . ."

"That's what I'm worried about," Aster mumbled. Not finding Madison alive was beginning to seem like a real possibility. In the heat of summer, everything in the desert looked like death—smelled like death. She prayed they wouldn't discover Madison as another piece of that decaying landscape.

"Oh my God—did you guys see that?" Layla said, at the same time Aster's bars disappeared and she lost her connection with Javen.

Aster followed the arc of Layla's pointing finger, but all she could make out were rocks, shrubs, cactus, and darkness, more darkness, always darkness, all of it unfolding to the soundtrack of howling coyotes on the prowl.

"I saw something running!"

"Some*thing* or some*one*?" Ryan asked, his voice gone suddenly tense.

"There it is again! Straight ahead! Did you guys see it?" Layla had picked up the pace and was heading right toward it, as Tommy cursed under his breath and followed.

Aster desperately tried to reach Javen again, but the connection was lost. He'd told her to forge straight ahead, or at least that was what she thought he'd said, and since that was more or less the direction Layla was headed, she figured they must be on the right track. Still, a better connection and a little more encouragement from the home base would be greatly appreciated.

After another attempt to reach him, Aster gave up and went back to chasing after Layla, who was several steps ahead, sending a spray of rocks behind her as she led them toward whatever it was she'd seen running.

In her rush to catch up, Aster nearly ran headfirst into a towering Joshua tree that seemed to appear out of nowhere.

"Careful." Ryan reached for her arm in an attempt to steady her as her phone began ringing again.

She slowed enough to answer it, though she could barely make out what Javen was saying. "Aster!" he screamed. "Shit . . . Aster! I'm at . . . W . . . didn't go home . . . and now . . . sorry . . . so sorry . . . We're screwed!" She heard what sounded like a commotion, and then muffled voices, and then the line went dead.

"Javen!" she shouted. "Javen!" She was just about to try him again, when Layla screamed. The bloodcurdling sound echoed through the night, as Aster and Ryan raced toward her, then stood gaping in dismay at the grisly scene laid out before them.

# FORTY-FIVE

# DON'T FEAR THE REAPER

Madison limped toward the boulders, only to discover they weren't really boulders. It was a tree—a large dead tree with mangled bare branches protruding from a wounded, rotted, dry trunk.

She squinted into the darkness and looked all around, wondering what else she'd gotten wrong. From what little she could see, the landscape appeared to be getting tamer, less wild. Which could possibly mean she was creeping closer to civilization and ultimately finding someone who might be able to help her.

Carefully, she maneuvered around the tree carcass, practically rendered delirious thanks to the unbearable pain shooting from her ankle and reverberating through her body. Chances were it was broken, which meant walking on it was only making it worse. Still, with her very survival at stake, there was no stopping now. The prospect of a future spent nursing a bum leg could only pale in comparison to what would amount to a certain gruesome death if she stayed.

Guided by the barest sliver of light, courtesy of the waning moon, Madison stumbled on. Determined to clear her mind of all the things she had to fear, she focused instead on all the wonderful things she'd indulge in once she was safe.

A long, hot bath with her favorite scented bath oils and salts made the top of the list. And even though she rarely drank, a nice cold glass of champagne would also be nice. Then, after a good night's sleep on her wildly expensive Sferra sheets, she'd rise to a cup of perfectly brewed cappuccino made with whole milk, not skim, since she could afford the extra calories, and with her beloved dog, Blue, by her side, she'd begin collecting evidence, and answers, and plotting revenge.

James, Ryan, Aster, Layla, Tommy, Ira, that nosy Trena Moretti—none of them were above suspicion. Reluctantly, she added Paul to the list. If there was one thing she'd learned on her rise from the ashes to the top of the Hollywood heap, it was that when it came right down to it, the only one she could count on, the only one she could truly trust, was herself.

She was so mired in vengeance fantasies, she missed the sound of staggered breathing, of shoes kicking up dirt—the telling signs of someone rushing up from behind her—until it was too late and they were already on her.

A strong hand grasped her by the arm and yanked her up hard. The fingers circled and pressed into the burn scar in a way that saw her howling in pain, as a hot ragged breath blasted her cheek and a familiar voice said, "Nothing out there but coyotes. You'll meet your end, you keep going." Slowly, they started trudging through the sand, dragging Madison back in the direction she came from. "They don't call this Death Valley for nothing, you know."

# FORTY-SIX

# SUGAR, WE'RE GOIN' DOWN

"What *is* that?" Layla cried, staring into what could only be described as a shallow open grave scattered with bones and other unspeakable bits that appeared to be human in origin.

Aster appeared to be all out of screams, all out of breath, like it took all her will just to sag against Ryan. "*Omigodomigodomigod!*" she whimpered. "Tell me that's not Madison!"

Layla watched as Aster sank to her knees, looking as distraught as she had the day their world turned upside down when she was arrested for Madison's murder.

Or maybe their world had turned long before that. Maybe it had happened when they'd first started working for Ira, but they'd been too caught up in the thrill of competition to notice.

Layla sought refuge in Tommy's arms, allowing herself to be soothed until her reporter's instincts kicked in and she went to kneel beside the remains in order to better examine them.

"Dude, this is so messed up!" Tommy spoke to no one in particular.

Ryan looked on in shock, seemingly struggling to process the horror they'd stumbled upon.

"Guys, I—I think I found something." Layla's voice was edged with panic, as she fought back the bile that rose high in her throat. "Tommy, hand me that stick."

"How can you be sure that's a stick?" Tommy remained rigidly in place.

"Just—" Layla sighed and shook her head, as Tommy tentatively reached for what did indeed turn out to be a stick, and passed it to her.

"What on earth are you doing?" Aster looked on in a mixture of horror and fear as Layla pressed her lips together. Determined to disturb the scene as little as possible, she tapped the suspicious piece and used the pointed end of the stick to drag it toward her.

"Ryan, Tommy, shine some light on this." Carefully, she pinched the object between her forefinger and thumb and dropped it on the center of her palm. "It's the tracker," she said, her tone lacking any hint of triumph. The moment instead resembled one of staggering defeat.

"And so . . . that's it. It really is Madison." Aster's words rang as flat and broken as her expression.

"This is pretty much the worst news ever." Tommy glanced between the microchip and Layla.

"Maybe." Layla bit down on her lip, not entirely sure that was true, but wanting a moment to weigh her words before she tried to explain. "Assuming those are Madison's bones in there, then yeah, it's truly bad news."

"Well, who else would they belong to?" Aster said. "Clearly Paul went rogue and killed her. He buried the bones in the desert where he expected no one to find them, other than the coyotes, and he's probably on some remote island somewhere. In fact, has anyone looked into Madison's finances? Because if not, they should. I bet he's bilked her out of millions."

"Of course the cops are watching her finances," Ryan said. "It's one of the first things they do. Not to mention how other than a nagging suspicion fueled by a few pieces of circumstantial evidence, we really don't have any valid proof that Paul's responsible for any of this. The way the cops will look at it, the whole thing can be made to point right back at Aster. So what if Paul fixed Madison's past and had access to her deepest, darkest secrets—it certainly doesn't mean that he killed her. What we need to do is find him and approach him. Only not in a suspicious way— we'll act as though it's purely out of concern for Madison. But first, we need to get the hell out of here and away from these bones, before someone blames us for putting them there." Ryan jumped to his feet and took one last look at the grave. "I mean, don't get me wrong, I'm hoping that's not Madison, but with the tracker right there, it's not looking good."

Without another word, Layla wiped the tracker against the leg of her jeans, placed it back where she found it, then stood up to leave.

The four of them were hurrying back the same way they came, when Layla's phone chimed with an incoming text.

Seems the day of reckoning is finally here

You should've listened when I warned you had plenty to fear

But since you insisted on doing things your way

You left me no choice but to make sure you pay

And to think your star once burned so bright

Funny how much can change in the course of one terrible night.

"What the—?"

Layla didn't even have a chance to finish the thought before the area suddenly flooded with light and a booming voice shouted, "Stop right there and put your hands in the air. One move and I'll shoot."

# FORTY-SEVEN

# DIRTY LAUNDRY

Trena Moretti settled into the makeup chair and closed her eyes as the stylist, Jasmine, fussed over her hair. There was something so relaxing about the ritual of being tended to. It reminded her of when she was a kid and Noni Moretti spent countless hours taming Trena's wild mane into obedient rows of sleek, glossy braids.

"Do you think they did it?" Jasmine asked, to which Trena just shrugged.

Where she once would've sworn a definitive *no*, she was no longer sure.

Or maybe she no longer cared as much as she used to.

Leave it to the detectives to solve the mysteries.

She was being paid to report the story—and lately, she was being paid very well. While part of her job involved uncovering the truth, the way Trena saw it, no one was ever as innocent as they seemed—herself included.

It was the first day of filming her newly announced televised news show, *In-Depth with Trena Moretti*, and though she was plagued with the usual nervousness that came from being a perfectionist, she was mostly focused on how improbable such a moment might've seemed just a few months earlier, back when she'd first arrived in LA fresh from a devastating heartbreak and looking to rebuild her life.

Practically from the moment her plane had touched down at LAX, Trena's star had taken off on the sort of awesome trajectory she never could've imagined, and she had Madison's disappearance to thank.

Her interviews with both Ira and Aster, along with the connected stories she continued to break thanks to Detective Larsen, her source in the LAPD, Trena had become the face of authority on the one story that showed absolutely no sign of abating.

The longer it took to solve the mystery of Madison Brooks, the better it was for her.

It was job security—akin to having a good insurance policy.

"Did they ID the bones?"

Trena peeked an eye open and regarded Jasmine through the mirror. "They're not Madison's," she said. "That's all I can say for now."

Jasmine nodded, though her lips jerked in a way that

barely contained her excitement at being handed such a juicy piece of insider gossip. Trena assumed the moment Jasmine was finished arranging Trena's curls, she'd run off to a corner and text all her friends with the news.

Well, they'd find out soon enough anyway. It was one of the big reveals for tonight's show. Besides, she was pretty confident Jasmine wouldn't hesitate to credit her as the source. And more than anything, Trena liked taking credit. Liked the power that came from revealing lies and dispelling secrets.

The important thing was not to give it all away at once. Like any good storyteller, Trena worked hard to build just the right narrative pace to lure the audience in. Then she held them captive and kept them riveted with the spattering of bombs she dropped along the way.

At this point, there was no doubt she knew more about the case than Detective Larsen. After all, she had the kind of intel and resources he couldn't even begin to penetrate with his meathead ways.

Layla had wasted her one permitted phone call to connect with Trena, having no idea that Trena wasn't the least bit surprised by the news, that she'd stood right there when Larsen had forced his way inside Aster's apartment and scared her little brother Javen into revealing their whereabouts.

And more—so much more—none of which looked good

for Aster, who could now face the death penalty for multiple homicides among other crimes, while Layla, Tommy, Ryan, and Javen were charged with aiding and abetting and accessory to the crime.

Maybe Trena would break the case. Wouldn't that provide an exciting boost for the ratings? After all, there was so much more to it than anyone yet realized . . . and she was so close to fitting all the stray pieces together.

Funny how she'd been seconds away from firing Priya when the girl finally came through. Had Priya been holding the intel all along—just waiting to see how far she could push it? Trena certainly suspected as much, yet in light of the reveal, she was inclined to let it go.

Turns out Madison spent those shadowy months between the West Virginia house fire and her move to Connecticut living with a certain Eileen Banks, who Priya revealed was Paul Banks's mother. As it also turned out, Paul Banks was first on the scene the night Madison's parents died. None of which, on the surface, seemed to ring any alarms. But for Trena, who could smell a cover-up from a decade away, it was a potential game changer she was quietly looking into.

Still, there was no need to rush the reveal until she was absolutely sure there was no stone unturned. She was so far ahead of the game, she could afford to milk it until she was confident the audience belonged entirely to her.

After all, Hollywood was a binge-and-purge culture,

where celebrities were expelled as quickly as they were consumed. Now that she was on her way to the top, Trena didn't plan to be discarded and forgotten anytime soon.

"Beautiful," Jasmine said, nodding approvingly at Trena's luxuriant curls, before leaving her to a few minutes of silence to look over her script.

**ANNOUNCER:** Tonight—the first of a multiple-part investigation going deep inside the secret world of Hollywood nightclubs, the teens hired to promote them, the stars who frequent them, and how it all might have led to a missing celebrity. This is *In-Depth with Trena Moretti*.

[Cut to clips of Hollywood Boulevard, the Night for Night facade, a billboard featuring Madison Brooks, and a dead and barren Joshua tree]

**TRENA MORETTI:** Good evening and welcome to *In-Depth*. Tonight, join us as we take you behind the velvet rope for a deeper look into what really happened to A-list celebrity Madison Brooks. While there have been over 215 reported murders in Los Angeles County this year alone, there is no denying that the Madison Brooks case is one of the most controversial, most talked-about crimes the world over. While many strive for a spot on the coveted guest list, few will ever get to experience what really goes on inside the gilded walls of Hollywood's most exclusive hot spots. It's a secret world of privilege and wealth, its doors carefully guarded by bouncers well trained on who to let in, and who to keep out.

Tonight, you'll hear from club owners, self-described nightlife impresarios, bouncers, bartenders, and promoters who worked alongside Aster Amirpour, Layla Harrison, and Tommy Phillips, who were recently charged for their involvement in the Madison Brooks case. You'll also hear from those closest to former teen heartthrob Ryan Hawthorne, who's also been implicated in the crime.

There are those who view the clubs as no more than a fun, uninhibited space where one can freely express oneself and blow off some steam. While others will paint a much darker picture, claiming that the world of nightclubs is not nearly as innocent as it seems. They say it's a dangerous, drug-riddled, crime-ridden world that's run by adults who prey on the young.

**BRITTNEY LANCASTER** (from video): I worked as one of Ira Redman's club promoters right alongside Tommy Phillips, and let me tell you, I had no idea what I was getting myself into. That world is totally corrupt, and I'm lucky I got out when I did.

[Aerial shot of Ira Redman's Unrivaled nightclubs lined up along Hollywood Boulevard]

**TRENA MORETTI:** You'll meet the critics.

**MATEO LUNA:** My older brother Carlos collapsed outside a club and died. They dumped him there like trash, so they wouldn't have to deal with him. Those club owners don't give a crap about the kids who are making them rich.

[Footage of police cars swarming outside Night for Night, zooming in to examine the line of crime-scene tape surrounding the terrace where Madison disappeared]

**TRENA MORETTI:** And you'll meet the supporters.

**IRA REDMAN:** I provide opportunity and the kind of well-paying jobs that work well around class schedules and other priorities young people have. Unrivaled Nightlife Company employs over two hundred people, the majority between the ages of eighteen and twenty-five. I ran a contest where the winner got to walk away with fifty percent of the door earnings—that's a boatload of cash—enough to pay a few years' college tuition. No one else out there can claim that.

[Footage of the long line of hopefuls waiting for a chance to interview for the Unrivaled Nightclub Promoter competition]

**TRENA MORETTI:** While there's no denying some of Hollywood's biggest stars can be found tucked away inside the VIP rooms, not all of them make it out of there.

**ANONYMOUS MADISON BROOKS FAN** (crying as she places a small stuffed pink bear outside Night for Night, where the Madison Brooks shrine grows increasingly larger each day): I still can't believe it. I just can't. To think that Madison was inside there, scared and alone … [needs a moment to continue] … Madison meant *everything* to me. When will they find her?

**TRENA MORETTI:** Stay with us, as we trace the events of the final days before Madison Brooks went missing, tonight on *In-Depth with Trena Moretti.*

[COMMERCIAL BREAK]
[*In-Depth* logo]

"Ms. Moretti?"

Trena glanced up from her script, trying to remember the name of the young gofer standing before her. Catherine?

Caitlin? It was a blur of young faces, and they all looked the same—bright-eyed, hopeful, and eager to make their mark on the world.

"You almost ready?"

Trena nodded. Ready, amped, her star meter was on the rise and she couldn't wait to get started.

"Great, we'll begin in three. In the meantime, this was delivered for you."

She handed Trena a large rectangular package normally used to hold long-stemmed roses, then shouted into her headset as she made her way toward the soundstage.

Trena set the script aside and studied the box. Her name was written on the front in a large boxy font, though there was no indication as to where it might've come from.

Grabbing a pair of scissors from the makeup table, she sliced through the tape to reveal a dozen thorny rose stems, all of them missing their heads, the arrangement tied with a gauze bandage roll tied neatly into a bow.

The small card tucked inside read:

> **Break a leg!**
> **Best-case scenario,**
> **that's all that happens to you.**

With shaking hands and a pounding heart, Trena carefully replaced the note, closed the box, and stowed it under the table.

"You ready?" The gofer was back and stood fidgeting before her.

Trena took a moment to steady her breath and settle the wild fluttering that had overtaken her belly. Then, nodding firmly, she rose unsteadily from her chair. "Did you happen to see who delivered that package?" She fought to keep her tone as casual and even as her frayed nerves would allow.

The gofer lifted her shoulders.

Trena had expected as much, but still, she had to ask.

"Everything okay? You look sort of shaken." The girl cocked her head in a way that saw a spray of frizzy bangs spilling over her forehead and into her eyes.

"Do I?" Trena turned toward the mirror. It was true. Her checks were flushed while her eyes looked wild, too bright. "Just some preshow jitters, I guess." She forced a laugh. "Don't worry, I'll get over it."

The girl shot her a worried look, then led her to the soundstage, where another crew went to work hiding the mic under her blouse, removing lint from her blazer, and doing a last-minute powder.

"Ready?" The director motioned to her from behind the camera.

Trena took a deep breath. Had James sent the message? With no hard evidence, she could only suspect.

Though whoever sent it had sorely underestimated her. Trena hadn't come this far only to fold right when the going got good.

No, this was her moment to shine—the moment she'd worked her whole life for—the moment she deserved.

Whoever was bent on bringing her down had no idea what she was capable of.

She settled onto her seat and took a moment to center herself, when she spotted someone who resembled Priya leaving the set. Trena was surprised to see her, since she hadn't exactly invited her. Still, now that she was there, she might as well hang around and watch. Trena would've killed for an opportunity like that at her age.

She was about to call out to Priya when the countdown to broadcast began, and Trena immediately switched gears, cleared her throat, looked directly into the camera, and in her most composed voice said, "Good evening and welcome to *In-Depth.* I'm Trena Moretti. . . ."

# ACKNOWLEDGMENTS

I owe so many thanks to so many people, but first I want to thank the winners of the *Unrivalled* preorder contest: Heidi Berenkuil (who also got a character named after her!), Pamela Fattorelli, Rochelle Garcia, Jennifer Görzen, Amber Hook, Mary-Beth Pearson, Jacklyn P., Annamarie Smith, Emily S., and Becca T.

Also, many thanks to the wonderful team at HarperCollins/Katherine Tegen Books, including but not limited to: Katherine Tegen, Claudia Gabel, Melissa Miller, Kelsey Horton, Stephanie Hoover, Rosanne Romanello, Alana Whitman, Lauren Flower, Valerie Shea, Julianna Wojcik, and Jean McGinley.

One of the highlights of my career so far was seeing *Unrivalled* launched in a simultaneous global release, and I'd like to thank the following HarperCollins teams for their efforts in making that launch so amazing: HC Japan, HC UK, HC Poland, HC Sweden, HC Canada, HC Norway, HC Netherlands, HC Australia, HC Brazil, HC Czech Republic, HC Latin America, HC Denmark, HC New Zealand, HC Portugal, HC Spain, HC Germany, HC India, HC Italy, HC France, HC Hungary, HC Finland.

And, as always, thank you to my agent, Bill Contardi, for the continued guidance, wisdom, and humor.

And to Sandy for pretty much everything.

# HQ Young Adult
## One Place. Many Stories

YOUNG
ADULT
HQ

The home of fun, contemporary
and meaningful Young Adult fiction.

Follow us online

 @HQYoungAdult

 @HQYoungAdult

 HQYoungAdult

 HQMusic

HQYA_Social Media